SOCIAL SKILLS

Sara Alva

DEDICATION

For my husband, who hopefully does not regret the day he said, "Babe, you should write a novel."

ACKNOWLEDGMENTS

Endless gratitude goes out to:

The wonderful people who helped me during the writing and publishing process: Anyta, Jay, Raevyn, Andra, Jenny, Yvette, Tim, Cole, Daniel and Dani.

The staff and readers at GayAuthors.org, for helping me find my passion.

And to Dani (again), for shouting encouragement from up on his soapbox and for creating the beautiful cover.

FIRST SEMESTER

CHAPTER ONE

Connor Owens stepped onto the newly waxed floor, and a rare moment of calm settled over him. The sweet scents of resins and polish, the gently curving stage, the warm weight of his violin in his hands—all of it comforting and familiar in the midst of a tumultuous few weeks.

He tightened his bow and fished out his rosin, smiling at the simple pleasure he took in making long, even strokes to coat the horsehairs thoroughly.

This, he knew. This felt right.

In a college life full of unknowns, orchestra would be his sanctuary. He could already feel it as the hum of tuning instruments filled the air, as the winds broke into arpeggios, as the rustle of sheet music on stands alerted him to the new piece they'd be playing: Rimsky-Korsakov's *Scheherazade*.

He was itching to play it. He wouldn't have the solo, of course, but the entire piece was lovely, and really at that moment it didn't matter what he played so long as he *could* play, surrounded by the myriad of sounds from all the other instruments. This was the kind of group in which he could belong without having to try so hard it literally made his head hurt. This came naturally.

"Hi!" A female voice greeted him, and he followed a peasant skirt up to the face of a tall, willowy girl with hair that hung to her waist. "I'm Rebecca." She gathered the dirty-blond wisps behind her head and tied them into a low ponytail as she sat next to him. "Looks like I'm your stand partner. You must be Connor."

He nodded, extending his hand for her to shake and battling a blush when her grip was much firmer than his.

"You're a first year, right?" she continued.

"Yeah."

"Must be pretty good, then, to be up here in the first violins already. It took me two years to fight my way up here."

He shrugged. Praise never sat well with him, no matter how many times his mother chastised him for not politely accepting compliments.

"Well, when we have sectional practice, don't let Vidar intimidate you. He's a bitter, bitter, Scandinavian man. I bet he thinks he's too good to be hired staff for a college orchestra, but I would guess that he's not, or else he'd have found another job."

Connor let out a low chuckle with a nervous glance to where the man in question sat five stands away, running scales with a pinched expression on his face.

Rebecca followed his eyes. "You see what I mean, right? You can totally tell he's got a stick up his ass."

This time Connor laughed openly, and when Rebecca joined in it gave him an instant shot of elation. Maybe music could be more than just the solace he was looking for. Maybe it would give him the chance to form a new friendship as well. It shouldn't be so hard—even for him—to build upon the connection between stand partners, on the way they learned to play as one, moving and bowing in complete synchronization.

"We can practice together, if you like." Rebecca tightened her bow. "You know, try our best not to incur his wrath."

Connor opened his mouth slowly. "Oh…um…"

Tap-tap-tap from a baton interrupted, and a hush fell over the assembled crowd. The conductor raised his arms, and as if an invisible string tied his tiny stick to every instrument, all rose in unison.

Rebecca smiled at Connor one more time, and he returned it. Maybe Rebecca, older—and wiser, no doubt—could become his liaison into the world of college…provided he could beat back his shyness long enough to give her a chance.

It was a good thing she was a girl.

***

He headed back to his room in a better mood than usual, letting *Scheherazade*'s melodies play through his head. If he kept up the tempo, he'd have time to make it through the first movement and at least part of the second by the time he reached his building. Hereford was a lot further out than the regular first-year dorms, but the newer construction meant air conditioning, something his mother had uncompromisingly demanded for her asthmatic son.

Just as well. He wouldn't have fit in at the first-year dorms, anyway.

Of course, there really wasn't a practical way to avoid passing by those hubs of social interaction. He averted his eyes from the gaggles of students lounging about the quad, laughing and sharing food, gossip, and in quite a few cases, saliva. *Scheherazade* picked up speed with his footsteps. With any luck, he'd look like someone who needed to be somewhere in a hurry, and not like an outcast who simply didn't know how to belong.

As he neared Alderman Road, a blue and orange Frisbee with the familiar block "V" for Virginia landed by his feet.

"Hey!" An olive-skinned boy waved at him. "Toss it here, will ya?"

Connor picked up the Frisbee and turned it over in his palm. He contemplated throwing it, but by now a group had formed around the boy, and he had no desire to make a public display of his weak throwing arm.

He crossed the distance between them and offered the disc with an outstretched hand. "Um, here you go."

From the gathered crowd, a familiar-looking face with a popped-collar polo shirt stepped forward. "Hey, you went to my high school. You're that violin player, right?"

Connor blinked rapidly. Had someone popular actually recognized him? But then he returned to his senses and felt the strap of his violin against his shoulder. It didn't exactly take a brilliant deduction to pin him as *that violin player*.

He nodded. "Uh, yeah. Connor."

"Tim," the former classmate said, though that was unnecessary because Connor already knew his name. He was good about affixing names with faces, even if hardly anyone ever did the same for him. "Hey, you wanna join us?"

Connor forced a smile. He didn't, really, but there probably wasn't another way to go about making friends. "Um, maybe I'll just…watch."

Tim and his friend exchanged bemused glances. "Sure. Okay."

Connor sat down on a patch of grass by a small cherry-blossom tree, and a few other onlookers planted themselves beside him. A girl with tight blue shorts announcing their school across her bottom—UVA—turned to him with a friendly smile.

"So, you play the violin. What's that like?"

"It's…it's fun, I guess."

"Cool." The girl nodded, and continued to stare at Connor until his pulse raced. *His turn to speak.* He tried to open his mouth and force more words out, but nothing happened.

Tim jogged over and tagged someone sitting by the sidelines. "You're in man, gonna take a break." Then he grabbed the UVA-bottomed girl and yanked her into a kiss.

"Get a room!" someone shouted.

"Maybe we will!" Tim shouted back, and he and the girl took off. Connor watched them go with a knot growing in his stomach, because with Tim went his very tentative connection to the group currently surrounding him.

"Hey, I'm gonna go grab a snack at the Treehouse," another unknown person announced, and suddenly the entire mass of people began to rise and shift away.

"Yeah, sounds good."

"Me too."

"I'm gonna head in, catch you guys later."

Connor said nothing, and within a few seconds he found himself alone.

For all his efforts, he'd wound up making friends with a tree.

***

His door clicked into place and he leaned heavily against it, letting the worst of the anxiety drain from his body. He was safe now; the world and all its strange rituals of socialization were locked away on the other side of the wall.

Here it was only *him*—his books, his music stand, his metronome, his bed…and the barren mattress across the room.

Life would have it he didn't even have *that* friendship-of-convenience to fall back on, because his college roommate had dropped out without notice. And despite all the meet-and-greets and the unmistakable air of camaraderie during orientation, he still hadn't been able to make any great strides in socializing. How could he, when the cliques he had so detested in high school had made

5

their way to college after all? Maybe they weren't as overt, but they were still there. The pretty girls still held fast to each other, the jocks still slapped each other's backs and guffawed loudly at inappropriate jokes, and the misfits had redoubled their efforts to find a way to fit in. Worse, many of them seemed to be succeeding where he clearly was not.

As was usually the case, a hundred options for what he *could* have said to keep the conversation with the friendly girl alive flooded his mind. *Do you play an instrument? Have you ever wanted to learn one? What kind of music do you listen to?*

But those thoughts were never available when he needed them.

With a sigh, he grabbed one of the textbooks off his desk. Might as well throw himself into acquiring knowledge instead.

***

"All right." Rebecca flexed her fingers and twisted around in her chair, stretching her long back. "I think we've covered everything Vidar's gonna bug us about in sectionals. When's your next class?"

Connor gathered his bag from the corner of the tiny practice room. The closet-like space felt far too sterile for music, but at least Rebecca's presence brought life to the otherwise stale air.

"Uh, I have my Theory and History of Anthropology class in New Cabell at two...I should probably go finish the reading for it. I didn't get a chance to last night."

Rebecca raised one of her pale eyebrows at him. They were so fair, in fact, that if he didn't look closely he might have missed them against her light skin. "You do know that no one does all of the reading for their classes, right?"

"Yeah, I know. But I took a summer course with this professor before I started school here, and she seemed to really like me. I kinda don't want her to have a reason to change her impression…" Connor trailed off. Of course he just *had* to sound like the giant geek he actually was.

Rebecca laughed, though she was good about not mocking him with her laughter.

"A summer course before you were in college? Wow, slow down! You're supposed to slack off a little, while you still can. Pretty soon you'll *have* to think about real-life things, like finding a job." She groaned and tossed a rust-colored knit scarf around her neck with a dramatic flourish. "Anyways, let's enjoy the freedom we have left, okay? You have an hour—let's go grab lunch at Newcomb. A bunch of my friends eat there around this time."

Connor rearranged his bag at his hip so he could slide his violin across his other shoulder, buying himself time to consider his response. This was exactly the kind of opportunity he'd been looking for, but it still took an extra burst of effort to put aside his nearly automatic desire for solitude.

"Okay. Sounds good."

Newcomb meant noise. Shouts, laughter, rattling trays and clanking silverware. Too many people, too much movement. And plenty of chances for Connor to make a fool of himself. He scanned the crowded tables, some filled with students grabbing a quick bite, others whose occupants were enjoying a more leisurely paced meal. The clusters reminded him of the groups that dominated the high school cafeteria, though lines were slightly blurred and labels not quite so easy to place.

Rebecca touched his shoulder lightly and led him to a table. A couple of blond girls already sat there with pretty smiles and tight tank tops, chatting with a brunette who seemed to share Rebecca's bohemian taste in clothing. Two guys with longish hair and oversized t-shirts joined them as Rebecca and Connor walked up.

"Hey guys," Rebecca called out cheerfully. "This is Connor, my new stand partner. Do us a favor and watch our violins while we grab some food?"

"Oh." Connor instinctively wrapped his arm around his instrument. "Uh, that's okay, I'll hold onto it."

Rebecca waved off his protest. "I swear to God, you can trust these guys. They'd die protecting my baby, so they'll do the same for yours. Isn't that right?"

One of the t-shirted guys at the table rolled his eyes. "Whatever you say, Becca."

Connor flushed, anxiety crawling along his skin. It wasn't as if his violin was a Stradivarius, but he'd grown accustomed to never letting it out of his sight. Over the past four years it had become like a fifth limb—the substitute for the best friend he'd never found. The thought of having to develop that level of intimate knowledge with some other instrument made his heart skip several beats.

But this was college, after all, and he was supposed to be going with the flow. He drew in a deep breath through his nostrils and dropped the strap from his shoulder. "Thanks."

A quick scan of the day's offerings led him to the line for chicken parmesan. Rebecca chose the salad station, and her long blond ponytail swung its way back to their table before he'd even received a plate. Restless, Connor drummed his fingers against a plastic tray and considered jumping ship. Maybe a simpler meal, like a bowl of cereal, was in order.

Someone bumped into him as the line started moving again. "Sorry," a voice above him said.

He shifted his gaze to the speaker and quickly looked away after a brief nod. Though he'd never gotten a name, he recalled the face from his anthropology class. Black curly hair, full lips, warm chestnut eyes.

In his peripheral vision, he caught the guy stretching and was momentarily lost in the lean but sharply defined muscles along his tall frame. Was he an athlete? Either that, or he just took really good care of his body. Prone to people-watching, Connor kept his eyes lowered but intensely focused.

"Son?" A warm plate of chicken parmesan, the oil bubbling away from the melted cheese, shook in front of his face.

He mumbled an, "Oh, sorry," even if no one with human ears could've heard it. Dish in hand, he stepped away from his classmate, who continued to stare ahead without a second glance in his direction.

It was for the best. If the guy *had* tried to talk to him, he was pretty sure he'd have turned into a stammering idiot. That was just how things went for him.

When he reached Rebecca's table, the two preppy girls had left, and he now clearly stood out from the group as the only one wearing an undeniably new button-up shirt and crisp khakis. He probably needed to start shopping at a local thrift store, so he'd blend in a little better with his crowd.

If this was to be his crowd.

He made certain his shirt was at least untucked and set his tray down, foolishly pleased to see his violin right where he'd left it, its gray case looking slightly dirty alongside Rebecca's earthy brown one.

"So, a fresh soul ripe for the picking." The brunette across from him leaned forward, dragging the sleeves of her coarse knit tunic across the table.

Blushing, Connor took his seat. By the time he realized he should have said something in response, it was too late, and he floundered with his fork while opting for a shrug.

"Connor's already in the first violin section. I bet if he wanted to, he could beat out the Scandinavian Devil in a few years," Rebecca chimed in for him.

"You and your hatred of tall, thin, very white men. Methinks the lady doth protest too much," responded the taller of the t-shirted males, running a thumb over his own pale cheek.

Rebecca rolled her eyes and the banter continued, right over Connor's head. He chewed and swallowed methodically, nodding and smiling when he felt it appropriate, and silently wishing he were a more interesting person so he could quit being a shadow on the sidelines of his own life.

***

Laptops unfolded, instant-messaging windows flew open, and classmates began chatting all around Connor. They didn't even stop when his anthropology professor began her lecture.

Connor didn't join in. He never joined in. Instead, he opted for a plain spiral bound notebook where he furiously scribbled notes if things interested or confused him, and doodled in the margins when he already knew the material. Although today, he was allowing his thoughts to wander a little. Wander all the way to the side of the room, where he could observe one particular classmate from a safe distance.

It was actually pretty easy to stare, because the guy was looking up, as if he could see the sky through the ceiling tiles of the small room in New Cabell Hall. With practiced peripheral vision and the cover of bangs, Connor watched him lean against the window, where he always sat. A beam of sunlight hit his hair.

Dark brown...not black.

Connor's visual target yawned and shifted down in his seat. His lids began to droop, his blinks became longer and more frequent, and then his eyes shut completely, showing no signs of opening any time soon. His lips parted as he slept.

Connor smiled to himself. Now he could *really* stare.

A slight snore and resulting giggles eventually startled the guy from his slumber. He looked around sheepishly and wiped his mouth clean of the tiny bit of spittle that had gathered in the corner.

"Connor, could you stay and talk with me for a minute?"

Turning abruptly, Connor faced his professor, embarrassed he'd been distracted enough to miss the last few minutes of class. But as the rest of the students filtered out she perched on the end of her desk, smiling warmly enough to quell any fear that he was about to be chewed out for his inattentiveness. After all, it wasn't like he had fallen asleep.

"You're doing really top notch work." Professor Abrahms gestured to the written assignment on his desk, which bore an "A" as well as "excellent" in red ink across the top. "You have wonderful insights into the reading material, and your theories are quite well reasoned."

Connor blinked. Should he thank her for her contribution as his teacher, or keep quiet to avoid sounding like a brown-noser?

He chose quiet. Or ended up with it by default, anyway.

"I wanted to ask you whether you have any interest in tutoring."

"Oh…" He took several seconds to process her request. "Why, does someone need help?"

Professor Abrahms smiled again, but it seemed less than genuine this time. "The athletic department has asked me to recommend someone they can hire as a tutor. There are a few students on the football team who could use help in this course, and unfortunately the Anthropology 101 tutors are too swamped this semester to cover the specific reading material."

He nodded slowly. He'd worked with little kids before, volunteering as a reading coach for elementary students during summer school. But he'd never considered working with someone his own age, mainly because he assumed his social ineptitudes would get in the way. And working with *athletes*, cool and confident and completely unlike him in every way, seemed like an even more disastrous idea.

"It's ten dollars an hour, and for now they're only looking for a commitment of about two hours a week, but if it works out they could hire you for other subjects as well."

He couldn't stop nodding, mostly because he was using the time to think of a polite way to suggest she find someone else.

"I usually don't recommend first years, but in your case, you showed me such maturity in your work over the summer...I really think you could be of assistance."

A sinking feeling in his stomach told him he was already stuck, and over his head at that, unless he wanted to prove to himself he really was a coward—and worse, disappoint Professor Abrahms. Would she hold it against him for the rest of the semester? He hated how much he cared what she—or anyone—thought of him, but the idea that her friendly eyes might one day hold him in contempt made his insides squirm.

Dazed, he nodded yet again. "Yeah, okay."

Professor Abrahms beamed. "Great. I'll call them and let them know you're interested. They'd like you to start tomorrow, if possible. Here's the contact info."

He took the offered paper and mumbled his thanks, praying he hadn't just made the worst mistake of his life.

***

For the first fifteen minutes of his maiden tutoring session, no one showed up. Connor sat in a small, barren room with a rectangular table and four burgundy-cushioned chairs. On one of the bare walls, a large clock worked away audibly.

He would have been perfectly content for the next forty-five minutes to have gone by the same way, since he was making decent progress on his assigned reading, but a quiet knock at the door meant that would not be the case.

Curly brown hair and chestnut eyes greeted him. "Hey, you're the tutor? Cool, dude. I'm Jared."

Jared. Finally, a name to the face.

Jared stuck out his hand. "Michael's on his way in. Kinda had to drag his ass. He needs this class for his major, in case you're wondering why you got hired. Though why anyone would major in anthro is beyond me."

Connor was already shaking the offered hand by the time Jared flashed him a contrite look. "Sorry. Maybe you were planning on it?"

"Uh…" Connor's doomed attempt to come up with a response was cut short by the arrival of another classmate, this one a little taller than Jared and much bulkier.

The new arrival—Michael—planted himself in a chair without a greeting. "All right, dude, let's see if you can help me figure this shit out. Because right now, it all seems like a waste of my time."

The blood drained from Connor's face, but a furious blush quickly replaced the pallor when Jared smirked at him as if they shared some sort of inside joke.

Suddenly aware he hadn't said a word since Jared and Michael had arrived, Connor sat down heavily and grabbed the book in front of him. He couldn't think of any pleasantries to utter that wouldn't sound completely useless, so he launched right into the text, where he felt safe, carefully explaining the main points from their assigned reading.

Every so often he tentatively made eye contact with his tutees, and was greeted with a bored expression from Michael and a tired one from Jared. He made sure to stop after each page to check if there was anything they didn't understand or to see if they had any questions, and each time they both answered in the negative.

Of course, when he got to the end of the chapter and asked for either one to reiterate the main ideas, he received blank stares.

Michael finally shook his head. "I gotta be honest with you, man. I don't know why I picked this major. I think it's 'cause everyone was saying it was easy, and it wouldn't be too much extra stress on me since our schedule is so rough. But this shit ain't easy. I mean, not if you're really trying to learn it. I guess I could just coast on through and buy papers off people and shit, but what's the point of even getting a degree then?"

When Connor didn't respond, because, as usual, he found himself at a loss for words, Michael continued. "Take it from me, dude. If you're not into this, pick something else."

That last comment was directed at Jared, who gave a little shrug. "Yeah, I haven't really decided what I'm gonna major in yet."

"Huh. Well you better think of something, 'cause the way you play, you'd never make it pro," Michael jeered, and Connor was surprised when Jared just scoffed.

"Yeah, well, at least I have my youth. You're getting pretty old there, fifth-year."

"I'll show you old." Michael retaliated with a swift jab to Jared's ribs.

Only ten minutes of their session remained—which meant Connor should be doing something to rein them in and return them to the tenets of Boasian cultural anthropology. Unfortunately, telling two large athletes to stop their bickering and get back to work was just not within his abilities.

He waited until the two had had their fill of fake-fighting before hesitantly glancing back at his book.

"W-would…would you like to go over the prompt for the next writing assignment?"

Michael sighed, making no effort to hide his displeasure, but Jared regarded him with a raised brow and a grin. "Yeah, sure, Connor. You're the boss."

CHAPTER TWO

Connor took his normal walk to the athletic hall in the hazy light of dusk, frowning at the pumpkins and ghosts that had suddenly appeared in dorm room windows. October was sure to be filled with even more lively parties he wouldn't be invited to…not that he would know what to do if he actually were invited anywhere. He kicked a pebble toward the mocking grin of a jack-o-lantern, then crossed the street to avoid an oncoming group of people.

Jared arrived for tutoring a few minutes after him, clutching at bare arms that stuck out from his orange UVA t-shirt.

"It's fucking cold already. Couldn't we have had a few more days of the nice weather? People say it's great we get all the seasons, but I still say Virginia sucks. Most of the time, it's either too hot or too cold. Or raining."

Connor grinned, but didn't say anything. Michael was usually there to spare him from the small-talk.

"So, I got some bad news." Jared plopped down in a chair. "Michael withdrew from the class. He talked to his advisor and decided it'd be better to take it next semester, or maybe over the summer. I dunno. I think he just wants to put it off as long as possible."

Connor nodded slowly, wondering if his tutoring days had come to an end. Michael was a defensive lineman, and one of the team's star players. He *had* to keep his grades up. But Jared was only a first-year, and he wasn't as important to the team yet. Besides, he wasn't likely to destroy his GPA with all the general education requirements in his course load. So he'd probably withdraw from the class now, too.

"You frown when you think." Jared broke into his speculation. "And you think a lot."

Connor's pulse quickened, his abrasive inner voice immediately taking center stage, reminding him he wasn't even close to normal— and that everyone around him could see it. He stared down at his textbooks and willed the feeling to pass, unsuccessfully.

"I'm not dropping the course, if that's what you're thinking. Wouldn't want to put you out of a job."

Despite efforts to continue studying the fake wood grain of the table in front of him, Connor found his eyes drifting up toward Jared's. He fully expected to see derision or mocking.

Instead, Jared met his gaze with a gentle smile. "So, you gonna tell me about the chapter?"

"R-right, right," Connor stammered. He flipped open his book and silently cursed the way his fingers trembled against the pages. In a last ditch attempt to steady himself, he drew in a deep breath, careful to keep his chest from expanding and making his discomfort any more apparent.

It was a wasted effort. The breath was trapped in his lungs when Jared stood and walked around the table to grab the seat next to him.

"You don't have to be so nervous around me, you know. I don't bite."

Really? In the instant before his anxiety took over, Connor had a moment to feel annoyed. It wasn't like it was a *choice*. His skin began to tingle, first with warmth and then with cold, rising and ebbing in waves along his arms.

17

His heart pounded, his palms grew clammy, and the constricting muscles in his throat blocked off any hope of even excusing himself from the situation.

Jared regarded him quietly, mouth tilted in a half-smirk. After a few seconds he slid his hand over to the textbook Connor was mechanically creasing open with his thumb.

"All right, so I read the last chapter, but I got a little confused when they were talking about the British structural-functionalism approach," Jared said, his low voice gentler than Connor could ever remember.

"Oh, y-yeah." Connor swallowed gratefully, his mind kicking back in now that it had something solid to hang on to. "No problem. We can go over that."

The rest of the session went by without any off-topic conversation, but Connor still couldn't bring himself to feel at ease. Perhaps it had to do with Jared's proximity, or perhaps it was because Jared was acting differently without Michael around. He seemed more genuinely interested, asking questions and trying to formulate his own—albeit less than stellar—conclusions.

Any semblance of calm was shattered when Jared stood at the end of the hour, stretching and causing his t-shirt to ride up over his toned stomach. His hand came down and settled on Connor's shoulder.

"See ya in class, bro." Jared's fingers pressed into a light squeeze before he took off.

Bro? Actual physical contact and now he was a *bro?* With a flash of clarity, Connor recognized that nervous feeling in the pit of his stomach. That jittery, ticklish feeling that had the potential to turn into something different—and something far worse. Something that often made male friendships a particular challenge for him.

He frowned at his train of thought. Friendship? With Jared? A highly unlikely scenario. And since he did have to work with him twice a week for tutoring, it probably wasn't a good idea to make use of him in his fantasies, either.

***

Keeping Jared out of his fantasies was easier said than done. Especially since Jared never returned to the spot across the table, but instead spent the next two sessions right beside him, often leaning in and pointing to the text as they spoke. Sometimes their fingers brushed, sending little pinpricks of shock and pleasure rippling through Connor before he was able to rein in his thoughts.

He could tell Jared had biked over to the athletic hall the following Thursday, because the earthy scent of his sweat blended perfectly with the clean smell of his shampoo. Before he could stop himself, Connor inhaled deeply and cracked a little smile.

"You can't tell me that's not ridiculous," Jared mused, evidently taking the expression to mean Connor was listening to his latest—and mostly futile—attempt to drag them into a casual conversation. He tilted his chair and rocked on the back legs. "The guy literally drew on his application in *crayon* and got accepted into the Brown dorms. I mean, it's like they try to get the weirdest people they can possibly find to fill that place. Maybe they just want all the crazies in one location, so they can keep a better eye on them?"

It did seem a little odd. Connor had no idea how the applications to get into the desirable housing facility were processed, but there was no denying the Brown residents tended to possess certain "artsy" qualities. Rebecca and her friends were no exception.

For once, he found the power to open his mouth. "Um, m-my friends live there," he answered in an effort to remain loyal, though he wasn't quite sure he could refer to Rebecca's entourage as *friends* just yet.

Jared flopped back on all four legs of his chair. "Those people you eat lunch with? Shit, I'm sorry. I should have figured they did. I mean, they all kinda have that weird artsy look...shit, I'm insulting them again..."

A bubble of laughter welled up in Connor as he watched Jared fidget and trip over his words in the attempt to backtrack.

"And shit, you probably want to live there, too, so I should just shut up now. I didn't mean to offend you." Jared thrust a hand into his hair to twist one of the loose curls into a tight ringlet, and Connor's laughter finally escaped.

"Um...I'm not really very good with crayons."

Jared relaxed, chuckling as well. His grin faded as the laughter died off, though, and he turned to Connor with his brows drawn thoughtfully. "You know, your eyes look more gold than green when you laugh."

The air in the room grew heavy as Connor labored to draw in his next breath. *His eyes?* Jared was looking at his *eyes?*

They weren't green, really, because they had small flecks of a murky brownish-yellow obstructing them. From far away he'd always thought they looked a dull olive color.

But Jared had just said they looked *gold*.

Movement startled Connor as Jared stood. "Well, time's up. I gotta jet—got a paper to write for my English class." A hand dropped down on Connor's shoulder and gave it a gentle rub. "See ya later, bro."

***

Jared smiled at him the next day in class, a fleeting grin so brief before he took his customary chair by the wall Connor wasn't sure it was meant for him. But he smiled again during the next class, and the one after that, and the one after that—sometimes even adding a brief nod of recognition to the friendly expression, making his warm eyes seem even warmer.

Maybe Jared knew, Connor reasoned—or hoped, actually—that such uncharacteristic *humanness* from a jock would put him at ease. Each smile became like a spoonful of medicine, used to help him get a grip on handling himself like a normal eighteen-year-old while in Jared's presence.

Once or twice, though, alone in the quiet of his dorm room, he thought of Jared and handled himself in an entirely different way. He never meant for it to happen, but their time together was so private it was all too easy to gaze at Jared intently, memorizing bits of his astounding physique for later use.

He worked his way down, from the unruly curls to the broad shoulders to the firm midsection, and on the day before Halloween he was just about ready to concentrate on Jared's lower half when the sound of clipping heels echoed through the athletic hall.

She strode in before Jared, wearing fishnet stockings and a tight black mini-skirt, along with a glittery purple top. Sparkles covered her face and chest.

"It's a *Halloween* party, Jared. You're supposed to dress up."

"Maybe I'll just wear your butterfly wings, then," Jared replied, looking like his normal self in jeans and a hoodie.

"Ha ha. Very funny." The girl rolled her eyes and pulled out a chair across from Connor. She lowered herself into it carefully—a difficult task given the restrictiveness of her skirt.

"Yeah, I guess you're right. Without those, no one would know what you're supposed to—" Jared cut himself off at her glare.

Whatever sense of camaraderie Connor had tricked himself into feeling rapidly disintegrated. He couldn't

21

forget now, even for a second, how different he was from Jared—how much they didn't belong together as friends, let alone anything else.

"Connor, this is Ronnie—Veronica. Ronnie, Connor." Jared pointed between them.

Veronica thrust her hand into Connor's for a shake. "The girlfriend," she stated.

Jared's shoulders twitched and he coughed. "Listen," he cut in. "I know I'm not supposed to bring in friends, but we have this party to go to afterwards down Barracks Road, and she—we—just thought it'd be easier to go directly, rather than have to drive all the way back to grounds."

"Yeah, that's fine." Connor nodded absentmindedly, trying not to stare at Veronica's bedazzled top as she leaned forward on her elbows.

"I promise, I won't be a bother," she said sweetly. "Just do your normal brainy thing. Maybe I'll even learn a thing or two."

Veronica was wrong. She was a bother, both unintentionally, as she continually ran her hand over Jared's arm or along his thigh, and intentionally, as she interrupted their conversation with random irrelevant comments. When Connor began discussing the tenets of British symbolic anthropology, she decided it pertinent to inform them that the British had bad teeth. When he moved on to American cultural materialism, she started talking about the material her faux-leather boots were made of.

Even more disconcerting than her asinine chatter was the lack of Jared's presence beside him. He couldn't detect Jared's scent at all with Veronica's perfume blanketing the room, and he longed for those accidental touches they usually shared. Only the apologetic glances Jared shot his way every time Veronica opened her mouth helped him retain his cool.

"It's almost nine." Veronica intruded on their discussion for the umpteenth time with a sigh. "Can't we just leave now?"

"Ronnie, no one gets to a party right at nine. You're being ridiculous."

Veronica graced Jared with another glare. "Why do you have to go over the reading right now, anyway? You only need to understand the stuff for the papers that get assigned. Why don't you just pay him to write them for you?"

"Ronnie!" Jared snapped, his eyes flashing.

Veronica's demeanor changed immediately, the haughtiness draining away as she feebly crossed her arms over her chest. "Sorry."

"Look," Jared said, though he looked at no one in particular, "maybe we should go. I don't think I'm absorbing much today, anyway." He reached into his pocket and handed Veronica a set of car keys. "Go get it started. I'll be out in a second."

"Thanks, baby," she whispered, loud enough for Connor to hear, then leaned over and pushed her pink-glossed lips into Jared's mouth.

Jared waited until she had disappeared down the hallway before wiping the leftover shine on his sleeve. "Hey, I'm really sorry about her. She's not always like that, but lately she's been having these weird mood swings or whatever. Maybe it's just that female time-of-the-month thing."

Connor shuffled through a series of response ideas. *Yeah? It's okay?* Or better yet, change the topic entirely, as that felt safest. "You...you have a car? I, uh, didn't think first years were allowed to have a car on campus."

"I got this dude who went to my high school to buy me a parking permit. It comes in handy when I want to leave grounds."

"Oh, that's...cool."

"Yeah." Jared stood. "So you know, if you ever need a ride anywhere in town, let me know."

Connor strained a smile and nodded, but there was no way he'd ever take Jared up on that offer. He rose as well, overwhelmed by the need to be in the safety of his room, where he wouldn't have to face any more surprises.

Perhaps it was because he was already standing, or because Jared was in a hurry, but for the first time in a month Jared did not drop a hand on his shoulder to say goodbye. And the fact that Connor noticed, and bitterly missed the contact, meant Jared was beginning to have far too great an effect on him. He was going to have to do some serious damage control to prevent the problem from getting any worse.

***

Connor sat alone in the dining hall on Monday afternoon, his European history text open in front of him as his shield against the world. Reading was an excuse to remain withdrawn, and it was the only way he felt safe eating in the crowded cafeteria when Rebecca and her friends were not around to give him a place to belong.

At a particularly juicy part about the Medici family, a familiar weight landed on his shoulder.

"Hey, what's up, bro? Eating alone today? Where are your friends?"

"W-what?" was the best thing Connor could stutter out, caught off guard at hearing Jared's voice outside of their tutoring sanctuary.

"The friends you eat with—that tall girl—she's your stand partner in orchestra, right?" Jared used his elbow to gesture to Connor's violin, which sat in the chair next to him. He'd wrapped the strap around his arm loosely as he ate, more out of habit than anything else.

For a split second, he wondered how Jared knew Rebecca was his stand mate, since he was pretty sure he'd never mentioned it. But he lost that line of thought the instant Jared's fingertips pressed into his shoulder.

"Oh…they…they have an earlier lunch break on Mondays."

"Oh," Jared replied, his hand still resting on Connor's shoulder.

Connor held his breath. Was Jared actually going to sit down and eat with him? His heart began to beat faster, first with familiar nervousness, and then with excitement.

"Jared! Hey, our table is over here!"

Veronica. She was dressed normally today, but that didn't do anything to hide her hourglass figure and classically beautiful features. She squinted at them for a second, then offered a half-wave in Connor's direction before sitting at a table that rapidly filled with people.

Jared sighed. "Okay, well, I'll see you in class."

Connor nodded, but Jared didn't take off immediately. Nor did he do his customary squeeze-of-the-shoulder as he hesitated a moment longer, eyes transfixed on the air above them.

The fibers of Connor's sweater shifted against his skin. It was impossible to be sure, but it *felt* like Jared's thumb was brushing soft arcs along his back.

"Later," Jared said, and finally walked away.

As soon as he'd vanished behind a sea of people and trays, Connor tossed his remaining food into the trash. Disparate emotions ripped through him—humiliation at being caught eating alone, and unwelcome arousal from the thought of Jared's fingertips on his skin. Of course, they hadn't *actually* been touching his skin just then, but that wasn't stopping his imagination.

And imagination like that demanded an outlet.

***

Despite the chill in the air, Connor was sweating by the time he arrived at his dorm. He could've taken the bus, but the walk back was supposed to help him clear his head from the fog of his growing—and irrational—infatuation.

It hadn't worked, though. Now two hours after his encounter, he still found himself straining in his jeans at the mere thought of Jared. He unbuttoned his pants and let them fall to the floor, and then, because he was still hot, stripped off his sweater and undershirt as well.

That was a mistake. When he turned to grab the clothes and shove them into the hamper he caught sight of himself, short and pale in the full-length mirror affixed to his closet door.

His straight blond hair, so very unlike Jared's dark and lively curls, stuck out at odd angles from his head. Too-skinny arms folded across a pale chest, and he frowned at the slight outward curve of his stomach. Maybe it would be a good idea to skip more lunches, and perhaps spend some time outdoors to get rid of the pasty shade of his skin.

God, what was he thinking? Not even in his fantasies could he imagine Jared wanting to touch someone like him. The high from earlier was gone. Closing his eyes, he feebly tried to recapture it, until the ringing of the dorm room phone interrupted him.

He almost didn't answer. There was only one person it could be…but this particular caller would not give up easily, and if she didn't reach him there, his cell phone would ring constantly for the next hour.

"Hi, Mom."

"Hello, dear," she responded in her syrupy tone. "I haven't heard from you in such a long time, and I just wanted to check to make sure everything is okay."

"Yeah, everything's fine." Connor sighed, pulling the ancient corded phone as far as it would go so he could sink onto his bed. *Such a long time* was about six days.

"Well, you could call more often, you know. Are you going to all your classes? Keeping up with your homework? Getting good grades?"

"Yes, Mom." He always had. So why did she feel the necessity to ask him this same question at least once a week?

"And are you eating healthy? Remember you're short, so you'll need to watch yourself closely to make sure you don't gain the freshman fifteen."

Connor chose not to respond to that and instead stared at his ceiling.

"You should really take up a sport, you know. It would be good for you."

"Hey, is Melissa there?" Talking to a teenage girl was never high on his list of priorities, but at least his sister's child-like concerns offered an escape from his mother's scrutiny.

"No, she's at a friend's house."

Of course. Where else would Melissa the social butterfly be?

"But your father's here. He wants to speak to you."

After a few seconds of shuffling, Connor heard his father clear his throat. He didn't have to be there to see the scene in his mind—his father's reluctant hand gripping the phone, his mother's stern glance ordering him to be the backup singer for her parenthood performance.

"You keeping your grades up?"

"Yes, Dad."

"Good, good. I was reading up a little on your school...you should join this debating group they have...called the Jefferson Society. All the prestigious grads were in it. It'll look good for getting into law school."

Connor had to suffocate his bitter laugh by biting down on his forearm. How was it possible he'd spent eighteen years of his life under the same roof as his parents without them knowing a single thing about him? Maybe it was because he'd never told them, or maybe because they'd never asked. Either way, if they thought he was going to join a debating society, they had serious delusions.

"Sure, Dad. I'll…look into that."

"Mmph," his father mumbled. "Okay, well…uh, take care."

"Yeah, you too," Connor replied in the same monotone before gratefully hanging up.

If staring at his body in contempt hadn't put him out of the mood, then talking with his parents certainly had. He abandoned all hope of sexual release and opened his violin case instead.

At least he'd always have that.

CHAPTER THREE

"Hey, is that the guy you're tutoring?" Rebecca stole a few french fries off Connor's plate to accompany her usual lunch of tofu and salad. Her friends Tate and A.J. took their chairs across from her, cutting into Connor's line of sight.

"What?" he mumbled, ducking his head to continue his no-longer clandestine observations.

Across the crowded room, Jared took a neat bite of his hamburger. The guy next to him—another football player, from the looks of it—already had a mouthful of some sort of casserole, and seemed content to display the half-masticated bits to the world around him.

Veronica said something and everyone at the table laughed, but Jared only joined in after he swallowed his food. Connor narrowed his eyes and studied Veronica's form. She looked thinner than the first time he'd seen her, and didn't really have much more weight to spare.

"She means the guy you're staring at," came the helpful clarification from another of Rebecca's friends. Chrissy set her tray down, completing their usual lunch crowd. She tossed her wavy brown hair over the shoulder of her hemp shirt. "Isn't he the guy you tutor?"

"Oh." Connor finally managed to look away. "Yeah…he's…yeah."

Tate leaned toward him with a snort. "Athletes. I find it pretty insulting they get to come to this school for free just because they can throw a ball around. And then when they can't pass the courses, they get extra help and don't have to pay for that, either."

Connor frowned while he considered a response. His contributions to the discussions at lunch were limited at best, but he had a strange impulse to make sure Jared was not unfairly judged. "Um…Jared didn't get a full scholarship. He came to UVA because he wanted to."

"Well, I suppose when you get paid for their lack of intelligence, it's easier to see the good in them."

"Hey," Rebecca snapped at the same time Chrissy threw in, "Don't be rude. They're people too."

Tate shrugged.

Connor's cheeks burned, and he was torn between defending Jared further and backing away from the conversation very carefully. One slip of the tongue was sure to reveal his schoolboy crush.

Rebecca solved the problem for him, though not in the most helpful way. "You okay, Connor? Your face is kinda red."

"Mmm…uh, yeah. I'm fine."

Thankfully, A.J. cut in with his preparations for the upcoming Brown dorm crawl, and the talk shifted into safer territory. Having no stake in the activity, Connor felt perfectly justified retreating into silence.

But his gaze wandered again. It was hard to look anywhere else when Jared was smiling.

Tate kicked him under the table a few minutes later. "C'mon, you can tell me, is he dumb as nails?"

Connor jumped up, tripping over the leg of his chair and causing four pairs of eyes to stare at him in alarm. "I…I just remembered, I have to finish a…a take-home quiz for my last class today. I gotta run."

"But you haven't eaten your lunch!" Rebecca called after him.

Connor blinked back at his abandoned tray. "I...I really have to finish my work."

"All right." She nodded, concern obvious in her drawn brows. "I'll put it up for you, it's okay. Go ahead. Catch ya later."

He escaped into the sunlight. *Stupid, stupid, stupid.* If he kept this up, he'd out himself in no time, not to mention be completely humiliated in front of the closest thing he had to a group of friends. Newcomb was starting to seem less like a place for sustenance and more like a lion's den.

He wandered to UVA's historic Lawn with a bag of chips from a vending machine, looking for the least populated spot to settle down. A secluded tree beckoned to him, and he scurried behind it to let out a pent-up sigh. *You and me, tree.* His fingers traced the crevices in the bark. Maybe it simply was his destiny to continue his friendships with plant life. It was a nice enough tree, after all, and a couple of nearby squirrels looked happy to call it home.

Definitely a safer place to eat lunch from now on.

He finished his chips, fervently avoiding the world around him by dint of an open book in his lap.

***

Connor arrived early to his anthropology class the day before Thanksgiving break, taking his time adjusting the strap of his violin case against the back of his seat. Sometimes he pulled the entire case under his desk and propped his feet along the edge, but today he noticed the dusty stains gathering on that part of the gray fabric. He bent over and wiped the smudges, having little effect on them.

A pair of legs slid into the seat next to him. Familiar legs. When he looked up, he was greeted by large brown eyes.

"Hey," Jared said with a grin.

"Hey," Connor managed to say back, much too softly for his liking.

"You'll never guess what I saw after tutoring yesterday," Jared whispered conspiratorially, like they sat next to each other and shared little conversations in class all the time.

Only, they didn't.

"Like fifteen streakers on the Lawn. It was barely eight o' clock! Man those guys have balls." He paused to shudder. "And I had to see them, flapping in the wind!"

Dumbfounded, Connor forced a weak nod.

That was all they exchanged for the remainder of class. Professor Abrahms beamed at them both, probably because she reasoned that with Jared away from the wall, he wouldn't be able to fall asleep as easily. She looked genuinely shocked when Jared raised his hand to participate a few times, and after one comment even shot Connor a little wink, which had him sinking down in his chair with embarrassment.

Still, it'd been a fairly successful day. A little attention from Jared, an exchange of cordial greetings, and no major incidents of anxiety. He retrieved his violin and gathered his books at the end of the hour with the happy notes of Dvorak's *Humoresque* bouncing through his head.

"So, I don't see you in the dining hall anymore," Jared's voice cut in.

Humoresque slipped into a minor key. "Oh." Connor licked his lips and drew himself back into the moment. The room was nearly empty. "I...I kinda stopped eating there. Sometimes I have work to do during lunch."

Jared frowned as they made their way into the hall. "Listen, don't take this the wrong way...but it doesn't seem like you have a lot of friends. Maybe it's not such a good idea to quit hanging out with people during lunch."

A sudden cloud of heat enveloped Connor. *Escape*, his brain told him. Humiliation that threatened to turn into tears clawed at his throat, and he took quick steps to exit the crowded hallway as fast as possible.

Jared was faster.

"Wait, Connor, wait. I'm sorry, that came out wrong. I'm sorry."

He only stopped because Jared forced him to with a firm grip on his arm. But he still couldn't say anything, and chose to focus on the wall just past Jared instead.

Jared dropped his arm and pushed a hand through his curly hair. "Look, sometimes I don't think before I speak. I didn't mean to imply you were some kind of loser or anything."

Wincing at the choice of words, Connor tried to school his gaze on a corkboard papered with colorful flyers, but Jared ducked into his line of sight.

Surprisingly, his cheeks seemed reddened by a blush. "Listen, you want to come over to my dorm and do our homework together? I mean, I missed a few classes, so I could use your help..."

No. That simple response would suffice. Or rather, *no, thank you, I have some work to do.* But as Connor prepared to excuse himself and retreat to the safety of things he knew, Jared flashed him a smile so full of bright white teeth and warm eyes that he was left wanting to stare at it for however long he could get away with.

"Y-yeah...okay."

"Cool." Jared grinned impossibly wider, hitching his bag up on his shoulder. "Let's go."

Connor had to take longer-than-normal strides to keep up, as Jared had at least a good ten inches on him. He was embarrassed to find that after several minutes of walking like that with his bag and violin banging at either side, he was slightly out of breath.

"You want me to carry that for you?" Jared asked, motioning toward the violin.

"N-no, I'm fine."

Jared reached over and grabbed the strap off his shoulder anyhow, yanking the case away. "Really, it's no problem. Now I can pretend to be a musician for five minutes."

He grinned and Connor bit back his panic, letting the infectious smile win him over.

They reached Jared's building and entered a lounge area filled with people munching on snacks and typing away on laptops. A guy about Jared's height, but much leaner and with a hooked nose, stood and gave Jared's hand a slap as a greeting.

"Yo, Jared. Whaddup? You starting a new hobby?" He eyed the violin on Jared's shoulder.

"Nah, man. This is Connor's. He's my anthro tutor. Connor, this is Ben, my roommate."

Connor received a hand slap as well. His arm flailed from the unfamiliar greeting, and he dropped his head to hide a grimace.

Ben smirked, clearly having noted his difficulty. "Cool, dude. You gonna study?"

"Yeah, we'll be in the room. Let me know if anything fun is going on tonight," Jared threw over his shoulder as he walked away. Connor trailed after him and nearly smacked into Jared's chest when he abruptly turned back around. "Oh, and Ben? If Ronnie comes by...tell her I'm at the library or something."

"No problem, dude. I'll give you a break from the crazy chick."

The crazy chick? It was times like these Connor wished he were the kind of person who could pry. But he wasn't, of course, so he just quietly followed Jared into a room at the end of the hallway.

Like all the other dorm rooms, two twin beds lined the walls. One was a mound of covers, books, food wrappers, and clothes. Some of the clothing spilled onto the floor, but as if an invisible line had been drawn, the encroaching mess stopped just left of the center of the room. The other bed was neatly made with an organized desk beside it to match.

Jared dropped onto a smooth dark blue comforter—on the tidy side—and leaned against the wall, closing his eyes.

For a moment, Connor stood awkwardly and waited to be directed, but when Jared didn't acknowledge his presence he took a seat at a desk and pulled a few books from his bag. "What would you like to go over first? The reading from last week, or what we covered today in class?"

Jared shook his head, finally reopening his eyes. "Neither. Actually, it just occurred to me that having you help me off the clock is like cheating you out of money or something. I shouldn't be taking advantage of you just because you're a nice guy."

Connor blinked rapidly in a few seconds of silence before stumbling into a response. "I...I can study with a friend without getting paid." As soon as the word *friend* was out of his mouth, he blushed, but Jared only smiled. A warm smile, not a teasing one.

"Well, friends do more than study together. I just want to unwind right now." Jared grabbed two video game controllers from the top shelf of his desk. He kept one in his lap and tossed the other to Connor, then turned on the twelve-inch TV that sat nestled between some books in crates against the wall.

"Yeah, I know," Jared said, even though Connor had said nothing. "It's a tiny-ass screen, but luckily I still have my eyesight. What do you want to play? Between me and Ben we have just about everything."

"Um...anything's fine..." Connor mumbled, picking up the controller and eyeing it warily. He'd never played any electronic game that wasn't educational, at first because of his parents' steadfast rule, and later because he realized he had no aptitude for them.

"Cool." Jared fidgeted with the TV and the box above it. A moment later a game lit up the screen, and Connor was caught between staring at Jared's hands, desperately trying to mimic their movements, and watching his tiny figure get shot over and over again. His tongue found a notch between his teeth and he accidentally bit down several times in his intense concentration.

By the fifth time his character died, Jared turned to him with a grin. "Dude, have you ever played this before?"

"No...I...we weren't allowed to have video games," Connor admitted. It had to be less humiliating for Jared to know the truth than to think he was totally inept, right? "I guess I don't have very good hand-eye coordination."

Jared laughed and crawled over to the end of the bed so he could take Connor's controller. "I don't know about hand-eye coordination, but you have decent hand coordination at least, or you wouldn't be able to play violin as well as you do."

"What?" Connor's mouth dropped open, and this time there was no mistaking the blush on Jared's skin. *When had Jared heard...*

"I mean, I assume so. I guess I haven't actually seen you play up close, but I passed through Old Cabell Hall a few weeks ago while you guys were having practice. I was too far away to really see your hands, but the stuff you were playing...sounded awesome."

"Oh." Connor breathed out slowly, mulling over the first thought that popped into his head—that not many people had a reason to be "passing through" Old Cabell Hall during an orchestra rehearsal.

"Hey, why don't you show me?" Jared interrupted before Connor could reach any reasonable conclusion.

"Show you?"

"Yeah, play something for me. You have your violin here."

"Oh...I...I don't have my music."

It was a blatant lie. Jared had to know that. Anyone with half a brain could tell there was music stored in the outside pocket of his case, or realize that having achieved the level of professionalism to be in a university orchestra, he could obviously play at least a few pieces from memory.

"Let's go to your place then."

Connor opened his mouth to object, but Jared had already grabbed his violin case by that time and was halfway out the door.

***

"Seriously, dude. No roommate? That's fucking awesome." Jared breathed with a sigh, settling himself on the empty bed across from Connor's. "I mean, don't get me wrong, Ben's a cool guy and all, but...wow. No roommate. I wouldn't mind that."

Connor shrugged. He'd only grown less and less sure of how to behave as their strange day together wore on, and now Jared was in his space—his sanctuary—and there'd be nowhere to run to if things got awkward.

Or with his track record, *when* things got awkward.

"All right then, no more excuses. Play for me, maestro."

Ordinarily, Connor hated playing for private audiences. But at this point, it seemed like the safest thing he could possibly do with Jared in the room. At least it would offer him a much-needed break from his anxiety.

He took out his violin and set some sheet music on his miserably bent wire stand, just so he wouldn't be caught in his lie from earlier. Then, with only a deep breath to bolster him, he launched into the first thing he could think of—the solo from *Scheherazade*.

It was a haunting melody, wistful and yearning, yet with a touch of hopefulness to it at the same time. The room and the tension slipped away as he drew the bow across the strings, his fingers vibrating with emotion—a simple task given what kinship he felt with the piece. It was so *easy* in this space to express himself, to make perfectly clear who he was and what he wanted from life. If only it were possible to speak with these notes in the real world.

He pulled the last sweet note to completion and kept his bow poised on the string, soaking in the final drops of security.

"Jesus, that was incredible." Jared's awestruck whisper dropped into the charged silence. "You're fucking amazing."

Connor shook his head. "N-not really…I'm not playing the solo for the concert or anything."

"Well you should be," Jared declared, standing and walking toward him.

Connor blinked a few times as Jared was suddenly taking hold of his violin. He rarely if ever let non-musicians handle it, but he couldn't seem to find the willpower to either stop Jared or put the violin away himself.

With great care, Jared took his instrument and bow and laid them on the bed, then walked back to him. He grasped Connor's left hand and turned it over in his open palm. "What did I tell you—you have great hand coordination." His thick fingers flitted over Connor's more slender ones. They paused to feel each fingertip, lingering in the faint grooves from the violin strings.

Connor closed his eyes, his mind reeling. Jared stood far too close, and the *touching* was beyond any contingency he'd ever planned for. If he didn't keep a grip on himself, his body might decide to do something without his consent. Something he'd never live down. Something that would force him to drop out of school and move to a cabin in the middle of the woods, where he wouldn't have to face this ultimate humiliation ever again.

"Your fingers are so nice," Jared murmured. "Mine are like bear paws…"

Still hiding behind closed lids, Connor didn't realize a tear had slipped out until a rough thumb brushed his cheek. And he certainly didn't realize how impossibly close Jared had gotten until he felt pressure against his lips— soft, pliable skin, sliding over his, with the hint of a tongue begging for entry into his mouth.

"Wh…what?" he gasped, eyes flying open as he struggled to stand.

Jared backed up quickly. He looked nearly as panicked as Connor felt, with pupils dilated into pools of deep black. "Oh…oh…I'm sorry. I'm really…I just…sorry."

He rushed to the door and was almost out before Connor summoned the ability to make a sound.

"Wait!"

Jared turned around hesitantly, gaze on the floor and one hand still on the doorknob. "Yeah?"

Even on his best days, Connor would have had a much better chance of making a coherent point in a research paper. At the moment, his vocabulary seemed to have dwindled down to nonexistent.

"I…I am," he finally managed to get out.

"You are?" Jared shook his head.

Connor tried for a shrug, but his body had gone too stiff to allow it. "Yeah. I am."

Jared closed his eyes. "Oh, you are," he exhaled softly, and this time, it wasn't a question. He shut the door and in two steps was flush against Connor's chest. His arms encircled Connor and he tugged upwards, leaning over to close the gap between their faces at the same time. He succeeded in parting Connor's lips with his own seconds after they connected.

Mouth filled and mind flooded, Connor had no choice but to surrender to Jared's advance. This was *nothing* like anything he had ever experienced. Jared was not at all like the lonely violist on the back of the Regionals bus who'd begged and pleaded and guilted him into his first—and only—kiss. And unlike Clarissa Maddox, Jared didn't have braces or breasts or breath that tasted like peanut butter. Jared tasted like mint and his lips were firm and strong, his tongue warm, and the way it darted around Connor's mouth probably meant he was pretty damned experienced in the art of kissing.

Experienced. The thought that broke the moment.

"Jared, wait." Connor fell back on his heels, realizing he'd been on his toes for most of their kiss.

"I don't want to wait," Jared groaned. He ducked his head back in again to continue, but to Connor's surprise, his own tongue was quicker.

"Ronnie," he said.

Jared froze. "What about her?"

"Sh-she's…she's your girlfriend. We can't…I can't…"

Jared backed up a few steps and rubbed his hand over his face. "Yeah. I know. You're…you're right." He continued toward the door. "Sorry again, then."

Shaky, labored breaths kept Connor from responding. Jared grabbed the door and opened it, but paused with one foot in the hallway. "I didn't mean to, you know."

"K-kiss me?"

"No. Have a girlfriend."

He left with his head bowed and shut the door behind him.

Connor stood still for the next two minutes before reclaiming his instrument. He mechanically loosened the bow and put his violin away in its case. Then he threw himself onto his beige comforter, open-mouthed, and gagged on the taste of his pillow.

Of all the times in his life to have a conscience, this had to be the worst.

CHAPTER FOUR

"Mrs. Hasker asked you to pass the stuffing."

The thick put-on sweetness of his mother's voice shook Connor from his thoughts. "Oh, sorry," he mumbled, finding the dish and handing it off to her plump friend.

Mrs. Hasker opened her mouth as if to continue speaking with him. To avoid the onslaught, he quickly lowered his eyes, and in his peripheral vision caught her scrunching her chubby cheeks up in defeat.

"Connor's gotten too used to daydreaming through dinner while at college, I'm afraid." His mother turned to her guests around the Thanksgiving table with an apologetic smile. "I'm sorry he isn't being more sociable."

Connor slumped down in his chair and used his fork to make a path through his mashed potatoes. He could have said something to placate his mother and stop the reproving glances from his father, but there didn't seem to be much point now that he'd been called out. He was sure to get a lecture after dinner anyway, and it wasn't as if the Haskers—old family friends—weren't used to his behavior by now.

"Melissa's been learning a new piece for this year's competition," his mother continued in a lighter tone. "Maybe she'd like to play it for us while we have some coffee?"

The room erupted in murmured consent, and Melissa nodded happily. "Sure, Mom."

Mrs. Hasker and her husband shoveled in a few more mouthfuls of food before rising stiffly. Connor stood as well, but before he even had a chance to grab his own plate, his mother pinned him with an icy glare. "You can clear everyone's dishes, Connor, since you don't seem to want to be here at all."

That suited him well enough. Because the truth was, he didn't.

He thought of at least ten places he'd rather be as he tossed the cranberry-stained plates into the dishwasher. Maybe everyone else at school had been thrilled about the chance to return to the comforts of home, but sometimes being around his boisterous and sociable-to-the-point-of-exhaustion mother was harder than being in a room full of strangers. At least strangers didn't pierce him with that frown of disappointment for failing expectations of being a *well-mannered* son.

He scraped away some turkey skin remains and stuffed them down the garbage disposal, then watched as the blade made quick work of dissolving the refuse.

If only he could so easily dissolve the tangle of thoughts in his head.

For the thousandth time in the past few days, he tried to make some sense of the jumble. *Why* had Jared kissed him? And even more importantly, why had he turned away the first guy who had ever shown any interest in him?

Veronica, he told himself. But that wasn't the whole story.

Per his mother's ingrained instructions, he fetched a used lemon from the refrigerator and tore off a chunk to liquefy in the disposal. It whirled angrily as the citrus scent rose up from the drain.

There was no possible way Jared could actually be interested in him. Jared was probably just experimenting—and safely, at that. He knew Connor would never breathe a word. Besides, even if he tried, who would believe him?

Guys like Jared were supposed to belittle and mock him, or, at best, ignore him. Things couldn't have changed so drastically in the six short months since high school.

Or had they? Jared wasn't exactly like other jocks. He was friendly. Very friendly. And he had *kissed* him.

Connor flicked on the garbage disposal one last time for no other reason than to attempt to drown out his thoughts. "Idiot," he muttered to himself. He knew why he'd turned Jared away.

As usual, it was fear.

The sounds of one of Chopin's Waltzes drifted out from the living room, followed by a round of applause. A few minutes later Melissa flitted in, rubbing her knuckles on her shirt. She blew on them with a self-important smirk.

"Mom says to bring out the pumpkin pie, but you should warm it up first. It tastes better that way." She perched on a kitchen stool while Connor wiped stray water drops off the counter. "So listen, I kinda want to duck out early and go to Jamie's house. Her family is having a holiday movie night. Should be more fun than hanging around here."

Connor grabbed the pumpkin pie from the fridge and wrinkled his nose. His mother could cook, but baking was not her specialty. The pie was a muddy brown color and far too soupy to ever hope to congeal properly, even with a little extra time in the oven.

"Connor, I'm talking to you." A wadded-up ball of paper towel sailed past his face.

"Yeah?"

"I'm saying, I want to go to Jamie's house. Can you help me out?"

"How can I help?" Connor mumbled, sliding the pie into the oven. His mother's voice drifted closer as footsteps sounded in the hallway, and he headed for the dining room to get out of sight.

Melissa followed. "You can help by pulling some of the weight around here. Go get your violin and play something, and maybe Mom won't mind me leaving. Or just go out there and talk to them about college. Adults love talking to kids about college."

Connor skirted around to the foyer and grabbed the handrail to the stairs. If he left now, he'd have a good ten minutes to hide in his room before he'd have to return for the pie. "Just ask Dad while Mom's not around. I'm busy right now."

"Busy?" Melissa scoffed. "Doing what? Gonna go hang out with your friends? Oh, wait." She paused to throw a hand on her hip. "That's right, you don't have any."

He pushed past her and took the stairs two at a time. Halfway up, his mother's voice stopped him.

"Connor? The pie! And put on another pot of coffee, please. Melissa, Mrs. Hasker would like to hear you play Mozart's Sonata 14."

Melissa crossed her arms and glared at him. "Thanks for nothing."

***

Four whitewashed walls greeted Connor back at school, as he'd never bothered putting up any decorations in his dorm room. Decorations were an advertisement of who you were, and he had no one to advertise to.

But as he stared at the vacant walls, he began to reconsider that stance. It would've been nice to have something up there to distract him from his thoughts. At one time, his room had seemed like the only safe haven on campus, but not anymore. Now it was tainted. Tainted by the memories of a broad chest, strong arms, and warm lips.

He glanced at his cell phone display. Seven o'clock. The tutoring session would be starting now, but he'd already called in sick. And this after skipping his anthropology class on Monday—his first time ever playing hooky—all in an effort to avoid Jared for as long as possible. Layers of guilt weighed heavily upon him, but they couldn't overpower his panic. He was way too off his game to interact with anyone appropriately, let alone Jared. The safest thing to do would be to eschew all human contact.

Squeezing the blue foam ball he'd received during orientation—as a stress reliever, ironically—he began formulating excuses for quitting at the tutoring department. If he told them he needed more time for his studies, they couldn't fault him, could they?

He threw the ball up in the air a few times and on the third attempt missed catching it by an inch. It rolled off into a corner of the room.

Stress reliever, my ass. He yanked open his astronomy book. Maybe he'd have better luck memorizing facts from the dry text.

Footsteps padded down the hallway outside his room, and he ignored them, like always. But the loud knock that came a few seconds later startled him half-off the bed. Straightening his twisted t-shirt, he edged his way toward the door, as if whoever was on the other side could jump out at him without warning.

"Hey, Connor?"

Jared.

Connor pressed his face into the door. The cool surface felt even colder against his skin—skin that had heated the second Jared's mellow voice sounded from beyond the safety of his room. For a moment, he considered pretending he wasn't there...but he had a nagging suspicion Jared could already hear the pounding of his heart through the wall that separated them.

He cracked the door open a few inches. "Yeah?"

"Hey, the tutoring place told me you called in sick, so I brought you some chicken soup from the dining hall. It sucks being sick and alone, doesn't it? I had a really bad cold my first week here, and I know it kinda makes me sound like a sissy…but I actually missed my mother taking care of me."

Jared's smile shone in the hallway, almost blinding Connor as he peered out from his darkened room. The tiny reading lamp wasn't bright enough to combat the shadows of evening. He reached back to flick on the overhead light, and Jared took the opportunity to slip through the unguarded door. He closed it firmly behind him.

"So, whaddaya got? A cold? A fever?"

"N-no. It's just…a bad headache."

That, at least, wasn't a lie, because in the last several seconds, a staccato pulsing had started behind his eyes.

"Oh, like a migraine? I used to get those."

Jared put down the chicken soup and took Connor by the hand, dragging him onto the bed. He made himself comfortable against the wall, then thrust both hands into Connor's hair.

"My mom used to give me these head massages. They really helped."

Connor was forced to agree. Jared's strong fingers did amazing things to help him forget about the pain and the panic—until one of Jared's legs snuck around him and two strong arms pulled him against a muscular chest.

Jared went back to his massage without skipping a beat.

"Wh-what…what are you doing?" Connor's voice shook, and he added embarrassment to the list of bombarding emotions. He coughed to clear his throat and prepare it for a less humiliating sound the next time he had to speak.

"I dunno." Jared's shoulders shrugged against his back. "I just...wanted to be close to you."

"Why?"

A blast of warm laughter tickled Connor's neck. "I dunno. I mean, yeah, you're really shy and all, but that's better than being one of those snobby geeks. I just got the feeling that if I got to know you better, you'd be pretty cool. And so far, I've been right."

Connor snorted. Self-deprecating thoughts staged an upsurge, but his tension eased as Jared's hands continued their work. And if this was to be his second opportunity for...for *something*, he was going to have to grow a pair. At least *pretend* to be normal.

"Jared?" he whispered.

"Mhm?"

"I...I wasn't really sick. I was just..."

"Freaked out? Yeah, I guess I did come on a little too strong," Jared mused with a chuckle. "I don't think I'm usually that forward. Or that much of a gambler."

"What...what made you think that...that I was..."

"Caught you staring at me. Lots of times, in fact." A proud smirk touched his lips. "I guess it was something in that look. Or maybe it takes one to know one, or something?"

Connor wasn't sure about that. *He* obviously hadn't known about Jared...but then again, he was no expert judge of character. "So, um, Veronica," he pressed, unable to forget how she played into this picture. "Does that mean you're...bi?"

Jared pulled away. He leaned all the way back on the bed until he was lying down and staring at the ceiling. "No, I don't really think so. I used to kinda wish I would be, because then I could just choose the path of least resistance and be done with it. But I guess that's not the way things turned out. I'm more interested in...in hanging out with you now than I am with Ronnie."

Connor felt his face turning crimson, and he lay down next to Jared so he could at least partially hide it in the curve of his pillow. "Oh. S-so why are you with her then?"

"I meant what I said the other day. I didn't mean to be."

That wasn't enough of an explanation, though Connor couldn't bring himself to ask for more. But he couldn't change the topic, either, and after a few beats of silence Jared grimaced and sighed like he'd been pressed to go on anyhow.

"We were friends first, and when we hooked up over the summer she was on the wait-list for UVA. Then she got in at the last minute, and before I knew it she was telling me and everyone else we knew that we were together. She's pretty hot, so I didn't turn it down because I thought it'd look weird. But lately she's been...sorta strange. I actually have been trying to break up with her, but it's like she mentally checks out and we just get into these fights that end with her crying and me apologizing...and my father told me never to make a girl cry..."

He trailed off for a moment, fidgeting with a bit of fuzz on the edge of his sweater. "But I'm gonna have to try harder to make things clear to her now."

"Why?" Connor blurted out his confusion before he had a chance to check himself. Still, it seemed a legitimate question—until Jared burst into laughter.

"You gotta stop that. You sound like one of those little kids who keeps on asking how the world works. And you're short enough to pass for one from the back."

Connor frowned. He wasn't *that* short.

In a blur of rapid movement, Jared dropped a kiss on his lips. "Sorry." He backed up quickly. "I don't think you know how cute you look when you frown like that."

"Wh-what? I...do?"

Jared chuckled, reaching out to push back a strand of Connor's hair. His knuckles brushed Connor's cheek and then stayed there.

In a deafening silence, Connor's pulse sped up, his mind more captive to Jared's touch than it had been the first time they'd kissed. He couldn't look away, even if his fear wanted him to. He couldn't blink. He couldn't draw in his next breath. Because *this*…this was all searching eyes and gentle caresses, and somehow, unbelievably, a *connection*.

A shudder broke the moment and he pulled back, as hard as he'd ever been—and deathly afraid to let it show.

"You okay?" Jared asked.

"Yeah. I'm…I'm good. It's just that…I've never…I mean…"

"You've never been with a guy?"

Connor nodded, grateful for Jared's strange ability to make sense of the drivel that came out of his mouth. Now, if only Jared could apply that skill to his reading assignments, he'd have no trouble understanding even the most convoluted text…

"Don't worry. I haven't either." Jared's voice dragged him back from the tangent. "I promise we'll take things slow, okay?" He shifted a few inches away, leaving a hand on Connor's arm so he could stroke it softly. "We could watch a movie or something if you have any on your laptop…or we could just talk."

Rock and a hard place. Watching a movie was safer, but…it involved having to move. If Connor got up from where he was pressing his lower half firmly into the mattress, there was no way he could hide his erection. "Um, t-talking's fine."

"Really?" One of Jared's eyebrows tilted up to mock him. "I thought you hated talking. It always takes me so long to get you to loosen up during our tutoring sessions."

"Well…we're supposed to be working then."

"Nah, you're just shy."

Connor frowned.

Jared bit his lip, his eyes dancing. "If you ever want me to kiss you, just make that face and I'd be hard pressed to resist."

When wouldn't he want Jared to kiss him? But that pathetic thought could never see the light of day, so Connor said nothing.

Jared grinned at him for few seconds before his lips straightened into a more serious line. "I guess we need to talk about this." He squeezed Connor's shoulder. "Just so you know, no one knows about me. Well, no one but you, I guess. That's okay, right?"

"Uh huh." Connor nodded readily. "M-me too. I mean, uh, no one, um…"

"No one knows about you either, you mean."

Connor blushed, but as Jared scooted closer he found his tongue unexpectedly loosening. "I have enough trouble talking to people as it is, so I didn't really want to have another reason to feel awkward."

Oh, brilliant. A blatant admission to his lack of social skills. Maybe his tongue was best left tied.

His face sought a deeper spot in his pillow and he muttered on through the fabric. "I-I've…I've thought about it, though. Since I got here, I mean. I've seen flyers for meetings and stuff."

Thought about it was as far as he'd gotten. There was a certain allure to the idea of finally belonging to such a "group", but it was just plain unrealistic to expect that to magically strip his social anxieties away.

Jared stopped rubbing his arm. "Oh. Really?" He rolled over to stare at the ceiling again, his voice dropping into a mumble. "Because I'm not really ready to…you know, with football and all."

Connor frowned again, but Jared wasn't looking at him, so there probably wasn't any danger of a kiss. "I was only thinking about it. I'm not…I'm not ready to do it."

"Yeah, I get that." Jared turned back to him, a half-smile nowhere near as inspiring as his full one tugging at his lips. "I guess I'd better get going. You probably have work to do."

Having finally regained control of wayward body parts, Connor stood with Jared and they made their way to the door. But before he could open it, Jared reached down to peck him chastely on the lips, murmuring, "See ya tomorrow, bro."

***

Connor's fingers whipped through the fastest, most difficult runs he could think of in every piece of music he had ever learned. He just didn't have the discipline to slow himself down and give due respect to anything softer or more delicate. Excitement radiated from within, and pouring it into the music felt like the only way to keep from literally bursting.

Jared. Jared liked him. Had kissed him. Maybe even wanted to *be* with him.

It seemed like the life he'd always been waiting for was about to begin.

A tap on the glass door of the practice room registered at the edge of his consciousness, but he waited until he'd completed the last measures of a run before turning to see who was there.

"What's up?" Rebecca entered as he rested his violin on his lap. "What are you practicing? Whatever it is looked like fun."

Connor hadn't been able to wipe the smile away since he'd woken up that morning, and faced with Rebecca, he had no more success.

"Oh, just some old stuff. You want to rehearse for sectionals?"

"Sure." Rebecca cocked her head and regarded him with a grin. "You're looking chipper this morning. Get another A on one of your essays?"

"No." Connor tried for a frown but failed miserably. "Let's just practice, okay?"

"Okay, okay." Rebecca put her hands up in defeat. "Keep your happy secrets, by all means."

They practiced together for the next thirty minutes, but unlike their previous sessions, any time Rebecca paused to make a comment about college or Vidar or the music, Connor allowed himself to get dragged into the conversation. Or rather, he *participated* in the conversation. All his nervous energy had the strange effect of making him *want* to talk to her, to share anecdotes of high school orchestra mishaps, or laugh freely at her latest theory as to how a high-brow Scandinavian had ended up stuck in a rural southern town surrounded by cows and corn.

They kept talking all the way to Newcomb Hall, and Connor was so caught up in Rebecca's pinched-face impersonation of Vidar berating the eighth stand for their out-of-sync bowing, he completely forgot there was a chance he'd run into Jared in the cafeteria. He froze just after they stepped inside and darted his head around wildly.

When he did spot Jared, his heart sank. Jared was sitting by his suite mates, laughing and talking with animated hands. Veronica was at his side, her arm casually lying on his thigh. She was considerably less made-up than the last time Connor had seen her, her hair sloppily shoved in a ponytail and her eyes clouded with a disinterested look.

That was, until she turned to Jared and planted a kiss on his cheek.

Connor paled.

"Hey, space cadet." Rebecca nudged him. "You gonna get that burger or what?" She pointed to the plate the service lady was impatiently shaking in front of him.

"Oh, yeah, thanks." He grabbed it and shuffled away, forcing his eyes straight ahead.

Chrissy, Tate, and A.J. sat in their normal spots, but he decided to switch to the other side of the table so he'd have his back to Jared. That didn't help as much as he had hoped, though, because he still found himself turning around every so often to steal worried glances.

"You in trouble with the law or something?" Chrissy asked suddenly, lowering her veggie burger from her lips.

"Huh?" The ungraceful syllable left his mouth before he could process her question.

"She means the constant twirling around you're doing, checking behind you. You look like you're being followed," Rebecca explained.

"Um...just keeping limber." Connor forced himself to shrug, searching for an excuse to cover yet another example of his awkwardness. "My back gets stiff, sitting in little desks all day."

Chrissy nodded. "I agree. It's stupid to keep us cooped up in those little cages. We should be learning outside, in the fresh air, where we'd actually have a chance to make connections between what we learn and how it affects the world."

Tate snorted, but A.J. gave her a rueful smile. "I'll support that petition, if you want to get it started."

"That is an excellent idea," Chrissy said brightly.

Rebecca was the only one who didn't seem caught up in Chrissy's joke—if that was what it was. She stared at Connor for a few more seconds, one pale eyebrow raised questioningly.

***

Amazingly, a single word from Jared managed to erase any anxiety or guilt about being in a love-triangle and turn all of Connor's thoughts into complete mush.

That one word was "hi," and Jared said it kind of quietly as he slipped into the desk next to him before their anthropology class.

"Hey," Connor replied, then bit his lip to keep from smiling so idiotically.

Jared smirked and turned away, busying himself with dragging a notebook out of his bag. "So, I'm sorta tied up for the rest of the week. Coach has us doing extra stuff to make up for getting lazy over Thanksgiving...but I was wondering, if you don't already have plans, maybe I could come by on Friday?"

"Um...sure," Connor whispered back, trying not to scoff out loud at the thought of already having plans for a Friday night. But maybe all that was about to change. Maybe from now on Fridays would be about Jared's incredible smile and soft, strong lips.

A blush crept up his cheeks, and he quickly turned his thoughts to the safer territory of French structuralism before his body could get any more ahead of itself.

Friday. He'd have to wait till Friday.

CHAPTER FIVE

Connor opted for a bag of chips and a soda for dinner, too nervous to do anything other than peruse the Internet for mind-numbing entertainment. He half-expected Jared not to show; after missing both a tutoring session and class that day, it seemed possible Jared had changed his mind about whatever-it-was they were doing.

He'd just started compiling a list of all the reasons for Jared's rejection when the knock at his door came in a familiar rhythm. *Rap-rap-a-tap-tap, rap rap.*

It was cheesy and so unlike anything he could imagine Jared doing. But then again, he'd never imagined being kissed by him, either. Looked like he was going to have to adjust some of his stereotypes about jocks.

"Hey, you," Jared said as he entered. He walked past Connor and settled on his bed. "Sorry it's kinda late. Did you already eat dinner?"

"Um, yeah." Connor hovered awkwardly until Jared grabbed his hand and tugged him down.

"Yeah? I never see you at the Observatory dining hall for dinner. Do you go all the way to Newcomb?"

"Oh…I…I don't usually eat dinner at the dining hall. Sometimes I just grab a snack or whatever to save time."

"Save it for what?" Jared prodded, a smirk playing on his lips.

Connor shrugged and looked away. Why couldn't Jared just drop it?

"Okay, so you gotta tell me, what's with the shyness? Were you like, the fat kid in elementary school or something?"

Resentment spurred Connor into a retort. "What? I wasn't fat. Maybe I wasn't as athletic as the other kids, but that doesn't mean I—"

"Whoa, whoa, I was totally kidding, dude. But it looks like I struck a nerve."

Now embarrassment did rear its ugly and familiar head, but as soon as the blush hit Connor's cheeks, Jared threw an arm around him and pulled him close against his side. "Hey, hey, I'm just kidding. You gotta take me with a grain of salt, you know."

"Y-yeah...whatever," Connor mumbled.

Jared chuckled and squeezed him a little tighter into the side-hug. "All right, as much as I'd like to have you all to myself right now, it's Friday night, and we should really go out."

"Out?"

"Yeah. Some friends of mine are throwing a house party. It should be pretty low-key—right up my alley. You in?"

Connor hesitated, sucking in a deep breath as he gathered his wits. "I...I don't really party much."

"I figured. Which is exactly why we should go. You trust me, right?

Not exactly sure if he did, Connor nodded.

Jared hopped off the bed and took his hand. "Well, let's go then."

The handholding stopped as soon as they stepped out into the hallway, but Jared's smile did not. Connor used that to sustain him as they left the familiar behind and trailed down dark, off-campus streets. Jared chatted amiably along the way, doing much more than his share of keeping up the conversation.

"So what sorts of things do you do for fun?" he asked.

"I…I like practicing…violin, I mean."

Jared halfway rolled his eyes, but the accompanying grin made it easier to bear. "Well I coulda guessed that. And it's definitely cool, you know. But what else?"

"Um, reading?"

"I said for *fun*."

Connor knit his brows, wondering if he should just make something up that sounded more interesting. Nothing believable came to mind, though, and the silence between them dragged on to the point where it seemed too late to respond.

"Okay…well, what kinds of stuff do you like to read then? And don't just say the stuff for class."

Again, Connor had the urge to lie, but who was he kidding? He was worse at lying than he was at speaking in general.

Staring at his feet, he mumbled the truth. "Uh, sometimes, sci-fi."

"That's cool. My dad used to…well, he kinda got me into comic books when I was a kid. Some of that is a little sci-fi."

Connor looked up to give a grateful smile, but his attention was soon captured by something else.

"Low key?" he blurted out, the first thing he'd said that wasn't a direct response to one of Jared's questions.

They'd stopped in front of an old house with peeling paint and warped siding that was bursting at the seams with people. The front porch and lawn were already littered with red plastic cups as the partiers milled about, laughing and shouting over the pounding bass from the music playing inside.

"Okay, so it's a bit crowded, but it's still more chill than a frat party. Don't worry, I'll watch out for you—make sure you don't get lost."

And Connor hoped he would do exactly that, even though Jared's tone told him he was being teased. He followed Jared in and was greeted by a slap on the back so forceful it pushed him into a wall.

"Little anthro dude!" Michael slurred after the violent welcome. "Good to see ya. Sorry for bailing on you, but you know, that really ain't my shit. Gonna go pro, so I won't have to worry about any of this shit anymore."

"You keep telling yourself that." Jared chuckled, and Michael turned on him with a drunken glare.

"You only wish you was this good." Michael thumped his chest menacingly and then dissolved into the crowd. He returned a few seconds later with two of those red plastic cups. "Drink up, guys. Especially you, little anthro dude. You definitely need to loosen up."

"Don't mind him." Jared leaned in close to murmur in Connor's ear. "It's surprising how fast a big guy like him can get drunk."

Connor shifted away instinctively—not that he didn't want to be close to Jared, but how could Jared want to be seen so close to *him* while they were surrounded by football players, other athletes, and their gorgeous friends?

A moment later, when Jared tried to say something else, he rolled his eyes at his own stupidity. Of course. The music was so loud, no one could be heard without shouting if they were more than an inch away.

Jared led him further into the house, encouraging him to drink his first and then second warm cup of beer while introducing him to various people who would surely forget he existed in the next five minutes. He didn't really talk to anyone, but decided he looked engaged enough as he nodded and sipped at his beer.

He was just the token charity case, anyway, and he could see that in the eyes of the people he met—*Oh isn't that nice, Jared let his little tutor tag along.* No one seemed particularly surprised, probably because Jared came across as the kind of friendly guy who would be prone to such a thing. And for once it didn't really bother Connor what people thought. As long as Jared was next to him, he felt safe—an unfamiliar sensation in public, though definitely a pleasant one.

Jared was like a security blanket. A tall, muscular, dark-haired, strikingly handsome security blanket...that was about to be ripped from his side.

He spotted Veronica standing by the makeshift bar with a lost expression, wearing a faded t-shirt that hung off her shoulder and a pair of sweatpants. Eventually she began wading through the crowd, yelling at various people who pointed her in the direction of where he and Jared were standing.

"Shit," Jared mumbled, not really loud enough to be heard, but Connor could read his lips as well as his expression. "I'll be right back, okay?" He took off to latch onto Veronica's arm and steer her toward the front door.

A few minutes of separation felt like an eternity as Connor stared out into the sea of unfamiliar faces. He found a darkened corner and took up residence there, more secure within the partial embrace of the walls.

"Hey." A tiny blond girl startled him by wrapping an arm around his waist. "I don't think I know you." Her breaths came out with little puffs of beer-smell mixed in with the scent of cherries, probably from the red shimmer that covered her lips.

"Um, I'm Connor."

The girl giggled sloppily, nearly dropping to the floor before she used her grip on Connor to stabilize herself. "Yeah, I didn't know you."

"Well...now you do?" He craned his neck over her high ponytail to catch a view of the front door.

"I need a beer pong partner. You wanna play?" She pushed in closer, apparently glossing over the need to introduce herself.

"Uh, I don't really know how…"

"Hey, Con," Jared's voice cut through. A momentary thrill enveloped Connor at hearing the newly assigned nickname, but his elation was quickly dampened by the frown on Jared's face. "Ronnie needs someone to take her home. She's acting kinda weird. Think maybe she's high or something."

"Oh, pooh," the little blonde said. "He was gonna be my beer pong partner."

Jared smirked. "Don't worry, he can still do that."

Connor started to shake his head, but Jared clamped a firm hand on his shoulder. "Hey, I promise I'll be back in like thirty minutes. I don't want to stop you from having a good time, okay?"

He shook his head even more frantically at that, eyes shooting wide, but Jared just smiled and disappeared into the crowd.

Little Blonde still had her arms around his waist, and she tugged on his shirt. "Well, come on then, let's go play!"

Just as he'd suspected, Connor was terrible at beer pong. Onlookers laughed themselves under the table at his miserable aim, as the tiny Ping-Pong ball repeatedly shot wide of its mark. His opponents, a boyfriend and girlfriend duo, had considerably better acuity. Little Blonde chugged the first beer in which the other team successfully landed their ball, and Connor reluctantly gulped down the rest. After the first few minutes of craving an escape while mentally cursing Jared, he grew more resigned to his situation.

When they finally lost, Little Blonde dragged him over to the kitchen and poured him a shot of vodka in his now-emptied last cup of beer.

"Here's to losing with style." She attempted a clink of her cup but missed, tipping precariously until Connor reached out to support her. "You *were* so bad, it was hysterical."

"Well…I aim to entertain," Connor said with a sudden burst of levity, surprised by the way his lips had trouble catching up with his words. He swallowed the shot and grimaced uncontrollably as it burned down his throat.

Little Blonde giggled and stretched to drape her arms around his neck. "You're adorable," she cooed.

"Having fun?" a voice interrupted.

The music wasn't as loud in the kitchen, and Jared's deep tone carried better there.

Connor shifted toward him, some of his earlier annoyance returning in a rush. "You *left*," he said, pointing an accusatory finger.

Jared cocked his head and raised an eyebrow. "Yup, but it seems like you had a good time despite yourself."

"Oh, yeah," the blonde piped in. "He sucks at beer pong."

"I bet." Jared laughed, reaching out to untangle her hands from Connor's neck. He propped her up against the kitchen counter, ignoring the pouting sound she made at being so summarily dismissed. "C'mon, let's go get you some fresh air."

"What about her?" Connor asked as Jared maneuvered him away.

"What, she's your new best friend now or something?"

"She said I was adorable," he muttered defensively.

Jared leaned in close, as they'd reached the din of the main room, and chuckled into Connor's ear. "She's not too far off at that."

The fresh air did feel good as it hit Connor's face, drying the drops of sweat that had gathered on his brow from the drinking and the proximity to masses of other people. He stood with his eyes closed for a moment, letting the wind rock him back and forth.

At least, he thought it was the wind, until he opened his eyes and saw the world seemed to be rocking as well.

"Mmm," he mumbled, a tiny inkling of distress worming its way into what had otherwise turned out to be one of his most successful social experiences. "Feel a little dizzy."

"How much did you drink?" Jared asked, bending down to peer at his face.

"Not sure…five more little cups of beer maybe?"

"And how much do you usually drink before you get drunk?"

"Drink? Drunk?" Connor repeated, then giggled, something that ordinarily mortified him. Now it just had him giggling further.

"Okay." Jared laughed, too. "I think we'd better call it a night."

They started off for the dorms, and Connor was soon faced with a dilemma. Putting one foot in front of the other wasn't so simple a task with the dizziness factored in. He really needed to watch his legs to ensure their placement…but he didn't have the self-control to maintain that focus. Not when he could be admiring Jared instead.

He stumbled and was caught three times before Jared apparently lost his patience.

"Dude, this is going to take forever if you can't stay on your feet. Come here." He scanned the empty streets, then squatted down and dragged Connor around behind him. "Get on my back."

"What? I can't let you carry me. I'll…be too heavy or something."

"I can pretty much assure you that you won't." Jared snorted. "Now climb on or we'll never get back."

Reluctantly, Connor threw his arms around Jared's neck and hopped onto his back. Jared stood with ease and began trotting down the road at a much faster pace than they'd achieved earlier.

It was good to be off his feet, but each bouncing step jarred Connor's skull and added an up-and-down vertigo to the already-whirling scenery. *Don't throw up. Just please, don't throw up.* He closed his eyes and rested his chin on Jared's shoulder, hoping the bad feelings would go away soon.

"We're here." Jared's voice startled him back to full consciousness outside his dorm. "Gimme your card."

Connor slid off Jared's back, sure he was headed for a puddle on the ground until Jared grabbed him firmly around the waist. He smiled with only mild embarrassment, the usual intensity of the feeling smothered by alcohol-drenched senses.

"Here." He fished out the card and handed it to Jared.

Jared passed it through the electronic lock and headed inside, dragging Connor in behind him. "Jesus you're a lightweight. Guess I shoulda figured that, though."

"I'm not tha'little," Connor slurred, his lip thrust out angrily as Jared pulled him up the stairs.

Jared rolled his eyes. "I wasn't talking about your size. I meant with the drinking. Have you ever even drunk before?"

"I've tried some beer…and some wine, thank you very much." Connor frowned, swaying into the wall. They'd reached the door to his room, and he rooted around in his pockets to pull out his keys, which he also handed off. He didn't have the patience to squint at the lock until it came into focus.

Jared's supporting arms left him, and so did Connor's last remaining will to stand. He sank down against the wall as Jared opened the door.

"You gonna get up?" Jared asked.

Connor thought about it for a moment. It seemed like a good idea, but the floor also seemed strangely inviting, and it was closer. He folded over and placed his head on the ground, leaden eyelids drifting closed. "Nope, I don't think so."

A second later, arms slipped under his limp body and he rose off the floor. He opened his eyes to find himself cradled against Jared's chest. Wafts of Jared's cologne hit him, mixed in with sweat and just a hint of beer, and Connor's lips parted to release a sigh. "I like the way you smell," he mumbled, twisting one of the buttons on Jared's shirt.

"Yup. Lightweight." Jared shut the door behind them with a backwards kick and set Connor down on his bed.

Somehow recharged by Jared's scent, Connor flopped around on the mattress, taking several attempts to shuck off his pants.

Jared stood back and grinned. "I have a feeling you're gonna regret this in the morning."

He disappeared from view for a few seconds, but returned with a cold bottle of water from Connor's mini-fridge. "You'd better drink this." He pulled Connor into a sitting position. "I guess I shoulda kept a better eye on you."

"Hey, I may be shorter than you, but I...I'm notta kid." Connor's lower lip thrust itself out again. "I don't need an *eye* kept on me."

Jared brushed his thumb over the pouting lip, smiling softly. "Yeah, I know, but I kinda like the idea of taking care of you. Now drink."

Connor obeyed, and the water did seem like a good idea as it trickled down his suddenly bone-dry throat. It also eased some of the nausea, and when he was finished he gratefully sank his head into his pillow.

Hovering between sleep and wakefulness, he felt one of Jared's fingers trace the contours of his face, from his jaw line to his cheekbones and down the straight slope of his nose.

After a minute, the hand drifted away to arrange the blankets before Jared leaned in and pecked his lips. "'Night, Connor."

CHAPTER SIX

Sometime around dawn, Connor opened his eyes and let out a soft moan. His breath tasted bitter as it escaped his mouth, his tongue dry and inexplicably hairy-feeling. Adding in the fierce headache and the rolling queasiness in his stomach, he'd never felt more miserable.

"Hey." Warm hands stroked his forehead. "Sit up and take these." A water bottle along with three white pills was thrust into his palm, and he dutifully swallowed the medicine. He tried to hand off the water after a sip, but it was pushed back. "No, finish it."

He did, and then lay down again to drift into an exhausted sleep.

When he next awoke, the clock by his side read half past twelve. A slight rustling from across the room alerted him to Jared, who sat curled up on the empty bed with a book in his lap.

"What...what are you doing?" Connor croaked, his voice thick from disuse.

"I know, me doing my reading for class. Crazy, huh?" Jared chuckled. "You feeling any better?"

"Um, I think so." He tested his theory with a slight shake of his head. "It's just a little headache now."

"That's good."

Connor rubbed the crust of sleep from his eyes, still confused by his surroundings. "Y-you stayed? The whole night?"

"I was afraid you were gonna get sick." Jared closed the textbook and crossed the room. "But I slept over there. For a little guy you sure take up a lot of space when you sleep."

An *I'm not little* retort faded from Connor's mind as he settled on a more important fact: Jared had spent the night, and it sounded as if he *would* have slept in the same bed with him had there been room. Without fully realizing what he was doing, he began scooting back against the wall.

"Oh, is that for me now?" Jared asked with a knowing grin.

Connor shrugged and grabbed his pants from where they'd been sloppily discarded the night before. Jared was fully dressed, and it didn't seem appropriate for him to be in only a t-shirt and boxers.

After waiting patiently for him to do up the button, Jared took the offered space. "This bed has sheets. Much more comfortable."

"I...I coulda slept on the floor," Connor stammered. "I don't think I would have known the difference last night."

"It wasn't that bad. I was only kidding. Although I do think I would have rather been here, but I didn't want you to think I was taking advantage of your drunkenness."

Connor snorted and almost choked on his saliva when Jared grabbed him and rolled him over in one swift move. He suddenly found himself lying directly on top of Jared's body, floundering like an oxygen-deprived fish from the unfamiliar contact with another human being. He conked his forehead against Jared's before deciding to scoot down so he could more safely rest on Jared's chest, and, as an added benefit, avoid his eyes.

He was only lying there for about ten seconds before something hard pressed into his stomach. Alarmed, Connor placed his arms on either side of Jared and lifted himself up so he could sneak a look to confirm his suspicions.

"Sorry," Jared said, his cheeks tinted pink. "I can't really help it with you squirming around on top of me like that."

Connor sank back onto Jared's body, his arms going weak while his mind snapped with sudden strength. "You really like me," he breathed out slowly.

"You know, for a smart kid, you can be a little thick sometimes."

"I'm not thick," Connor mumbled.

"All right, fine. Then you think maybe you might like me, too?" Jared laughed, his breath warm against Connor's scalp.

"Um...yeah." Connor pressed his lips together to stop himself from adding something stupid, like *obviously, who in the hell wouldn't?* "But...what...what does that mean? I mean, for you...and me..."

"It means I'd like to be with you."

"Be with me? L-like just for today? Or like friends with...with...um...benefits?"

Jared laughed again. He was really laughing *at* Connor a little too much for comfort. "You're kinda old-fashioned, aren't you? Why don't we take things as they come? Right now, I just know I'd like to keep seeing you."

Connor said nothing, and Jared's confident smile faltered as a flash of something vulnerable slid across his eyes. "That is, if you want, and if you don't mind keeping it between us."

"Um, what about Veronica?" Connor rolled off Jared and onto his side.

"Remember when I took her home yesterday? I finally convinced her we needed to take a break."

"A...a break?"

"Yeah, but everyone knows that's just a way to save face when you're breaking up."

"Oh." Connor nodded. He obviously wasn't *everyone*, but that seemed logical enough.

"So, I'm gonna stay friends with her"—Jared leaned in closer and dropped his voice to a mellow whisper—"but it's just you and me now, I promise."

This time, it was perfectly clear where things were going. Jared's eyelids were lowering and his mouth was coming closer, and in a second their lips would connect.

Connor shot up from the bed, ignoring Jared's startled eyes.

"H-hold on." He snatched his bathroom caddy and ran all the way to the dorm restrooms, not bothering to breathe until he was standing safely inside.

A shockingly pale face met him in the mirror. Before he could analyze his reflection any further, he deliberately forced his gaze away.

Don't think, he told himself. *Don't think.*

Thinking would only screw things up, so instead he grabbed his toothbrush and gave his teeth the most thorough scrubbing of his life, fighting to rid his mouth of the stale beer taste. He splashed some water on his skin and relieved himself before scurrying back to his room.

"Hey, where'd you go?"

"Sorry…just had to brush my teeth." Connor climbed back onto his half of the mattress.

Jared regarded him with a slow sweep of his eyes. "I hope that means you're going to kiss me now."

Connor let a dazed nod be his answer, and Jared surged forward to wrap him in his arms.

But he didn't dive into the kiss immediately. He stayed an inch away, watching in a way that made Connor's skin burn much like his anxiety attacks did. Only in this case, the dousing of cold fear that usually followed never came. He simply burned.

Finally Jared brushed his lips—more the touch of breath than body. Ticklish waves passed through Connor's mouth and hummed all the way to his toes. His arms and legs tensed, and then his whole body was trembling, the vibrations rising up like a crescendo and hovering at the climax.

And God, that was barely even a *kiss*.

Jared didn't notice the shaking—or if he did, he didn't seem to mind. He gripped Connor tighter, punctuating the softer kisses with a much more solid one. His tongue slipped between Connor's lips, gliding along his teeth and pressing into his skin. In fact, every part of Jared was pressing against him, firmly enough to take the breath from his lungs.

Connor shifted to relieve the pressure on his chest, and Jared tried to roll him on top again. The sheets, though, had other ideas. They caught on Connor's legs, tightening around his ankles and leaving him in a tangled mess.

Frantic, he fought to kick his way out of the beige prison and ended up entrapping Jared as well. Jared started laughing, and the more frenzied Connor's kicks became, the harder he laughed, throwing his entire body into it so that he covered Connor's as they rolled around in search of freedom.

And Connor found himself laughing, too, drunk off the warmth and the rocking rhythm and the pounding of his own heart…although there was a distinct possibility he *was* still a little drunk. He was barely controlling his lower half, struggling to keep from thrusting against Jared's hips.

Jared pulled back, his lips red and swollen, his curls sweaty and plastered to his forehead. "Connor," he groaned. "I know I said we could take it slow, and we can, but…please…I want to touch you. Do you think we could—"

"Yeah," Connor said before Jared could even finish his thought, far too aroused to care how needy or pathetic he sounded.

Jared didn't care, either, evidently, because he threw back his head and grinned. "Thank God." He yanked off his shirt and tossed it aside forcefully.

Connor gaped, higher thought suspended by the sight of Jared's tanned skin, with its fine dusting of dark hair and deeply-defined muscles. Never in his life had he been so close to someone so physically stunning.

Then Jared shifted even closer, and he broke free from his stupor. Of their own volition, his hands drifted forward, nearly touching Jared. He managed to jerk them back only at the last possible second.

"This'll probably be hard for you," Jared murmured, leaning in and resting his arm on Connor's hip, "but stop thinking so much. This…this feels right to me. Let's just do what feels right, okay?"

Swallowing, Connor lifted an unsteady hand. He *did* want to touch, and Jared was so close now all he had to do was stretch a few more inches to be doing exactly that…if only he could shut out his fearful mind long enough.

His eyes sank into an extended blink, and when he next opened them his palm was flat against Jared's chest. After another blink his left hand joined in, and together they ran in halting strokes down the length of Jared's body. "Wow," he whispered.

"I'll tell Coach you appreciate all my hard work." Jared laughed at Connor's mortified blush, then wrapped his fingers around the hem of Connor's shirt and tugged upwards.

"Wait, wait!" The music in Connor's mind abruptly faded into a dissonant chord.

Jared stopped, his hands tightening into fists in the fabric. "Why? What is it?"

Connor pulled free from Jared's grasp, edging back against the wall. His heart pounded so fiercely he was having trouble thinking over the sound of rushing blood. "I'm not…I'm not like you."

"What?" Alarm crossed Jared's face, and he sat up. "What does that mean?"

"I mean...I don't look like you."

Jared breathed deeply, shaking his head. "Connor." He let out a long sigh. "I know that. I'm not trying to make out with myself here. I thought we'd already established that I *like* you."

Faced with Jared's amazing half-naked body, the only thing Connor could summon to his lips was a confused, "But *why?*"

Jared rolled his eyes dramatically and scooped Connor up, despite his further attempts to meld into the wall. "You have some serious self-esteem issues, you know that?"

The words stung, even though there was mostly gentle concern in Jared's voice. Connor twisted around to try to hide his head in the pillow, but Jared's arms stopped him.

"I like you, Connor. You're smart, and funny sometimes, even if you don't know it...and...and when you concentrate really hard on something you stick the tip of your tongue out between your lips...but when you play the violin you look so relaxed and...peaceful...and..." He trailed off, brows lifting as he waited for a reaction.

All Connor could do was stare at him, slack-jawed.

"And you've got this whole, I dunno, boy-next-door look going on, with those cheekbones, and those eyes..." Jared stopped again to chew on his lip, a faint blush coloring his skin.

Connor swallowed, his mouth dry from letting it hang open for so long. "B-boy next door?"

"Shut up," Jared grumbled. Setting his jaw defiantly, he tossed Connor over on the bed and pulled off his shirt.

Connor stiffened as Jared appraised him, choosing to stare at a spot a few inches below Jared's firm pectoral muscles so he could avoid eye contact. He was holding himself so rigidly that he started to tremble from the effort.

Jared leaned in to kiss his chest. "Relax."

Connor blinked and mistakenly looked up, and what he found in Jared's eyes was nothing short of amazing. He couldn't begin to fathom why, but there certainly *appeared* to be attraction there.

He used that thought to guide him as they pressed themselves together, chest to chest. Jared's hands flitted down his sides, leaving hypersensitive trails along his skin that had him writhing. He forgot all about his body and its inadequacies for the next few minutes, until Jared's hands traveled down to the button of his pants.

Panicked again, he jumped back, then cursed inwardly at his cowardice.

"You all right?" Jared's lips twitched into a slight frown.

"Yes...yeah, it's nothing." Connor rushed to assure him, wondering if he would die of embarrassment before the day was over. In all of his fantasies about sexual exploration with another man, he never imagined he'd be screwing things up every other second. Although...that really was just par for the course for him.

"Don't tell me nothing if it's something," Jared said flatly. "I don't want you to resent me or whatever."

"I won't...I don't...I want this...but...j-just so you know...I haven't ever..."

Jared let out a low chuckle. "Jeez, Connor. I already know that. And I told you, this is my first time with a guy, too. It's okay."

"No...I haven't ever...with anyone."

Jared blinked at him for several seconds, during which Connor wished he actually *would* die from embarrassment. Why had he suddenly been possessed by a need to confide all of his insecurities—the ones he usually tried so desperately to hide—to the very person he should be trying to impress?

"Not with anyone? You've never been with a girl at all?"

Numbly, Connor shook his head.

"Not even a hand job?"

Another shake of the head.

"Didn't you ever get…curious?"

"No." Connor shrugged. "I'm…I'm gay."

Jared chuckled again, but it was strained. "Um, okay. Not that I'm a male slut or anything—I mean, I've only been with a couple of girls. And I always used protection, you know, so I'm clean, or whatever, but…you weren't like…saving yourself, or something, were you?"

The responding laughter that sprang to Connor's lips edged on hysterical, but it served its purpose as Jared relaxed.

"Okay…so, you still want this, right?"

"Yes," Connor breathed, glad he could finally latch onto something with conviction. "Yes."

Jared rested his hand on Connor's chest. "Okay," he said softly.

He traced a slow line down Connor's stomach, pausing to run his fingers through the silky golden hair below his navel. He didn't aim for the button of Connor's pants again, and instead let his hand wander on top of the fabric—cupping Connor's balls and running his thumb over the length of his erection. Connor moaned and Jared gripped him again, this time with more force.

Wracked by a sudden spasm, Connor had just a few seconds to pull away and flop over. He shoved his face into a pillow as his body tightened and then released.

"Connor?" Jared's tense voice cut through the strange moment of elation and misery.

"I'm s-sorry."

"What's wrong? Seriously, talk to me."

Face burning with shame, Connor rolled back over and stared at his crotch. Why hadn't he worn jeans instead of cargo pants? The stain would've been far less noticeable then.

"Wha-…Oh." Jared cut himself off as he followed Connor's gaze. He started to laugh, but when Connor squeezed his eyes shut to stop the tears, Jared wrapped both arms around him and pulled him close. "Hey, it's okay. Kinda speaks highly for me, doesn't it?"

Connor buried his head in Jared's broad chest as words came tumbling out with unprecedented speed. "Okay? How is it okay? I'm an eighteen-year-old virgin, about to be touched by the hottest guy I've ever known, and I fucking came in my *pants*."

Jared laughed some more, his chest rhythmically bouncing Connor's head. "Well I for one hope there'll be other chances. The day's not over, either. I could still…"

Connor twisted out of the embrace. "I'm…I'm good. Let's…just forget about me for a little while, okay?"

"Uh, okay…"

Determined to steer the day away from all of his failures, Connor found an unexpected wellspring of motivation. He pushed back on Jared's chest until he had him lying flat against the bed.

Jared looked up at him with a dopey smile. "Yeah, okay," he said again.

Connor grinned back, but only because it was hard not to when Jared smiled. Inside, he was quivering, struggling to latch onto the momentum from earlier in the hopes it would carry him to his next move. So far, he'd only been reacting, and it had been easy to let Jared take the lead while he rode the mindless wave. Now, though, Jared was still, and it was his turn—his turn to take control, and he had just as little experience in taking control as he did with sex. He had only a meager helping of porn to rely on, and how realistic were those things, really?

But there was also something else—a tiny voice in the back of his head that had previously been silenced by his nervousness. A voice that was telling him what *he* wanted, a thrumming inside that demanded he take action and fulfill his own undeniable desires.

He used a hand to trail Jared's body for a few minutes, while the voice inside got stronger and stronger until fingers on skin was no longer enough. Then he began kissing Jared's chest, as Jared had done to him earlier. Jared squirmed under him, letting out pleased gasps, especially when he added a small amount of tongue to the mix.

By the time his trail of kisses had reached the belt line, Jared was panting, his stomach rippling and contracting with labored breaths. The carnal response encouraged Connor to continue, and he stared down with intense concentration, soaking in the area he was about to know intimately. Slowly but deliberately, he unbuttoned Jared's pants, feeling the tip of his tongue against his teeth as he bit down in anticipation.

Jared was hard, and Connor wasn't so much uncovering his dick as releasing it, since the moment the zipper was down it sprang out from his boxers. Connor pulled down the elastic band to make Jared more comfortable, then sat back to study the scene.

He was pleased to find he wasn't panicking to the point of a complete meltdown by this point, as he'd rather expected. Maybe he would have been if he'd been straight—if he'd been faced with some foreign piece of anatomy he could never truly understand. But Jared had a dick, and so did he. And he could have laughed from the relief, because at the very least, he had some knowledge of what one did with a dick.

He breathed in through his nose and out through the space his tongue created between his teeth, an internal debate now raging. Think, or don't think? Think about what he usually liked when getting off, or don't think, since that seemed to be the best way to calm his nerves? The seconds ticked by as Connor weighed his options.

After a while, Jared wiggled restlessly underneath him.

Fuck. He couldn't just leave Jared there now, dangling on a precipice. Why had he never been the type of kid to jump into icy water? Wading in was always that much more agonizing.

Fuck, he thought again, and forced himself into action. He gripped Jared firmly, and he could tell Jared was just as surprised as he was by the move, because he let out a wordless stream of noise that ended in a shudder. Relieved the sound seemed to be one of pleasure, Connor continued to stroke, pretty much as he would for himself, until that voice got in the way again.

Fingers on skin is not enough.

Jared had probably had a hundred hand jobs, if not more, not to mention all the times he must have fulfilled his own needs. If there was ever a chance of making Jared *want* him the way he wanted Jared, it was probably now. And if he wasn't going to be enough for Jared because of his lack of experience, he should really figure that out now, too, before he grew any more enamored.

But please, don't let it be that.

For once, something stronger than his usual fear overtook him, spurring him to dive into the deep end—the fear of losing what he was only just now discovering.

So he inhaled deeply, leaned down, and brought Jared's dick into his mouth.

He couldn't take it all the way in, but he used his hand to compensate, and the first time he closed his lips and sucked Jared gasped, thrusting his hips upwards.

"Jesus," Jared said.

The spoken word distracted Connor enough that he looked up, something he'd been trying to avoid for as long as possible. He'd had the notion Jared would be eyeing him skeptically, but now he could see Jared was far too gone to be judging. His face was flushed, his eyes were nearly jet-black, and his reddened lips had curled into a small *o*.

"Connor, I'm gonna…"

Fierce pride welled up in Connor as he didn't flinch at all, and instead swallowed the strange warmth that shot into his mouth. It wasn't entirely pleasant, but it wasn't horrible, either, and thankfully his gag reflex was one of the few things he did have control over.

Jared's strong arms pulled him up after a second, and his lips were smothered in a kiss. "You swallowed," Jared said hoarsely. "You're fucking incredible. That was so much better than—" He stopped and kissed Connor again. "You're incredible."

Connor grinned, but a sudden realization hit him that caused a clenching in his gut. *Better than Veronica.* The image of her sticky pink-glossed lips wrapped around Jared's penis popped into his head, and he blinked several times to clear it and dispel the queasiness it left in its wake.

Jared was kissing him again, though, and he wasn't able to dwell on the feeling for long.

CHAPTER SEVEN

Jared shuffled into class late on Monday. By that time only his old desk near the wall was open, and with an apologetic nod in Professor Abrahms' direction, he took his seat.

Connor's eyes trailed after him, uncertainty plaguing his every breath.

Waiting for the chance to see Jared again had been hard enough. He'd spent the remainder of the weekend staring off into space, reliving every moment of their time together. He wanted every touch, every taste, and every scent to be permanently logged in his mind, and any time he thought he might be forgetting something, he replayed their encounter yet again, from start to finish.

He'd almost forgotten how improbable the whole thing was, but in the harsh light of day his doubts began to pile on top of each other, mocking him for his lack of caution at becoming entangled with someone so far out of his league. Maybe it wasn't likely to be an elaborate hoax, but that didn't mean Jared hadn't already had his fill. His foray into gay experimentation could very well be over, or he could be ready to move on to bigger and better romantic prey.

Through the veil of his bangs, Connor glanced in Jared's direction. He could see Jared's face, but he couldn't quite make out the expression. It took him nearly a full minute to convince himself to look up.

Jared was smiling. Connor returned the grin shyly, then quickly turned away.

Five minutes later, his eyes traced the same path. This time, Jared smiled even wider, and Connor let his gaze linger, taking in the strong lines of Jared's face and the slight shadow of stubble along his jaw.

While he looked on, Jared pulled a sliver of his bottom lip into his mouth, bit down and then released it slowly.

Connor's pencil fell from his grip and clattered to the floor. He hurried to retrieve it and wound up knocking a book off his desk as well, which landed on the ground with a much louder thump.

The snickering he expected as he scrambled to reclaim his belongings never came. Evidently, everyone was too engrossed in their personal musings, or in Professor Abrahms' lecture.

Jared was the only one watching, chewing on his eraser tip with a cocky grin.

For the next hour they continued to share occasional flirting glances, and Connor was so elated he'd pretty much worked up the courage to approach Jared by the time class was over. He didn't have any idea what he was going to say, but so far Jared had been good at taking the initiative. All he could really focus on was that he wanted to be *close*.

He stood and gathered his books, but before he could take even a step forward, Jared's roommate came barreling in from the hallway.

"Dude, I brought your car. You ready to go? We only have like half an hour to get all the goods. Oh, and Brendan says he wants Cheetos, to match his hair. The spicy kind."

Jared chuckled. "All right man, let's go." He gave Connor a little shrug and a smile as he moved past.

The wind knocked from his sails, Connor trudged out. In his fantasy-filled mind he'd temporarily forgotten that, unlike him, Jared had an active social life. Chances were even if Jared *did* like him, hanging out with a shy, awkward outcast wasn't going to be at the top of his priorities.

Which was why Connor would just have to fall back on his old priorities. He headed to the library and tucked himself away deep in the stacks, surrounded by books and silence, where he read until little neck jerks alerted him he was starting to doze off. By the third time he was forced to admit defeat, and he drowsily made his way home.

In the darkness of his room, a tiny blinking red light greeted him. He snapped back to his senses in an instant, his usual cynicism abandoning him as he trampled across the room to check the phone message.

His free hand closed into a fist when it was not from Jared. It was Karen at the athletic department, informing him his services would no longer be needed because Jared Brothman had decided to forgo aid for the remainder of the semester. She kindly offered him a position with the anthropology tutors next fall, and asked that he keep her informed if there were any other subjects he felt comfortable tutoring for the spring semester.

Bewildered, Connor replayed the message. A dark voice suggested Jared might be trying to break off contact with him, but rationally that didn't make sense in light of the whole *I'd like to keep seeing you* discussion, and the way they'd spent class locking eyes, darting them away, then locking them all over again. Perhaps Jared was just sick of anthropology.

When the phone rang a second later, Connor still had his hand on the receiver, and given his train of thought, for once he didn't answer with, *"Hi, Mom."*

"So, did you get your layoff notice?" Jared asked.

"Uh, y-yeah. You…don't need tutoring anymore?"

"Um, *need*, well, that's a separate story. But what I *want* is time to spend with you. I'm pretty booked most days, so this solves the problem perfectly. It gives us a built-in block of time to spend together twice a week, and no one will wonder where I am."

"Oh." *Oh, thank God.*

"I hope you're not mad. I know I should've asked you first. You didn't need the money, did you?"

Connor barked a nervous laugh. "Um, it was just twenty dollars a week. I think I can live without it."

"Great. Listen, I gotta go. We're having a Madden tournament in my suite. But I'll see you tomorrow night, during our regular session time, 'kay?"

"Yeah…okay."

Jared hung up but Connor kept the phone in his hands, pressing it against his chest. He was afraid if he put it down, he'd think he'd dreamed the whole thing up.

***

He opened the door on Tuesday and stood back a few feet, waiting for Jared to settle on his bed like he had the last two times they'd been together. But Jared stayed in place and stared at him, a curious expression somewhere between anticipation and annoyance on his face.

"Hi," he eventually said.

"Hi," Connor replied, and waited some more. Jared still didn't move.

They watched each other for several seconds, while Connor's mind swung in so many directions trying to interpret Jared's behavior that he grew dizzy from the effort.

"All right, bro." Jared finally broke the silence. "The shy act was kinda cute in the beginning, but it might start to get old. You had my dick in your mouth the last time I was here, and now you're acting like we're strangers. Aren't you going to talk to me at all?"

Connor steadied himself with a hand on the nearest object to him, which happened to be his wire music stand. It wasn't up to the task of supporting his weight, and it bent a little more toward the ground as he stumbled and finally grasped his bookshelf in his quest to remain upright.

Jared didn't even crack a smile. He just kept staring earnestly.

"Um…it's not an act. It's just…h-how I am."

"Yeah, I know." Jared sighed. "But I'm hoping you'll be able to make an exception for me. I want to get to know you better, and that probably won't happen if I'm the one talking all the time. And I don't want to have to get you drunk every time I'd like you to open up."

Connor's tongue popped through his teeth and he chewed on it as he nodded. "O-okay."

"So let's start right now. You tell me what you want to do."

"D-do? Do where?"

"Here, with me. What would you like to do right now?"

"Um…I…I…" Blood tingled in Connor's cheeks, and if he hadn't been holding onto his shelf, he probably would have sunk to the floor.

Jared heaved another sigh. "Okay, okay, don't have a panic attack." He edged closer and wrapped Connor in his arms, running comforting hands along his back. "Just relax."

On the verge of tears from the unexpected confrontation, it took Connor a second to ease into the contact. But once he did, the proximity to Jared's steady heart rate began to settle his anxiety.

"Better?"

He nodded against Jared's chest. "I'm sorry."

"Nah, don't be sorry. I didn't mean to scare you. I just want you to be comfortable around me."

SARA ALVA

"I'm starting to be," Connor mumbled, unable to resist burying his head deeper into Jared's warmth.

"Well if this is all it takes, I'd say things'll work out fine." Jared's hands settled at Connor's waist. "Got any ideas about what you'd like to do now?"

"Um…this is nice."

Jared leaned down and pressed his lips into Connor's. He stayed close when he was done, whispering, "Okay, what else?"

One kiss was all it took to get Connor's body surging almost to the brink, and he was pretty sure Jared could feel that, as he was pressed up against his thigh. Would there ever come a point when he'd be desensitized to Jared's touch? So far, he could barely deal with his hand being held.

He shifted to glance down, and Jared began pulling him toward the bed. "Let's take care of that." Jared grinned. "I'm sure it'll help you relax."

Connor tensed again, the memory of his previous failure springing to mind. Strangely, that turned out to be a benefit, throwing him into his head instead of his body and keeping him from fully focusing on what was happening.

Jared pushed down on his shoulders until he was lying flat on his back and staring up at the ceiling, praying for stamina. A hand slipped under his shirt but he hardly noticed it, even as it began running along his chest in slow circles. The pressure gradually increased and the circles widened, sliding further and further down his torso.

As distracted as he was, he managed to do a better job of containing himself. He remained composed until Jared yanked his slightly loose pants down without unbuttoning them and wrapped surprisingly hot fingers around his dick. Warmed from the friction, the fiery temperature of Jared's hand shocked him into a squeak.

Jared paused. "This is okay, right? I'm not entirely sure what I'm doing here. Just thought I'd try what I usually like."

"O-okay?" Connor's voice scratched out while most of his mind remained frozen in ecstasy.

He came less than a minute later. Jared expertly caught the stream in his hand and wiped it off in a tissue while Connor floated back into his body. He couldn't remember a more blissful release in all of his life—though that probably had a lot to do with the fact that it was only the second time someone else had led him to it. And this time Jared had even managed to make skin-to-skin contact.

After a brief recovery time, he tried to shift Jared into a convenient position to return the favor, but Jared resisted.

"Nope. Time for you to talk, remember? You gotta be relaxed enough now."

Connor smiled, the endorphins still traveling his body. "Yeah, maybe."

"So, what's on your mind?"

"Well…that was…the best hand job of my life." A sigh escaped Connor's lips without his approval.

"That was your only one," Jared pointed out, chuckling.

"Yeah, but it seemed like you were an expert. I mean, it always seems like you're so completely…confident in everything you do. I'm not like that."

Jared shook his head. "Don't put me on a pedestal, Connor. I'm still figuring things out, the same way you are."

"Not the same way I am," Connor scoffed. "You may be just figuring out what it means to be gay, but what about everything else? You're an athlete, you're popular, you're amazing-looking…"

Jared cut him off with a wave of his hand. "I hope those aren't the only reasons you like me." A frown crossed his face. "'Cause I'm a mediocre player at best, and looks don't last forever. I act the way I do because my father raised me to be assertive even when I'm not entirely sure of myself. So I can present a confident image, you know? Maybe you should try it sometime."

"Uh...um, okay," Connor replied weakly. An awkward silence descended while he worked on swallowing the lump in his throat.

Jared's expression softened. He leaned in, his lips grazing Connor's temple. "Sorry. I didn't mean to interrupt you like that. So, you were saying, you like me because I'm a popular athlete?" Despite the teasing smile, something sober colored his voice.

"N-no. I mean, th-those weren't the reasons I like you. Just why I was so shocked you liked me."

Jared rolled his eyes. "We've covered that territory. Let's move on."

Nodding, Connor slipped his hand up Jared's chest, absentmindedly tracing an infinity sign along his ribs. When he realized what he was doing he hurriedly tucked the hand away, as it clearly could not be trusted out in the open. "Well, you're a lot more than just good-looking. You're...nice to me. You're nice to everyone, as far as I know. And you're really...patient." He hid an embarrassed smile in a convenient lump of comforter.

"I don't know that I'm always so patient...but you're worth it." Jared pushed in to kiss Connor's nose. He yawned when he was through, arching his back against the bed and giving Connor a glimpse of tan skin peeking out from under his shirt. "Hey, would it be really weird if we took a little nap? I'm feeling kinda beat today." He didn't wait for a response before pulling Connor against him in a near-smothering embrace. "Wake me in like fifteen."

Jared drifted off easily, his breaths slipping into an even rhythm, his dark lashes fluttering every so often beneath twitching lids. Not wanting to miss a minute of his sleeping form, Connor fought to keep his eyes open. He wasn't exactly comfortable, but he remained still so as not to disturb Jared. Besides, comfort was overrated if the alternative was being in Jared's arms.

At some point he must have dozed off, though, because the next thing he knew Jared was sitting up and stretching.

"Hey, I'd better get going. But I'll be back for our next tutoring session." He chuckled. "This is a lot more enjoyable than hanging out at the athletic hall—not that I minded that all that much."

Connor sat up as well, already missing the proximity to Jared's body. "If...if you want, I can still help you...with your anthro stuff."

"I'll probably take you up on that." Jared leaned over to plant what was quickly becoming his customary goodbye kiss on Connor's waiting lips. "See ya later, bro."

***

For the first time since they'd met, Rebecca's familiar form was missing from the lunch table the next day. Connor approached hesitantly, his feet slowing as the distance narrowed. He considered hanging back for a while to see if Rebecca came late, but Chrissy looked up and caught sight of him.

She patted the empty chair by her side. "Becca's working on some project for her film editing class, but she told us not to gang up on you for joining that hive mind of music called orchestra." She paused, putting a thoughtful finger to her lips. "Or maybe she just told me that."

Connor blinked.

Tate shook his head. "Seriously, you know you just ignore her when she says stuff like that, right?"

There was no way to escape now, so Connor shrugged and took his seat.

"You know, Connor, you've never really told us that much about yourself," Tate continued, stroking the coarse hair of the goatee he'd recently begun growing.

A.J. snorted. "Yeah, 'cause he can barely get a word in edgewise between you and Chrissy."

Tate whirled to glare at him. "What is that supposed to mean?"

"It means the two of you are conversation manipulators," A.J. answered, unfazed.

Chrissy stabbed a piece of tofu with her fork. "Don't include me in your unsupported theory!"

Tate ignored Chrissy and dismissed A.J. with a flick of his middle finger. "Dude, whatever. I'm not manipulating anything right now. All right, Connor, center stage. Tell us about yourself."

After watching the conversation with darting eyes and praying that, as usual, the three friends would talk themselves in circles and forget all about him, Connor suddenly found himself the focus of their undivided attention.

"Not much to tell," he muttered.

"Everyone has a story," Chrissy countered. "Everyone and everything. From the largest mountain to the smallest stone."

"Really, Chrissy. Like that's helpful. I'm trying to give the guy a chance to talk here."

"So am I! I'm just explaining that while he may not think his story is remarkable, it is."

Connor's gaze drifted past Chrissy to zero in on Jared and Veronica, who were laughing as Jared's lanky roommate related what looked to be some hilarious story. *Taking a break* evidently didn't involve changing seats at lunch, but there was no evidence to suggest they were acting as anything other than friends.

Out of habit, Connor began to tune Chrissy and Tate out, imagining how much happier he would be if he were sitting next to Jared instead. Or rather, next to Jared, but without anyone else around. And in his dorm room. On the bed. And maybe Jared would have on very little clothing.

Tate rolled his eyes. "No one is saying anything about remarkability. I'm just asking him the basic getting-to-know-you questions."

"And I'm saying that even though it may seem basic to you, it *is* remarkable. We're all interconnected, all important...you know the old butterfly flaps its wing adage."

"There are too many butterflies flapping around in your head if you ask me."

A.J. cut in with a broad smile. "See, what did I tell you? Conversation manipulators."

That sent both Tate and Chrissy off on another round of protests, leaving Connor in the clear. He stared at Jared for several more minutes before it suddenly occurred to him he should have been putting the time to better use.

Tate, A.J., and Chrissy were experts at conversation. If he were smart, he would take note, and hopefully pick up a few things to use with Jared. Sure, Jared liked him, but how long would he put up with a mute?

There was little hope of jumping back into the conversation now, though. Chrissy was prattling on about the butterfly effect, which launched Tate into a discussion of a movie by the same title. Annoyed at the hijacking of the topic, Chrissy resorted to tossing a few peas at him, while A.J. leaned back in his chair with his usual smug look.

They were each so different...how could he know which would be best to emulate?

Chrissy and Tate eventually met somewhere in the middle of their disparate subjects, landing in friendly banter. And whenever A.J. opened his mouth, it was with complete confidence, as though he'd been listening carefully and waiting for just the right moment to make the fullest impact with his few words.

All Connor felt as he prepared to speak was a crawling uncertainty along his skin, and a deep conviction that whatever he was about to say was going to be insufficient.

He seriously doubted any amount of studying his lunch mates could alter that fact.

"Well, we gotta go. See ya later, Connor," Chrissy announced cheerfully amid the clatter of scraping chairs and clanking trays.

Connor eked out a smile as they left him to his thoughts.

CHAPTER EIGHT

The pacing started a good fifteen minutes before Jared was due to arrive. Connor ran through a hundred possible conversation starters, ranging from the mundane to the absurd, and rejected each thought that crossed his mind. He worked his fingers through his hair as he strode, straightening it out and ruffling it back up again, unsure of which look was best.

He finally stopped to peer into the mirror and test both styles. The clean-cut look made him appear a little too juvenile, so he thrust his hand back into the blond strands and flung them around until they were thoroughly mussed.

One challenge down, one to go. His reflection gave him a doleful smirk. After a moment he tried to get his mind back on his plans to keep from sounding like a complete imbecile in Jared's presence, but something in the mirror held his attention.

Narrowing his eyes, he studied his features for longer than he had in some time. The same face he always saw stared back at him. He hadn't changed, so why was it he thought he caught a glimpse of something a little less meager than what usually seemed to be there?

Of course, he was still frustratingly short, but maybe his eyes weren't all that bad—they did have the rarity in color going for them. His lips were a decent shape, as lips went, and hadn't Jared said something about his cheekbones?

A group of students trampled down the hallway outside his room, their laughter shattering Connor's reverie. Realizing the precious minutes he had wasted, he resumed his pacing route and focused on the more important conversation front. Nothing he could come up with sounded natural, though, and he felt just as clueless as always when Jared's knock sounded at the door.

"Hey," Connor said first. That, at least, was a small step forward.

"Hey, bro. I brought my anthro stuff this time, but I gotta tell you, not so sure I wanna do any work right now."

Connor nodded, and because Jared was still standing in the doorway, gestured hesitantly. "C-come in."

"Thanks for the invite." Jared smirked as he kicked off his shoes and dropped his bag by the bed.

Only a small amount of air from a weak, shallow breath made its way to Connor's lungs. For all his attempts at preparation, he found his mind nearly blank. *Open up!* he screamed at himself. *Talk! Act normal!*

"Um…h-how were your classes today?"

Jared's eyes bounced with suppressed laughter. "They were all right, I guess. Yours?"

"G-good, good." Connor licked his lips and bit down fiercely on his tongue when he was through. *How were your classes today?* He sounded like his mother, and that was a horrible image to put in his mind, now or anytime.

"What's that face for?" Jared asked, mouth twitching into a grin. "You look like you're in pain."

If he'd looked like that before, Connor could only imagine the expression had just gotten worse.

He closed his eyes. "I'm trying," he mumbled, his sense of failure a palpable tightening in his chest. "I just...I can't think of the right things to say."

"You know there's no handbook on how to hold a conversation. There's no right and wrong thing to say. You just talk."

"No." Connor crossed his arms. "I do it wrong. I *know* I do it wrong. And it's not because I don't like you, because I really do. I'm bad at talking to everyone, and—"

Jared came closer and wrapped him in a hug. "Don't be so hard on yourself. You're not doing that badly."

"Right. Because asking how your day went doesn't make me sound like some kind of fifties housewife."

He felt the rumble of Jared's laughter in his chest. "I think you put too much pressure on yourself. The stakes aren't that high in every casual thing you say to people. No one has a scorecard and no one is judging. If you'd just be yourself, you'd be fine. You're a very likeable person."

Yeah, right. "You're the only person who's ever liked me."

"Maybe like this." Jared pulled him onto the bed. "But you have friends. I see you with them at Newcomb all the time."

Connor's head naturally rested on Jared's muscled shoulder, and he curled into the space under his arm. "They're kind of hard to miss, huh. Tate's nearly seven feet, and Rebecca's really tall for a girl. And Chrissy dresses like a flower-child from the sixties...I guess A.J.'s the most normal one."

"Mm," Jared agreed, running his fingers up and down Connor's side. "Have you noticed you tend to talk a lot more when we're close like this?"

"Yeah...I've noticed." Connor sighed, too pleased by the feeling of Jared's hands on his skin to be embarrassed.

"Well, then maybe you should just come hug me as soon as I get here."

"Really? That wouldn't be...weird?"

"You are a little weird." Jared laughed. "But I think I can handle it."

That comment probably should have been upsetting, but for whatever reason, it wasn't. Connor just found himself curling a little tighter into Jared's embrace.

"Don't stop talking yet," Jared prompted after a moment.

"Wh-what do you want me to talk about?"

"Hmm. Well, what's it like hanging out with the artsy Brownie crowd? Do they drag you to lots of arts exhibits and film festivals and stuff?"

"Oh…I don't really hang out with them all that much. Just Rebecca, and that's mostly when we're practicing for orchestra."

"Connor." Jared shook his head with a gentle *tsk*. "Come on. This is your college experience here. You really need to get out of this room more."

"I know." Moisture sprang to Connor's eyes, and he scratched restlessly at a freckle on his arm. "I…I should try harder."

"As quirky as they seem, it should be easy to be yourself around them," Jared added thoughtfully. "Not that I'm saying you're quirky. Just that I doubt they'd be the judgmental types."

Quirky. That really was a good word to describe them, and Jared did have a point. A smile crept onto Connor's face. Maybe there was hope for him yet. "So…I guess you've always had a big group of friends. It must come naturally to you."

"I guess."

"That…that must be…nice."

Jared stared off at the bookshelf across the room. "Yeah. I guess." After a moment he turned back to Connor and gave his arm a squeeze. "This is nice, too."

His voice had gone soft and deep, his lids were half-lowered, and suddenly there was no more pressure to talk.

They observed each other silently as a minute ticked by, Jared's eyes locking Connor's in a steady gaze.

The staring went on far longer than Connor expected. Was he supposed to be doing something? Did *he* need to take the initiative to bring things to a more physically intimate level? It wasn't something he'd ever imagined doing—wasn't even something he was sure he *could* do—but the atmosphere seemed right, and he was dying for there to be less clothing between their bodies.

Thankfully, Jared was a mind reader. Either that, or he had a perfectly good set of eyes and could see his casual touch already had Connor hard. He stretched and peeled off his shirt. "Okay, enough talking for now. Clothes off. All of them."

"All of them?"

"Yup. Here, I'll turn off the lights, so you feel more comfortable." He made his way over to the light switch, shedding his pants and boxers as well. All that was left by the time he got there were his socks.

Even in the dark, Connor could make out the long muscles of Jared's thighs and the high, firm curve of his butt. After that sight, it'd probably take only the lightest touch for him to wind up coming in his pants, yet again. He closed his eyes and tried to shut out Jared's impressive body, using the notes of a tedious etude to distract himself.

"Need some help there?" Jared murmured playfully, then began to strip off Connor's clothes.

Connor repeated the etude in his mind until he was completely naked and Jared was lying close at his side.

"Open your eyes," Jared said. "I like your eyes."

His lids fluttered open and he swallowed hard. "Would…would you like me to…um…for you…first?"

"Nuh uh." Jared shook his head. "I want you right there."

Jared's fingertips coasted along his skin, and somehow, the contact made the normally incessant voices of his self-doubt grow quieter. They faded to the dullest of roars as Jared wrapped a powerful thigh around both his legs, then drew their bodies together with a grunt.

Connor latched on to Jared's shoulders, trying to pull him even closer—to be wholly enveloped by the warmth of his skin. It was almost possible, too, given how much larger Jared was than him. Their lips met in an extended kiss, until the necessary gasp for breath forced them apart. Jared used his leverage to grind them together, his thrusts coming faster and faster until Connor's breath quickened and he released, all over Jared's stomach.

The thrusts kept coming, with Jared's thigh clamped firmly around him so he couldn't back away. Jared gripped himself and started pumping. A gasp became a moan, and the warm spurt hit Connor right above his groin.

"Mm." Jared planted a soft kiss on Connor's jaw. "Yeah, I can definitely handle this."

He shifted away after a moment, grabbing a handful of tissues from the desk to wipe first Connor's stomach and then his own. When he'd cleaned them off to his satisfaction, he threw the wadded ball of paper into the trash and flicked on the lights.

Connor scrambled to redress, managing to get on his boxers before Jared donned his own and returned to the bed.

"Hey, that's enough clothes." Jared yanked the faded high school orchestra t-shirt out of his hands.

"Um…" Connor tried to recapture the clothing, but Jared easily held it out of reach. "I was going to go over your paper for anthro. You brought it, didn't you?"

Jared threw his shirt into the corner of the room. It only lay there for a second before he snatched it back up and placed it in the hamper instead. "Yeah, but you don't need a shirt to do that."

Connor folded his arms across his chest. "Um, I guess not."

"Good." Jared grinned victoriously. He grabbed his backpack and handed off a stack of papers. "Hope it meets with your approval."

"I'm sure it's fine." Connor gave him a nervous chuckle. "If you incorporated the stuff we covered in tutoring, it should be all right."

He launched into his review, but kept his arms crossed, all too aware the lights were on and Jared was staring at him. In an effort to remain covered, he pulled his knees up to his chest.

Jared snuck a hand under his arm and attacked his ribs with a few tickling jabs.

"Hey!" Connor squirmed away. "I can't concentrate."

"Do you usually curl up into a little ball and hide your body when you concentrate?" Jared asked with another jab. "I'm bored here. The least you can do is let me look at you."

Connor sighed. How was it Jared's teasing could both unnerve him and set him more at ease?

"Fine." He uncoiled, and to his relief, Jared pulled him close. The feel of Jared's body against his made the tension slip away once again.

"Much better. But hurry up."

Despite the order, Connor was thorough in his notes. He couldn't let Jared's grades slip just because they'd co-opted the tutoring time for a much less academic purpose. By the time he was finished, their hour together was almost up, and he silently cursed the clock as Jared shifted out of his embrace.

Two loud beeps sounded before they could stand. Jared reached down to pull his cell phone from his pants pocket, then laughed as he read the screen. His thumbs danced across the buttons with practiced speed.

"Man, Ben is such a riot. He's always texting random-ass shit. You should hear him sometimes, when he gets going—" He cut himself off abruptly and shoved the phone back into his jeans. "Anyways, speaking of going, I guess it's time for me to do that."

A hollow space opened up in Connor's chest as soon as the word "going" left Jared's lips. In a sudden bout of desperation, caution flew to the wind.

"Really?" He pressed in closer. "I thought…I thought maybe you could spend the night."

Was he actually being *forward?* Apparently he'd discovered the secret to getting his voice to work—just dangle the carrot of having Jared close to him for a few more minutes.

Jared nuzzled his shoulder. "Not tonight, bro."

"Oh." Connor found a stray piece of lint on his comforter and devoted a good three seconds to picking it off. "I just thought, since winter break is coming and we won't be able to see each other…"

"I know." Jared pressed in for a quick kiss. "I would, but now that Veronica and I split it'd be kinda weird for me to be away all night. Ben'd get curious, and I'd rather not have to invent a bunch of stories for where I am."

"Oh. Yeah. That makes sense." Connor scoured his comforter for more lint.

"But hey, I was thinking…" Jared shook his arm to get his attention. "How 'bout I give you a ride home for break? Manassas is on my way. We could stop and get lunch at this really great barbecue place. I mean, it's kind of a hole-in-the-wall, but I promise the food is awesome. And there's this shack nearby where they sell custard ice cream cones…we have to get some of those."

Little bits of glee barreled through Connor's disappointment. It almost sounded like he was being asked out on a *date.*

"Yeah, okay. I'd…like that." And, for the very first time, *he* did the leaning in, meeting Jared's lips without hesitation.

***

Humming the romantic theme from Borodin's *Polovtsian Dances*, Connor found his friends for their last lunch together of the semester.

His friends, he realized suddenly. Not just Rebecca's. Whatever had sparked the change in his mind, he had to believe it was progress.

"Hey." Rebecca used her tongue to suck out a piece of spinach from between her teeth. "I forgot to ask, do you need a ride home for break? I think you're only about a half hour away from me, so it wouldn't be a problem."

"Oh, thanks, but not this time." Connor took his seat by her side, grinning at his macaroni and cheese. He almost regretted having to turn her down…almost. "Jared said he'd drop me off. I guess I'm on the way home for him."

"Jared? The football star?" A.J. asked, leaning in on his elbows.

Jared wasn't really a star yet, but that didn't seem worth sharing, so Connor just smiled.

Tate tugged on Rebecca's ponytail as he joined the conversation. "Wow, I'm surprised you still eat with us lowly peons, now that you're best friends with athletic royalty."

Connor glanced up, his good mood undiminished, and a boldness took hold of his tongue. "Yeah, well…I thought maybe some of my newfound coolness would rub off on you."

Tate choked on his chocolate milk. Clearly, he hadn't expected a comeback from the heretofore mostly-silent Connor. He chuckled after recovering and rolled his eyes.

Rebecca shot Connor a surprised but pleased smile, and he had to bite back his own proud smirk. Maybe he wasn't exactly ready to write the book *How to Succeed at Social Interaction Without Actually Trying*, but there was no denying things were getting better every day.

***

"Connor."

Jared's voice sounded different. Connor was just growing accustomed to the way the static from the airwaves added a gentle rasp to Jared's low, resonant tone, but today there was no playful lilt to it. Jared's voice was flat and weary.

"Listen, I need to give Ronnie a ride home. She hasn't been doing so well…missing a lot of classes and stuff. I guess maybe the college thing is too much for her or something. But anyway, her parents are really pissed and she doesn't want to ride with them, so…"

He trailed off while Connor sank onto his bed, jealousy and disappointment battling for their spot at the top of his emotional response.

"I mean, I can still give you a ride if you want, but it'll be…different. You know."

"Yeah." Connor frowned and rubbed at the resulting crease on his forehead. "Um, I think I'll just get Rebecca to give me a ride then."

"I'm really sorry. We're gonna leave now, so I won't be able to say goodbye…but you'll call me, right?"

"Um, okay."

"Promise?"

"Yeah."

"I gotta run, she's just in the bathroom. Talk to you later."

Jared hung up, and Connor stared wistfully at the phone, wishing there were some way to erase the last few seconds and the unfortunate news it had brought him.

But maybe this kind of thing was just the price he'd have to pay for someone like Jared.

CHAPTER NINE

"So then Rick totally likes you!" Melissa squealed from the kitchen. Having been denied a cell phone for the tenth time that evening, her chosen act of rebellion was to carry on talking with her friends where she could be of maximum annoyance.

Connor sat on the floor at the base of the couch, biding the time he had left of forced socialization with his parents. If he could just make it through the half-hour of Jeopardy, they'd be less likely to bother him the rest of the night.

"Who is Pontius Pilate!" his father yelled at the T.V. screen.

"I knew that one. I was going to say that, too," his mother put in.

At least they couldn't see him rolling his eyes from where he sat.

A commercial break gave his mother a chance to redirect her attention. "Connor, I was thinking, you should use this vacation time to go with your father and visit nearby law schools, just to get a feel for the campuses. Doesn't that sound like a good idea?"

"Mhm."

"Connor! Are you listening?"

"Yes, Mom. Sure."

"Will you be doing tutoring again next semester?"

Connor shifted, fingers restlessly scratching at the worn carpet. "I'm...I'm not sure yet."

"Well, I think you should. You enjoyed it, didn't you?"

A small chuckle escaped him. "Yeah, I did. Actually, I was thinking maybe I could look into taking some education courses next year to see if—"

"That's nice, dear. It's an excellent activity to put on your applications for law school. Especially for UVA Law."

"Mom, I—"

"What is curium!" his father bellowed.

"Oh! I knew that!" she exclaimed, turning back to slap his arm.

Melissa's voice rang out over them as she bounced through the foyer. "Maybe Danny will ask me to the dance and we can go together!"

"Honey, please keep it down, we're trying to watch here. Connor, why aren't you guessing any?"

Connor snapped his mouth shut, folding his arms across his chest. Being home was frustrating, stressful, and sometimes even demeaning, but above all, it was *lonely*.

So why was it he was putting off the one thing that might be able to offer him some relief? A week had gone by, and he still hadn't worked up the courage to call Jared. Instead he sat home alone, or worse, home with his family, seething at the ill-timed vacations of his school calendar.

Perhaps he hadn't called because he was still disappointed about their cancelled drive. Or maybe it was just that calling Jared now, while they were away from school, made what they were doing seem much more like a *relationship* than ever before.

Except...that should've been exactly what he wanted.

His mother startled him by throwing her arms out in triumph. "Marie Antoinette! Ah ha, I got that one!"

"You have to answer in the form of a question," his father responded calmly.

"I still knew the answer!"

Connor sprang up from the floor. "Mom, can I go to my room? I'd like to check the online course catalog again to see if anything new has been posted for next semester."

She sighed. "But you'll miss final jeopardy."

He couldn't bring himself to respond to that one, so he just waited with one foot already planted in the hallway outside the family room.

"Fine, Connor. Just make sure you're keeping pre-law courses in mind. It's never too early to start preparation."

He ran to his room and shut the door with a thud, ignoring his mother's harried yell requesting he not slam things that didn't belong to him.

"Hey, you," Jared answered on the second ring.

At those simple words—back in Jared's usual tone—Connor blushed, but not in the bad way he was so used to.

He collapsed onto his bed in relief, almost positive he'd made the right decision. "Hey...I...I hope it's okay to call right now."

"Of course it is. I actually thought you woulda called sooner, but I figured you must've been busy."

"No. I mean, yeah, a little."

"Well, I'm glad you called now. It's funny, but I...I really miss you."

Connor couldn't help but giggle. "You seem about as surprised at that as I am."

"Shut up," Jared grumbled. "It's just, I never really used to miss any of my girlfriends when they weren't around...but I shoulda known it'd be different with you."

Connor lay back and put a hand on his chest, wishing it were Jared's. "Maybe that's because you're gay."

He hadn't meant to be funny, but Jared laughed anyway. "I guess, huh. I always hoped I'd find someone in college. Just never thought it'd happen so fast. I'm glad, though. Glad I didn't have to wait too long."

"Um…I'm glad you didn't have to wait so long either."

Jared let out a sound somewhere between a sigh and a groan. "Man, three more weeks. I mean, I love my family and all, but…I *really* miss you. Wish I wasn't all the way up at my Uncle's place in Jersey now, or I'd try to come see you."

"I miss you too." Connor grinned so hard his cheeks started to hurt.

"Well, I guess I went eighteen years without kissing a guy, so what's three more weeks?"

"Yeah…but wasn't that before you knew what you were missing?"

"What's this?" Jared's tone rose with feigned shock. "Is my little Connor done eating humble pie?"

"I'm not little," Connor retorted at the same time his insides turned to jelly. Jared had just referred to him as *his*.

"Not where it counts."

The bedroom door suddenly flew open, sending Connor scrambling back in a vain attempt to remain hidden among the pillows and comforter.

"Hey, doofus." Melissa watched his antics with her hands on her hips. "Mom wants to know if you'll come down and practice that concerto with me, because the Mitchells are coming over tomorrow and they're bringing their kids, so we're the entertainment."

"Get out!" Connor pulled a pillow onto his lap, hiding the erection he'd been growing from the sound of Jared's voice. "Can't you see I'm busy?"

Melissa eyed the cell phone cupped against his chest. "What, you're talking on the phone to a friend? Wow, I guess wonders will never cease."

"Melissa, if you don't get out I'm going to…"

"All right, all right." She backed up slowly. "I'll tell Mom we'll practice it tomorrow, 'cause you know there's no way you're getting out of this one."

"That's fine." Connor sighed. "I'll do it, whatever. Just...I'm busy right now, okay?"

"Okay." She grinned mischievously. "I'll leave you to your obviously very important *friend.*"

As soon as she'd shut the door, Connor unfolded and brought the phone back up to his ear. "Are you still there? I'm really sorry."

"Melissa, huh?" Jared's throaty chuckle put him at ease. "I take it she's the younger sister."

"Yeah, she's just hitting those really annoying teenage years. Sorry about that."

"No worries. I have two younger brothers, so I know how it is."

Connor relaxed his body the rest of the way and took up his earlier position, staring at the ceiling. "Are they a lot like you?"

Jared laughed affectionately. "I guess they are. They're really into football...although I'm starting to think they're gonna be way better than I am when they grow up."

Connor frowned. Emboldened by their physical distance, he opened his mouth without thinking. "Why do you always do that?"

"Do what?"

"I dunno. Call yourself mediocre. And...and when Michael used to come to tutoring, you'd let him tell you he's so much better than you, that you'd never get to play in any games..."

"I'm *not* as good as Michael, not by a long-shot, even though we play different positions. I guess I was good in my little fishbowl of a high school, but not at the college level. I'm fourth string, Connor."

"Fourth string?" The only strings Connor knew anything about were the ones used to tie things, and the ones on musical instruments.

"It means I'm not that great. Means I'm mostly used so that the real players have someone to practice against."

"Oh."

"Sometimes I think about throwing in the towel, you know?" Jared's sigh crackled through the line. "Concentrating more on my studies…on figuring out what I want to do with my life…but my dad played at UVA when he was in college, and he always really loved following the college teams. I guess it's just important to me that I…"

He fell silent, and Connor pulled the phone back from his ear to check if he'd lost the connection. He hadn't.

"I guess it's kinda weird I haven't told you yet," Jared continued after the pause.

"Told me?"

"That…that my dad passed away. He died last year, right before graduation."

"Oh," Connor breathed out slowly, wishing more than ever that Jared were beside him so he could offer more than stupid verbal condolences. "I'm so sorry. Was he…sick?"

"Yeah, for a while. Cancer. It sucked, but in a way I guess it was also good, because we had time to adjust, you know? He always used to say God gave him that time to groom me for my takeover as man of the house."

A short burst of static could've been either a sad chuckle or a pained sigh. Connor balled his useless hands into fists around his comforter. "I'm sure you're living up to his expectations."

"I guess. Football was important to him, and even though I'm never gonna go pro, it's important to me that I keep his memory alive this way. You think that's stupid?"

"No." Connor shook his head, even though no one was there to see it. "I think…I think if it's something you love, you should give it all you've got."

"Thanks, Connor." Jared's voice dropped close to a whisper. "I don't really tell many people that. Or any."

A few moments of silence passed while Connor pondered whether to change the subject or take the opening he'd been given. Sharing personal information wasn't something *he* was prone to...but then again, if he'd ever had someone around to truly listen, there were one or two things that would've been good to get off his chest.

"It must have been hard, losing your dad your senior year," he finally said, and then wanted to kick himself. Of course it was hard.

This time Jared's sigh was long and drawn out, like he was reluctant to speak. "It'll probably sound stupid...but I think one of the worst parts was all my friends."

"What do you mean?"

"You know how you asked if I've always had a big group of friends? Well, I have. It's just that...they expected me to be the same guy, you know? The life of the party, the star athlete, the lady's man...I guess part of it's my fault for always playing into that, but to be honest with you, I would have traded the whole crowd for just one good friend. Just one person I could chill with and not have to *be* anybody for. Things were tough enough after I realized I was gay, but when everything happened with my dad...between that and having to be there for my mom and my little brothers...it was fucking exhausting."

"I can only imagine," Connor murmured. A trite response, but true enough. He'd never come anywhere near to being in Jared's shoes. "It sounds sorta like you were there for everyone, but no one was there for you."

Jared let out his breath in a quick puff. "Don't get me wrong. I'm really glad I could be there—*can* be there—for my family. And, well, friends can be a good distraction sometimes. I shouldn't really whine about it." He inhaled sharply. "Anyways, I feel like I'm dragging us down here. I'm sure you didn't call to listen to me complain."

"I don't mind. You can complain to me whenever you want."

Another rush of air sounded against Connor's ear. "You're a good guy, Connor. I...I wish you were here."

"Me too."

After a few seconds of heavy breathing, Jared cleared his throat. "Well"—a reluctant note crept into his tone—"my aunt and uncle want us to have a family game night, so I guess I'd better get going."

"Oh, okay." Connor pinched a chunk of skin on his forearm to keep the disappointment from his voice. "Guess I'll talk to you tomorrow."

"Guess? It should be more than a guess."

"Okay, I *will* call you tomorrow. Or, you know, you could call me. Either way. I...I just like to hear your voice."

Like to hear your voice? Conner punished his mouth for releasing the saccharin comment with a swift bite to his tongue.

"Sure thing, bro," Jared responded immediately. "My voice may not be as good as my kisses, but I'll do what I can."

"Your kisses?" Connor giggled.

"Yeah, that was sappy. Deal with it," Jared growled. Then his voice grew muffled. "I'm coming, Mom!" Some shuffling noises followed, but when they were done Jared's voice was right next to Connor's ear again, low and soft. "Goodnight, Connor."

"Goodnight, Jared," he whispered back.

Before he could even set the phone down his door sprang open and a wild-eyed Melissa stepped in. "Goodnight Jared? Goodnight *Jared?*" She flapped her hands about dramatically with each word.

A stabbing pain hit Connor in his ribcage, making his breaths come out ragged. "What do you need, Melissa?"

"Jared?" She continued, green irises small in the whites of her blown-wide eyes. "Jared is not a girl's name."

"I don't know what you're talking about." Connor turned away from her as the pain grew stronger. He focused on a smudged fingerprint that marred the wall.

"Uh, yeah you do. I've been standing out there for the last few minutes, listening to you flirt on the phone, and then you just said 'goodnight Jared'. Wow, Connor…you like *boys?*"

Connor dropped the cell phone on his pillow and saw his hand had started to shake. *Fuck, fuck, fuck,* echoed in his head.

"Wow. Is that why you've always kinda been a freak? What do you think Mom and Dad will say?"

He flung himself back around to face her, desperation overriding his panic. "Melissa, please don't…please don't tell them…"

"Oh, so you want my silence?" She tapped a finger against her lips. "What can I get for that?"

"W-what do you want?"

"Hmm…well, I'm going to the movies tomorrow with Amanda. I could use twenty bucks for some popcorn and a soda."

Wordlessly, mindlessly, Connor grabbed his wallet from his pocket and handed over a bill.

"Wow, that was easy." She folded her ill-gotten gain in half and tucked it into her pocket. "But are you sure you don't want me to try to find out what Mom and Dad would say? I mean, I could just bring up the topic…"

"No. No. Don't say anything. Please."

"All right, fine. Whatever you say." She whirled around and headed for the door, but then suddenly froze. Glancing over her shoulder, she pinned Connor with an odd look. "Thanks for the money, Connor, but you know I wouldn't really tell them anything. You may not be the greatest brother, but I still wouldn't do that to you."

She tossed her hair with a flick of her wrist as she left.

***

Connor descended the stairs cautiously the next morning. As usual, his mother was already up, sipping a cup of coffee in her pajamas while she watched a morning talk show.

"Connor, will you have time to dust the furniture?"

Nothing out of the ordinary there.

"Yeah, I can do that."

"Good. Because we're having guests for dinner, so I have to pick up groceries and cook today. I'll probably need help tidying up some other areas, too. And don't forget Melissa wants you to play a concerto with her. You know how she loves to accompany you."

"She told me last night."

He poured himself a bowl of frosted flakes as Melissa came dashing down the stairs, fully dressed. She blew past him without a second look, running over to their mother and pecking her on the cheek.

His pulse picked up speed.

"Morning, Mom!" She chirped in an exaggeratedly sweetened voice. "Can I go down the street to Amanda's? Her dad's gonna take us to see an early movie."

"Melissa, you remember we're having guests for dinner, and you said you would play—"

Melissa threw her arms around her mother's shoulders. "I remember, Mom. I'm all ready to perform, and I promise I'll be back in time."

"Oh, all right. Eat some breakfast, though."

After another kiss on the cheek, Melissa danced back to the kitchen to grab a banana from the fruit bowl on the table.

"Oh, hey, Connor." She gave him a funny little smile and touched his arm lightly. He stared back at her for a second, trying to read her intentions, but he couldn't see anything in her green eyes other than an eagerness to leave.

He kept watching as she bounded out the door, wrapped in a puffy winter jacket. He'd always believed no one in his family really knew him, but maybe the reverse was true as well. Maybe he *could* trust her to keep his secret...or maybe she just had other, more exciting thirteen-year-old things on her mind than outing her brother.

Either way, it seemed he was safe for now.

CHAPTER TEN

Connor closed his eyes, pulling out a trill in the Andante from Tchaikovsky's violin concerto and dropping it into a quick succession of thirty-second notes. Though he was beginning to tire, his fingers continued sliding gracefully over the strings. He had to take full advantage of these occasions whenever they came—with everyone out of the house, the only sounds that infiltrated the silence were the ones *he* created. Through his instrument he could command the most furious of tirades or the most romantic of appeals, and the longer he went without anyone interrupting him, the more powerful he felt.

Of course, there was one interruption he could tolerate. His cell phone buzzed once and he *glissandoed* to a stop as he cleared his throat and tried to tamp down on the happy butterflies in his stomach.

But it was only a text message from Rebecca.

Hey, just thought I'd get my NY greetings out now in case I'm too toasted after 12. Happy NY!

His eyes flew to the clock. Still twenty minutes to go, which meant at least an hour of solitude before his family returned from the Haskers' party. Sure, he'd have passive-aggressive hell to deal with for skipping out, but it was worth it, especially given how few days there were left until freedom.

He rested his instrument for a moment and scrolled through his saved messages. A few were polite *how is your break going* inquiries from Rebecca, but the rest were from Jared. He wouldn't dare delete a single one of those.

Hey, what're you up to?

Man, if I have to hear one more story about me in diapers from my Gma I'm gonna hurl.

The next one was far from his favorite, but he held onto it anyway.

Going skiing with my uncles and brothers. Won't be able to talk for a few days. Don't miss me too much.

An impossible request. Their nightly calls were about the only thing he looked forward to each day, especially since he was getting so much better at them—the words flowing with greater ease, the silences between them dwindling to only the occasional awkward pause.

The last text from Jared had come a day ago. Just a simple *hey*, it still caused his heart to skip a few beats. The way they messaged back and forth, the way Jared was so open with him—it was almost like Jared was his *boyfriend*.

He resumed his practice with new energy, switching to the Allegro moderato. Quick strokes of his bow accompanied the playful notes as they bounced off the walls, the slight echo encouraging him further.

Several minutes later, his phone buzzed again, and this time, the buzzing continued.

"Hello?" He nearly dropped his bow in his haste to answer.

Shouting and laughter greeted him on the other end of the line, but it gradually faded.

"Sorry, that was loud. I'm upstairs now. Happy New Year, Connor."

Connor hugged his violin against his chest. "Oh, is it New Year's already?"

"It's five past twelve. Where have you been?"

He yawned. "Practicing."

"Figures." Jared chuckled. "Anything I'd like?"

"Um, I dunno. Just dusting off some pieces I've learned for fun."

"Play me something." Jared's voice was distorted by his own yawn. "Not a lullaby, though, 'cause I might fall asleep."

"Are…are you sure?"

"Connor," Jared said simply, but his tone conveyed it all. *Stop doubting; stop second-guessing. Just go with it.*

So he did. He set his phone on speaker and rested it against his music stand, thankful again the house was his for the night.

The Allegro moderato was a plucky enough sort of piece, and he whipped through the best parts with few mistakes. He wasn't able to fully concentrate on the music, though, what with the little rustles from Jared's breathing coming through the phone line. He'd give anything to feel those rushes of air along his skin.

"How was that one?" he asked when he was through. "Not too sleep-inducing?"

"Nah." Jared laughed. "You were awesome as always. Although it sucks that it gets sorta static-y on the phone. It's so much cooler to watch you in person, like the first time I heard you play."

"The first time," Connor repeated involuntarily, his body rushing back to the sensations of that moment. *Hot skin, embracing arms, demanding lips, tongue…*

"Yeah, the first time." Jared's voice teased, like he knew just how starry-eyed Connor had suddenly become. "Hey, was that your first kiss?"

"What?" Connor blinked the memory—and the associated arousal—from his mind. "No, of course not!" *Second, thank you very much!*

"It's okay if it was. I mean, you're a pretty good kisser, so it's not like I have a problem with it."

"Well, it wasn't."

A couple of rapid clicks emerged from the phone, and Jared huffed. "Shit, Ronnie's calling. She's been trying to reach me all week—I guess I'd better see what she wants really quick. You wanna hold on, or should I call you back?"

"I'll…I'll wait."

"Okay, be right back."

Feeling empty as soon as the line went dead, Connor stared intently at the phone. Somewhere, hundreds of miles away, *she* was talking to him, monopolizing his time…but it had been comforting to note Jared sounded frustrated with the interruption. He was just being a good friend, and friends accepted New Year's greetings from other friends. So long as they were brief greetings.

"Back." Jared switched over, and the wave of adrenaline that passed through Connor drowned out his concerns. "Guess what? I have some good news."

"Oh?"

"Ronnie's sick, or in trouble or something—I'm not sure—she was sorta vague just now. Or drunk or whatever. I mean, it is New Year's."

"Um…okay," Connor mumbled. Veronica was far from his favorite person, but he didn't exactly want to take pleasure in her suffering.

"Fuck, that wasn't the good news. What I mean is, she's gonna stay at home a few extra days. And, well, I was thinking, if you wanted, we could go back to campus early. Like, maybe, the day after tomorrow?"

"Together?"

"Yes, *together.*" Connor could almost see the roll of the eyes that accompanied Jared's response. "So, do you want to?"

The day after tomorrow. One more day—one more day and he could feel Jared's arms surrounding his body. One more day, and the first and only balm for his insecurities would be near him again.

He bit his lip. "Yeah. I do."

"Good." Jared chuckled. "I thought so. Then it's set. See you in a couple of days, okay?"

"Okay."

"I'd better get back to the party. My whole extended family is down there—it's why we came up here for the break. Mom didn't want to be alone over the holidays 'cause it's the first time since…well, you know."

"Yeah. I get it. Have fun, then."

"I will. Bye, Connor."

"Bye."

Connor picked up his violin and played until his fingers were raw.

***

He awoke early on the long-awaited morning, taking extra care in grooming and dressing himself before plastering his face up against a window to watch and wait.

A beat-up Chevy station wagon pulled into his driveway. He stared at it for a while, forgetting his plan to rush outside as soon as humanly possible. He'd never seen Jared's car before, and for some reason, he'd always imagined it as a trendy sports car, or at least a manly SUV.

But as soon as the wobbly door flew open and Jared's long legs stepped out, the shock was broken. Connor grabbed his bags, screamed "bye, everyone," over his shoulder, and bolted out of the house.

Jared was standing a few feet from the car by then, and Connor practically had to pull himself backward to keep them from colliding. He stopped only inches away, smiling stupidly. "Hey."

"Hey," Jared said, his own smile shining in the light of the clear winter day. "Ready to go?"

A piercing voice suddenly erupted from the house, plainly audible through the open front door. "I don't even know, sometimes. I don't even know what I did wrong that he's so impolite like that. I guess he's moved on, and he can just come here and use me to cook him meals and do his laundry and then leave without looking me in the face to say goodbye."

Connor raised a hand to his forehead. "Fuck," he muttered.

"What's her problem?" Jared shifted his weight, his brow crinkling.

"Um, she's big on etiquette, I guess. I kinda just ran out of there…"

The sound of the swinging door alerted them to company, and Connor turned around to see his father standing on their front porch.

"Uh, your mother is upset that you didn't say goodbye properly," he mumbled, darting his eyes between Jared and Connor. "You, uh, need to go apologize."

"Yeah, okay, Dad." Connor sighed. "I'll just be a minute, Jared. I'm really sorry."

"Nah, don't be sorry." Jared grinned. "C'mon." He surprised Connor by dropping a hand onto his shoulder and steering him toward the door. "Let's go say goodbye."

They entered the foyer together and Connor called out right away, hoping to settle things quickly. "Mom? I'm sorry I left in a hurry, it's just that I wanted to get back to school so I could buy my books for next semester."

"Yes, I'm sure you have an excuse, Connor," she spat back, her voice cutting. "You always have an excuse, and you don't even care how you—"

She stopped abruptly as she rounded the corner and saw Connor was not alone.

"Oh, I didn't realize…" The tone of her voice turned on a dime from angry to sickeningly sweet. "Well, aren't you going to introduce me to your friend?"

"Um…"

"I'm sorry." His mother directed her attention to Jared. "Politeness has never been Connor's forte. I'm Mrs. Owens." She extended her hand for him to shake.

"Jared," Jared replied, taking it and shooting a bewildered glance in Connor's direction. "Sorry I rushed Connor, ma'am. I guess there really isn't a need to be in that much of a hurry."

"Oh, don't be silly," she replied smoothly. "It's just that I was making an omelet for Connor to have before he left, and I didn't want it to go to waste. I've made so much, you see. Would you like to join us for breakfast?"

Unable to warn him off in front of his mother, Connor resigned himself as Jared nodded. "Sure, that'd be great, Mrs. Owens."

They sat at the island in the kitchen while his mother dished out the omelet and then, to Connor's chagrin, took up a chair opposite them. "So, Jared," she began, "how did you and Connor become acquainted?"

"Oh." Jared swallowed a mouthful of eggs. "He tutored me in anthropology last semester."

"Ah, you're an athlete. How wonderful. Football?"

"Yeah."

"Maybe you could teach Connor here how to play. I've always wanted him to take up a sport, but he just out and out refused. He should have an activity to help him maintain his physical health, don't you think?"

Jared's lips twitched. "Uh…"

Softly padding footsteps on the carpeted stairs caught Connor's attention. Grateful to have it diverted from the humiliating conversation at hand, he watched Melissa tread into the kitchen in her two-piece teddy bear pajamas.

"How come everyone's so wide awake?" She ran a hand over her hair, which was tangled in a bird's nest of a bun and sticking out from the side of her head.

"Oh, Melissa, dear. Come over and say hello to Connor's friend Jared."

Melissa's eyes widened and darted over to Jared. Then, though it hardly seemed possible, they got even wider, and it seemed just a tiny inkling of *envy* flitted across them before she was back to shock.

"Mom!" she shouted, backing up the stairs. "I'm not dressed!"

"She's getting to that age, I suppose." Connor's mother shook her head. "You know girls. I'm sure she'll be dressed in a few minutes, if you have the time to stay. She plays the piano and—"

"Mom, we really have to go," Connor interrupted. He got a disappointed huff as a response.

"Well, all right then. It was nice meeting you, Jared. Remember to call, Connor. Don't let us worry too much." She enveloped him in a stifling hug.

"Okay." Connor counted to ten before pulling away. "Bye, Mom."

Once outside, he dove straight into the station wagon and took a deep, steadying breath, ignoring the old-car mustiness that greeted his nostrils.

"So...your mom is kinda intense," Jared said as he got in beside him.

"Yeah." *If only there were some way to wipe the entire last fifteen minutes from existence...*

"Or maybe the word is 'overbearing'. I wonder if that played a part in you being the way you are...so shy and all?"

"I...I don't know. I think maybe I was just born that way." Connor shrugged, his face growing warm.

"Well, she's strange, that's all I'm saying. You and your sister are like musical geniuses, and you're a regular genius, too, getting A's in all your classes...I would think she'd be grateful instead of complaining."

A smile pulled at the ends of Connor's mouth. "I knew I liked you for a reason."

They drove on for a good twenty minutes, until the neighborhoods they passed grew sparser and the trees denser. Far from civilization, Jared pulled onto a little dirt trail that probably led to a house deep in the woods. He cut off the engine after traveling a few feet.

"Sorry," he said as Connor looked to him for an explanation. "I can't wait any longer." He unbuckled his seatbelt and threw himself over Connor's body. "Missed you," he muttered in between kisses.

Home and all of its oppressive memories faded as they continued to reacquaint themselves, until Jared pulled back with a rueful glance at where his erection was pressing against the zipper of his jeans. "Fuck, we still have like two hours of driving left before we can…"

Connor focused on the strained zipper, then cast his eyes on the trees that shielded them. "Who says we have to wait?"

"Are you serious?" Jared drew in a sharp, excited breath. "Please don't tease. I'm…I'm like dying for you here."

Nibbling on his lip, Connor reached for Jared's zipper. "I'm n-not. I'm not."

Jared lifted his hips off the seat so Connor could work his pants down and then settled back once he was exposed. "Connor…you're…you are just…"

Connor could have waited for whatever sweet thing Jared was going to say, but he had other things on his mind. They'd been separated far too long. He bent over and drew Jared in, deeper than he'd been able to before from this new angle.

"Sh—…oh, yeah," Jared grunted. His fingers wove into Connor's hair and he tugged and pushed a few times, following up with quick, breathless apologies.

The seat in the old station wagon squeaked. The whole car squeaked, actually, as Jared squirmed, his knees banging into the steering wheel. Connor pulled away for a second of rest, flicking Jared with his tongue as he went.

"Oh shit," Jared moaned. "Oh…"

Connor quickly reopened his mouth to receive the stream. No sense in ruining Jared's car.

"Oh, shit, Connor." Jared said again. "Sorry."

"It's"—Connor swallowed—"it's okay."

Jared chuckled, pulling his pants up and redoing the button. "That was more than okay. And I think…I think maybe it's your turn for, uh, for that. I mean, if you want."

Connor said nothing, his body quivering like a plucked string with the rush of desire. Of course he *wanted*. Maybe he couldn't have asked for it on his own, but if Jared was even half as good at blowjobs as he was at kissing…

His zipper clicked its way down, and he braced himself against the doorframe and the center console until his pants slipped to his thighs.

"Y'know," Jared remarked, "you actually have more experience at this than I do, so, uh…"

"Please," Connor murmured before he could stop himself.

"Hey, I didn't say I wouldn't try." Jared kissed him, a mischievous glint in his eye. He reached over and jerked at the seat adjustor, throwing Connor back so that he wound up staring at the drooping fabric roof of the car.

"Uhh…" Connor gasped. He wanted to be more coherent…maybe call out Jared's name, or something hot like that, but he couldn't form words once Jared had his lips on him. Jared's tongue darted out to lick down his shaft, and any chance for speech was gone. Slippery warmth enveloped him and Jared's dark curls bobbed up and down to an ever-accelerating tempo. Eyes rolling back in his head, back arching, Connor shot out down Jared's throat.

"Mm." Jared sat up and wiped his mouth. "You taste saltier than me."

Still shaky from the release, Connor returned his seat to its normal position. "Y-you…you've tasted yourself?"

Jared pulled him into a hot-breathed kiss. "Only on your lips."

They resumed driving with sated smiles, in a comfortable kind of silence Connor had never experienced before. And when Jared slid a hand into his lap, palm up, he took hold of it, and they stayed hand-in-hand all the way until the Charlottesville city limits.

SECOND SEMESTER

CHAPTER ELEVEN

"Quit trying to distract me," Connor reprimanded.

"Distract you?" Jared glanced up innocently, as if he hadn't been tracing a line from one of Connor's hipbones to the other—a line that was dipping suspiciously lower with each pass.

Connor rolled his eyes and went back to reviewing the paper in his hands, until Jared slipped low enough to catch a tuft of pubic hair with his fingers. "Jared," he groaned. "You're the one who asked me for help with this. If you want me to look it over, you're gonna have to actually give me a chance to read it through."

Jared huffed and pulled away. "Yeah, but that was before I knew you were gonna get all crazy with the red pen."

The pen was blue, actually, but Connor put it down anyway and shifted to catch Jared's eye. "I'm only trying to help."

"I know." Jared developed a sudden interest in his cuticles. "But you're not even in this class. Are you sure my paper sucks that badly?"

Sucks wasn't the word Connor would have used. But disjointed, unsupported, and unclear would probably translate to that in Jared's mind.

"I know I'm not in the class, but I've taken history classes before, and I have a general sense of what makes a good paper. I'm sorry if this sounds mean, but I've gotta say—"

"Hold it," Jared interrupted, throwing up both his hands. "Are you gonna make me wish for the days when you were too scared to talk to me?"

Accustomed to Jared's brand of teasing by now, Connor hesitated only a moment before continuing. "What I was going to say is, you're smarter than this. How much time did you spend on the reading before you wrote the paper?"

"The reading?" Jared parroted back, then gave Connor a rueful smile. "Connor, if I did all the reading for my classes, I'd never see the light of day again. And I'd never see you, either. We barely have any time to spend together without the tutoring excuse now, and you know how busy I am."

"I know." Connor fought to contain a sigh. "It just sucks, 'cause I know you could do a better job. I can edit the paper for you, but you really need to go back to the sources and try to make your ideas more cohesive."

Jared closed his eyes and scooted down on the bed, draping an arm around Connor and resting on his body.

"I'll see what I can do," he mumbled. "And thanks for helping. To be honest, I spat that out in like thirty minutes, which obviously wasn't enough time. I've just been sorta stressed, and practice hasn't been going that great." He reached down and scratched at the ace bandage on his knee. "I'm beginning to think I'm doing more of a disservice to my dad's memory—" Cutting himself off abruptly, he burrowed into Connor's chest. "Never mind. If he were here he'd just tell me to buck up and be a man."

Connor set the paper down and placed his hand on Jared's back, feeling how taught the muscles were. He was terrible at massages, so instead he dragged his fingers up and down the contours of Jared's body. After a few gentle caresses, Jared's tension dissipated, his shoulders relaxing and his breaths becoming deep and even.

A flash of confidence shot through Connor. *His* touch had that power—the power to comfort Jared in a time of need. "I'm sure your dad was a man in more ways than just football," he said gently. "Like in providing for his family, raising you and your brothers…I mean, I know football is important to you, but if you ever did want to move on, I don't think you should feel guilty about it. Your father may have told you to be a man, but I doubt he ever said to be the exact same man he was."

Jared considered the words for a moment before breaking into a sly grin. "Maybe you should be a therapist. Then you could dole out advice on a regular basis."

"Hah." Connor snorted. "Like that wouldn't be the blind leading the blind."

Jared tickled him, jabbing a whole hand into his ribs. "Don't sell yourself short. You have a lot to offer, you know. If you don't want to be a therapist, how 'bout a teacher? I got a B minus in anthro, and I definitely owe that to you."

"I'm supposed to be pre-law, remember?" Connor shooed Jared's pestering fingers away. "And anyway, we have some time yet before we have to worry about jobs. Let's just enjoy our free time while we have it."

"Finally!" Suddenly revived, Jared bounced up and tore off his shirt. "I thought we'd never get to the fun stuff."

***

"You're not sleeping, are you?" Rebecca's voice greeted Connor through his cell phone later that night. "It's only like twelve-thirty!"

"Mmm?" Connor grumbled, rubbing the crust from his eyes. Before college, twelve-thirty had been the middle of the night. "No, I wasn't."

"Good. Get your ass over to Newcomb, then. We're going steam tunneling."

"Steam tunneling?" he asked warily. "Isn't that illegal? I'm pretty sure we had a special meeting during orientation about how it's dangerous and—"

"Connor, there is no way you can graduate from UVA without going steam tunneling. You might as well get it over with. Now hurry it up. We'll be waiting."

She hung up, and Connor was left trying to adjust his eyes to the darkness.

Evidently, friendships involved phone calls out of the blue, encouraging him to do things he would have once considered dangerous—or criminal. But he was pretty sure he could trust Rebecca, and now that he was awake he'd just wind up tossing and turning, wishing Jared had stayed the night instead of disappearing with a wistful kiss.

So he threw aside his blankets and dressed.

Even with the heavy winter coat, he was shivering by the time he arrived. He found Rebecca, A.J., Tate, and Chrissy waiting for him with one of the preppy girls who'd happened by their lunch table a few times that semester. He searched his memory for her name and landed on Beth.

All five of them were visibly freezing, arms wrapped around themselves in a futile attempt to protect their barren skin, because they were all wearing t-shirts.

Rebecca frowned as he approached. "What t-took you so long?" she exclaimed through chattering teeth.

"Um...I have a fifteen minute walk to get here. Your dorm is only like five steps away."

A.J. shook his head. "Dude, you can't wear that in there." He grabbed a handful of Connor's jacket. "You'll roast. They're steam tunnels, you know."

After a quick stop at Rebecca's room to drop off his coat, they headed for the closest entrance to the tunnels. They had to wait several minutes, hopping around to keep up body warmth, as a slew of passersby made entry risky.

Once the coast was clear, A.J. and Tate grappled with the manhole cover, grunting with the effort it took to remove it. Connor almost went to lend a hand, as he was the only other male present, but he ended up staying back. He doubted he'd be of much help, anyway—Rebecca was probably stronger than he was.

The guys managed the feat and Tate dropped in first, then whispered for the others to follow. Rebecca jumped down without hesitation. A.J. and Chrissy struggled a little, and evidently needed help from either Rebecca or Tate, because by the time it was Connor's turn, he could hear them joking about being sexually molested. Apparently, they'd been aided by "hands on the ass."

Flashlights switched on below, and Connor started down the rungs on the side of the tunnel. They stopped short of the ground, though, and he waited there to gauge the distance he'd wind up falling if he let go.

"Don't freak," Tate said. "I'm gonna grab you."

Hands wrapped around his waist, and Tate deposited him on his feet.

"Okay, Beth, hurry up!" Rebecca called out.

The tiniest of the bunch at barely five feet, Beth almost made Connor feel tall. She came down in the glow of the flashlights, her shiny strawberry-blond hair catching and reflecting the beams. Tate grabbed her the same way he had grabbed Connor, then shimmied up the ladder, followed by A.J., and together they pulled the cover back into place.

Without even an inkling of moon or streetlight present, it was clear the flashlights were necessary, or they would have been plunged into complete darkness. It was also hot—extremely hot—and Connor had already started to sweat. A cockroach scuttled by his feet and he jumped back reflexively.

"Don't worry," A.J. said with a grin. "They're about the only living things we'll run into down here."

Beth let out a frightened squeak. "Kill it!"

"Don't!" Chrissy shouted at nearly the same time. "It's one of earth's creatures. What has it ever done to you?"

Beth stuck out her tongue. "Carry diseases…and creep me out. You guys didn't tell me there were going to be bugs down here."

"There aren't," Tate countered. "Just cockroaches. It's Connor's first time, too, and you don't hear him bitching."

Beth's cheeks reddened as she crossed her arms, turning away.

The embarrassment in her downcast eyes was all too familiar, and an urge to comfort overtook Connor. "I really hate roaches, too," he whispered in her ear. "I'll kill them for you if I can."

She smiled gratefully.

Tate led the way, skillfully ducking and crouching when the ceilings dipped lower. Graffiti, Latin quotes, riddles, and artwork appeared as their flashlights trailed the walls. After ten minutes of meandering through the narrow passages, Connor finally had to ask for their destination. He'd soaked through his shirt, and as he breathed in the thick, heated air he began to wonder if it wouldn't have been prudent of him to bring his inhaler.

"I'm taking you to see Jesus," Tate told him.

"Umm," Beth cut in, her voice tense. "I'm agnostic. How much longer is it?"

"Not much," Tate responded cheerily. "We've just gotta crawl through this one tunnel."

"Crawl?"

The tunnel in question was only large enough for one to get through on hands and knees. Tate, A.J., Chrissy, and Rebecca dropped down on all fours like seasoned pros and started to squirm their way through, but before Connor could follow, he felt a frantic tug on his arm.

"Crap," Beth whispered. "I can't go through there."

Connor tried his best to sound encouraging. "If Tate fit, you and I sure will."

"No, I mean, I can't. I'm...scared."

The flashlights, held by the four senior members of their group, were rapidly disappearing down the tunnel. In a moment, they'd be left in darkness.

"Hold up!" Connor shouted down the narrow opening.

"What? Why?" came the agitated response, from Tate.

"Just give us a sec," Connor found himself demanding, something he doubted he would have done if he and Tate had been face to face. He turned back to Beth. "I have no idea where we're going either, but...if you want, maybe you could hold onto my ankles while we crawl through. Maybe that would help?"

In the shadows, he couldn't make out Beth's expression, but he heard her exhale softly. "Okay."

She gripped him firmly as they began, occasionally letting out little whimpers of fear. The whole crawling part only took about a minute, but by the time they emerged even Connor was feeling slightly claustrophobic.

He turned around to help Beth to her feet and she fell into his arms, her body trembling. "Thanks, Connor."

Tate put the flashlight up to his face so that he looked like an eerie ghost-version of himself. For the first time, he stood completely straight, making whatever space they currently occupied the one with the highest ceilings yet.

"And now, ladies and gentlemen, I present...Jesus."

In concert, A.J. and Tate turned their flashlights to the wall, which was indeed graced with a huge Jesus-face. Or, at least, it was Jesus if Connor took their word for it.

Though artistically done, it was hard for a floating head in the darkness to look like anything other than a creepy apparition.

"Pretty neat, huh? It's been here for a while now."

Beth still had her arm around Connor, and she raised a dainty eyebrow. "Um, yeah, I guess so. A spray-painted Jesus. Is that all we came here to see?"

"We came for the experience," Chrissy said. "And to add ourselves to the history." She reached into a small pouch at her waist and pulled out a can of spray paint. "Time to make our mark!"

They traveled further to find some relatively less-crowded patches of wall, then took turns painting their initials. Beth stayed close by Connor's side, though she seemed to relax a little until everyone was done and it was nearing time to go.

"Please tell me we don't have to go through that tunnel again," she whined.

"Nah," Tate said. "We'll leave through the chem building entrance. That'll put Connor closer to his place, anyways."

The cool air felt amazing, and even though Connor knew he'd be freezing in a few minutes, courtesy of sweat-drenched clothes, he'd never been happier to see his breath than when they finally climbed their way out. All in all, he was glad he'd gone; there was something to be said for having *the experience*, but he wasn't ready to make it a regular nighttime fare.

Beth didn't seem too enthused, either. As they stood shaking out the cramps from their legs and waiting for Tate and A.J. to re-cover the hole, she murmured to him, "Never again! That was scary...and really uncomfortable. I'm so glad you were there, Connor. You were a real sweetheart." Without warning, her appreciative smile turned into a peck on his cheek.

He darted his eyes around to see if anyone was watching, and caught Rebecca's smug look from a few feet away. "Uh, no problem…well, I'll see ya later. We'd all probably better get indoors before we catch pneumonia."

"There's the responsible Connor we know and love." Tate clapped him on the back.

"Wait, you're not coming to Brown to hang out?" Beth asked. "Your jacket is back there. C'mon."

"I'll get it tomorrow." Connor shrugged away from her beckoning arm, growing more and more apprehensive about the attention she was giving him. It wasn't the same kind of friendly acknowledgement he got from Rebecca or Chrissy. "You guys have fun. I'll catch ya later."

He waved as the group chorused their goodbyes, then took off jogging toward his dorm.

***

Apprehension met its cause the next afternoon, when he approached the lunch table to find Beth sitting there. Her appearances at Newcomb were rare and usually brief, but today she seemed settled in for the count, wearing a pink turtleneck sweater that brought out the rosiness in her creamy complexion. Her hair was carefully done in a French braid.

"Hey," she chirped as he set his tray down. "It's my tunneling hero. If it weren't for him, I'd still be rotting down there." She shot dirty looks to the rest of the table.

"Connor is very dependable," Rebecca agreed. "The least flighty of us all, for sure."

"Hey, I'm not flighty," Chrissy protested, and everyone, including Connor, scoffed.

"You are, but it's a deep sort of flightiness." A.J. patted her hand.

Beth leaned closer to Connor. "Well, I for one am thankful he decided to stick around with you lot." Her fingers brushed his arm, and she grinned at him through strangely dark lashes for her hair color.

He gave her a meager lip twitch as a response, his anxieties cropping back up with a vengeance. Something about her attitude and physical proximity reminded him of the way he'd seen Veronica hang all over Jared…and if that was anything to go by, he was approaching dangerous territory.

He chewed his food slowly, remaining silent throughout the meal.

After thirty minutes, Beth rested her hand on his thigh. "Well, I have to get all the way to the Physics building, or I'd hang out longer." She slumped her shoulders and gave a rueful wave. "Bye, guys."

As soon as she'd walked off, Rebecca shot out from her seat and latched on to Connor's arm. "Let's grab some dessert."

He let himself be led away, but Rebecca wasn't heading toward the food. She dragged him out on the patio to a partially secluded corner.

"She likes you," Rebecca said. "You should definitely go for it."

"Go for…what?" Connor tried to skirt around her. "I could go for some ice cream."

Rebecca rolled her eyes. "C'mon, Connor. You've done so well coming out of your shell this past month, don't go back there now."

Crossing his arms, Connor attempted to settle his gaze into a glare, even though his stomach churned at her rather accurate observation.

"I mean, you know…adjusting to college can be hard for some people…I'm just saying. Why not Beth? She's smart, cute, funny…a little panicky in stressful situations, but hey, you can work on that. You seem to have a calming effect on her."

He shook his head. "Honestly, it's nice of you to care, but I'm good."

"Well, what's the problem? You're not seeing anyone, are you?"

Connor's breath stopped mid-intake.

So there was one more caveat for developing friendships: friends expected to *know* things about each other's lives. And now the best thing that had ever happened to him had suddenly become, to Rebecca at least, *the problem*.

He opened his mouth slowly, and only with the greatest degree of willpower. He couldn't say yes. If he did, he'd be faced with an onslaught of unanswerable questions. But for some reason, the lie was not forthcoming, either.

"N-no." He finally forced his vocal chords to move. "B-but I'm not looking for anything right now."

Words had never tasted more bitter as they'd left his mouth.

CHAPTER TWELVE

Connor forced his eyes from the time display on his laptop to the blinking cursor on the screen. He managed to type his name and the course number in a steady rhythm before his gaze carelessly drifted back to the time again.

Not even a minute had gone by.

Familiar insecurities chipped away at him with new strength. What if Beth didn't give up so easily? Or Rebecca, for that matter? Dealing with the situation seemed like it would require finesse, something he obviously lacked. Terrified of making the wrong move, only one thing offered any hope.

Jared would know how to handle it. And Jared already knew all his insecurities, so it wasn't like he needed to keep up the pretense of holding them back. Jared would have just the right words, or just the right amount of gentle teasing to make him feel like his problems were not nearly as insurmountable as they seemed.

Connor gave up on writing and stared at his clock, willing the time to change. A minute finally passed and he let out a sigh of relief before starting the waiting game all over again. Once a week—or twice, at most—was not enough time to spend with Jared.

When the familiar knock finally came, he flung open the door and immediately sank into Jared's arms.

Jared hugged him back approvingly. "I know. I missed you too."

Connor gave him a wan smile, tugging him onto the bed and then resettling in his arms. "I wanted to call, but I knew you wouldn't really have time to talk for long."

"Yeah." Jared patted his chest. "I'm sorry. But I have time now. Four or five hours, in fact. Told Ben I was driving out to Madison to meet a friend from high school."

Connor nodded, chewing on his tongue as he pondered how best to direct the conversation.

"You obviously have something on your mind." Jared scooted a little closer. "Spill."

Taking a deep breath, he launched into his tale of the tunneling adventure and Beth's unexpected attention. Jared listened attentively, a quiet smile playing on his lips.

"See, I told you you're attractive," he said when Connor was through, reaching out to ruffle his hair.

Connor pulled away, strangely irritated Jared was not feeling any of the jealousy *he* experienced when catching a glimpse of Veronica. Apparently, Jared was all too aware he had nothing to fear from a petite strawberry-blonde.

Jared crossed his arms and regarded him with raised brows. "Still haven't learned to take a compliment?"

"It's not that," Connor mumbled. "It's just…it was an awkward situation. Beth flirting, and Rebecca asking me if I was seeing someone…I mean, wouldn't you have been uncomfortable if it'd happened to you?"

"Uh…" Jared quickly found something near the ceiling of the dorm room that required his attention, and the realization hit Connor mid-sigh.

"Oh, right. I guess that happens to you all the time."

"Maybe." Jared shrugged. "But you have nothing to worry about. I have enough trouble with Ronnie still, and we're not even dating anymore. I would never get myself into that again."

Connor drew his knees up to his chest, hugging himself to dispel the slight chill in the air. This wasn't exactly the solution he'd hoped for. Then again, he didn't know what would be.

"Hey," Jared said quietly, pulling Connor's legs down so he could crawl closer and sneak a kiss. He tried for a playful smile, but it slipped away when Connor couldn't muster the emotion to return it. "Why don't we do something together tomorrow?"

"Do something?" Connor repeated doubtfully. He and Jared never *did something.* They stayed indoors, where it was safe—safe to touch or kiss each other whenever they felt the urge. And he understood Jared's desire for secrecy, he really did, but there *were* times when he wished...

"Yeah, just you and me." Jared covered his foot with a warm hand. "How 'bout around three?"

"I have two classes after three."

"So do I. Skip 'em. I don't have anything else to do tomorrow, so I'll be able to spend the whole afternoon and evening with you."

"Skip class?"

"Yeah, brainiac." Jared chuckled, tickling his ribs. "We both know you'll survive, and I doubt it'll put a dent in your 4.0."

Connor tried to protest for a few more seconds, until Jared grabbed him by the waist and threw him down on his back. "All right, all right," he groaned, struggling for breath as Jared's knee pressed into his stomach. First steam tunneling, now skipping a day of classes. College was turning him into a regular delinquent. "So, what something are we going to do?"

"It's a surprise." Jared winked, then shifted his leg so he could press himself against Connor in a much more enjoyable fashion. Too aroused to continue the interrogation, Connor gave in to his hormones. Handling reality would just have to wait.

***

Jared showed up at a quarter to three the next day, wearing jeans and a red flannel shirt. It was his footwear, though, that had Connor questioning his decision to go along so readily.

"Hiking boots?"

"I know you probably don't have them. You can just wear sneakers."

"But what are they for?"

"Uh, hiking," Jared replied smugly. "And don't give me that face. I'll go slow so you can keep up."

Connor continued to stare. Did he stand any chance of seducing Jared into forgetting about their afternoon plans?

He almost laughed aloud at the thought.

"C'mon, get ready," Jared prompted, giving him a little shove.

Reluctantly, Connor pulled on his shoes, and when Jared was distracted with a text on his cell, surreptitiously grabbed his inhaler and shoved it in his pocket. If there could be anything worse than trailing after the obviously fitter Jared as they scaled a mountain, it would be him trailing while having an asthma attack, without his inhaler.

Eager to get on the road, Jared ushered him out the door and down to the cul-de-sac where he'd left his station wagon illegally parked. The sight of its warped tan siding and fake wood-grain interior instantly made Connor smile. It was only the second time he'd had an opportunity to ride in Jared's car, and despite what a wreck it was, the privilege made him feel giddy.

He yanked at the rusted handle to get in and flew forward into the window when the door refused to budge.

"Oh, yeah, sorry about that." Jared gave him a sheepish grin. He leaned over to open the passenger door from the inside. "Ben slammed it really hard the last time we all went out, and now it doesn't open very well."

Connor rolled his eyes. It was amazing Jared managed to spend as much time with his careless and messy roommate as he did. Or maybe it was just *annoying,* since it was far more time than Jared spent with him.

He pushed back the flicker of less-than-pleasant thoughts as the radio came on and an unfamiliar twang filled the car.

Country music?

"I didn't know you liked country," he remarked, and at least a little dismay slipped through.

"Guess I'm not as sophisticated as you are." Jared laughed. "It's not gonna bother you, is it?"

"No, of course not." Connor resigned himself to suffer in silence.

The chorus of the tale of two young lovers began to play, and Jared started humming along. His voice matched the pitch surprisingly well, even though he'd sworn up and down he had no musical sense whatsoever.

Connor bit his lip to stop his smile, but couldn't keep himself from leaning in to peck Jared on the cheek.

"What was that for?"

"Um…the humming is…cute. And it makes this music a little easier to handle."

Jared shot his eyes skyward, flushing a pale pink. He was quiet for the next song, but a few minutes later the humming was back, this time louder and with a broad smile in Connor's direction. Connor giggled, and by the end of the forty-minute drive, found he was tapping his foot to the beat despite himself.

"Here we are." Jared pulled off the scenic byway and into a parking lot surrounded by broad oaks. The outstretched tree branches hung over the car, casting shadows across his face. "So, you ready?"

He'd probably follow Jared anywhere, but Connor decided it best to stick with a simple nod.

Jared tugged on a backpack and began leading him up the dirt path, chatting nonstop about the flora and fauna all around them.

"Check out this ant trail!" He pointed to a wide swath of ants traveling the stump of a tree. "They're probably just coming out of hibernation."

"That's cool," Connor replied, less enthusiastic about the ants than he was about the look of little-boy wonder on Jared's face. "They're such social creatures."

Jared turned back to him with a crooked smile. "You don't think maybe, every once and a while, two ants sneak off by themselves to have a little fun?"

"Maybe." Connor shrugged. "But they'd have to rejoin their colony sooner or later, right? Could...could they survive otherwise?"

Jared knit his brows, but before he got the chance to respond, a man and a little girl came bounding up the path.

"C'mon, or we won't get to the top by sunset, Daddy!"

The father gave them each a polite nod as he hurried past, and Jared stepped away from the ants.

"Well, you heard the girl. Let's get a move on."

The dirt path gave way to rocks as they ascended, and the rocks began to pile on top of each other with increasing steepness. Connor resorted to scrambling up on all fours a few times, but when Jared skipped ahead and turned back to watch, he attempted a difficult part of the trek while standing upright.

Which, of course, only led him to slip, banging his knee on a jagged rock as he fell.

"Shit, you okay?" Jared backtracked and helped him to his feet.

"Yeah." Connor dusted himself off. "I guess I should've told you I'm pretty clumsy."

Grinning, Jared squatted down and pulled up his pant leg. "Skinned your knee pretty good."

140

Spots of blood poked through the crisscross pattern of scrapes on Connor's skin. "Oh…it's okay. I'm fine."

Jared rooted around in his backpack and pulled out a first-aid kit. "Always be prepared," he responded, then tore into an alcohol pad and gently pressed it onto Connor's wounded knee. He applied a Band-Aid as another group of hikers bypassed them. "There you go. All better."

Heart fluttering mercilessly, and strangely, given all Jared had done was fix up a scrape for him, Connor struggled to come up with a response. "Y-you were a boy scout, weren't you?"

Jared offered him a hand to help him traverse the rough patch of rock. "Guilty as charged."

Five minutes later they reached the summit, where the rocks flattened out and provided the travelers with a stunning view of the surrounding peaks and the valleys below. In the distance some of the trees on taller, neighboring mountains were still covered with a dusting of snow, and as the sun began to descend it touched their caps with fiery brilliance.

Jared settled on a slab of rock and pulled two turkey sandwiches out of his backpack. "Made us dinner," he said, handing one over. "Guess I should have thought to bring something warm to drink in a thermos, but I'm not that advanced in the whole planning department."

Connor grinned and sat beside him. "This is fine."

It *was* cold, though, and as he chewed his sandwich he found himself leaning toward Jared's side. He really wished he could just *snuggle* against Jared—throw an arm around him like he did when they sat alone on his bed—but instead he contented himself with staring out at the natural wonder before him.

He'd seen beautiful sunsets along the ocean when he was a child, but something about watching the sun disappear among the mountains was more powerful than that gentle sinking into oblivion. Here the sun left waves of burning color in its wake, turning the green trees into a multi-colored spectacle—its last gasps of magnificence before it left that particular span of earth for the night.

Jared's hand inched closer to his along the rock where they sat until their pinkies touched. Checking to make sure no one was near enough to notice, Connor linked those fingers loosely, and Jared let out a thoughtful sigh.

"My dad took us here, when we came for one of his reunions. I was only like thirteen then, but I remember knowing I was going to come to this school, come to this mountain again, because of him." He swallowed, his Adam's apple bobbing up and down violently. "I miss him."

Connor rubbed Jared's pinky, willing comfort through that tiny amount of contact. "I know I shouldn't say this," he began slowly, "but sometimes I'm jealous of what you had with your dad."

Jared turned toward him, eyes brilliantly lit from the colors in the sky. "What do you mean?"

"I mean, I know I still have my dad, so I should just shut up, but we're not...close. And you and your dad obviously were. You're still close, and he's not even with you anymore."

Jared nodded, the shadow of sadness lifting from his face. "Yeah." He smiled. "I guess we are still close. That was actually a really sweet thing to say."

Connor stared into Jared's eyes, the sunset all but forgotten. Whatever beauty it offered was nothing compared to the intensity of watching Jared watch him, knowing they felt something so perfect for each other. The emotion was so overwhelming it almost made him want to cry—joyful tears, though—and scream from this or any mountain he was pretty sure what they'd found together was *real*.

"You're cold," Jared murmured, their eyes still locked.

"No, I'm fine."

"Your lips are turning blue. I don't want you getting sick. Come on, let's head back."

The stars were out in full force by the time they reached the car. Under the protective cover of night, Jared leaned in to buckle Connor's seatbelt and give him a teasingly soft kiss. "That's all until we get back," he said.

***

Even with every inch of Connor's body geared up in anticipation, Jared still managed to surprise him. He grabbed Connor's shirt collar before the door to his room even fell closed and pinned him against the wall, the kisses anything but soft now. Clothes were shed with little care where they fell as they twisted against each other and toppled over onto the bed.

Not a word passed between them, but at times like this, words weren't really necessary. Relying fully on that fact, Connor tore himself away from Jared's embrace long enough to walk over to his desk drawer and grab the items he had hidden there weeks ago.

Jared blinked up at him, until Connor stretched out the hand that held the lube and condom. Then he recoiled as if he'd seen a snake.

"What's that for?"

Connor stared at his open palm, taken aback by the intrusion of words into their passion. "Um, w-what do you think it's for?"

"You're not happy with what we're doing?"

Of all Jared's possible responses, that had to be the furthest from Connor's mind. He sank onto the bed, panic squeezing his stomach and making bile rise up in his throat. After spending the last two months building the courage to push the envelope on their physical relationship, the rebuttal had him about ready to find a corner to hide in. He hadn't felt that way around Jared in a long time.

"O-of course I'm happy," he mumbled. He closed his eyes, praying Jared would come to his senses and take the lead. It was only natural, wasn't it? "But...r-remember when we first talked about...stuff...and you asked if I was ever curious? Well, I am."

Jared sighed, rubbing his hand over his face. "It's not that I wouldn't want to, um, be with you that way. It's just that...I don't know I'd ever be comfortable with anyone...you know...to me...and it doesn't seem fair to take without reciprocating."

"Oh. O-okay." Humiliation burned Connor's skin, and he began to tuck the offending objects away under the bed.

Jared stopped him. "Wait, hold on. Have you...have you really thought a lot about this?"

"N-no, it's okay, it doesn't matter."

"Don't do that," Jared chided. "If it's important to you, then let's talk about it."

"I-it's n-not. I didn't m-mean to—"

"Connor!" Jared grabbed his shoulders and shook. "Stop. Take a deep breath and talk to me."

Connor obeyed, closing his eyes again and finding relative peace in the darkness. "Fine. It's just that...I thought you might want to. I'm not unhappy, and we don't have to...but if you ever did...I...I wouldn't mind being the...the...you know. It doesn't matter to me if you never want to be."

Jared scratched his chin. "You may feel like that now, but who's to say you won't change your mind?"

"I won't," Connor replied firmly. And he was fairly certain that was true. He'd prepared himself—assuming Jared would be in charge, of course. After all, Jared was in charge of their entire relationship. "I just"—his voice dropped closer to a whisper—"I just...want it to be you...with me...my first time..."

Oh, no. He'd said too much. Now he sounded desperate, and if he kept on talking, he'd probably wind up giving it all away—that deeper desire for much more than what he was asking for.

And he didn't even want to give that away to himself.

Jared hesitated a moment longer before taking the items from his loose grasp. "You're sure you're ready?"

"I'm...I'm sure."

He lay on his back with his hips propped up as Jared's much larger frame hovered above him. That would have been intimidating, once, but now he knew better. Knew better than most—maybe even better than *anyone*—that beneath the big football-player exterior, Jared was an incredibly gentle person at heart.

But even with all his preparation, he still gasped when Jared's cold, wet fingers slipped into him.

"Does it hurt? Am I doing it wrong?" Jared asked, retracting quickly.

"No, no, you're doing fine," Connor reassured him. It felt odd, to be in the reassuring position for once. "J-just keep going. I'm fine."

He suffocated his first whimpers when Jared entered, so he wouldn't startle him. Still, Jared paused until Connor gave him a small nod to continue. Then he moved in a little further, and the process repeated itself. The eternity of *move-wait-move* made things feel cold and technical, and Connor lost his erection as he focused on accustoming himself to the foreign object inside of him.

Another eternity passed, while Jared pulled at him to coax him back to life. Jared was still completely firm, his chest heaving, his pupils blown wide. Clearly, he had no need for the lengthy pause. He was just waiting patiently for the okay to move on.

Connor pushed his hips up, tightening himself around Jared, and realized his own chest was now heaving in sync.

Moving as one, he thought as Jared finally began to thrust.

The thin line between pain and pleasure shattered. Suddenly, instead of the rawness, there were sparks— sparks that made the fireworks on his now-closed eyelids explode with new dimension. What was responsible for that startling radiance? Was it just the physical sensations, or was it this absolute *intimacy*, beyond any connection he'd ever had with another human being?

Jared's thrusts grew more forceful, throwing him back into the physical. Into deeper pressure, faster movements, and harder collisions between their sweat-coated bodies. Fingernails dug into his shoulders, and Jared's thighs rippled with the contraction of his muscles as he tensed and then released.

The moan of pleasure—and the reflexive tightening of Jared's hand on his erection—drew Connor to the edge. He came in a stream against Jared's chest.

Jared collapsed onto him. They gasped together for a while, riding out the aftershocks of post-orgasmic pleasure, before Connor realized his breathing was not approaching the normal pattern Jared's was. He squirmed free of the tangle of arms and legs and retrieved his pants from the floor so he could dig out his inhaler.

"Shit, I didn't know you had asthma." Jared leaned on his elbow to watch. "Are you all right?"

Connor held his hand in a thumbs-up while he used the nebulizer. "Yeah." He coughed out gently when he was done. "It's really mild. I'm fine."

He headed back to bed, but even in the dark he could tell the concern in Jared's eyes had been replaced by a mischievous twinkle.

"What?"

The look was followed by a smirk, and as Connor stood a few feet away from the bed, Jared broke into an all-out fit of uncontrollable laughter.

"What?" Connor repeated, crossing his arms against his bare chest, which reminded him he was completely naked. Naked and standing in front of the person he'd just let take his virginity...and in no mood to be laughed at. He felt far too exposed for even friendly teasing.

"I'm not laughing at you, I swear," Jared subdued himself long enough to say, but a moment later, he was back to laughing.

"Then what is it?"

"I can't tell you. You'll probably hit me."

"Jared," Connor pleaded, that old insecure tremble slipping into his voice.

"All right, all right." Jared finally got himself under control as he wiped a laughter-borne tear from his eye. "I was just wondering...did I...did I take your breath away?"

Connor grabbed a pillow and aimed for Jared's head.

He fell asleep secure in Jared's arms, but sometime around midnight, awoke to movement as Jared tried to unwrap himself. Stubbornly, Connor clung tighter. "Don't leave, please," he mumbled in a sleep-induced state of honesty.

Jared sighed and settled back against him with a light kiss. "I'm right here," he whispered. "Go back to sleep."

Connor did, his pangs over separation momentarily eased. But the next time he awoke in the darkness, he found himself alone.

CHAPTER THIRTEEN

Connor rested his instrument at the conductor's swift motion, thankful for the break. He twisted in his seat, rotating his shoulder blades and trying to relieve the tightness in his back. The Baroque music selected for the spring concert was a little too precise for his tastes, as he'd discovered—especially of late—he was a romantic at heart.

Rebecca shared a similar disdain for the music, amplified by the multiple times Vidar had called her out in sectionals for not bowing cleanly enough. "I don't want to sound like Chrissy," she muttered while the conductor demanded more of a crescendo from the winds, "but sometimes I feel like this stuff is stifling my natural creativity. Maybe I need to break out of here and join a barefoot bluegrass band. I oughta be able to find one around here."

Connor grinned. Willowy Rebecca would fit in perfectly in such a setting. "Yeah, I was thinking of joining the pit orchestra for that theater group. You know, the one that's doing *Kiss Me, Kate*. Thought it might be nice to do something different for a change."

"Ooh, good idea. Just don't let Vidar hear you say that. I had a friend who asked for a day off from rehearsal once to practice with the pit, and he tore her a new one. I mean, he must have lectured her for a straight five minutes about making a commitment to *real* music and not wasting time with stuff a monkey could play."

"A monkey?" Connor chuckled. "Really?"

Rebecca shrugged. "What can I say, he's a foreigner."

The conductor tapped his stand. "Can I have quiet, please?"

Exchanging guilty glances, they waited a few minutes to resume talking, careful to keep their voices to a whisper.

"Hey, you gonna come by tonight? A bunch of us are gonna hang out and watch a movie in the Brown common room."

"A bunch of us?" Connor asked hesitantly.

Rebecca rolled her eyes. "I don't even know why I'm asking you. You're coming, period."

***

A bunch of us turned out to be the usual Brown-dorms crowd. Connor settled himself on the uncomfortable couch while Tate and Rebecca took their seats rather close to each other on a large, lumpy beanbag.

A.J. came up from behind them, his arms full with two bowls of popcorn. "What are we watching?"

"A classic. *La Cage aux Folles*," Rebecca answered. She reached out to take her share of the snacks. "You'll love it."

Busy studying the way Tate had casually thrown his arm around Rebecca and was now stroking her hand, Connor missed the exact moment when Beth entered the room.

"I know, sickeningly cute." She plopped down next to him. "You didn't know they'd started dating?"

"Oh, uh, I guess I didn't get the announcement." Connor turned slowly to face her. Why on earth had he chosen to sit in a spot that was so difficult to guard?

Rebecca stuck out her tongue. "Shut up. We're not cute."

"Nope, not at all," Tate agreed, but Rebecca looked less than pleased with his support.

"A girl as tall as me can't afford to be choosy." She sighed. "I have a limited pool to work with if I want to date someone who doesn't make me feel like a giant."

"I don't care, I'm sticking with cute," Beth said defiantly. "You're going to that dance at Newcomb this weekend, right? That's cute if I ever heard it."

Rebecca blushed. "I just want an excuse to dress in an eighties prom dress and crimp my hair." Then she perked up, leaning toward the couch. "Hey, why don't you come with us? It'll be fantastically cheesy."

Beth squirmed in her seat. "Aw, I would, but I don't have anyone to go with."

Connor's neck twitched. Something wasn't right here. Even after his years of abstaining from social interaction, he could tell something was off about the way Rebecca and Beth were speaking to each other. The words just didn't seem to be flowing naturally—they almost sounded...*rehearsed*.

He stared at his shoelaces. Hopefully whoever else they were waiting for would show up soon, so they could be distracted by the movie...although being next to Beth in the dark wasn't too appealing a thought, either.

"Hey, you wanna come with me, Connor?" Beth asked a moment later, solidifying his dread.

His pulse was already racing, and he knew he'd waited too long to respond when Rebecca shot him a concerned look.

"Oh...I...don't dance."

"You don't have to dance, silly." Beth laid her hand on his thigh. "We'll just hang out and have a good time."

"Yeah, man," Tate threw in. "I'm a ridiculous dancer. I mean, have you ever seen anyone this tall and this white try to find a beat? I can pretty much guarantee that if I attempt it, it'll be the pinnacle of entertainment."

Connor's stomach roiled, and he was hesitant to open his mouth as the bout of nausea overtook him. How was it possible that just as he was finding himself in the social world, he had to be waylaid by a five-foot-tall girl? It really wasn't fair.

"I'm just not much for dances," he finally mumbled.

Tate threw a piece of popcorn at him. "C'mon man, you're a musician. You gotta be able to at least sway to the music."

It was Rebecca who finally came to his aid, putting a hand on Tate's shoulder and silencing him with a look Connor couldn't quite figure out. "Hey, let's put on the movie, guys. It's getting late, and I have a nine-thirty class tomorrow."

Stumbling to his feet, Connor faked a stretch. "I...I think I'm gonna call it a night. I kinda have a busy day tomorrow, too."

Beth stared at him for a moment before darting her eyes away, but not before he caught the disappointment shining through them.

"Oh, no, Connor, please stay. We haven't even started the movie yet!" Rebecca pleaded. "I think you'll really like it."

Connor shrugged, unable to even make eye contact with her, and headed for the door. "I...I'm not really into foreign films. I'll see ya tomorrow."

He hurried away, wondering how long it would be before he'd feel safe being around his friends again. After this pitiful display, Beth would probably take the hint and stop pestering him, but what would Rebecca think of his actions? All his hard work for a decent friendship could very well be out the window if she thought his cold shoulder was unwarranted.

His phone rang as he neared the entrance to his dorm.

"Hey, you."

Still jittery, Connor pushed his ear against the hard bit of plastic, as if he could reach all the way through to Jared's warm skin. "H-hey."

"Everything okay? You sound a little upset."

"Actually…is…is there any way you could come over tonight? Just for a little while?"

Jared hesitated. "Oh…I thought you were gonna chill with the Brownies tonight. I'm supposed to be hanging out with Ben and some of the other guys."

"Right. I know." Connor sighed, hurting his ear with the rush of static-feedback from the phone. Moments of silence ticked by while his feet dragged to a standstill.

"All right, I can come for a few minutes. Just give me like half an hour, okay?"

"Yeah, okay." His lungs filled with breath again. "Thanks."

***

Jared stepped into the room, one finger held up for silence while he spoke into his cell phone.

"Okay Jake, here's what you do. Buy her yellow roses." He plummeted down on the bed. "Yes, yellow. Yellow is for friendship. Then, if she acts really excited by the gift, she probably likes you. If she doesn't seem thrilled, you can tell her it was a friend thing. That way you've made a good impression, but you don't have to feel embarrassed if she doesn't like you back right now."

He gave Connor an apologetic shrug. "Yeah, buddy, no problem. I gotta go now. I'll talk to you later."

"Sorry." He silenced the phone and tucked it away. "My brother has his first serious crush, and apparently I'm the love doctor. But I'm all yours now." He pulled Connor onto the bed and scooted around until he had him resting between his legs. "Tell me what's wrong."

Connor leaned back and closed his eyes, inhaling the comfort of Jared's scent. "Beth," he mumbled.

"The little chick with a crush? C'mon, Con, you can handle her."

"But I don't like hurting people's feelings," Connor shot back, though he really was beginning to feel like a whining child. Jared was right; he should have been able to handle the situation without running away. "She outright asked me to that stupid dance they're having at Newcomb."

"So?"

"So? So I had to say no…and now I bet both her and Rebecca are pissed at me."

Jared shifted behind him, but Connor didn't turn around, afraid he'd see frustration in Jared's eyes.

"You didn't have to say no," Jared replied calmly. "Just because you go to a dance with her and a bunch of friends doesn't mean she's expecting you to marry her." The comfort Jared provided rapidly vanished as he pulled away even more, leaving a gap between their bodies.

Connor finally moved to face him, his hands scrunching into fists around his comforter. Why was it he so desperately needed Jared to show just an *inkling* of jealousy? "Well I don't want to lead her on, either. It wouldn't be fair."

"You just have to make sure she understands you're going as friends. It's no big deal. Hey, do you know her number? Why don't you call her…or Rebecca, and make it like a group thing. Then you won't be uncomfortable."

"What? No! I don't want to go!" Connor's throat tightened on the words, making them high-pitched and strained. "I don't want her to like me. She's ruining my friendships!"

"Whoa, whoa," Jared scoffed. "Tune down the melodrama, man. You're starting to sound like a chick."

Connor ripped himself all the way out of Jared's arms, backing up to the corner of his bed. A smoldering anger rose in his chest, and he almost gave it voice to call Jared an asshole, or some equally vicious epithet. They'd never really had a fight before, but in his already-emotional state he could feel one brewing now.

Jared snatched his hand. "Okay, I know that was rude. I'm sorry. Don't flip out. I'm just saying, you can go with your friends and have a good time."

"Jared, I'm not going." Connor gritted his teeth and tried to hold back the storm.

There was a beat of silence, and then Jared dropped his hand. "I am."

"What?"

He shrugged. "I'm going. A bunch of my suitemates thought it'd be mildly entertaining, so...yeah, we're going."

"With your suitemates?"

Jared looked past him. And Connor knew then he wasn't going to like what came next.

"With Ronnie."

Fury and sickness rushed into him, heating his face and blinding out rational thought. "Why...why would you do that? Why would you go with her? Y-you told me...you promised me..."

"Calm down," Jared said. "We're going as friends. It's not a big—"

"Don't you dare say it's not a big deal!"

Jared recoiled, but Connor couldn't lower his volume mid-stride.

"It *is* a big deal, because if it wasn't, you would have told me before. You've obviously been planning it for a while!"

"Connor," Jared continued in a level tone. He pushed his hands out in the universal *calm down* signal, which only infuriated Connor more. "It slipped my mind, okay? But it's not like we're going on a date. Ronnie and I were friends in high school long before we started going out."

"Yeah, but does she know there's no chance? Does she get that? Because I'm pretty sure she doesn't. Maybe you don't even know that!"

"That's not fair. You know how I feel about you. Veronica is just a friend, nothing more. I swear to you. You don't even want to go to this stupid dance, so why are you so upset about me going with friends?"

"Because...because if you're going to go to a stupid dance, then it should be with *me*!"

The words flew out of Connor's mouth and whipped through the air, stunning him. When had he reached this turning point? When had he gone from gratefully taking whatever he could get to actually believing he deserved *more*?

Jared's shock held for a few seconds before his face crumpled. "Shit, Connor," he whispered. "It...it can't be. You know that. We have to keep this under control."

Under control? What did that even mean? Frantically, Connor tried to latch onto the rage that had filled him a moment earlier, but it was already slipping. Only pain lay underneath. "Yeah. Yeah, I know that."

They sat in silence, at opposing ends of the bed, while Connor tried to make sense of his own reactions. He *did* know how things had to be between them; he'd known all along. So why did he feel so different all of a sudden? Why couldn't he turn back the clock to when stealing kisses a few times a week was all he needed to sustain him? Everything was simpler then.

He could almost see the same thoughts behind Jared's downcast eyes.

"I gotta go meet up with Ben," Jared finally said.

"I know."

Jared stood to leave. He paused at the door for a second to look back, nostrils flared and lips pressed into a wobbly line. "Bye, Connor."

No kiss, no tousle of the hair, no hand on the shoulder—just goodbye. Connor sat frozen on the bed, replaying the argument in his head. How had things gone so far astray in only a few minutes?

You know how I feel about you, Jared's words hit him again. Most of the time, Connor thought he did. But what *proof* did he have? The only evidence anything existed between them was in his own memories. And even if Veronica was nothing more than a friend, she still got higher billing than he did. She could be seen with him in public. She could hold his hand, touch him, kiss him if she so chose—all the things Connor wanted to do, far more often than he got the chance. And to do it in public, for the whole world to see—to show anyone who was watching how much they *meant* to each other...

He exhaled slowly, the last seconds of the breath turning into a shudder.

That was it. He might not have known for sure what he meant to Jared, but he knew what Jared meant to him. He wasn't just infatuated anymore; he was deeply and emotionally connected. And from this point, there was no turning back.

But there was no going forward, either.

Connor pulled a pillow up to his face and pressed it against his eyes, hoping the flimsy bit of bedding would be enough to hold back the tears.

CHAPTER FOURTEEN

"Again!" Vidar barked, his thick accent and the force of the shout making Connor wince. Again, all the first violins raised their instruments—some more wearily than others—and launched into the difficult run.

It seemed baroque music *was* Vidar's musical match, and Connor's body ached from the tense way he'd been holding himself as he attempted to comply with the man's every demand. Fighting the empty feeling in his chest, he tried to hit the notes perfectly, pull the bow precisely and control every sound that emerged from his instrument in a way he could never control his life.

Vidar silenced them again and directed his attention to a mousy brunette who still hadn't gotten the fingering right. The poor girl wilted under his wrath, and Connor took the opportunity to sneak a sidelong glance at Rebecca.

She rolled her eyes, her lips twitching in an empathetic grimace. "*Yikes*," she mouthed to him at Vidar's harsh: "No! You must do it again! Do you practice?" She knew better than to speak out loud, though.

After avoiding her for the past few days, it was a relief to see she was treating him like nothing had happened. But as thankful as he was for the apparent reprieve, Connor simply didn't have the drive to act the same.

When the hour ended, Rebecca turned to console the now teary-eyed brunette, and Connor snuck away. He rushed up the steps from the basement of Old Cabell Hall and burst out into the cold night air.

Congratulations, his sarcastic inner voice told him. *You got through another day of functioning normally.* Or at least, as normal as he got, under the circumstances.

A bleep on his cell phone informed him of a missed call, from Jared. His heart leapt and then sank—there was no message, and he had no idea what to say if he initiated the contact. He knew what he *should* say—that he was still upset, that they needed to talk about where things were going between them—but he'd never have the guts to be that straightforward. What he'd probably end up doing would be begging for Jared to come and hold him, to make all the hurt disappear with kisses, to let the problem be buried in a deep, dark hole where they'd never hear from it again.

"Connor," Rebecca huffed from behind him.

Startled, he shoved the phone into his pocket and took two more steps before he realized he couldn't just walk away from her. "Uh, yeah?"

"Hey, I've been meaning to talk to you. You've been busy at lunchtime these past few days?"

"Yeah." He gripped his violin tighter and began walking again. It wasn't as if Rebecca was going to have any trouble keeping up if she wanted to continue their conversation.

"Beth hasn't been eating there, either. It's really too far for her to come for lunch. Observatory's much closer to the science buildings where she has class afterwards."

"Oh." Was she trying to tell him the coast was clear?

"Yeah...so, you know, it's a pretty small crowd. Hope you have more time next week."

Connor slowed his pace. He *did* miss hearing friendly voices. The silence was so much lonelier now than it had been in the past, when he hadn't known anything different.

He gave her a weak smile. "Yeah. Me too."

"Cool." She let out a little burst of breath, like she'd been waiting to exhale. "And listen, I'm really sorry about pushing the whole Beth thing. I hope you don't think I'm a complete bitch for pestering you. Beth's been my friend since my first year, and I was just trying to lend a hand."

"It's fine." Rapid footsteps resumed now that the conversation was turning in a direction he wanted nothing to do with. "Hey, I gotta run."

"What? Now? I was hoping we could grab coffee or something. We should hang out for a little while, ya know?"

Not if the conversation has anything to do with Beth. "I really gotta run right now...but maybe this weekend."

"Well, I've got the dance on Saturday," Rebecca started, then trailed off. "But yeah, sure, we'll catch up later. Maybe tomorrow...oh, but you're still going to join the pit orchestra, right? Don't they start tomorrow?"

"Um, actually, I'm not sure I have time for it."

Rebecca took two swift steps to reach him and brought her hand down on his arm, pulling him to a stop. "Connor," she said sharply—gone was the friendly tone from just a second ago. "Look, you don't have to say anything, but just listen, okay? I know something's up. I can always tell with you because you're...you're like a turtle. When something's wrong you retract into this shell that you have, and you stop hanging out with us and stop talking to people...and it kind of worries me, okay? So you don't have to tell me what's wrong—I get that you don't want to talk about it. But just don't drop off the face of the earth. And if it was the thing with Beth, well, I can promise you that won't be an issue anymore."

Connor bit down on his tongue and used the pain to distract himself for a moment, but he couldn't escape Rebecca's worried eyes for long. "O-okay."

"So, are you going to join the pit orchestra?"

Her gaze bore into him, making her intention clear. *It's not a question.*

"Um…yes?"

"With more conviction, please."

"Fine. Yes."

"That's better." She released him, and normal easygoing Rebecca was back with her innocent smile. "See you at lunch tomorrow!"

***

One, two, three, go.

Connor gripped the metal door handle to the Student Activities Building and pulled. A wall of noise immediately struck him. Everywhere he looked there was movement and sound—people laughing, pointing, singing, dancing, shouting, dragging set pieces and lights and costumes. The musicians were just as rowdy as the cast and crew, erupting in random bits of melody and harmony as they showed off their chops.

The smiles were rampant, the atmosphere rife with the feel of instant-camaraderie—very different from the classical music world he was used to. He'd stick out like a sore thumb if he didn't act friendlier than he ever had in his entire life.

Clearly, this was a terrible mistake.

He shirked back against the door, battling his instincts.

Leave. Leave now.

No. You promised Rebecca.

Get the hell out before they see you.

But they need a violinist. You gave your word.

Well that was stupid, now wasn't it.

He closed his eyes and quieted the voices in his head, but he couldn't shut out all thought. This sort of thing was exactly why he needed Jared. If he could have spoken to Jared, he would have aired all his concerns about socializing with a group of complete strangers. And Jared would have comforted him, told him he should just be himself, told him he was smart and talented and funny and had nothing to fear.

But he didn't have Jared to bolster his self-esteem right now…and maybe, after his emotional outburst the other day, he would never have him again.

A ball of pain rose in his throat. He turned on his heels to march back to his dorm—responsibility be damned— but a smiling girl suddenly appeared in his path.

"I'm Amy, the pit conductor. I'm gonna go out on a limb and guess you're the violinist?"

He blinked once as she slid an arm around his shoulder and pulled him into her slightly-padded frame. "Here, I'll show you where to set up."

Why had he ever thought girls were easier to relate to? Now all they seemed to do was foul things up.

He remained mute as he unpacked his violin and set up his wreck of a stand beside the stage. There was no actual pit, so the musicians just bunched up alongside the raised black platform, trying to make themselves as inconspicuous as possible. At least that aspect of playing in a pit suited him well enough.

"Only one violinist? Damn, my dream come true," he heard from behind him. Turning reluctantly, he locked eyes with a short and wiry French horn player. "Just kidding, man. I'm Ray."

"Connor," Connor offered with a curt nod.

"Nice ta meet ya. You really the only one of your kind here?"

After a brief look around, Connor shrugged. "I guess so."

"Now, no offense, but you could see where that'd be exciting for those of us who are used to bowing down to the sheer power of your numbers in orchestra." Ray smirked and ran a hand through brown hair frosted with bright blond tips.

Connor mustered only the faint echo of a smile. Being comfortable with friendly banter was not in the cards today.

"All right, everyone!" Someone—probably the director—clapped his hands several times. "Snap twice if you can hear me."

The actors and musicians complied, and everyone settled into position. But unlike in orchestra, giddy smiles stayed firmly in place. Apparently, there was no need to be as serious when performing a musical comedy as there was when churning out baroque masterpieces.

The house lights went down and they worked through the overture first. As soon as Connor's fingers touched the strings, his dread eased, his body finding comfort in the familiar actions.

If baroque music had stifled him, then the melodious stylings of Cole Porter seemed to set him free. Here, as the only violinist, he was able to move his body with the rhythms, bow however he chose, smile, frown, and just *feel* every note without worrying about how it made him look different from those around him. He was *meant* to be different in this setting, as he was the only one with that part to play. And no one would be able to see him in the dark, anyway.

After rehearsing the first three numbers multiple times, the lights flickered on for a much-needed break. Connor slipped away from the crowd and out of the building, seeking the safest place to wait out the respite.

He sat crossed-legged on the ground and took out his phone. There were no more missed calls from Jared, but he tried not to think about what that could mean. Perhaps Jared was just busy. Maybe he was doing schoolwork, since he'd be losing a large chunk of Saturday to the dance. He'd probably go out to dinner with his friends first, before he and Veronica would make their entrance in the grand ballroom, hand in hand…

Connor grabbed the rough brick wall of the building's exterior to haul himself up, then rushed back into the din before his musings led him any further down that dark path. At least the anxiety he felt inside was something he was used to. This other feeling—bitter jealousy—was still foreign and completely terrifying.

"Hey, lone violinist, you're pretty good." Ray bumped him with his horn as he took his seat. "This a cold read, or have you seen the music before?"

"Um…" Connor stared at the exit door, but it was too late to retreat a second time. "I listened to the instrumental music last night. It's…pretty catchy."

"Guess you probably picked it up by ear—bet that's a lot easier to do when you always have the melody."

"Oh my God," the trumpet player next to him cut in. "Will you get over your violin envy already? If you wanted melody all the time, you shoulda chosen a different instrument."

Ray smiled cheerfully. "I was only teasing. Connor knows that, right?"

"Break's over!" the director called out, sending the room into a flurry of motion as actors rushed the stage. "Back to your places for *So in Love*!"

Relieved, Connor took up his instrument and scanned the music. The violin had a small solo in this one and he readied his fingers for it, glossing over the slanted squiggles of lyrics written beneath the staffs.

But they were much harder to ignore when heard out loud.

"Strange, dear, but true, dear,
When I'm close to you, dear,
The stars fill the sky,
So in love with you am I.

Even without you
My arms fold about you.
You know, darling why,
So in love with you am I.
In love with the night mysterious
The night when you first were there.
In love with my joy delirious
When I knew that you might care.
So taunt me and hurt me,
Deceive me, desert me,
I'm yours 'til I die,
So in love,
So in love,
So in love with you, my love, am I."

Strangled emotions nearly rushed out of him, but he used the strength his instrument granted him and diverted most of them into the music instead. Only a small amount made its way to his eyes, blurring his sight until he rapidly blinked the moisture away. He played on resolutely, his notes ringing out at least an octave above the other instruments and sweetly filling the air.

When the number ended he swiped an arm across his face, grateful yet again for the dimmed lights. To his surprise, the actress on stage broke character for a millisecond and gave him a wink, while Amy the pit conductor placed a hand on her ample chest and mouthed, "*Perfect.*"

He rested his violin and sat still, torn between the depressing thoughts the song had conjured and an unusually strong sense of pleasure at a job well done. It wasn't clear which emotion would wind up in control.

"Hey." A finger jabbed into his side. "About before, I really was joking. You are *so* good. The pit's lucky to have you," Ray whispered.

A tiny smile of pride found its way to Connor's lips and stayed for about thirty seconds, before thoughts of

Veronica draped over Jared as they danced to some overdone love song washed it away.

***

By Saturday afternoon, he'd chewed a spot raw on the inside of his cheek. Unable to concentrate on a single thing other than what Jared—*his* Jared—was out there doing with just-a-friend Veronica, he remained in his room all day, consuming a box of Pop-Tarts for sustenance. At around eight o'clock he turned out the lights and stared at videos on his computer screen until his eyes hurt.

When sleep finally came, it was mercifully deep—the kind where his body pulled him down into slumber like a dead weight. Several hours later, the gentle knocks at his door blended into his dreams, adding a tap-tap-tap rhythm to the music playing through his mind.

Tap-tap-tap became *rap-rap-rap*, louder and faster. The music crescendoed into a fury of colors and noise, ending in an explosion that finally jarred him from REM.

Rap-rap-rap.

He bolted upright, adrenaline coursing through his body.

"Connor, open the door!"

The green glow of his clock read two-thirteen—hardly the normal time to expect a visit from Jared.

"What?" Connor mumbled, using his arm to shield his sensitive eyes from the hallway light.

"Can I come in?"

Without a word, Connor stepped back, and Jared entered, flicking on the lights behind him. Connor recoiled deeper into his arm and let out a groan.

"Sorry. Were you asleep?"

"I tend to do that at night."

Jared grinned. "I like it when you're sarcastic. It's such a rare treat."

Still caught in the fog of sleep, Connor struggled to focus on the significance of Jared's presence. "Jared...it's two a.m. What...what are you doing here?"

Jared fidgeted with something in his hands. "I got you something."

"You what?" Connor yawned.

"Here." Jared thrust a white plastic bag at him, and Connor peeked inside to find a matte-black collapsible music stand. "That one you have is like the Leaning Tower of Pisa, so I thought I'd get you a new one. This one looked more sturdy."

"Oh." Connor nodded, waking faculties slowly returning. "Um, thanks."

"I actually ordered it a little while ago. I was gonna save it for your birthday or something, but I just felt like giving it to you now."

Connor turned the stand over in his hands. Maybe he was still dreaming...but if he was, he hoped he wouldn't wake up. "Uh, I didn't know we were celebrating two o'clock in the morning, or I'd have gotten you something, too."

Jared shook his head and took a step forward. "I just don't want you to be mad at me anymore. If it makes you feel any better, I was miserable the whole time. All I could think of was you."

"Um...yeah, I guess that makes me feel a little better." Connor set the stand down and scratched at the corner of his mouth, wiping away some dried saliva.

"C'mere, baby," Jared said, and pulled Connor close.

Baby. Connor trembled against Jared's body, his heart melting while other parts of him became decidedly less soft. He only reached Jared's chest when he wasn't on tiptoes, and he rested his head there, closing his eyes and finding the rhythm of Jared's heartbeat. Jared stroked his back and they swayed together in perfect timing with the music in his head, driven by the percussion of both their hearts.

"Okay, I'm not mad anymore." Connor's lips pressed into the fabric of Jared's shirt.

Jared broke away and began toeing off his shoes.

"What are you doing?"

"Spending the night...if that's okay."

"The night? The whole night? Won't Ben wonder where you are?"

Jared paused. A flash of apprehension ran across his face, but he shrugged it off as he climbed into bed. "I'll...I'll just make something up. Don't worry about it, just get over here."

Connor relented, wrapping himself securely in Jared's arms, in that place where he just *fit*. For all that he pretended to be annoyed when Jared teased him about his size, there really was no better feeling than being wholly encompassed in Jared's embrace.

Sleep took hold of him despite his arousal, and he'd almost nodded off again when he heard Jared draw in a sharp breath that got trapped somewhere in his throat.

He sought Jared's eyes and found the pools of deep brown studying him. And there was a look in that gaze, one he couldn't remember seeing before, or at least not with such intensity. They shone with something dark, and definitely not happy. Confusion? Worry?

Jared threaded a hand into Connor's hair and stroked his temple. "I...I want to spend more time with you, Connor...do more things with you," he whispered, his voice hoarse. "I just don't know. I don't know if...I mean, I'm not sure if I could...if I could ever..."

Possessed by a need to erase the strange look from Jared's beautiful eyes, Connor stretched up and kissed him. A smile emerged as he drew away. He was far too tired to analyze what Jared was saying—or trying to say—and the only thing that mattered right then was that Jared was holding him. That *had* to mean everything was going to be okay.

"I have a concert coming up right before spring break. Maybe you could come to that." He snuggled back into Jared's body.

"Yeah, maybe," Jared murmured, mouth brushing against Connor's ear. "I love hearing you play."

Connor closed his eyes to drift off fitfully.

When he awoke, he found Jared kneeling by the side of the bed, the golden-yellow light of the dawn he so rarely saw casting a glow about the room.

He smiled drowsily. Jared really had stayed the entire night.

"What are you doing?"

Jared looked over with a sheepish grin. "My shoe went under the bed." He lifted the wayward sneaker to display it, then sat on the edge of the mattress. "Sorry, didn't mean to wake you."

"It's okay. I'm glad you did."

"Yeah." Jared leaned over and ran a finger along Connor's cheek. "I mean, I was going to say goodbye." He moved in for a kiss.

"Don't, I'll have morning breath!" Connor tried to squirm away.

But Jared nailed him squarely on the lips anyhow, his normal cocky smirk back in its rightful place. "Bye, baby. I'll see you later."

Connor fell asleep again with a smile, dreaming of a morning when they could wake up in slow luxury, still tangled in each other's arms.

CHAPTER FIFTEEN

"All right, let's get this show on the road!"

"I don't have to be there until five." Connor stepped back from the doorway to let Jared in. "You're like an hour early."

"So sue me. Maybe I wanted to catch you in your boxers." Jared dropped his backpack and reached out to snap the band of Connor's underwear.

Connor playfully slapped him away. "But I have to practice still. I always do a quick run-through to make sure I'm ready."

"As if you weren't," Jared scoffed. "I bet you could play that stuff in your sleep."

"Maybe, but I still like to have it under my fingers once before we go on. It's tradition."

Jared's hands came down on his shoulders, his strong fingers kneading deep into the muscle. "Don't you think we could postpone tradition? Just for a few minutes?"

"Jared…"

"What? You can't just stand there half-naked and not expect a response. I'm only human. C'mon, let's start a new tradition."

Without waiting for an answer, Jared plucked him off the ground and carried him to the bed.

"But…" Connor found himself flat on his back with Jared gloating above him. "But I should…I should really…" The protests were meek, even by his standards. Any real objection died the moment Jared's lips pressed into his chest.

"I sh-should…"

"Quiet," Jared commanded. He pulled down Connor's boxers and teased him with a couple gentle strokes until the only thing Connor could mumble were partially stifled pleas for more.

With one eyebrow raised smugly, Jared brought his lips to Connor's dick. "Don't tell me this isn't better than practicing," he whispered before slipping him into his mouth.

Left with only half an hour after their romp, Connor scrambled to shower and dress, opting to forgo the last-minute practice session. Jared was right; he didn't really need to rehearse anymore. The music had been burned into his head and his fingers for months now, and the truth was he couldn't wait to get it out and make room for newer, more exciting material.

Jared stared at him unabashedly as he fixed his cummerbund and bowtie, making him squirm.

"Shit," Jared said. "If I'd known how hot you were gonna look all dressed up, I'd have come even earlier."

Cheeks blooming red, Connor tried to turn away, but Jared caught him with a finger under his chin.

"Guess I'll just have to wait 'til afterwards," Jared murmured, his skin still flush with a post-orgasm glow. He tilted Connor's face up so he could press their lips together, and the gentle peck soon deepened into a full-blown, open-mouthed kiss.

A stirring in Connor's pants confirmed what he had realized for some time—it simply wasn't fair they so rarely had time for seconds. He pulled back reluctantly and smoothed out his clothes. "Yeah, afterwards."

Jared noted his erection with a sly smile, but let Connor finish getting ready in peace. Then he grabbed his backpack and Connor's violin, slinging them both over his shoulder before Connor could protest. "All right, *now* let's get this show on the road."

***

Connor took a program on his way into the hall—his mother liked to collect them—and frowned once again at the concert's offerings. Baroque music would probably end up putting Jared to sleep. He just hoped it wouldn't turn him off from orchestra concerts altogether.

"Hey." Rebecca greeted him as he reached the backstage practice room. "You're five minutes late. I was about to send out a search party."

He rolled his eyes and bit his lip to stop the smile. "I was practicing."

"Sure you were." She braced her violin against her thigh, and her D string warbled around until she brought it to the right pitch. "Aren't you going to warm up?"

"Yeah, yeah." Connor snapped into action, a smile spreading despite his best efforts. He planted himself on the ground with his case, but before he could open it, an unfamiliar bulge in the outside music pocket caught his eye.

He unzipped it quickly and drew in a sharp, startled breath.

A single red rose lay inside, slightly crushed, but still beautiful. Attached to it was a small note card, and across that was Jared's unruly handwriting, springing about the paper like his dark curls tumbled from his head.

Just wanted to wish you luck, even though I know you don't need it. Break a leg, and all that good stuff.

There was no signature, but that didn't really matter. It was more than enough, just as it was. Connor held the notecard to his lips, closing his eyes and filing the moment of happiness in the stores of his mind to be relived over and over again.

"You have a secret admirer!" Rebecca's voice exploded near his ear.

His hand clenched around the note, crushing it, and he frantically shoved the rose back inside his case.

"Or do you know who it is?" she pressed.

"What? N-no...no...I..."

His face burned, his tongue became clumsy and heavy in his mouth, and his brain sputtered to a complete stop, offering nothing of intelligence for him to say.

"Connor," Rebecca said, giving his shoulder a light shake. "Connor."

If only he *had* been born with a shell to hide in whenever life became too uncomfortable to bear.

"Connor." With a flash of dirty-blond hair, Rebecca whirled him around. He stumbled to his feet as he was dragged out of the room.

She pulled him into a tiny practice module and shut the door behind them. "Connor, listen, I know it's none of my business, but I'm gonna say it anyway. It's okay."

"What?" He shook his head.

"I mean, it's okay if you're gay."

It's okay if you're gay. That rhymed. That rhymed and Rebecca had just said it. Out loud. To him.

Dizziness consumed him and he collapsed into a chair.

"I just wanted you to know that. It's okay by me. It'd be okay by all my friends, too. Even Beth. I promise you."

"Wh—" He wheezed, swallowed, and tried again. "Why...how...how'd you..."

"How'd I know? Well, honestly I've been suspecting ever since the thing with Beth...but really that note sealed the deal. I have lousy handwriting for a girl, but that was guy handwriting if I ever saw it."

"Oh...r-right."

"And I'm totally not trying to pressure you or anything, but just so you know, if you ever wanted to get involved with gay life on campus, a friend of mine is the president of the Queer Student Union."

If he wanted to get involved? She must've taken leave of her senses—just as he had.

"Um...I...I d-don't think..."

"Don't worry, I won't say anything to anyone. I just wanted you to know the option was out there. I promise, I'll butt out. Like I said, I know it's none of my business."

Connor put his head between his knees, concentrating on his breathing. He didn't have his inhaler with him, and the last thing he wanted to add to this calamity was a panic-induced asthma attack.

"I'm gonna go get warmed up," Rebecca said quietly. "And Connor? I'm glad you have someone."

"Yeah," he mumbled into his lap. "I'll...I'll be right there."

He spent five more minutes sitting in the dark before fear of being late pushed him out. Rebecca smiled at him but kept her distance, granting him the much-needed time to process things on his own.

Making sure no one was near, he straightened out the crumpled note and folded it neatly, then tucked the white square into his pocket.

Rebecca knows, his mind whispered. *Rebecca knows and it's okay.* He wanted to smile, to feel relief, but he couldn't just yet. She may have made it clear it wasn't going to change their friendship, but she also knew he *had someone*—a someone who didn't want to be found out.

They filed onto the stage with all the other musicians and took their seats as the concert began. After a quick scan of the audience, Connor spotted Jared sitting only a few rows out from the front.

Jared gave him a goofy little wave, and despite his unease, Connor smiled back.

"Oh my God," Rebecca interrupted the moment of relief. "*Him?*"

"Rebecca...n-no..." he stuttered, but he could see by her face she already knew. *If there were ever a moment for a shell...*

She opened her mouth to say more, but was cut off by the applause as the conductor took the stage.

For once, Connor was grateful for the technical demands of Baroque music. If they'd been playing something that required less precision, he might not have been able to stay focused on the performance. But the little sixteenth notes that marched across the page kept his mind occupied and off the small disaster that had just unfolded. And as long as he didn't think about it, there was a chance he could go on pretending like it had never happened. Maybe Rebecca would even go along with that, too.

He kept himself on track all the way until the middle of Sammartini's Symphony in C Major, when his eyes drifted from the page at a part he knew from memory. They were immediately drawn to Jared—for comfort, maybe, or for one more reassuring smile.

But the sight that greeted him made his fingers slip, and it took several seconds before he was able to locate his place in the music again.

Rebecca shot him a startled look; she'd never heard him mess up in a performance before. As soon as they had a measure of rest she whispered, "Don't worry, no one heard it."

He ignored her. He didn't care if anyone had heard his mistake or not. His gaze was stuck on Jared, and on the figure by his side—dark-haired, delicately-featured Veronica.

Her thin arm stuck out from an oversized t-shirt and wound around Jared's. In a few seconds, she'd probably be holding his hand.

Connor turned back to the black notes on the white sheet music in front of him. They were neat and orderly, clear and easy to follow. They made sense to him. They had one meaning each, and if he followed all the rules, he was rewarded by the correct sound emerging from his instrument.

Life was nowhere near as clear…but then again, maybe that was because he'd gone and broken the rules.

***

He threw his violin in its case with as little care as he ever had and ducked out the back entrance before Rebecca could find him at the close of the concert. Even then he didn't feel safe, and he raced across the parking lot toward Jared's car, half-expecting to see Jared and Veronica seated in it, driving away. No one was there when he arrived, though, so he leaned against the brown monstrosity and let his lids fall closed.

"Hey, there you are. I was looking everywhere for you."

He opened his eyes again to see Jared standing in front of him, alone. Some time must have passed, because the parking lot was filling with the well-dressed patrons.

Jared hadn't dressed any differently than normal, but the expression he wore was an aggravated one. "I thought we said we'd meet by the stairs."

Clinging to the echoes of sixteenth notes to remain calm, Connor shook his head. "Had to get out of there."

"Uh, okay." Jared scratched his temple. "Well, let's go then."

He unlocked his door and stretched across to open Connor's, which still refused to budge from the outside. Connor tossed his violin into the backseat and sat with his body pivoted away. They made the drive in silence, but once they'd reached his dorm, Jared parked in a shadowy alcove and leaned over to get his attention.

"Hey," he said softly, moving in for a kiss. "What's the matter?"

"Nothing," Connor muttered. Better to keep his useless anger bottled up than to let it out, where it might cause...

"Huh." Jared backed off and crossed his arms. "Right. Well, your lips are usually a lot more malleable when I do that. And you've been in a pissy mood since the concert let out. What, you messed up or something?"

The cork popped. "What was *she* doing there?"

Jared rolled his eyes. "Uh, it was open to the public, wasn't it? She asked me what I was doing tonight, I said I was going to the orchestra concert for a class assignment...and she just showed up. It's not like I invited her."

"But...she...she was touching you!" The words grew louder by the syllable. "She was trying to hold your hand!"

"Well, I didn't let her!" Jared retorted, voice rising in volume to match. "She's just really needy right now. She's having some sort of fight with her suitemates...she thinks they're all out to get her...Hell, I don't know. I don't want to tell her to piss off, but I swear to God I'm not sleeping with her. That's what you're really afraid of, isn't it?"

Was it? Connor didn't know. He didn't even know if he *was* afraid...or just fed up. "You're not even dating her, and she still gets to be such a big part of your life."

"I spend time with you, too. I just have to keep things balanced."

"Yeah, so no one finds out."

Jared fell silent, a frown cutting through his handsome features. Then he shrugged. "Yeah. But like I said, I'm still gonna hang out with you."

"And you don't think that will tip them off?"

Jared barked an angry laugh. "This isn't high school, Connor. I can be friends with whoever I want."

"Are you telling me your friends don't think it's weird you spend time with me as it is?"

No answer this time.

"Oh, that's right," Connor continued for him. "They don't even know, do they? You make things up to keep your dirty little secret hidden."

Jared gritted his teeth. "Are you about to give me some sort of ultimatum? Because let me tell you, I'm not into being bossed around."

Connor opened his mouth to fire back, but his retort died as the thin veneer of Jared's anger evaporated into a much more pitiable—and familiar—emotion: fear.

"No." The fury slipped away. "Of course not. I would never force you into anything. But what happens if people do find out?"

"They won't."

"They might, Jared. And sometimes…it worries me. I don't know that anyone would care if I'm gay, but your life is…different. You're a football player…you're popular…and I don't want to be responsible for ruining all that for you, but what if—"

"Quit being so melodramatic," Jared huffed. "I have things under control. No one is going to find out."

Connor closed his eyes. "Someone already has."

"What?"

"I said someone already has. Rebecca."

A frantic gasp sent Connor's eyes shooting open again.

"*What?* You told her?"

"Did I say I told her?" Connor snapped. "I said she *found out.* You have boy handwriting, apparently, and she caught me watching you. For like the tenth time. She's not stupid, you know."

"You could have told her nothing was going on." Jared stuck both hands into his hair and pulled. "What the fuck, Connor."

"So, what, you want me to lie to her? I mean, more than I already am?"

"Yes!" Jared flopped back, banging into the seat. "No...shit, I dunno." He folded over and rested his head against the steering wheel. "Shit, Connor. I don't know."

The lump in Connor's throat promised tears, and he struggled to keep it down. "Yeah. I know."

They sat in silence for several minutes as Jared ran his fingers over his face, smashing his features into parodies of themselves. "Look, I think I'm gonna get going," he finally said.

There was something off in Jared's voice—something distant and strained—something very different from his usual warm tone.

Connor's pulse jumped.

"But...I thought...I thought you didn't have anywhere to be right now."

Jared shook his head. "Not tonight. Just go on up. I'll talk to you later."

"Um...yeah...okay."

Connor pulled his case off the backseat and stumbled from the car.

Once in his room, he set himself on autopilot. His violin went against the wall beside the bed. Wallet and keys went on top of his nightstand. The tux came off—first bowtie and cummerbund, then pants and ugly pleated shirt. He hung them all the way in the back of his closet, but putting them out of sight didn't help him forget the rejection.

He sank into his desk chair, clutching his stomach. It threatened to upheave its limited contents, and the feverish chills racking his body made the churning even worse. Things were all wrong—more wrong than they'd ever been before. Jared wasn't supposed to push him away like that. Jared wasn't supposed to look at him with fear in his eyes, wasn't supposed to speak to him with that cold, unfamiliar voice. Jared was the one who had an upbeat solution for every problem, the one who made every obstacle seem surmountable. He was supposed to tell Connor everything was going to be okay.

So how could Connor think or do anything else right now without hearing those words?

An hour of staring and dozing with his head on his desk produced no answers—because only Jared had those. He gathered himself up and dialed Jared's phone. It rang several times, but eventually went to voice mail. He tried it again, and again got no response.

All the sixteenth notes in the world couldn't keep back his panic. The music in his head was a cacophony, violins shrieking up the E string and piercing his stupor.

Only Jared could stop it. Only Jared could fix him.

He threw on jeans and a t-shirt and took off into the darkness.

***

By the time he reached Jared's suite, he was trembling. Just raising his arm to knock left him weakened.

A redheaded boy with freckles opened the door and peered at him. "Who do you want?"

"I…um…is J-jared here?"

The guy shrugged and let him pass, then took off down the hallway.

Connor made his way to Jared's room—a room he'd only been in once before. The door was halfway open and the faint click of keyboard keys came from inside.

As before, half the room was in disarray while the other half was relatively pristine. Jared's roommate sat hunched over at his desk with the tiny white buds of earphones firmly rooted in his ears, bopping his head to the music and tapping his foot against the floor to an uneven beat. Jared was nowhere in sight.

Connor backed up, but it was too late. Ben turned at the movement, his face first registering confusion and then recognition.

"Hey," he said, his voice louder than necessary. He removed the earphones and continued at a normal volume. "You were Jared's tutor, right?"

"Y-yeah."

"I thought Jared quit going to tutoring." Ben cocked his head. "After last semester."

Connor swallowed, but there wasn't enough saliva to moisten his dry throat. "H-he did. I...um...I just look over his papers sometimes."

"*Ohh.*" Ben nodded slowly, eyes widening as if he had received a sudden burst of clarification. "I get it. Well, he's not here right now. Some of his teammates came and snagged him...think they went out to CiCi's Pizza for dinner."

Bitter disappointment sapped Connor's last powers of discourse. He stared blankly into space.

"So, do you want me to give him a message? Or like, do you have his paper to drop off?"

Connor glanced down at his empty hands, then back up at Ben, who had an eyebrow raised and was beginning to give him a look he was very familiar with. A *hello? Are you retarded or something?* look.

Noise erupted in the suite as a good six pair of footsteps trailed in, coupled with booming masculine voices.

"You sure you won't come with us, Jared?" one voice said. "Last hurrah before spring break, man. After that your first year is almost over, and I really don't think you've been drunk *nearly* enough."

"Nah, man, some other time," Jared responded with a light-hearted chuckle.

Connor shirked back against the doorframe. How could Jared sound so carefree? What had happened to the heavy, sad tone he'd had earlier?

But once Jared caught sight of him, his brow furrowed—in concern, or maybe even in anger.

"Hey, the little anthro tutor," Michael announced from behind him, and suddenly Connor found himself the focus of five football players, Jared, and Ben, who popped out from the room to stand beside him. "You still getting tutoring, Jared? Man, you must be dumber than I thought."

Jared's laugh was strained. "Whatcha doin' here, Connor? Need something?"

"Right." Ben snickered. "Like he doesn't *help* you with your papers."

"Nice." Michael guffawed, slapping Jared on his back.

Connor stood frozen, like a *fermata* had descended upon him, drawing out the agonizing moment. What could he do to steer things in the right direction? Toward him and Jared alone, preferably in each other's arms? He stared at Jared, silently pleading for him to do the work. If Jared would just look at him with a smile, or move a little closer, his paralysis could be cured, and he'd at least be able to say *something*.

But Jared was barely making eye contact, and when he did, it definitely wasn't with a smile. "You're finished looking over that history paper for me?" he eventually prompted.

"Uh, y-yeah," Connor rasped.

Michael turned with the rest of Jared's teammates and began to walk away. "As thrilling as this sounds, we're gonna head out. See ya, man."

That left Connor alone with Jared and, unfortunately, Ben, who didn't seem to be going anywhere.

Jared sighed. "You need a ride home or something? We were using my car, so I left it at that little lot down the block."

Connor nodded, skin hot but insides shuddering with cold.

Jared moved abruptly. "Let's get going then."

Silence reigned for the first minute of the walk. When less people were passing by, Jared finally turned to him. "What were you thinking, coming here like that?" He tugged at his curls. "I mean, that was just...really not cool on your part."

They reached the car, and Jared got the door for him as usual, but nothing else felt as it usually did.

It was wrong. All wrong.

"I'm sorry. I just wanted to talk to you."

"Then you should have called."

"I did. You didn't answer."

"Because I was *busy*, Connor. You're smart. You could have figured that out before you came over to my dorm and started talking to my roommate. And what exactly did you tell him, anyway? That I buy papers off you?"

"I didn't tell him anything, I swear. I didn't say anything at all! He jumped to that conclusion on his own!"

"Yeah, okay. Sure. Now what do you want?" Jared pulled into the lot nearest Connor's dorm. He left the engine running and kept both hands on the steering wheel.

"I just...today...you were upset...and I ..."

Jared shook his head. "Can we talk about this some other time?"

No. No, they couldn't. Not if it meant another minute with this weight in the pit of Connor's stomach—the terrible fear that he was *losing* Jared...and probably himself in the process. "C-can't you come up? Can't we talk tonight?"

"I don't really feel like it."

"Please, Jared—"

But Jared wasn't listening, and his next words had that sick feeling crawling up from Connor's stomach and into his chest. "Connor...maybe we should cool it."

"W-what?"

"I think...I think we need to take a break. Maybe I didn't think this all through. I just got so caught up in...I dunno. I just got caught up. I don't think I'm handling things the right way anymore."

An intake of breath turned into a hiccup as tears filled Connor's eyes. "J-jared...no...I...I won't let anyone else find out, I promise."

Jared blinked, staring straight out his windshield and into the darkness. "You were right before. My life *is* different from yours. And I'm just...I'm not ready for it to change."

"Jared, please. I don't want...I don't want to take a—"

"What do you want, then? Because the truth is, I don't really know if this *should* be what you want...and I don't have much else to offer. Look, I like you. I like having fun with you...but...that's all. I think maybe this whole time I've only been thinking about what *I* want...not what's best for you."

"N-no, I want this, too! Please, I n-need—"

"I'm sorry, Connor. I've been trying to figure this out for a while now, but it's just not going to work." Jared turned to face the window, his knuckles white as they grasped the steering wheel. "I'm so sorry. I...I never meant to hurt you."

An instinct of self-preservation guided Connor to dash from the car before the tears could overtake him. They sprang freely as he ran off toward his building, though, blurring his vision and smearing the world into an impressionist painting.

He reached the safety of his room and slammed the door behind him. With his eyes closed, he was able to still his breathing and stop the crying, but he knew it was only the calm before the storm.

The moment his lids fluttered open, the repose crumbled away. Ninety percent of his relationship with Jared had taken place within the four walls of his room, and every piece of them now echoed with memories that mocked him for his foolishness. He'd gone and fallen for someone so unattainable, so unavailable—he should have expected an end such as this.

Because everyone knew taking a break was just a way to save face when breaking up.

His tears pulsed back to life. As if subconsciously seeking more pain, he unzipped his case to retrieve the rose. The red petals were just beginning to darken with the first signs of death, and he held the flower tightly in his hand, willing it to last just a little bit longer.

A thorn that had escaped the removal process pricked his palm, and the sharp physical pain brought his tears to a standstill. He uncurled his fingers to look at the tiny circular pool of blood that formed. After a moment, he pressed it into the sheet and let the blood seep into the fabric.

He stared at the spot of red on white until sleep came.

CHAPTER SIXTEEN

Even when his mother was whispering, her voice still carried. The hushed murmurs were spiked with just enough attitude to make it clear she was complaining, and most likely about him.

But it barely registered. Connor retrieved the pitcher of water to set at the dinner table, ignoring how the room grew silent again as he took his seat. Even Melissa kept her mouth shut for a change.

"Richard." His mother broke the quiet. She shot his father a prodding look over the plates of brisket and potatoes.

He coughed, then addressed Connor directly for the first time that day. "How are your classes going this semester?"

"Fine." Connor shredded a piece of meat with his fork, but didn't bring any part of it to his mouth. He'd had no desire to eat, lately.

"We really need to start trying to find you a summer job. Something that will help in getting into law school."

"Fine."

"And maybe we could even start looking at specific programs, so you can begin tailoring your applications."

"Fine."

"Look at your father when he is speaking to you," his mother snapped.

Connor managed to bring his eyes up for a second, but his father did not meet them. "May I be excused?" he mumbled in his mother's direction.

"No you may not!" She brought her palm down on the table, making the silverware clatter. "We eat together as a family. You may be able to do whatever you like at college, but don't forget your father and I are the ones paying for that experience."

Connor said nothing. He turned his attention back to his meal and took a slow bite, just so it was clear to everyone that his mouth was occupied with food.

His mother placed her hand against her temple. "I just don't know what I did wrong."

Again, he ignored her. He couldn't be bothered with her right now. Not when simple acts, like waking up each day, were so much harder. Not when his body ached, his skin so sensitive even the shirt on his back felt painful. Not when every forced social interaction reminded him of how alone he truly was.

"I'd like a summer job," Melissa threw in.

His mother's glare seemed as though it would bore into him for ages, but after a few seconds she turned away. "You're too young, Melissa. You can volunteer at the library, with me."

"Oh." Melissa blinked once before continuing. "Sure, Mom. That sounds like fun. But I'd also like to learn some more difficult pieces for next year's piano competition, and summer's the best time for that...so I might not be able to help a whole bunch."

"Of course not, dear. Maybe just a couple of hours a week, if you're not busy."

"Sounds great." Melissa beamed.

Connor redoubled his efforts to keep his eyes on the brown and beige of his meal. Melissa's smiles were like one stabbing insult after another. He couldn't even remember the last time he'd seen her frown.

Thankfully, she filled the void for the rest of the meal—at least she was good for that—by chatting on about how ready she was for ninth grade and was far too mature to have to spend another day within the confines of middle school.

Connor rose when everyone else did and made his way into the kitchen to complete his chores. He was lucky it had been a brisket night, even if he didn't care for the food. It meant there was no pile of pans to be scrubbed, and hopefully, within a few minutes, he could be safely ensconced in his room once again.

He cleaned the inside of the crockpot, running the water hot enough to make his skin splotch red. He studied the marks that formed—strange blobs of color against too-white skin. Skin that stayed indoors. Skin that *should* stay indoors, away from the normal, happy people who found life something worth living.

Before he could finish clearing away the juices from the meat, a hand reached over to shut off the faucet. Connor stared down at it, his eyes skirting along the blue veins, thin fingers, and protruding knuckles.

His mother let out a sigh, and though he tried not to look, he didn't miss the grim expression on her thin-lipped face.

"I gave birth to you, you know," she said, pressing her palm to her heart. Connor had to bite back an acrid smile—his mother had always had a flair for the dramatic. "And now you can't even be bothered to carry on a conversation? You've barely said a word to us since coming back for break."

This time, he couldn't control his reaction, and his eyes rolled of their own accord. His mother's pupils flashed in outrage and her arm flew up, as if preparing for a strike.

He shrank back. It wouldn't have been the first time her temper had gotten the better of her.

A moment later, she dropped her hand and pulled it tightly against her side. "Connor, you will show respect so long as you are in this house." She shook her head, muttering as she walked away.

Connor stood still as the shock from the confrontation slowly abated. As soon as it had, though, he wanted it back—she'd robbed him of some of the numbness he'd acquired that day.

Why wouldn't she just give up already? He'd never be the son she wanted. He didn't even have the energy to pretend anymore.

He finished the dishes and retreated to his room, firmly closing the door behind him. He would have locked it, but on the off chance his mother returned to pick up where she'd left off, he'd never hear the end of it. He was not meant to lock doors that didn't belong to him.

It would be hours before he'd be able to fall asleep, so he debated his options: random Internet surfing, reading, or staring at the ceiling. Whichever he chose, he promised himself he wouldn't cry anymore. It made his eyes look terrible—all dark and puffy in a gaunt, ashen face.

Not that he had anyone to impress.

He took a book off his shelf—making sure it contained no romantic storylines—and lay on his bed with it. But the written words weren't enough to drag him out of his life, and he hadn't even made it through a single page when his door creaked open a few minutes later.

"Can I come in?" Melissa asked. Without waiting for an invitation, she planted herself at his desk.

He didn't greet her, praying that would be enough to get her to go away.

It wasn't.

"So," she began, running her palms along her pink bunny pajama pants. "What happened to the guy?"

Connor turned away from her and back to the book in his hands. He couldn't remember a single word he'd just read. "What are you talking about?"

"Oh please. I know you were dating that hot guy who was over for breakfast."

Abandoning the book, he began idly pressing his fingernails into his palm and staring at the crescent moon shapes they left behind. "Get out."

Melissa crossed her arms and set her jaw in defiance. She looked a little like his mother when she did that. "Jeez, Connor. You don't always have to be such a jerk to me. I didn't tell anyone anything, you know."

"There's nothing to tell."

"Nothing to tell, huh? So you're switching back to girls, then?"

Connor squeezed his nails in even deeper. How hard would he have to press to draw blood?

"Really, I don't know what the big deal is," Melissa went on. "I said I wouldn't tell Mom. Why don't you want to talk about the guy? I mean, he's hot. Way hotter than I thought you'd ever get. If I were you I'd be bragging all over the place."

He focused on the pain in his hand. Hot tears prickled at his eyes, but he managed to keep them at bay. There was no way he was going to cry in front of his sister.

"What, he dumped you?"

His silence wasn't going to sway her, it seemed, but it was all he had to offer.

"He did, huh," she surmised. "So that's why you're acting all crappy again."

A tiny flame of anger ignited within him, and he actually welcomed it. Anything was better than complete desolation. "Melissa, get out."

"Yup, back to your usual stupid self." Melissa made no move to depart. She stretched out against his desk, arching her back like she was trying to enhance the appearance of her barely-there breasts. "So, what are your plans now?

Hide in your room and piss off Mom until you die of old age?"

"I said, get out."

"You know, I'm not surprised things didn't work out with that guy. You have to actually carry on conversations with people if you want to keep their interest. Why don't you ever talk like a normal person?"

A normal person. He released his clenched fist and something broke free inside him, turning the flame into a full-blown fire. Thank God Melissa was the only one there.

"Jesus Christ, Melissa! You're a fucking *moron.* Didn't it ever occur to you that I don't *want* to be like this? That it's fucking *hard* for me to talk to people and say the right things? That I berate myself far more than any of you ever could?"

She blinked at him a few times, then broke into a grin. "Do you suffer from depression?" she quipped, mimicking the voice of a commercial spokesperson. "Maybe you should try the pills that make that bouncing blue ball happy."

He drew in a deep breath, but not to calm down. *"Get the fuck out of my room!"*

Melissa curled in on herself, wincing. "Whoa. You're serious, huh? I always thought you acted all strange and unfriendly to piss off Mom."

Drained, he sagged against the bed. The rage was gone, but the embers were still smoldering. "Why the hell would I *want* to piss off Mom?"

Melissa snorted. "I can think of more than a few reasons."

"What?" He looked up sharply. "What are you talking about? You're like her best friend."

"Please." Melissa puffed out a breath that sent her bangs flipping off her forehead. "I know Mom's crazy. She wants to control everything we do, 'cause she thinks if we're great, it'll make her look great, too. I just know how to handle her, is all. The trick is to do what she wants while she's watching, so she'll leave you alone more, and you can do what you want when she's not."

Connor gaped at her. So her perfect fit in their family was just an act? Maybe there was more kinship there than he'd thought.

Her sudden candor had him opening his mouth again when all common sense told him to keep it shut. "I...I guess I don't know how to do what she wants. But I don't do it to piss her off. I don't do it to piss anyone off. I just...I'm not good at...dealing with people. And just when my life was actually starting to get better—"

He stopped short. What was he thinking? He couldn't say it out loud—*he* didn't even want to hear it, let alone have it revealed to his little sister.

Melissa furrowed her brows, the levity gone from her expression. "I'm sorry about the guy, Connor. But you know, you'll have other...*boy*friends." She giggled, then straightened her lips out with some effort. "I mean, I'm only thirteen and I've already had two."

Connor resumed making little moons, now along his forearm.

"You wanna know what I think?" Melissa twirled around in his desk chair.

"Of course not," he muttered.

She rolled her eyes and continued anyway. "How'd you get good at violin? How'd you learn all the pieces you know?"

"What?"

"How'd you learn the difficult parts?"

He lay back in his bed, staring up at the ceiling. It hadn't been his first choice for how to spend the evening, but it looked like the direction he was headed now.

"Practice, right?" Melissa answered for him.

"Sure. Practice."

"Practice," she repeated, nodding her head like a bobble-head doll. "You have to practice to get better. 'Cause sometimes, you kinda suck when you first try, and when you hit those high-pitched notes slightly off it makes me feel like someone is scratching fingernails against my brain."

Had he any venom left, he might have brought up how she pounded at the piano keys in frustration when she messed up a run. But he didn't, and she was prattling on again within a couple of seconds anyhow.

"So to get better at something, you have to practice. At first it's hard, and you kinda suck, but eventually, you make progress. That's what you should do with people. Just practice being normal until it starts to sink in. You won't get any better if you keep hiding from them." She smiled proudly as though waiting to be praised for her conclusion.

Connor closed his eyes and counted to ten. "Melissa, please get out of my room."

"See, that was better already! Much more polite than 'get the fuck out'." She spun around in the chair once more. "Keep it up, though, you've got a ways to go."

"*Connor!*" His mother's shout carried down the long hallway that led to the master bedroom. "Come here, I need to speak to you."

Melissa met his weary gaze for a moment before he rolled to face the wall and bury his head in a pillow. He pressed his fingernails deeper into his arm than ever before, actually *wanting* to draw blood. Heat rose in his skin and quickening breaths caught in his chest. It was too much. He couldn't handle any more of his mother—not this day, maybe not even this month. Or ever.

But a moment later, the cool comfort of darkness blanketed the room. Melissa had turned off the lights.

"Connor's asleep, Mom," she hollered. "He said he had a headache. Do you think you could help me with the poetry assignment Mrs. Eddleton wants us to do before we get back to school?"

A few long seconds ticked by.

"Yes, Melissa. Bring it over here. We can take a look at it."

Relief washed over Connor, the power of it causing a few tears to fall, though the pillowcase immediately soaked them up.

Melissa left the room and shut the door behind her.

***

He awoke far too early. Sleep was the only release he had, and he tried to keep his lids closed so he wouldn't have to face the day just yet.

But it was a lost cause. His parents were stirring downstairs, and in a little while they'd be knocking at his door, wanting to know why he hadn't shown his face yet. He absentmindedly reached up to feel how swollen his eyes were, though he'd cried less that night than he had in several days.

Stretching, he tossed his blanket aside and knocked his cell phone off his nightstand. It immediately buzzed to life.

He stopped breathing, his mind exploding with insane hopes. *It could be Jared.* It could be Jared, calling to make things right, calling to apologize, calling to pull him from his depression and make it seem like nothing more than an awful dream. He almost started to cry again, just from the sheer stupidity of his fantasies.

Still, he couldn't reach out to the phone for several seconds, wanting to keep that hope alive for as long as possible. When he finally did grab for it, he kept his thumb over the screen for one more instant.

Please, God. Please. He moved the finger away slowly.

It wasn't Jared. It hadn't been the last eight or nine times his phone had rung since that day, either. It had been and still was Rebecca.

He hovered over the ignore button. He couldn't talk to her. He couldn't talk to anyone. He would just continue to avoid everyone, returning to school and finding a whole new way of life, without anyone else in it.

He could keep hiding.

How had everything fallen apart so quickly? Everything he'd worked so hard to attain—a meager social life, a relationship...*happiness*. All gone in the blink of an eye.

His phone stopped ringing and then bleeped with a missed call. A second later, it rang again.

An *accelerando* took control of his heart, making the beats come faster and faster, sending a nervous energy coursing through his body. He knew what *it* wanted—for him to curl up into a ball and stay there, indefinitely. But his mind was screaming as well, telling him something else: *You can't give up, not yet!* And as much as he wanted to ignore everything that had happened—was happening—and chalk it up to purely external forces...he couldn't. There were still a few decisions left for him to make.

He closed his eyes and answered. "H-hello?"

"Oh!" Relief flowed through Rebecca's voice. "I didn't know you were there. I was just going to leave a message. But I'm so glad I got a hold of you."

"Um, yeah."

"I didn't see you that whole week after the concert, you know. I've been trying to reach you. I guess...I guess I just wanted to make sure things were okay between us. I've been thinking, it was such a stupid move on my part to open my mouth like that. I'm really sorry."

"It's...um, it's okay."

"So, we're cool then?"

If she hadn't found out... He cut off the thought before it could go any further. It didn't really matter, anyway. Someone would have found out sometime.

"Connor? You still there?"

"Y-yes."

"Is...is everything all right?"

The seemingly never-ending supply of tears sprang back into action. *No, everything is not all right.*

"Connor?"

He took in what felt like the longest breath of his life and held it, hovering on the edge of a decision before finally releasing.

"Rebecca...I think...I think I need someone to talk to."

***

She sat on the corner of his bed, her long legs drawn up to her chest, her dirty-blond hair draped across one shoulder.

It was weird seeing her there. Actually, it was weird seeing anyone there—he so rarely had friends up to his room. But he wasn't really surprised she'd offered to rush right over. The drive was only about forty minutes, and she was just that kind of person.

She had been all along.

"It's not my fault, is it?" She spoke softly as she arranged her long flower skirt around her ankles. "Because I opened my big mouth?"

He shook his head, pulling the desk chair over so he could sit in front of her, until she grabbed his arm and yanked him onto the bed. "N-no. It...it just happened. It would have happened eventually."

She removed her Birkenstock sandals and nudged him with her foot. "Well, I'm sorry anyways. Sometimes I meddle too much for my own good—I thought you knowing that I knew would make things better, not worse."

"You didn't do anything wrong." He sighed, situating himself a little closer to her tall shoulders than he ever had been before. "Besides, it's probably better that it was you finding out and not someone who could cause trouble for him."

Rebecca scowled. "You shouldn't really be thinking about what's best for *him* right now. He hurt you, Connor. It's okay to be mad."

He found the strength to put on a weak smile. "I'm...I'm fine."

"Really? You're okay?" She peered at him with one of her pale brows arched doubtfully.

"Yes."

"Really?"

"Yes. I just...needed to get what happened off my chest, and you're the only person I can talk to." He bit his lip, cursing his choice of words. "N-not that you're not a good person to talk to. You're a great person, in fact."

Rebecca narrowed her eyes. "So, you're totally fine now."

He nodded.

"Because you don't look it."

"W-what? What do you mean?"

She scrunched her lips to the side, studying him. "Well, you've got big dark circles under your eyes, like you've been crying. And you look like you've lost weight since the last time I saw you, which was less than two weeks ago."

He backed up, stunned by her bluntness. "I...I..."

A few tears fell, and, still in shock, he didn't push them away. Two more followed before he pressed both palms into his face to cover his shame. He'd managed to keep from bawling in front of Jared, in front of his mother, in front of Melissa...and now here he was letting his closest friend see how *weak* he truly was.

Rebecca wrapped her arms around him and pulled him against her chest. "I'm so sorry, honey. I'm so sorry this happened to you."

He tried to back out of the embrace, shaking his head as he finally regained some emotional control. "I'm sorry. I don't know why I'm being so stupid right now."

"How you feel is not stupid," Rebecca countered, refusing to release him. "I said it before—it's okay to be upset, it's okay to be mad, it's okay to be hurt. You can't help how you feel."

Connor gave in, melting into the embrace. "I just...I just miss him so much. And I know I'm an idiot, but there were times...there were times when I really felt he might...he might actually l-lo—"

He had to stop to avoid hiccupping the words. Words that shouldn't be said, anyhow.

Rebecca stroked his hair. "I'm sure he cared for you, but if you ask me, he was being selfish. He should never have made you feel like you had to lie for him, or like you didn't deserve to be recognized."

"I...I knew it couldn't last. But I was just so happy to find someone...and Jared, he's so far out of my league that I—"

Rebecca cut him off. "Connor, you're an amazing guy. You deserve more than what he had to offer. I don't care how good looking or popular you think he is."

Connor fell silent, pushing a little harder against her. Rebecca's closeness calmed him, and it wasn't often he got that sensation around people. Jared had been the only other one to inspire those feelings of *safety*—and what he'd felt there might not even have been real.

She eased up on the hug and he wiped off the remains of his earlier tears.

"I guess I knew things couldn't last the way they were," he finally spoke, relieved to hear his voice settling into a normal tone. "I just didn't want to face reality."

"Well, it's his loss. He's missing out on something great."

Connor pulled away, unable to give her the smile he knew she was looking for. "Thanks."

"Don't mention it." She grinned for him, giving his shoulder a little shake. "Now, what are we going to do about this?"

"A-about what?"

"I'd say we need a plan of action."

"A what?"

Rebecca frowned, then exhaled heavily through puffed-out cheeks. "You're probably going to hate me when this is all over…but when we get back to school, I'm not going to let you hide in your room, all depressed and alone. We need to get you out, as much as possible for as long as possible."

He closed his eyes. "No. I'm no good to anyone right now. I wouldn't be able to act right or enjoy anything…"

She clapped both hands on his shoulders, forcing him to look at her. "Then you fake it."

"What?"

"You go out there, and just *pretend* like you're having a good time, and you're bound to actually have some fun, eventually. The main thing is that you're distracting yourself, keeping your mind off being hurt by him."

"You want me to fake that I'm having fun?"

"Exactly. I know you might not feel like being around people now, but trust me, being around friends is one of the best ways to move on from a bad breakup. And you do have friends, you know." She gave him a pointed look.

He swallowed. "Yeah, I know, but –"

"No buts. Like I said, you may hate me, but if you try and hide I'll be at your door, pounding on it until you're forced to open it and get out of that room."

For some reason, he had no doubt she was telling the truth.

"You'll go out, you'll have new experiences, you'll meet new people…eventually maybe even a new guy…"

Connor's snort interrupted her, and though he quickly silenced himself, she waited patiently for an explanation. He sighed. "Rebecca, I'm sure you've noticed…but I don't exactly have the best people skills. Jared's the one—" He swiped angrily at his eyes. Why couldn't he even say Jared's name without tearing up? "Jared's the one who encouraged me to hang out more with you guys—to get to be better friends."

"Well, he got one thing right, then," she said brightly.

He refused to be cheered by that, as true as it was. "And meeting a new *guy*…I just don't see…I don't see how that would ever be possible."

"Yeah, I guess it would be kinda difficult to meet a guy when you're…" Trailing off, she glanced around the room as if searching for insight. "Have you ever thought about coming out? Not that I'm trying to force you into anything—I'm just curious."

He shrugged. "I guess I've *thought* about it."

"Well, are you expecting a bad reaction, from your parents, maybe?"

Shaking his head, he grabbed a fistful of comforter and began twisting. "My parents don't hate gay people. It's just…they have all these plans for me…and they don't like it when things upset their plans."

Rebecca laid her hand on his to still his restless fingers. "Connor, at this age, I really feel like the only one who should be making plans with *your* life…is *you*."

His cheeks burned. He *did* sound like a pathetic little boy, waiting for his mommy and daddy to decide his future. But he'd never really known any other way.

"What about just at school? Ever thought of that? Or do you think someone there might tell your parents?"

His lips twisted in a bitter smirk. "If anyone at school cared enough to do that, I'd almost be flattered."

"Okay, so, that's something to think about. You could join the QSU—you'd meet lots of people there."

"I…I don't know." His skin began to prickle with his usual anxiety. "I don't think I could…"

She leaned back as she nodded. "I understand. It's your choice to make. I just feel like the bigger the change, the easier it is to get past a low point in life. It's worked for me in the past."

"Really? Y-you've had low points?"

She rolled her eyes with a droll smile. "Nobody's life is perfect. I know it'll be hard for you to believe, but back in high school, I was a bit of a nerd."

It *was* a little hard to imagine. Rebecca definitely wasn't the blond cheerleader type, but nothing in the confident, composed way she held herself spoke of being a *nerd*.

"The thing is, I had a crush on this guy…and I went through this phase where I just really wanted to be popular, so he'd like me. I wore stupid clothes and put on tons of make-up…but it just wasn't me, you know?"

He tried to keep his incredulous brows from shooting up too high.

"Anyways, the guy was a jerk, I was heartbroken…and by my senior year, I figured, fuck it, I'm just going to be myself. So yeah, I got called a dirty hippie a few times, but I also made great friends—Chrissy went to my high school, you know—and since then, things seem to be working out."

"Yeah, you have Tate," he added, quashing the bit of jealousy that rode in with the statement. "Things are good with him?"

She blushed, her cheeks turning a delicate shade of pink. "Well, he's no Rico Suave, but he's a good guy, and he treats me well. And I'm happy."

Connor's eyes watered again, but he kept any tears from slipping out.

She noticed anyway. "Oh, Connor, I'm being stupid. Let's talk about something else."

He swallowed and nodded slowly. "Um, so…what does that group do? The one you're talking about?"

Rebecca perked up. "Oh, all kinds of different stuff. They organize a lot of social gatherings."

He frowned.

"But other times they get together and discuss things related to gay life. Sometimes they have guest speakers come and give lectures." Rebecca paused, tapping her chin as she regarded him with a thoughtful expression. "Hey, you love lectures. It could be a perfect fit! Bet you could even write an essay on what you learned. They'd like that."

She grinned widely, and he laughed—for the first time in nearly two weeks. It gave him an odd sensation, tickling his throat as it escaped.

Rebecca laughed, too, and wrapped an arm around his shoulders. "Well, whatever you decide, I hope you know I'm here for you."

He smiled his most genuine smile in days. "I do now."

CHAPTER SEVENTEEN

T-shirt or button-down? Blue or black?

Connor cast all rejected options to the floor of his dorm room, trying not to think about how Jared used to scoop up his clothing—after ripping it off, usually—and place it in the hamper. Jared wasn't one to abide mess for very long.

He pinched himself to keep his mind on track and settled on jeans and a blue button-down. His fingers were already trembling, though, and he had a hard time guiding the little white buttons into their holes. He'd also started to sweat, causing bits of hair to stick to his forehead. It was not a good look.

One glance in the mirror and he felt close to vomiting.

I can't...I can't do it.

The idea of failure was familiar, and he almost dove into it, hot shame guiding the way. What a stupid, stupid thing for him to even consider. Rebecca was wrong. Going out into the world would only prove what a misfit he truly was—*being* out would probably help even less. Jared didn't want him, and no one else would.

He tore off the shirt and added it to the pile on the floor, half-aware he was letting his mind cycle through the kinds of thoughts that would only lead to more crying and more misery. But it was hard to stop once he got going.

Jared doesn't want you, he told his reflection. *He was the best thing in your life and now...*

His heart jumped at Rebecca's knock, even though it sounded nothing like Jared's. He just wasn't used to having any other visitors.

"Hey, Connor, ready to paint the town red?" she sang out from the hallway.

With a quick swipe to dry his damp forehead, he pulled on a grey t-shirt and hurriedly kicked the discarded clothes into the closet. He took his time answering the door, though, the guilt at having to let her down slowing his movements.

Rebecca stood in the hallway with a hand on her hip and a bag on her shoulder, her bright smile slipping once she saw his face. "I'm guessing from that look"—she bent over to meet his downcast eyes—"that it's a no-go."

"I'm s-sorry," he stuttered, his cheeks burning. "I'm sorry I dragged you all the way out here. I wanted to be ready…but I just…I can't."

"Connor, it's all right." She squeezed his shoulder. "No pressure, remember? There'll be other chances if you change your mind."

He shifted uneasily, staring down at her well-worn sandals.

"Listen, why don't you grab your books and come back to Brown with me? A.J. and Chrissy are watching some old film…or we could just study in the lounge."

He shook his head, his mind still a mess of self-deprecating thoughts. "N-not tonight. Some other time, okay?"

She pushed past and entered his room. "Good thing I brought my stuff, then," she announced, setting herself up at his desk.

He blinked as she unzipped her bag and pulled out a hefty book. "Rebecca, I…"

"What, you've already done all your schoolwork?"

"N-no, I have stuff to do, it's just that—"

"You don't want my company?"

He sighed, sinking down onto his bed. "I appreciate what you're trying to do, really. I may be a little...depressed, or whatever, but I don't need a babysitter. I mean, it's not like I'd ever do anything...stupid." He quirked his lips up in a half-smile, to at least look like he could handle joking about the situation. "I'm much too cowardly for that."

"Mhm." Rebecca raised a brow. "Why don't you take a minute and think about how that is not the most reassuring response you could have given."

Now his face flamed even hotter, and he clutched the edge of his mattress for stability until his temperature returned to normal.

"You need any of these?" she asked, gesturing to the books stacked on his desk.

"Uh...no, I guess not." He shook the cramps from his fingers. "Just hand me my laptop, please."

She did, then grabbed a pencil and began scribbling notes in the margins of her book. Connor wasted a few more minutes before tucking into an outline on an upcoming paper. By the third Roman numeral, though, he noticed the rustle of Rebecca's pages had come to a stop.

"So, can I ask what made you change your mind about tonight?" She peeked over her book at him.

Did she *always* have to be so nosey? And what exactly did she expect to hear—a confession about how pathetic he was?

"I...I couldn't think of what to wear."

She choked on a laugh. "Connor, what you're wearing is fine."

"Yeah, but..."

"I mean, there's no gay bouncer there, waiting to turn you away for not meeting style requirements." She broke into a fit of giggles. "But if there was, lord knows I'd never get through the door."

Rolling his eyes, he stifled his own laugh so as not to appear too insulting—not that Rebecca seemed to care much about what people thought of her. If there was anything he hoped to pick up from knowing her, it was that. Too bad it was much easier said than done.

"All right." She creased her page open again. "Now that we've covered the dress code, if you ever reconsider, you'll have that part down." She opened a drawer at his desk and propped her feet up on it. "Back to work. Though I say we take a study break in a few and go for a smoothie."

Connor nodded and resumed typing, until one Roman numeral later, when Rebecca sneezed. Her long arm stretched out in front of him to grab a tissue from the box on his nightstand.

"Allergies." She shrugged as he glanced up at her. "I swear, I'm not contagious."

But Connor remained focused on the tissue box, suddenly immersed in memories of Jared's hand reaching out to that very same box—after they'd spent themselves against each other's bodies. Jared's hands, slowly and gently cleaning him off, making a sort of ritual out of it that only had him dying to do it all over again…

And *Jesus Christ*, he needed to get a grip. Now even tissues reminded him of Jared.

He leapt up, startling Rebecca into banging her knee on his desk. "Okay."

"Okay? Okay what?"

"Okay, let's go."

"For a smoothie?"

"No…to…to the thing."

"Really?" She rubbed her knee. "Are you sure?"

Connor stalked over to the closet and yanked out a jacket. "No, but I'm never sure of anything. Let's just go before I change my mind."

***

A sea of legs had to part around Rebecca as she led him down the cobblestone sidewalk. He stuck close to her side, overwhelmed by the mass of bodies—there was a good reason he'd never been to The Corner at night. Any locale known for being a popular college hangout was a place best avoided. The restaurants and bars were spilling their clientele—and their noise—into the streets, and the large Tex-Mex place they approached was no exception. Through the windowed walls of the building, he could see the throng of energetic people inside, and he abruptly drew to a halt.

The first few guys he glimpsed were wearing skin-tight pants and obviously had on eyeliner, if not mascara. Two of them had tattoos, and one had a series of piercings down his ear and along an eyebrow. As Connor stood there gaping, the tattooed ones moved in close and groped each other into a quick kiss.

Rebecca linked her arm with his. "Ready?"

He pulled back, almost cowering against her body. "Wait, wait," he begged, his breaths growing shallow as he stared down at his attire. There was no way he was going to fit in with this crowd. "P-please don't be mad, but I don't think...I don't think I can do this."

"Why would I be mad?" She pursed her lips. "You don't have to do anything you don't want to."

"But I've wasted your entire night..." he began, trailing off when a guy and girl, holding hands and exchanging loving glances, walked past to enter the restaurant.

Confused, he looked to Rebecca for an explanation, and she rolled her eyes. "They don't rent the place out for social gatherings, they just reserve tables. I'm sure there are other people in there as well. Karaoke night is popular here."

"Oh. Oh, right. That makes sense."

"So, you know, we could just go in and take a peek around. Then if you still want to go, we can walk out and no one would know a thing."

"Oh," he said again. He took a few steps forward without thinking, and suddenly the door was being opened for him and he was walking inside.

Dimmed lights and off-key music set the mood for all the lively patrons. Connor scanned the room and was relieved to find his first impression had been wrong. Not all the guys had tattoos and piercings or wore skin-tight pants; most were actually dressed normally for UVA's preppy atmosphere. And there were girls there, too—some looking like they were ready for a night on the town in dresses and heels, others in pants and t-shirts. Two with very short hair were singing *Summer Nights* in the background with little care for pitch, but the audience still hooted and hollered their approval.

"How are you doing?" Rebecca whispered in his ear. She pointed to a couple of chairs up at the bar, and he quickly took a seat. He'd blend in better there than he would just standing around and staring.

"Um…okay so far, I guess."

She ordered him a coke and herself an ice-tea when the bartender breezed by. "We can get some chips and guac, too, if you like. They make it from fresh avocadoes at this place."

He took a long drink of his soda. "No thanks. I'm…I'm way too nervous to eat. I think maybe I shoulda waited for those other types of meetings you were talking about…the ones with the lectures."

Rebecca smirked. "Think of it this way—if you get to know a few people tonight, you'll already have some friends when it comes time for those."

Before he could respond, a guy in a salmon-colored polo shirt, khakis, and flip-flops—the unofficial UVA uniform—approached Rebecca and pulled her into a hug.

"Becca, I haven't seen you in forever!" They exchanged quick pecks on the cheek.

"Hey, Adam." Rebecca shot a glance at Connor and he gave her a slight nod. "I want you to meet someone. This is my stand partner, Connor. Connor, this is Adam. He's president of the QSU."

Connor shook Adam's hand while Adam and Rebecca had a silent conversation with their eyes. He translated it in his mind. *Is he? He is. Oh, I see.*

"Nice to meet you, Connor." Adam rested his elbows on the bar. "Were you thinking about joining?"

"Um…" Connor scratched his head. Where was the momentous emotional reaction he'd expected at his first voluntary 'outing'? He waited a few more seconds, but nothing came. "I guess. I mean, I'm not…I'm not out at home, yet…or anywhere, really."

Adam nodded. "Yeah, man, I get that. This is your first year, right? There's a lot of other people here in your boat. You've come to the right place. We have all the resources for any support you feel you need…or if you just feel like kicking back and hanging out for a while, that's fine too. Whatever you want to do, we're all here for you." Adam deliberately sought and held eye contact, way too long for comfort.

"Um…yeah, thanks."

Rebecca scooted back her chair. "Sorry guys, tiny girl bladder," she shouted over the sounds of *Dancing Queen.* "Be right back."

Great. Now he was alone with a stranger. Connor stared wistfully at the bottles of alcohol up on the shelves, remembering the last time they'd eased his stress in a social gathering. Too bad he stood little chance of being served underage at this place.

Adam took Rebecca's place at the bar. "So, you're a musician then. I used to play clarinet, but I've sort of given it up since high school. Things get busy around here."

Connor made a noncommittal *mhm* noise, keeping an eye out on the hallway to the bathroom for Rebecca's return.

"You gonna sing a song for us?" Adam jerked his head in the direction of the music.

"I'm, uh, not really a singer."

Adam snickered. "Right. Like they are."

Chuckling softly, Connor glanced toward the Karaoke stage, where several boys were finishing their crooning of the ABBA song. Bright blond frosted tips caught his gaze. Ray spotted him, too, and as soon as the song was over, he tossed the microphone off to a friend and came barreling through the crowd.

"Hey! The lone violinist!"

"Uh, hi...French horn player."

Ray pulled up in front of him and surprised him with a quick hug.

"Cool." Adam backed away from the bar. "Looks like you already have some friends here. Well, I'll see you two later. I'm off to do my presidential mingling duties."

Ray jumped onto the stool as Adam took off. "So, I've never seen you 'round these parts before."

"Well...it's my first time." Connor forced his shoulders into a stiff shrug. *This* confrontation—with someone who knew him in his daily life—was one he was far less prepared for.

"Awesome, man. Awesome. I just love Karaoke nights."

"Yeah, um...it sounded good."

Ray smacked him on his arm, another bit of bodily contact Connor was not ready for. "Oh, shove it. At least you know I play an instrument a lot better than I sing. Honestly, I think I could do a better job, but when I'm up there with the guys and they're just belting out whatever, it's almost kinda fun to be terrible."

"I didn't think it was all that bad." Lying seemed like the socially appropriate thing to do, given the circumstances.

"Ah ha, but you *did* think it was bad," Ray pointed out, flashing a disarming grin when Connor blushed. "Hey, are you here alone?"

"Um, n-no, I came with my...my friend."

"Oh, that's cool." Ray shifted in his seat, his eyes darting away from Connor's face.

"Here she is," Connor added as Rebecca approached. He caught Ray's expression brightening as soon as the word *she* left his lips.

"Hey, Connor." Rebecca looked over at him expectantly. "New friends already?"

"Rebecca, this is Ray. He's in the pit with me."

She threw an approving smile in Connor's direction. "Nice to meet you, Ray. I'm Connor's stand partner in orchestra."

"Oh, no, another violinist!" Ray joked, a slight dimple showing when he laughed. He slid down from the stool and turned toward Connor, extending his arm. "My friends and I have a table in the back, and there's room for you two. Wanna join?"

Connor stared curiously at the offered hand while Rebecca brushed past to snap up her iced tea. "Sure, we'd love to."

Ray grabbed his wrist and began leading the way.

There actually wasn't much room at the table, and Connor slid into the booth after Rebecca, leaving only a tiny sliver of seat for Ray. Across from him sat two other guys, one with a full head of blue hair—and a bit of blue eyeliner—and the other with blond spikes probably held up with copious amounts of gel.

"These are my friends, Max and Kaden. Guys, this is Rebecca and Connor. Connor plays the violin in the pit." Ray settled into his seat, his thigh pressing up against Connor's.

Trying not to appear too obvious, Connor leaned a little more toward Rebecca's side.

"So, how are you enjoying the pit so far? Like it? Or are you just ready for the play to be over?" Ray asked.

Connor shrugged. "I'm ready to play the music, I guess."

Ray tipped his head in agreement but didn't speak, and Connor eventually realized he was waiting for more of a response. "So...it'll be nice to see the whole thing all put together...but when it's actually over...I think I might miss seeing that play."

"Ah, so you're the romantic type." Ray smirked. "Got a soft spot for the rom-coms, huh? I guess I have to say I'm with you on this one. I'm gonna miss seeing Fred and Lilli fall in love with each other over and over again."

Across the table, the blue-haired Kaden sneered. "If you ask me, that play could use a little updating."

Max lifted a hand to run it through Kaden's cobalt tresses. "Oh, don't mind him. Kaden just thinks every work of theater should include a gay storyline. But we'll both be there to see...err, hear you guys, when the play does go on. And we'll love it."

Ray rolled his eyes. "Yeah, thanks, guys. We appreciate your support."

Max's hand dropped back down to the table and conveniently landed on Kaden's, where it remained. The entwined fingers of deep tan and peachy-cream soon captured Connor's attention. He could hear Rebecca continuing the conversation, as she was so expert at doing, bringing up plays that would meet Kaden's criteria, but the only thing he could focus on were those two hands, locked together and on public display.

He wished he'd gotten to hold Jared's hand more. But holding hands was something people did when they were out in the world, as if to say, *even though we can't be in each other's arms right now, we still want to remain connected.* He could sense that emotion coming from the couple across the table.

Now that he thought of it, the only time he'd held Jared's hand for any significant time was when they had driven back from winter break. And he would never forget how magical those moments had felt—like they were actually going *somewhere* together, in much more than a physical sense.

But they hadn't really gone anywhere—*couldn't* go anywhere—and it was about time he truly faced that fact.

His eyes misted over until Rebecca gently squeezed his knee, reminding him to be more present in the moment. He shook out of the reverie with one last, longing glace at the hands across the table. Luckily, no one else seemed to have noticed his mental absence.

"So, to celebrate Connor here joining our little ragtag group—" Ray was saying.

"The QSU is the largest gay organization on campus," Kaden interjected.

Ray glared. "As I was saying, to celebrate, we should order one of those dessert nachos, with extra caramel."

"Dessert nachos?" Connor asked.

"Cinnamon-sugar-covered tortilla strips with ice cream, whip cream, honey, and caramel. I'm telling you, it's delicious."

"I prefer the chocolate to the caram—" Max began, until Ray kicked him under the table.

Throwing an arm over Connor's shoulder, he smiled sweetly. "So, what do you say—are you in? It may very well be the best nacho experience of your life, I swear."

Connor looked around at the familiar faces and the new ones, then at the room in general. And it hit him...he wasn't standing alone in the corner, bemoaning his awkward ways. He was sitting with a group of friendly people, talking, smiling and about to partake in a shared dessert—like he *belonged* there.

He nodded. "Yeah. I'm in."

CHAPTER EIGHTEEN

"Okay," Rebecca huffed. "Next time, you're coming to Brown." Her loaded bag slipped from her arm with a thud. "That really is a long walk."

Connor watched her drop her violin from her other shoulder and grimaced. Why hadn't she mentioned wanting to practice? Now he felt even worse. "I know. I'm sorry. It's just...I thought I might want to talk about...things, and with everyone else over there at Brown..."

"I'm only teasing, Connor." She patted his head. "I mean, your dorm *is* out in the boonies, but you make the walk to Brown all the time. I can handle it every now and then. Though a backpack instead of a shoulder bag might be a good investment—better for the long haul."

"I didn't know you were going to bring your violin, too, or I wouldn't have asked." He leaned against his nightstand and waited for Rebecca to settle on his bed. "Really, Rebecca. I'm...I'm sorry...I know I'm taking advantage..."

"So, you went to the QSU meeting yesterday, right?" She interrupted his bumbling apologies. "How'd it go?"

With a deep breath, he let go of his worry over troubling her. He had more important things on his mind, anyhow. "Um, it was all right, I guess. There were a lot less people there than at the social."

"Well, yeah, I'd imagine so." Rebecca stretched out, her legs taking up most of the bed. "What was the meeting about?"

He climbed onto the space that was left. "They mostly talked about club business…painting Beta Bridge, plans for next year's LGBT history month…that kinda stuff."

Rebecca nodded. "Painting Beta Bridge is a lot of fun. If they do that, you should definitely join in. I've done it a couple of times with Brown—it just sucks when it gets painted over the next night. You want at least a few days for people to revel in your artwork."

Connor shrugged. "I'm not really artistic."

"Everyone can paint a rainbow, Connor." She laughed. "But enough about that. Did you get to know anyone? Make any new friends?"

He focused on her toes for a moment, reminding himself she wasn't looking to chide him for failing at social interaction, the way his mother would have. "I talked to Adam a little…but everyone already knew each other and they seemed pretty busy covering the agenda for the day…" he trailed off as he ran out of excuses.

Rebecca frowned. "I'm sorry. Adam's usually really good about making everyone feel welcome. Maybe they just had a lot on their minds? I can talk to him, if you like."

"No, no." He shook his head emphatically. "Everyone was really nice to me. It's just…they were all regulars, and I couldn't really get involved in the stuff they were talking about. I guess I was sorta hoping Ray and his friends would be there."

"Oh." Rebecca nodded, her concern replaced by a knowing look. "Right, right. I get it."

"But he told me during pit practice he pretty much only goes to the social events."

"I can see that. He seemed like a social kind of guy."

"Yeah, he's pretty nice."

"Cute, too," she added with a sly smile.

Connor shot her a look. Just what was she getting at? "Um, Rebecca, I d-don't think—"

"Oh, no need to worry." She threw up her hands. "My matchmaking services are closed. I learned the hard way that's not where my talents lie."

Running twitching fingers through his hair, he gathered his scattered thoughts and tried not to blush. "Anyway, I think I want to do that, too—go to just the social events, I mean—before I decide if I want to be more involved in the club."

Rebecca made a strange squeaking noise. "Good God, Connor, did you hear what you just said?"

He blinked. "What?"

"You actually said you *wanted* to attend social gatherings, and with no prompting from me! I think I can die happy now."

"Shut up." He looked around for something to throw at her, but came up empty. Meanwhile Rebecca dissolved into giggles, and within a few seconds he had no choice but to join her.

***

"You guys must have some tough stuff coming up for the next concert, huh," Tate remarked, loading his lunch tray with two slices of pizza and an overflowing bowl of french fries. A few pieces fell off and landed on the ground, causing a cafeteria worker to scowl until Tate bent to pick them up.

Connor smirked and took a more modest handful of fries. "Not too terribly hard, no. Actually, I really like Ravel's *Bolero.*"

"Oh." Tate finished off his food pile with an apple. "I've heard that piece. It's nice. That why you're practicing so much?"

"Huh?"

"Practicing," Tate repeated. "Is that why Becca's been going to practice with you so much?"

Connor reached out and grabbed…*something*…from under a heat lamp without even looking at it, buying himself time to let Tate's words sink in.

Rebecca was lying to her boyfriend. And she was doing it for *him*. Practicing was probably the best excuse she could come up with to keep Tate from asking too many questions about the time they spent together.

His empty stomach gurgled angrily. Was it possible to get indigestion *before* eating? "It's…it's a hard piece to get out of your head…sometimes playing it is the only answer," he replied, rearranging his food on his tray. Turned out he'd selected a piece of bread pudding, which he hated.

More lies. He was amazed at how quickly the misleading words had emerged from his lips. When had lying become so easy?

Tate didn't seem to take issue with his response, however, and together they began walking off toward their seats.

"Oh no you don't." Chrissy stopped them before they could reach their usual table. "It's spring outside. Time to commune with nature. Go get takeout containers—we're eating on the Lawn."

Predictably, Chrissy discarded her sandals as soon as they had claimed their spot of grass and happily curled her toes up in the dirt. Rebecca and Tate sat cross-legged beside each other, their knees touching, while A.J. and Connor rested against a tree.

"Hey, guess what?" Tate bit into his second slice of pizza. "They're gonna have a midnight screening of

Donnie Darko at the Newcomb theater next week. We should go."

"Yeah, man. I love that film," A.J. added. "And it's got Maggie Gyllenhaal in it. She's hot."

"What?" Tate dropped his pizza from a height and almost missed the takeout box. "Are you kidding me? Maggie Gyllenhaal is *not* hot. She's just plain…weird-looking." He crossed his arms with a haughty smile, daring anyone to contradict him.

A.J. shook his head. "Well, I disagree." He stroked his chin and stared up at the tree branches. "I think she's…unique. She stands out from a crowd. There's something *different* to her. I kinda like that."

"Yeah, what's different is that funky nose and those huge cheeks."

Rebecca smacked Tate's leg with a resounding *thwack*. "Be nice," she ordered.

Tate rubbed his thigh sheepishly. He turned to give her ridiculous puppy-dog eyes, but she just laughed, gathering up her hair and beginning a loose braid.

"Men." Chrissy let out a disgusted snort. "Quit placing your superficial values on beauty. I think she's lovely."

"But you're a girl," Tate replied. "And besides, you'd never admit anyone was ugly." He shifted abruptly to face Connor. "What do you think?"

Connor picked a dandelion from beside him as he considered his response, but couldn't quite summon the actress' face to mind. "Um…" He smashed the yellow petals between his fingers. "Actually, I'm not sure."

Tate chuckled. "C'mon, man. You're a dude. Go with your, *ahem*, instincts." He cast a meaningful glance at his crotch.

Rebecca paused in her braiding, her gaze seeking out Connor's as if she sensed his rising discomfort.

"Uh…"

"I mean, take Drew Barrymore, or that other chick. I always forget her name…the one who plays Gretchen.

217

They're way better looking, right? Who would you rather do from that movie?"

Rebecca smacked Tate again, this time on the back of his head.

"What! I'm asking Connor! I have no interest in anyone except you, I swear!"

The normally stoic A.J. laughed heartily, his chuckles a deep throaty rumble.

"I'll rephrase," Tate said carefully, keeping his peripheral vision on Rebecca to watch for any more play-abuse. "Who would you rather *date* from that movie?"

Connor found Rebecca's eyes again, and he waited to see if she'd make a move to ease the conversation in a different direction. But she just smiled at him reassuringly, tying off the end of her hair with a long weed.

He took a deep breath and tossed the flower aside. "From that movie..." he began, but his voice faltered. He gave himself a little shake and made a second attempt. "From that movie, I guess I'd..."

The words failed him again, and this time he clamped his mouth shut, aware a stricken look had plastered itself on his face.

It was such a silly, easy thing to lie about. Considering how well he'd done earlier with a much more sensitive subject, there was no logical explanation for his sudden inability to speak. But all the same, the acids were churning in his stomach, burning their way up his esophagus and choking off any hopes of a glib response.

He saw Tate's face change from one of expectation to one of concern, saw his mouth open to say what Connor could only assume was going to be some form of *are you okay, dude?*

And in that split second, he decided to beat him to the punch.

He took one last breath. "Sorry, I was trying to think of everyone in the movie. Anyway...I guess I'd pick...Jake."

Tate waited a second before responding. "Jake?"

"Yeah…um, Jake Gyllenhaal. You know, Maggie's brother. He's…he's…" *Spit it out already!* "He's m-more…my type."

In a moment of silence, everyone exchanged looks—A.J. with Tate, Tate with Chrissy, Chrissy with Rebecca, and Rebecca with Connor. Connor couldn't hold her gaze for long, though, as she was sitting in front of Old Cabell Hall. How long would it take for him to run there and lock himself in a rehearsal room? He could practice scales until the only thing running through his head were the simple notes that always led to the next without error.

Then Tate grinned. "Yep. I guess Jake's a good-looking fella. He's got the whole blue-eyes, dark-hair thing going for him."

Dazed, Connor thought about nodding, but didn't actually move.

"Poor Maggie." Tate sighed. "It must suck to have such a good-looking brother when she's not all that, but I suppose my sis has the same burden to bear."

"Oh, please." Rebecca ripped a handful of grass and deposited it on Tate's head. "You wish."

The involuntarily-tightened muscles of Connor's abdomen finally relaxed. His body went limp and he fell back, letting the tree support his weight.

Normal conversation-flow resumed around him, filled with its usual blend of jokes, stories, and good-natured ribbing. A few extra smiles flew in his direction that seemed to say *don't worry, it doesn't change our friendship*, while also being considerate enough not to make a big deal of his revelation.

A small blush crept up his cheeks anyway. Not because of how anyone was reacting, but because of how foolish he had been, waiting so long to be honest. He should have known they'd take it in stride—probably even more so than he did. They were the kind of people who took everything in stride.

"So, we're on for Darko next week, right?" Tate asked as they stood to clear their trash. "A little something for everyone," he added with a wink in Connor's direction.

Rebecca shot Tate a warning glance, and for a moment, Connor thought embarrassment might overwhelm him again. How was he supposed to take that remark?

But a second later, the feeling passed, as a sudden realization whisked it away. Tate was merely treating him the same way he treated all his friends.

He shrugged. "Yeah. Whatever."

Tate elbowed him in the ribs, then gave Rebecca a brief kiss before leaving with A.J. and Chrissy for class.

"Well, that wasn't so hard, now was it?" Rebecca fell into stride beside Connor.

"No...I guess not," he admitted. "You were right. You've been right about everything, so far."

"Yup." She didn't bother to hide her smugness. "I do tend to be right like that."

Connor shook his head, grinning. "Well don't let it go to your—"

He stopped mid-sentence, his smile demolished by a crowd of passing students—because Jared's tall form was among them. Connor's heart fluttered from sheer habit, then plummeted into his stomach when he caught sight of an unkempt Veronica trailing a few feet behind.

As if he knew he was being watched, Jared suddenly looked up, and their eyes locked.

His gaze seemed almost...*vacant*. After a flicker of only the most basic level of recognition, he looked away again.

Connor had to stop walking, and he clutched at his chest to dull the gnawing emptiness inside. How could there be *nothing* left in those familiar eyes that spoke of what they'd shared?

Rebecca grabbed him by both shoulders. "It's his loss, Connor. His loss."

He swallowed and nodded, but couldn't keep from watching Jared as he disappeared from sight.

***

The director clapped his hands for attention and addressed the room for the final time that evening. "Call time for actors is six o'clock, pit and crew six-thirty…and my final note is for everyone to get a good night's sleep!"

Ray's hand dropped onto the small of Connor's back as he stood. He managed not to jerk away this time, since it was about the fifth time that day, and probably the fifteenth time that week. He was slowly becoming accustomed to Ray's hands-on approach to life.

"Can't believe this is our last rehearsal," Ray said, smiling broadly. Connor grinned as well—the thrill of being this close to putting on the production was contagious. "Just a few performances left and then we'll probably never play this music again."

At the reminder of the inevitable, Connor's smile faltered. Having a lot more spare time on his hands probably wasn't for the best.

"Hey, where do you always run off to after rehearsal?" Ray asked, removing his hand so he could pack up his horn.

"Run off? I don't run off."

"Sure you do. It used to be worse—you used to pack up and split like a bat out of hell. At least you hang around to talk to me a little now."

Connor turned away to place his violin in his case, hiding his blush. "I go to read or study, mostly."

"To study?" Ray's eyes brightened. "Perfect. Max and Kaden and I are meeting up at the Treehouse tonight for a mini study session. You should come."

"Uh…" Connor loosened his bow. "I usually go to Alderman library to study."

"Alderman? Why go all the way over there?"

"Because it's closer to Brown. That's where Rebecca and all the rest of my friends study, so…"

"Huh." Ray came around to stand in front of him. "I bet you they'd give you a night off, though."

Connor gathered his music. "Yeah...but I should let them know first, I guess."

Ray's hand was back to its touching, this time along Connor's forearm. "Okay, so call 'em and let 'em know. We'll meet in like half an hour, okay? See ya then!" He gave Connor's arm a little squeeze before departing.

Not sure whether to be flattered or wary of Ray's insistence, Connor obediently pulled out his cell phone to text Rebecca.

Ray wants me to go study with him and his friends.

A few seconds later he received her response: *Then you'd best get your butt over there and have a good time.*

Kaden's blue hair was easy to spot in a crowd. He and Max were seated next to each other at a booth, with Ray directly across from them, craning his neck toward the front door.

"Hey, Connor! Here we are!" Ray called out unnecessarily, waving his hands. "Did you bring your books?"

Connor made his way over and took a seat. "Yeah, I have a few chapters of anthro to read tonight."

"Cool. So, the rule is, we work for at least five minutes straight before we're allowed to talk."

"Oh...okay." Connor nodded slowly. He'd never had rules for a study session before. "And how long are we allowed to talk for?"

"No limit on the talking." Kaden chuckled. "The first rule just ensures that we get at least five minutes of work done before we start fooling around."

"Fooling around," Max repeated wistfully. "That's what I'd rather be doing right now, instead of reading this chemistry text."

"That can be arranged," Kaden said, and a second later Max let out a yelp, jumping around in his seat.

"Hands to yourselves, boys. We're in public," Ray admonished.

Kaden put up both arms innocently. "I am the very model of propriety."

"Sure you are." Max snatched one of Kaden's hands and held it in his lap. "I'll get you for that later, just you wait."

Heat rose in Connor's cheeks. Something about seeing Max and Kaden act like...like such a *couple* made him uncomfortable. Was it jealousy, or some buried issue regarding self-acceptance? He wasn't sure.

"Promise me you won't let the boys scare you off." Ray gave his leg a gentle pat. "I'll keep 'em in line."

Connor shook his head as Ray's warm smile dragged him from his thoughts. "I won't."

They got in about fifteen minutes of studying before Max started nipping at Kaden's ear, and Ray ordered them to get a room. That led to a discussion about what their rooms had looked like at various stages of childhood, and after transitioning into embarrassing confessions of boy-band crushes, they decided to call it a night.

They grabbed smoothies on their way out and took their time walking to the Alderman first-year dorms. Connor naturally fell into step beside Ray while Max and Kaden locked hands a few paces in front of them.

"Hope it works out for them this time," Ray said with a gentle shake of his head.

"This time?" Connor took a long drink of his smoothie to avoid the stares Max and Kaden received from at least a few passersby.

"Yeah, they're sort of on again, off again. You know how it goes. But I think they're a good couple, as long as they quit being stubborn long enough to see it."

"Oh," Connor mumbled. "I didn't expect that. They seem so happy together."

"Yup. But all relationships require work."

Longing tugged at a loose thread of Connor's heart. *If only Jared could have…*

"So, Friday, after the play…I was thinking we should go out to celebrate," Ray continued.

"Oh." Connor latched onto the distraction. "With Max and Kaden?"

"Actually, I could kinda use a break from them. I was thinking just you and me. Thought maybe we could grab some frozen yogurt at Arch's."

"Uh…yeah. Okay."

Ray grinned coyly and finished off his smoothie. "Just so we're completely clear on this, I'm asking you out on a date."

"Oh." Connor stopped walking, rapidly swallowing a lump of icy fruit, and a bout of brain-freeze stabbed him right between the eyes.

A date. A real date. His *first* real date. He tried to access his possible feelings for Ray, but all he could really get at was raw excitement. Someone *wanted* him, and it felt so very, very nice to be wanted.

A gust of wind blew past, creating goose bumps on his bare arms. "Yeah." He smiled at the remainder of his smoothie. "I get it."

"Cool," Ray said.

Max and Kaden turned to wave goodbye as they headed up the path to their dorm, but Ray hung back. "Guess I'll see you tomorrow evening, then."

"Yeah, okay."

Ray took a step closer. "I'm glad we got to spend some time together."

"Um, me too," Connor agreed quietly, and before he knew what was happening, cold lips met his for an abrupt kiss.

"Goodnight, Connor."

With one last flirtatious glance, Ray took off, leaving a stunned Connor in his wake.

CHAPTER NINETEEN

Strange, dear, but true, dear,
When I'm close to you, dear,
The stars fill the sky,
So in love with you am I

The lyrics still hit Connor, setting off an ache in his heart, but the feeling was not quite as piercing as it had once been. The adrenaline rush from performing for a sold-out crowd insulated him, and the notes absorbed the emotion as he played.

Ray leaned in during the applause, his thumb resting on the back of Connor's neck. "Nailed it," he whispered.

Ray's voice made him nervous. Not in a bad way, entirely, but not in a familiar way, either. It didn't create the same feeling Jared's voice had—that odd mixture of safety and comfort, touched with just a hint of danger at the same time.

But was he even supposed to feel the same way? Maybe those kinds of emotions could only be experienced once.

Another faint wave of sadness lapped against his consciousness, and he gave Ray a smile before returning his eyes to the stage.

As usual, Lilli and Fred tormented each other, verbally sparring in denial of their love while revealing their true feelings through soliloquy and song. After a series of comical turns, they finally capitulated to their undying romance, and the audience broke into wild applause.

"I'm gonna say hello to my friends," Connor yelled to Ray over the ruckus created by the final bows. The audience's appreciation was more enthusiastic than he was used to, adorned with whoops and whistles one didn't often find in a classical music hall.

Ray nodded and turned to high-five another brass player, and Connor took off. He darted through the advancing crowd, feeling sleeker in the all-black ensemble than he ever had in his orchestra tux. Rebecca and Tate were only three rows out, and they waved cheerfully as he approached.

Before he could reach them, a wrinkled hand dropped down on his arm, forcing him to stop.

"That was just lovely, young man," an unfamiliar woman said. "Absolutely lovely. You're a truly gifted violinist."

He struggled to make the appropriate eye contact. How had she recognized him? He'd thought he was supposed to be unnoticeable in the pit, dressed in black and shrouded in darkness...but it seemed people were noticing him more now, whether he liked it or not.

"Oh, uh, thanks." His voice was weak, but at least it was something. She patted his hand one last time before departing.

"Oh, wow, Connor," Rebecca said as she and Tate reached him. "The play was awesome! I wish I'd joined now...maybe next session. Unless of course you don't want me hanging around you all the time."

Connor rolled his eyes, bumping fists with Tate in greeting. "I sorta liked being the only violinist. Maybe you could take up viola?"

Rebecca made a gagging noise, strangling her own throat.

"All right then, Connor, awesome show." Tate interrupted her antics with a laugh. "We're gonna get going now."

"Right, right!" Rebecca nodded, clasping her hands together. "We are gonna get going, because you're *busy* this evening." She made no move to leave, though, even as Tate threw his arm around her shoulder to lead her away. She just kept staring at him with a big, goofy grin.

"Ahem." Tate yanked a little harder. "Leave the man to his business."

She still didn't move, and Tate finally resorted to curling a hand around her waist and pulling her out, comedy-routine style.

"Call me!" she shouted as she disappeared through the door.

Shaking his head with a soft chuckle, Connor returned to the makeshift pit. Most of the other musicians had gone backstage by then, probably making plans to head to one of the many after-parties thrown by cast and crew. Luckily for him, he had a perfectly acceptable excuse for skipping out.

He'd just rested his violin on the crushed velvet inside his case when the hairs on the back of his neck stood on end. Footsteps had approached but not departed. Someone was watching him, hovering only inches away.

"You were really good tonight," Jared said.

Connor whirled around to face him. *Jared? Here? Now?*

"I liked that I could hear just you, you know? When I was at that concert...well, I could see you, but I heard like fifty violins at once."

Nodding out of reflex, Connor went to secure the neck of his violin with its Velcro strap. His hands trembled and it took a few attempts before he got it right.

Jared shuffled his feet. "Um...so, I wanted to..."

Arms enveloped Connor from behind and a chin came to rest on his shoulder. "Okay, lone violinist, ready for our date? I stashed my horn under the stage, so we can just drop off your violin and go."

Jared's eyes widened as they shifted over to Ray's face, and then his expression went completely blank.

"Uh…" Connor twisted toward Ray, who seemed to have no idea he'd interrupted anything. "Yeah, j-just give me a minute, okay?"

But when he turned back around, Jared was nowhere in sight.

"Yeah, sure. Whaddaya need to do?"

Connor fumbled with the zipper on his case. "Um…nothing. Never mind. Let's go."

He followed Ray out into the warm night air, his mind spinning into overdrive.

Why now? Why had Jared picked this night, of all nights, to show up? And what could he possibly have wanted?

Connor didn't speak as they approached his dorm, even when Ray threw a couple of odd looks his way. He couldn't think of anything to say, still trapped in the shock of seeing Jared again.

"So…everything went really well tonight, didn't it?" Ray broke the silence.

Connor glanced up and realized they'd reached his building. "Hey, wait here, okay? I'm just gonna drop off my case." He didn't give Ray a chance to object before sprinting away.

Grateful for the time alone, he bolted into his room and tried to get himself back on track. Jared probably wanted to give him some sort of lame "no hard feelings" apology, which, he told himself firmly, he did *not* want to hear. Ray was a great guy, and he was waiting downstairs, offering him a chance at an honest-to-goodness, above-board *relationship*. He couldn't afford to look back right now.

Get it together.

He slammed the door to his room when he left. Too bad he couldn't slam the door to his past as easily.

"Hey, I'm back," he announced as he came upon Ray, a little breathless from running.

"Yes, you are." Ray looked relieved. "Off to Arch's then?"

"Off to Arch's."

***

"I thought Jenny was totally gonna blow it when she missed that cue," Ray said, scooting a couple inches forward in line. The frozen yogurt spot was packed, as always. "But she did a really good job recovering, don't you think?"

"Jenny?" Connor cast a few sidelong glances at the white tiled floor and at the tables and booths that sprung up from it. No one he knew was there—just as he'd expected, since he didn't exactly know many people. "Which one was she again?"

"Seriously? You never learned their real names? She plays Lois."

"Oh." He shoved his hands into the pockets of his slacks. "Well the director was always calling them by their part names, so that's all I've ever known."

"Didn'cha ever talk to them offstage? Jenny's a real darling."

Connor bit his tongue. No, of course he never talked to them offstage, and he couldn't really think of a clever reason to explain away his antisocial behavior. Jared's voice still echoed in his head. *Um, so...I wanted to...*

"Earth to Connor." Ray waved a hand in front of his face.

He blinked his way back into the conversation. "Oh, sorry. Didn't mean to zone out there. I think maybe the play wiped me out."

Ray grinned knowingly, tapping his fingers against the metal rail that bordered the line. "First date, huh."

The words doused Connor with a cold shot of reality. He was on a *date*. "Is…is it that obvious?"

"Sorta, but don't worry about it." Ray chuckled. "I promise, no crazy public displays of affection."

Connor's eyes widened. He hadn't thought about having to face *that*. "But um, non-crazy ones?"

"Well, sure. Like, I might want to put my arm around your shoulder."

Ray did, and standing close like that, Connor could see he was only an inch or so shorter than him.

"That okay?"

"Um, yeah." He mustered a smile. "That's fine."

Ray paid for both their selections and found them a small booth in the back. He had to drop his arm from Connor's shoulder to sit across from him, and Connor found himself sighing in relief.

"So…" Ray searched his face as they dug into their treats, openly studying him. "You gotta tell me some more about yourself. You're a quiet sort."

"Yeah, I guess," Connor admitted. He stared back at Ray, because it somehow seemed like it would be ruder to look away.

And Ray was fairly nice to look at, with small but proportional features. But no matter how hard he fought it, comparisons to Jared streamed through his mind—especially since Jared's dark and rugged looks were currently fresh in his memory. *Jared's so much taller. His hair is a nicer color. Maybe Ray shouldn't bleach his ends like that…*

"Well, I'm all ears now, so you'll have to tell me something."

Connor scooped some vanilla yogurt mixed with Heath bars into his mouth. "There's not that much to tell. I have a sister, I'm from Manassas, I'm a violinist, which you know…and my parents want me to go to law school."

"Oh yeah? I've been thinking about law. I'm an only child, though. My parents' pride and joy."

The opportunity to turn the spotlight onto Ray was a welcome one. "So, do they care that you're...gay?" Connor whispered the last word, darting his eyes around to make sure no one was near enough to hear.

Ray shrugged and licked his spoon clean of chocolate soft-serve. "They're adjusting. Told 'em back during my junior year, so they've had a while to get used to it. Weren't too thrilled at first, but there's not much they can do about it. I'm just gonna prove to them that being gay won't hold me back, and they'll be forced to accept me or wind up childless."

Connor frowned. "You say that so casually. Wouldn't it bother you if your parents turned their backs on you?"

"Of course it would. But I know who I am, and I can't change that for them." Ray pursed his lips. "Hey, this is getting sorta heavy for first-date talk. Let's get back on track." He leaned in so he could rest his hand on Connor's. "Can I try a bite of yours?"

"Sure." Connor pushed his cup forward, but Ray bent over the top of the table and sucked the frozen yogurt right off his spoon.

"Mm, I love Heath bars." Ray completed his swallow with a slow-motion licking of his lips, and Connor laughed.

"What, the seductive moves not doing it for you?" Ray feigned a hurt look. "Nah, man"—he stopped to giggle—"I'm not that cheesy. Unless you want me to be."

The only thing Connor could do was blush. Flirtation skills were not in his extremely limited social repertoire.

Ray seemed to take that as a good sign, though, because he straightened up with a satisfied smile. "You like it, just admit it."

"Huh, sure." Connor forced a chuckle. "You can finish it all off, if you want." He lifted his spoon to offer another scoop, praying he sounded cute or coy and not just plain ridiculous, like he felt.

"Maybe we should save some of that for when we get back." Ray winked, sending Connor into panicked silence once again. Ray just wasn't going to let him gain the upper hand.

A group of thin, sharply-dressed guys walked past the table, capturing Ray's attention. It was a relief to be off the hook for a moment—until two of the boys stopped abruptly to give him a once-over with their eyes.

"Hi, Ray," they both said, seconds apart.

"Uh, hey, guys." Ray gave them a stiff tip of the head in greeting. "This is Connor."

The two interlopers nodded, returning to a visual appraisal of Connor that had him twisting in his seat.

"Oh, he's cute," one said, smirking, and they both left to rejoin their group.

Sure he was near fire-engine red, Connor tried to cool off with several spoonfuls of yogurt. "Friends of yours?" he asked after recovering.

"Sorta." Ray shrugged.

"Were either of them…exes?"

"Yeah, kinda."

"Which one?"

"Uh…both, actually." Ray drummed his fingers on the table. "But not at the same time," he quickly added. "And we didn't really date…just sorta fooled around."

"Oh." Connor dug into his cup for a distraction.

"That doesn't bother you, does it? I mean, it was way back in the beginning of the year, and only a couple of times." Ray's cheeks turned pink as he looked on, waiting for a response.

Fooled around. That meant Ray was probably far more sexually experienced than he was…or than even Jared, for that matter. Still, it didn't mean Ray wasn't a good guy. In fact, maybe all that experience was a selling point. Maybe

Connor could benefit from it…if he could just get over the gut reaction of panic the thought caused.

His spoon hit bottom, and he no longer had anything to hide behind. "N-no, of course not."

"Good." Ray finished his yogurt off in a few large mouthfuls. "Anyways, I say we blow this joint. It's getting too crowded."

Connor stood and Ray came around to his side of the table, returning the possessive arm to his shoulder. "But just so you know, I'm really hoping the date's not over yet."

As they walked back to campus, Ray's arm gradually made its way from Connor's shoulders to his upper back, and from there to his waist, where it remained.

"I heard Jenny's madly crushing on Evan—uh, that's Fred, for you." Ray easily led the conversation. "But he's been dating the girl who plays Lilli for a month now."

"Maybe that's why their love scenes are always so touching," Connor remarked.

Ray scoffed, blowing his frosted tips off his forehead. "Nah, I betcha the lovey scenes're what made 'em *think* they'd be good together. They have no chemistry off stage."

"Oh." Connor nodded, though he really wished them the best. They'd reached the hill leading up to his dorm and he drew to a stop. "Guess we're here."

Ray grabbed his hand. "Yeah, we are. You gonna invite me up?"

"Oh, um, sure. Did you want to…to watch a movie or something?"

"Watch a movie? Sure, if that's what you want." Snatching his other hand, Ray pulled him into an embrace.

As they stood only inches apart, Ray's chocolate-sweetened breath washed over Connor's face—an unfamiliar sensation, since Jared had been so much taller than him.

"You know what else would be fun?"

"Hmm?"

The place where Ray's arms rested on the small of his back also felt strange, as did his much less-muscled torso.

Stop comparing!

"This." Ray leaned in for a deep kiss.

Connor made his lips move responsively, but he felt clumsy and out of practice. Besides, Ray's tongue didn't dart around the way Jared's did, instead taking a much a slower path, in and out, and in and out again.

Ray finished with a gentle peck, pressing his body in so there was now hardly any space between them. "So, we going up?"

"Um...uh, I...I..."

"Easy." Ray slid his hand down to Connor's butt. "We can do whatever you want, as much as you want or as little as you want. No pressure. I know you're probably new at this."

Connor stared at Ray's parted lips, which were pinker now than they had been earlier. He knew what they offered...but after a second, he also knew he couldn't accept. Even if his mind hadn't been filled with comparisons to Jared at the moment, he just wasn't ready.

For once, though, the truth seemed to have the potential to help him out. "It's not that. It's just...I got out of a relationship fairly recently...and I'm just not...not gonna be ready for...*that*...anytime soon."

Ray's look darkened. "Did he hurt you or something?"

"No, no. I mean, n-not like that. I just wouldn't want you to feel like...like the rebound guy or something."

Ray let out a sigh as he ran his hands up and down Connor's back. "Connor, I like you a lot. If you tell me I'm not the rebound guy, I think I can trust you." Without giving him time to respond, Ray occupied Connor's mouth with another lengthy kiss.

Cold fear set in as the bulge of Ray's erection pressed into his dress pants. "I'm s-sorry, Ray. I l-like you, b-but I…I…"

"Okay, easy, easy." Ray backed up, a tiny frown pulling at his lips before he switched to a smile. "I get it, you're not ready yet. My bad. Why don't we just rewind to the part where I kiss you goodnight?"

Near dizzy with relief, Connor nodded. "Th-that would be great, thanks."

"Okay." Ray moved in for a quick peck. "I'll see you tomorrow at call time, all right?"

"Y-yeah, see you tomorrow."

Ray stepped away and took off down the path, hands in his pockets and shoulders slumped.

Connor headed for his room, his insides still quaking. He reached the second level of the stairwell before someone grabbed his wrist and yanked him back, jolting his shoulder so forcefully he almost cried out.

Surprise overcame the pain at first, and he swung around, fully prepared to tell Ray he needed to be much gentler when dealing with a string player's arms.

But he should have known Ray's grip would never be so strong.

"You kissed him!" Jared spat, showering him with drops of saliva. His eyes were bloodshot, and from where he stood a few steps below, his alcohol-tainted breath wafted close enough to make Connor step back for air.

"W-what?"

"You kissed him!"

Connor shook free from Jared's grip and continued toward his room, heart pounding so hard he could feel it in his throat. "Jared, what are you doing here?"

"You fucking *kissed* him," Jared announced yet again, just as a neighbor poked his head into the hallway. The boy gave them a surprised look, and Connor frantically pushed his keys into his lock to get out of public view.

He opened the door and Jared barreled past, tossing off a backpack before flopping onto the bed. Connor fell back against the wall and stared at him, waiting.

Finally, Jared met his gaze. "Are you...in love with him?" The anger was gone now, his voice sunken into a hoarse, emotional whisper.

As dramatic as the situation felt, Connor erupted into a startled laugh. "Um, it was our first date."

"Mm." Jared stood and began taking off his clothes.

"What are you doing?" Connor remained frozen by the door.

"Don'think I can make it home," Jared slurred. He tripped over his pants as they sank to his ankles and rolled onto the bed with a muffled, "ooph."

Connor placed a hand to his temple. "How did you know he kissed me? Were you...watching me or something?"

"Was waiting for you," Jared said, then hiccupped. "Was drinking a little while I waited."

Connor took a few steps forward and retrieved Jared's backpack from the floor. Something inside sloshed around, and he opened it to find a half-empty bottle of vodka. "I think it was more than a little."

"I'm not little," Jared said.

Connor sighed and stepped closer. "Why were you waiting for me? What did you want?"

"I want..." Jared trailed off. Suddenly, and with surprising agility for someone so intoxicated, he bolted upright and pulled Connor onto the bed.

Connor tried to back up, but Jared locked him in place with an arm around his chest. He stopped struggling after a moment, a mental fatigue setting in as the adrenaline from Jared's unexpected appearance wore off.

"I want you to stop seeing him," Jared said.

"What? That's...you...you can't ask...y-you have n-no right—"

Jared laid a heavy hand on Connor's mouth, pushing it into his lips. "Shh. Shh, baby. It's okay."

Exhausted and overwhelmed, Connor squeezed his eyes shut. "What's okay, Jared? I don't understand. Why…why are you here?"

"Shh," Jared repeated, clumsily brushing Connor's cheek with his thumb. "It's okay, baby. It's okay." He leaned into Connor's lips until their mouths touched, but didn't kiss him. He just rested there, breathing heavy, liquor-laden breaths.

"J-jared, I—"

"Shh, baby. I love you."

Connor's mouth fell open, his own breath coming to a sudden stop. Words he'd never even dared to hope for rang in his ears, but all he felt was a confusion so deep it made his vision blur.

Or maybe that was because he'd forgotten to start breathing again.

He sucked in a mouthful of air. Even if he *did* figure out his emotions, the situation was so far from ideal it was almost laughable. A drunken declaration was hardly the stuff dreams were made of.

As if to emphasize the thought, Jared started to snore. Saliva trailed from the corner of his mouth and pooled on the pillow.

Connor retreated to the empty bed and curled up on his side to watch Jared sleep.

CHAPTER TWENTY

He awoke slowly, peeling back layers of dreams—dreams of Ray's lips sliding over his, and of Jared's much more familiar ones whispering *baby* in his ear. It almost seemed like the night's strange events could have been a dream as well, but the first thing Connor saw when he opened his eyes was Jared splayed out across his bed, arms and legs flung wide like he'd just landed there after falling from some height.

Jared was still snoring, but it was softer now. Didn't look like he'd be getting up anytime soon.

Connor stood and dressed. He kept a nervous eye trained on Jared the entire time, as though he were some kind of sleeping bear that might suddenly roar back to life. But Jared barely moved, and eventually he sat down at his desk and tried to clear his head enough to come up with his next course of action.

Throw Jared out? Demand an apology? Interrogate him until he dredged up exactly what it was Jared thought he was going to accomplish by this stunt?

And then there were those three pesky words—words he'd never expected to hear, words he couldn't trust, given Jared's intoxicated state. But was there a chance a kernel of truth lay behind them?

He sunk his head down and clipped his temple on the edge of a politics textbook. Rubbing the sore spot, he eyed the haphazardly piled books that littered his desk. He hadn't really been keeping his room in the best condition, partly because he spent less time puttering around in it than he used to.

Maybe it was time to straighten up. At least it would give him something to do.

He pushed back his chair and grabbed a couple of books to place on the shelf, glancing over at Jared as he went. Jared still hadn't moved.

Impatience was beginning to get the better of him. Sure, he could probably use the time to plan out what he was going to say when Jared awoke, but how much longer was he going to have to wait? He'd just get more anxious as time went on…and turn into a stuttering mess when they finally did get a chance to speak.

He lifted another book to put away, but instead of placing it gently, he brought it up over his head. Eyes still on Jared, he released his grip and let it crash onto the shelf. Jared didn't stir.

Annoyed, Connor picked another, heavier book and repeated the process. Still nothing.

Soon he was grabbing all the books from his desk—even ones he'd already put away—and slamming them down, one after another. Jared flinched a couple of times and he redoubled his efforts, adding a chorus of opening and closing drawers for good measure.

"Mm," Jared whined. He dug his head into the pillow. "What's all that noise?"

"I'm cleaning up." Connor sat innocently at his desk.

"Oh. Do you have any aspirin?" Jared peered over with bleary red eyes.

Connor tossed a bottle to him and watched silently as he swallowed a handful down dry.

A minute passed before Jared spoke again.

"I'm such an idiot."

Yeah. But the word wouldn't come to Connor's lips.

"It's just...I didn't get a chance to talk to you at the play, and after you left...well, I made a really stupid decision, obviously."

Obviously.

Jared sat up slowly, squinting in pain. "I've wanted to talk to you for so long now—"

"For so long?" A burst of indignation finally spurred Connor to speak. "I saw you the other day and you acted like you barely remembered who I was. Seemed to me like you didn't want anything more to do with me."

Jared let out a bitter laugh. "Jesus, Connor. You're way off. I haven't been able to stop thinking about you. I wanted to come talk to you sooner, but I just...couldn't work up the guts."

Raising his brows, Connor leaned forward to rest his elbows on his knees. "*You* couldn't work up the guts to talk to *me*?"

"Irony." Jared gave him a wry smile. "Gotta love it."

They fell silent again. To keep from meeting Jared's eyes, Connor focused on a beam of sunlight that streamed in through the window, illuminating Jared's dark curls. Eventually Jared got up and pulled on his clothes. When he was finished he sank down on the other bed, pushing his hair back with slow strokes of his hand. "So...I quit the team."

"What?" Connor snapped back to attention. "Why?"

"It was something you said, actually."

What? Connor stood and edged away from Jared, crossing his arms. "S-something I said? I never said—"

"About the kind of man my father was."

"I never—"

"He was a great dad...a great husband," Jared went on, his normally smooth voice marked by a tremble. "He was hard-working, and really responsible—he moved us into a smaller house when he got sick, so my mom wouldn't be in danger of losing her home...set up funds so me and my

241

brothers could all go to college…he made sure we'd all be taken care of, even after he was gone."

A tear slipped down Jared's face, but he quickly rubbed it away with his shoulder.

"Anyway, that's the kind of man I want to be—someone my family can count on. And to do that I think I need to start concentrating on my studies more. I gotta figure out what it is I'm actually gonna do with my life, you know?"

Connor nodded, on the verge of crying, too. Even with the anger that remained, seeing Jared in distress tore at his heart.

"I'll always love football, but I have just as much fun playing with my brothers, or my friends…hell, maybe even more fun."

"Yeah," Connor murmured, and another heavy silence descended on them.

A door opened somewhere down the hallway, and footsteps trailed past, growing softer and softer until they were out of earshot. More silence followed.

It was Jared who broke the quiet again. "So, the thing with that guy…is it…serious?"

"I told you last night." Connor shrugged uneasily. "It was only our first date."

"Oh." Jared bent over and fiddled with his shoelace. "Are you…going to keep seeing him?"

Connor opened his mouth to respond, but quickly closed it again. Was he? He paced a few steps away, stalling for time. Now that he'd been asked—and not ordered—he actually had no idea.

But he wasn't ready to admit that.

"Look, why did you come to the play last night? You said you wanted to talk to me—was it just about the football thing?"

"No."

"What then?"

"I came to tell you…" Jared stopped and closed his eyes, drawing in a deep breath. "I came to tell you…I made a mistake."

"A mistake?" Connor's arms shook as his pulse picked up, and he folded them tighter against his body to keep them still. "What was the mistake?"

"Letting you go."

The room spun a few times, white walls becoming a blizzard before they settled back in their places.

"Connor, I…I know I don't deserve another shot, but I miss you so much, and if we could just—" Jared stood slowly.

"Jared." Connor stopped him. Tears constricted his throat but he pressed on. "You…you really hurt me."

"I know, baby, I'm so sorry," Jared breathed out in a rush. He shot toward him with arms extended, but froze when Connor took a rapid step back.

Connor looked down to see his hands were up, palm out, as if to ward Jared away.

Why was he doing that? Slipping back into the relationship would be so easy, like putting on a comfortable, broken-in pair of shoes. If he took just a few steps forward, he could fall into the familiar—into Jared's strong, warm arms—just as he'd hoped.

But he didn't move.

"Things are different now, Jared. I'm…I'm out."

"Yeah." Jared worked his fingers into his pockets. "I sorta figured that last night. But I don't really think it has to make a big difference for…for us, right now."

Connor dropped his hands, and they curled into fists at his sides. Of course Jared didn't think it made a difference. It wouldn't if they never told another living soul what they were doing, slinking about in the shadows.

"Well it *does*, Jared." Bitterness turned his words into forceful jabs. "I'm not looking for someone to just have *fun* with."

Jared winced. "I said some stupid shit when we broke up. I don't even know why. I panicked, I guess. I felt like I was losing control…I just didn't realize how much I was going to like you."

Like. Not the other four-letter L word. No doubt Jared had forgotten he'd even said it. That was probably for the best, but it still fed the growing pit of resentment in Connor's chest. "You know, if you were out, you wouldn't have to settle for me."

"Jesus Christ!" Jared exploded. "You don't think I fucking know that?"

Connor gaped at him, and Jared clamped a hand over his mouth, shaking his head. "Fuck. I guess we know I shouldn't pick a career that relies heavily on public speaking. That came out completely wrong. What I meant was, I know there are other gay people in the world. I know I could…date them…or whatever, if I wanted to. But I don't."

He traversed the small space between the beds, stepping closer to Connor but keeping his hands jammed in his pockets. "I'm not going to lie to you and say convenience didn't have something to do with us getting together…but it's pretty damn far from convenient now. And no part of anything I've ever felt for you has been about settling. Maybe just the opposite, in fact."

Jared's eyes went glassy with the hint of more tears, and Connor loosened his fists, struck by the urge to reach out and comfort him. "Jared…"

"I can stop hanging out with Ronnie, if that's what it takes."

He blinked at Jared numbly. At one time such a suggestion would have thrilled him, but it no longer seemed to be the solution it once had.

"Please, baby," Jared whispered.

Connor closed his eyes, his heart racing. They'd reached the point where he'd have to make a decision, but he wasn't sure what he was going to say, even as he opened his mouth to say it. "Maybe—"

"Maybe?" Jared interrupted, his tone hopeful. "I can work with maybe."

"Maybe…maybe we should try being friends."

Jared's face fell, lips clamping into a grimace. "Friends? You just want to be friends?" His voice broke. "Don't you…don't you have feelings for me anymore?" A tear formed at the corner of his eye, teetering on the edge of his lashes.

What are you doing? A voice broke into Connor's head. *This is what you wanted!*

He reached out to grasp Jared's arm. "O-of course I do…b-but I just don't know if that's enough."

"What do you mean…enough?"

Connor stared at the place where his hand touched Jared, feeling Jared's body heat seeping into his skin. It made it hard to concentrate, and he had to draw his arm away so he could continue. "I get that you're not ready to come out, and I would never force that on you…but if we can't even be friends—the kind that hang out other places besides dorm rooms—then I don't see how we could ever have a decent relationship."

Jared swiped his eyes, catching the tear before it fell. "Oh."

"You know me, Jared. I have enough trouble getting out of this room as it is. I don't really need another excuse to hide away in here."

"Oh," Jared said again. "Yeah. Yeah, you're right."

What did that mean? Was there a chance they could work on a friendship? Or was Jared finally going to write him off for good?

Jared said nothing, but disappointment shone in his downcast eyes, and Connor had to look away.

Guess that's the answer.

His gaze drifted to the clock. "I have to go now. I promised Rebecca we'd meet up to practice for sectionals, and I'm late."

Jared nodded. "Right."

Connor turned away slowly, the tears he'd been keeping back fighting for release. *This is it. It's over.*

"Hey." Jared caught his hand and held it for a second before letting go. "Do you think we could talk some more later? Maybe you could call me when you're on your way back from practicing. We could meet up somewhere...grab coffee or something."

A mixture of fear and giddiness swept Connor as he was pulled back from the edge of despair. "Uh, yeah. Sure. I'd...I'd better get going now, though."

"Yeah, okay." Jared smiled, and the expression almost touched his eyes. "Duty calls."

***

Rebecca assessed him with one glance as he stepped into the practice module. "Who killed your cat?"

"Huh?"

"Did your date with Ray go badly or something?"

He'd almost forgotten about the date. "Uh, no, it was all right, I guess."

"Just all right? No sparks?"

He couldn't remember. "I'm...I'm not sure."

"Uh huh. Well, I wouldn't worry about that too much. Maybe they'll come later...or maybe they won't, and you'll move on. Either way, I just hope you know there are other people out there."

"Yeah." Connor sat heavily, pulling out his instrument and setting his music on the stand.

Rebecca gave him a searching look, but he warded her off by breaking into a scale. He played with rapid, powerful strokes, trying to keep his energy trained on the notes and not on the chaos of *what ifs* that had invaded his mind.

The technical warm-ups did hold his attention, but when they began to practice the more melodious *Bolero*, his thoughts inevitably wandered.

What was Jared doing right then? Waiting by the phone, perhaps? Maybe he was planning where they'd meet up for coffee. Would he choose one of the many places on campus, or the Starbucks down on The Corner? Either way, they'd be in public, surrounded by masses of other students.

"All right." Rebecca abruptly cut off her note, dropping her violin. "Out with it."

Connor blinked into her steady gaze. "Out with…what?"

"Whatever is going on in your head. And don't tell me it's nothing."

Caught, he thought sourly.

He tucked his violin under his arm, debating whether or not to tell her. It ended up being a quick decision—she'd figure it out anyway, either by persistent interrogation, or with her wily feminine ways. Besides, he'd need her advice sooner or later.

"Jared came by last night."

"Oh?" Rebecca said, her tone guarded. "What did he want?"

A tiny smile worked its way onto his lips. "Me, I guess."

"You?"

"Yeah. He wants to get back together."

Rebecca tugged on her ponytail, twisting it up in her hand. "I see. And what did you tell him?"

He could sense her disapproval, even if she kept her expression completely neutral. "I told him…we needed to see if we could be friends first."

Rebecca nodded slowly. "Uh huh. Well that's…a good start, I suppose. And what about Ray?"

"I…I don't know."

"Well if you're considering getting back with Jared, you should probably be truthful with him."

"I didn't say we were getting back together. I…I don't know what to do, honestly. What do you think?"

"Connor." She inhaled deeply, shaking her head.

He frowned. "You're not going to tell me, are you."

"Nope. I don't think it would do any good, anyhow. I think you already know what you're going to do."

"No, I don't."

Rebecca raised a skeptical brow. "I know how you feel about him. And I can already see it on your face."

She could? Was she reading him better than he was reading himself? "Look, I'm not rushing into anything. I know things might not work out…but you don't know him like I do. He's not some dumb jock—he's sweet, and caring…and…and…"

"And?" she prompted when he stalled out.

"And…he said he loved me. But he was drunk, so I know it doesn't count," he finished in a rush.

"That's right, it doesn't." Rebecca tapped her violin for emphasis. "Nor does it count immediately before, after, or during sex."

Connor sighed. "I know you're just trying to watch out for me. But…but if we can be friends—real friends—I just thought…I thought maybe there'd be a chance. I know he's not ready to come out, but if we could still do stuff together when other people are around, maybe…maybe then—" His voice rose in pitch as he spoke, and he cut himself off before he wound up an octave higher. "Crap. I have no idea."

"It's all right." Rebecca soothed. "Just take things slowly, okay? Don't make any hasty decisions. Promise me you'll think it through."

He released a shaky breath. "Yeah. I'm trying to."

"Good." She raised her instrument, plucking the strings with her pinky. "And he knows that I know, right?"

"He knows."

"So you can tell him, if he messes with you again...he'll have to answer to me."

Connor closed his eyes, tension fading as laughter escaped.

"Hey, quit laughing." Rebecca poked him with her bow. "I could totally take him."

"Yeah." Connor lifted his violin, ready to lose himself in the music again. "Yeah, I sorta think you could."

***

He left Old Cabell Hall with his cell phone in hand, but for some reason, couldn't bring himself to dial.

What was he getting into? *Think things through,* Rebecca had said. He forced his mind to attempt the task, his feet slowing as he reached the McCormick first-year dorms. The last time he'd been there, he'd been a walking zombie, embarrassing himself in front of Jared's roommate and friends.

Would things be any different now? He wanted to believe he'd changed—that he was stronger and more capable—but was he just proving himself a fool for considering Jared again?

Then there was the way Jared had looked at him that night, with anger, and maybe even a little fear. It didn't speak highly for their chances at a legitimate friendship. And what about the rest of Jared's friends? How would they react if they found out Jared was buddying up to an openly gay violinist?

Obstacles were mounting with each step he took, and he finally came to a stop. Maybe the whole thing was a pipe dream, and after dragging things out, he'd wind up even more devastated than before. Did he have the strength to withstand that? He wasn't so sure. And he didn't want to have to wait weeks to know if everything was going to fall apart—he needed to know *now.*

He started walking again, a frantic plan unfolding in his head. Instead of continuing down the road, he turned and took the path to Jared's building. He didn't know what he was going to say when he got there, but that wasn't really the point. The point was to see how *Jared* would react.

Real friends should be able to show up unannounced. If Jared was cold or distant after his arrival, then he'd know, right then and there, that they didn't have a chance. But if he was happy to see him, maybe told his roommate they were going to hang out...

He was just coming upon Jared's suite when a flash of movement caught his attention. The door swung out and Jared stood there, holding it open for Veronica.

"See you later, Ronnie." Jared's voice was tired but gentle, and he squeezed her shoulder as she moved past him.

Veronica paused, bringing a hand up to stroke Jared's face. Connor couldn't see their eyes from where he was standing, but it seemed they were staring directly at each other for a long, emotionally-charged moment.

Then Veronica leaned in and kissed Jared. Hard, and directly on the lips.

CHAPTER TWENTY-ONE

Connor whirled around and took off before even a second passed, a wild sob gripping his throat.

"Ronnie, what the—" Jared's voice reached his ears, but it barely registered as he was already at the stairs. "Connor? Fuck."

And then Jared's footsteps were after him, accelerating as he scrambled even faster to get away.

"Connor! Connor, hold up!"

Connor ignored him and ran on, his violin crashing painfully at his side.

"You don't actually think you're gonna outrun me, do you?" Jared clamped down on his shoulder, spinning him into a standstill.

Now that he was no longer moving, he felt the streams of tears traveling his cheeks. The urge to escape grew stronger and he twisted frantically to free himself from Jared's grip.

"Shit, Connor," Jared breathed softly. He brought his other arm down and lifted Connor by his shoulders, then pulled him behind the trees at the side of the building.

"L-let go of me!" Connor scratched out.

"Baby, please listen to me."

"No!" He tried again to break free, without success. "Y-you were kissing her. You were probably sleeping with her the whole time we were together!"

"Please, Connor." Jared gripped his shoulders so tightly it felt like they would crack. "I need you to listen to me. *She* kissed *me*...and I have no idea why she did that. Maybe it was like one last hurrah."

"What...what is that supposed to mean?"

Jared led him further along the side of the building before he spoke again, keeping his voice low. "I had her over today because...well, you were right. I don't think she understood things were really over between us, and I know how much that bothered you. I wanted to make it completely clear, so I told her there's no chance we'd ever be getting back together. I told her I wanted to be with someone else."

Too stunned to move anymore, Connor stood perfectly still as Jared lifted his high school football t-shirt and used the hem to wipe away his tears. Jared's well-toned abdomen was on display for a moment, and despite the whirlwind of emotions, Connor found himself getting aroused.

"A-and she accepted that?"

"Uh, I guess maybe not." Jared chewed on his bottom lip. "I mean, I thought she had, but we did spend a good portion of the conversation arguing. She kept bringing up all this random stuff, saying we were 'meant to be together' or some shit. That she'd been fucking told everything was going to work out between us—though I have no idea *who* would have told her that since as far as I know she's managed to push away most of her friends. And then the kiss...I don't know what that was all about...but after this, I'm just *done*. I'm done playing it nice, I'm done trying to be supportive. I don't know what the hell she's been smoking, but I don't have room for her in my life anymore. I need that room for you."

"O-oh." The last of the wild panic began to subside.

"You gotta trust me, Connor. I have never cheated on you, I swear. Please believe me."

Jared's chestnut eyes bore into his with an extra dimension of fiery conviction, leaving him momentarily speechless.

"I do," he finally responded. His knees wobbled, and Jared supported his weight by pulling him into a hug.

"Thank you. Thank you for believing in me," Jared whispered, rocking him gently.

The embrace was so warm and familiar that Connor instinctively leaned in. He burrowed his face into Jared's shirt, inhaling the scent he'd missed for so long. "I'm...I'm sorry I jumped to conclusions."

"It's okay. I don't blame you. I'm sorry you had to see that." Jared held him even closer. "When I saw you kiss that guy last night...well, it really sucked."

A chill of guilt ran through Connor, though another stern voice in his head—sounding suspiciously like Rebecca—reminded him he'd done nothing wrong.

"Hey." Jared reached out to brush back a piece of his hair. "What do you say we make a pact not to kiss anyone but each other from now on?"

Reality struck, and Connor pulled away. "Jared, I still think we need to—"

Jared yanked him close again, kissing the top of his head. "Sorry, I know. Friends."

This time Connor made no attempt to break away from Jared's arms. They weren't exactly out in the open, but they weren't completely hidden, either, and the risk of being caught made Jared's hold on him that much more intoxicating.

"What are you doing tonight?" Jared whispered into his hair.

"Um, I have the play, but nothing after that."

"Well, would you let me take you out for a late dinner? As friends?"

Connor's heart swelled with so much hope it nearly brought more tears to his eyes. "Uh, yeah." He nodded into Jared's shirt. "I...I should get going, then. I kinda have a paper to work on."

Jared dropped his arms with a grin. "There's the little bookworm I remember."

***

Connor arrived at his seat in the pit when the house lights flickered, at the last possible minute—on purpose.

His shoulders twitched as though they could feel Ray's questioning eyes boring into them.

"Cutting it a little close?" Ray murmured.

Amy raised her baton and the overture began, saving Connor from an awkward response.

He used the music to calm himself. Clear, predictable notes flowed as they transitioned into the opening number, and for a time, Connor drifted away from all the confusion in his life. He wove his song and tried to drink in the confidence that came through in his playing, hoping it would somehow be available after his fingers no longer touched the strings.

He was going to need it.

He let Ray grab him at the intermission and pull him backstage, just as the audience applause died down.

"Hey, I wanted to apologize about last night. I know I probably came on too strong, but you can't really blame me, can you?" Ray batted his lashes.

Connor's gut twisted. He looked around, hoping for a distraction—anything to delay the conversation he knew he had to have.

"Everything all right?" Ray stroked his palm with a thumb.

Connor pulled his hand away. "I...I have to tell you something."

"Yeah?" Ray lifted a worried brow. "Something wrong?"

"N-no...but I just felt like I should tell you this...to be fair."

"Tell me what?" Taking up a disinterested stance, Ray studied the fingernails of his left hand. "That you're not into me? Because I'm starting to get that vibe."

"It's not that."

What was it, though? He had no desire to lie anymore, but he didn't have solid answers, either.

"It's just...I told you I was with someone before, and I thought he was completely out of my life...but maybe he's not."

Ray took a slow, thoughtful breath. "You mean you're getting back together with your ex."

"No! I mean, I don't know. I don't know what I'm going to do. I just thought you should know I'm...I'm still trying to figure things out."

Ray nodded but continued staring at his hand as if he expected to find dirt under one of his immaculately clean nails. "Anyone I'd know?"

Connor shook his head.

"He's in the closet, isn't he."

"Uh...yeah. He is."

"Well good luck with that." Ray finally looked up, and despite the flippancy of the words, there was a softer expression in his eyes. "And just be careful. I've been there before—it doesn't always end up happily ever after."

"I...I know. And I haven't decided anything, but it didn't seem fair to keep this from you."

Ray shrugged, his buoyancy and self-confidence reemerging through a smile. "It's cool, man. You let me know if you figure things out...but I can't promise you I'll still be available."

"Of course not." Connor bit the inside of his cheek, feeling guilty at the relief that flooded him. "You're...really great, Ray. I don't want you think I don't like you—"

"It's all right, Connor." Ray put up his hands. "I get it. Wrong place, wrong time. But we should get back to the pit now. Amy was already stressing out when you showed up late, and I don't want to give the girl a heart attack."

Connor watched him tread off, his earlier relief darkened by a sudden realization.

Now there was every chance he'd wind up completely alone.

***

The brown station wagon sat waiting in the parking lot of the Student Activities Building, with Jared reclined leisurely against the open passenger door. He stumbled to life as soon as Connor approached and ushered him inside. "How'd it go? I wanted to see it again, but they were sold out."

"It went okay. About the same as yesterday."

"That's good." Jared jumped in his side, rocking the car. "Bet you're hungry, though. I picked a place out in Crozet—is that all right? It shouldn't take too long to get there at this hour."

"I'm fine, no rush," Connor reassured him, but Jared still drove slightly above the speed limit to the dark and sparsely developed Route 250.

Connor focused on watching his side of the road for any deer plotting to cross, and they were a good five miles in before he realized the car was strangely silent. Usually he felt responsible for such lapses in conversation, but when he glanced over at Jared he was pretty sure it wasn't entirely his fault this time.

Jared's jaw was locked, his upper body tense. He was obviously struggling with something, but he spoke up then as though he could feel Connor's roving eyes. "So, how have things been…with classes and stuff?"

"Um, good."

"Still doing the pre-law thing?"

"Uh, I guess."

"You don't seem too crazy about that."

"Yeah. Maybe not."

Jared drummed his fingers on the steering wheel as the forced conversation dried up.

Connor's never-too-distant anxiety crept up on him as he returned to his deer-watching. What if Jared didn't know how to relate to him anymore? What if he decided they had nothing in common—nothing left to share?

A moment later, he could have kicked himself for his selfishness. If he was really going to give friendship with Jared a try, then it couldn't be all about him.

"How about your classes?" he asked.

Jared shrugged, his shoulders stiff. "Eh. I let my grades slip a little, but I'll get back on track for finals I think."

Now Connor felt selfish and guilty.

"It's been sorta…tough…dealing with Ronnie. Trying to help her out while keeping her at bay, if ya know what I mean. I'm really glad that's going to be over with now."

Connor stared out the window and thought he saw a pair of almond eyes glowing from within the woods. "I guess it'd be rude to say I am, too."

"Nah." Jared shook his head. "It's not. I never meant to let her come between us at all."

It wasn't really about her, Connor wanted to add, but he kept his mouth shut.

They reached the first signs of civilization—a tiny strip mall with a few stores across the street from a gas station, and Jared pulled into a parking space. "We're here."

"Here?" Connor asked, raising a brow.

Jared pointed to white letters on a barn-style wood storefront that read *Crozet Pizza*. "It's supposed to be good."

"Well, they certainly have an original name."

Jared shot him a worried glance. "Did you want to go somewhere else? We can, if you like."

"No, it's okay." Connor tried to calm his nerves with a little chuckle. "I was just joking. I'm sure it's great."

"Seriously, I've heard they have like the best pizza."

"I thought Mellow Mushroom was supposed to be the best," Connor remarked as they entered, though he was surprised to find the restaurant fairly crowded. "You know, that place down at the end of The Corner?"

Jared's eyes darted away from his and dropped to the floor.

Oh. So maybe there were ulterior motives at play here.

"Wait, did you take me all the way out here because...because you didn't want anyone from campus to see us?"

Jared sank his head into his hands. "No. Yes. No. Shit...I came out here for a reason, but not because I'm ashamed to be seen with you."

"What then?"

An older Latina lady came to usher them into a booth and take their order, interrupting the conversation.

"You wanna get by the slice, or split something?" Jared asked.

"Sharing's fine," Connor answered quickly, eager for the interloper to leave so he could get back to his question.

"Cheese okay?"

"Sure. Whatever."

The waitress shuffled away after filling their drink orders, allowing Connor to return to his icy stare. "You were saying?"

Jared sighed. "I came out here because I thought it'd be easier for me to...to do date things."

"What?" Connor snapped his head back. "Jared, I told you—"

The waitress returned to drop off their sodas and they fell silent until she had departed.

"I know, I know." Jared jumped in before Connor had a chance to finish. "I guess I was just hoping...well, anyways, you don't need to worry. I was wrong. I think I feel even less comfortable out here. It was a stupid idea to begin with."

"What...what exactly did you think you were going to do?"

"I dunno. Sit close to you. Touch you. Hold your hand or something."

"Oh." Connor's cheeks warmed. Just what would he have done if Jared had pulled any of those moves? "S-so...why do you feel less comfortable here?"

Jared snorted. "Have you ever driven around Crozet? The people out here fly Confederate flags from their windows. I know that doesn't necessarily mean they want Black people to be their slaves, but it still sorta freaks me out."

"Well..." Connor scratched his head. "I guess I see what you're saying, but—"

"Oh, and the other day, Ben was out here doing a community service project and these old ladies gave him a really hard time about how he's not going to be 'saved,' because he hasn't accepted Jesus into his heart. I can only imagine what they'd think of gay people."

Connor stifled a chuckle. "Okay, so it's probably a good idea to be...cautious...but I wouldn't lump everyone into one stereotype. I mean, if you and I were our stereotypes, we'd probably have nothing to do with each other."

A smile eased onto Jared's features. "I guess. Well, then here's to breaking stereotypes." He raised his glass of coke and tipped it before taking a swig.

Connor grinned back, although underneath that expression was a tiny, wistful daydream of holding Jared's hand out in the open, where anyone could see. He quickly blinked it away.

Jared replaced his glass in the ring of condensation on the table. "You're different, you know."

"How so?" The pizza arrived and Connor leaned away.

"You don't…need me anymore." Jared shrugged. "Not like you used to. Guess that's why you're making things more challenging this time around."

"What does that mean?" Connor folded his arms defensively, even though the implication was perfectly clear—and true.

"I saw you with your friends…laughing, talking…looking so much more confident. And you're out now, too, which is good for you, I guess. I just mean you've come a long way."

"Oh." Connor blushed and directed his attention into removing a slice of pizza. The cheese trailed along the table, giving him an added excuse to avoid Jared's eyes as he dabbed it away.

"I'm proud of you," Jared added.

A lump formed in Connor's throat, and he swallowed a hunk of pizza to push it down. "Thanks, I guess. I…I owe some of it to you."

Jared scoffed. He picked at the crust of his pizza, but didn't eat it. "Why, because I broke your heart?"

"No," Connor responded immediately, although that probably did factor into it. "You…you were the first person I ever felt safe opening up to. You showed me that letting people see me could be a good experience. That I was missing out on things by being too afraid to risk my heart."

"So, are you afraid to risk it again now?"

Yes. "A little."

Jared nodded solemnly, his eyes sad but accepting. "Okay. Friends first, then, until you feel safe again."

***

Connor's ringtone woke him the next morning. He answered the phone groggily, coughing to force the raspy coating of sleep from his throat. "Hello?"

"You wanna come over to the quad and play Frisbee?" Jared asked.

Connor peered at his clock. Was it really almost noon? The emotional drain of the past few days must have tired him out more than he'd realized.

"Um…I dunno."

"Why not? What are you doing right now?"

Connor scratched at himself under the blankets. "Uh, working on a paper."

"Well an hour off is not gonna kill you. Come on, it'll be fun."

"Aren't you getting tired of me yet?" Connor rolled over and pressed his ear to the phone, like he'd done so many times before, just to feel a little closer to Jared. "You saw me like twelve hours ago."

"No, not tired yet. Won't be anytime soon, either. So, you coming then? Ben should be around in a little while. We could all hang out together and play."

Ben.

The image of Jared's roommate and his condescending smirk popped into Connor's head, with a flare of nervousness close on its heels. "To tell you the truth, I've always thought Frisbee was better suited to dogs than people. It's pretty mindless."

Jared's sigh filled the line and he cringed. He hadn't meant to sound so rude.

"Connor, how do you expect this friendship thing to work if you're afraid to hang out around my friends?"

"I'm not afraid!" Connor shot back, even as the jump in his pulse told him Jared had hit a nerve. "I just…don't care for Frisbee."

"Well it's not about the Frisbee. It's about hanging out, getting some fresh air…we could sit and talk for all I care. If you're really not afraid, then why don't you—"

"All right, all right." Connor kicked off the blankets. "I'll come. But not for very long—my paper is due this Wednesday and I haven't even written a word."

"I thought you said you were already working on it."

"I'll be there in like fifteen," Connor grumbled. "Bye."

***

"You're letting go too late," Jared said, apparently unmoved by the scowl on Connor's face. "It's like this." He released the neon green disc and it sailed through the air, slowly enough that Connor was actually able to catch it.

Connor threw it back, and once again, the disc shot wide. Jared dove for it anyway and grasped it as he fell. He landed on his side, still managing to make the move look graceful.

"That was better. At least I could reach it." This time, Jared launched the Frisbee from his position on the ground, and it ended up flying a little too high.

After a split second of consideration, Connor decided to lunge for it. People were watching—the first-year quad was always home to at least a handful of lounging students—and he probably hadn't imagined the snickers at his earlier failures.

Of course, he missed the Frisbee and wound up on the ground with a face full of grass.

He rolled over to stare at the sky, prepared for embarrassment or shame, but instead started to giggle. Jared trotted over to observe him with an amused expression, and the laughter grew so out of control he got stomach cramps. "I suck," he gasped out between spasms.

Jared grabbed the Frisbee and tucked it under his arm. "Yes, you do," he murmured, his eyes dancing. He pulled Connor to his feet. "There are some things you suck pretty well, in fact."

Connor groaned but couldn't stop the giggles—until Jared stepped closer, reaching out to brush a thumb along his cheek.

"You have a smudge of dirt," Jared whispered.

The air between them crackled, energy shooting out from the tiny space where Jared's skin touched his. Connor gazed up into Jared's eyes, and it no longer mattered that they were in full view of at least a half a dozen students, or that he was supposed to be maintaining a firm line of friendship. All he wanted was for Jared to grab him and kiss him deeply, like he had that very first time.

Rebecca was right. He didn't stand a chance against these emotions.

Jared brushed the dirt for a few more seconds, then kept his finger hovering by Connor's cheek. His lips tilted in a drunken-looking grin. "Connor, I—"

"Jared!"

Dropping his hand, Jared whirled to face his lanky roommate. "Yo, Ben. What's up?"

"What's up? *What's up?* Where the hell have you been? I've been trying to get a hold of you for like forever! Don't you know how to answer your damn cell phone?"

"Uh, I think maybe I left it in the room. Why?"

"Dude, Ronnie's been going around telling everyone that'll fucking listen that you're…that you're…that you're a…" He trailed off, his gaze shifting between Connor and Jared.

Connor's heart leapt into his throat.

"Jesus." Ben gasped. "The crazy bitch was telling the truth for once, wasn't she?"

Connor waited, suspended in shock, for Jared to deny it. For him to get angry, or laugh it off as a joke.

But Jared did neither; he just stared back at Ben with wide eyes.

"Wow, dude." Ben shook his head, pressing a hand to his temples. "Just…wow. That's…fucking nuts." Then he turned and walked away.

In the terrifying silence that followed, Connor opened his mouth, but only air came out. Had that really just happened? Everything Jared had worked so hard to keep secret, laid bare across the green grass of the first-year quad?

It took him thirty seconds to muster his voice. "Jared?" he whispered.

Jared spun around. "I have to get out of here," he said, and took off running.

CHAPTER TWENTY-TWO

When he could finally get his feet to move again, Connor sent them plodding toward his dorm. Thoughts crashed through his mind like so many forceful, final chords, and every step made him crave his previous shadowy existence that much more.

Because he knew what would happen now. Jared would hate him. He was to blame for placing Jared in the position to make a mistake—a mistake that had probably just cost him the only life he knew. And unlike Connor, Jared had actually *had* a life to begin with. He was the popular, good-looking, all-American boy. He was never meant to be a marginalized human being.

Jared would never forgive him.

A slumped figure by the entrance to Connor's dorm added his voice to the despair. "What took you so long?"

Startled, Connor jumped back. "Oh…I…I didn't know you were coming here."

"Where else could I go?" Jared stood and dusted himself off, then followed Connor into his room. He collapsed onto the bed and wrapped his arms around a pillow, burying his face there.

"Jared..." Tears gathered in Connor's eyes, hot and fast. "I'm so sorry, I'm s-so—"

"Don't," Jared growled.

"I never meant for th-this—"

"Connor, please stop. Just...just let me be right now. Do your work or something."

"B-but—"

"I said, stop." Jared rolled over to face the wall, effectively shutting him out.

For several seconds, Connor stared after him. He took in uneven gulps of air as he worked to keep the tears at bay. No one would comfort him if he did cry—and wasn't Jared the one who deserved the comforting right now?

But not from him, apparently.

After a few more wistful seconds, Connor sank down at his desk and opened his laptop.

In an hour's time he typed only a few disjointed notes. He flipped mindlessly through books, highlighting random phrases while the sentence *Jared's been outed and it's all your fault* streamed through his head like it was on an electronic marquee sign. After a while he could tell Jared had fallen asleep by the way his ribcage rose and fell with even breaths, but he still couldn't concentrate. He finally gave up and went to the only thing he could count on to grant him any relief. Without his bow, he tucked his violin under his chin and began wandering through familiar favorites.

He started out fast, his fingers just barely grazing the strings. When they tired, he went on to a few Hungarian dances, then shifted toward slower, sadder music. His hand trembled with a shaky vibrato, and after slipping into Barber's melodramatic adagio, he was forced to stop. The last thing he needed was more emotional fodder for his tears.

Jared stirred as he undressed. "Do you want me to move to the other bed?" he asked, his voice thick.

Connor sat on the edge of the mattress. "You don't have to."

With a grunt Jared scooted over to make room, and Connor lay stiffly beside him. Fear kept him from reaching out and making any physical contact. Instead he just whispered, "I'm sorry, Jared."

There was no response.

***

Jared didn't move an inch at the noise from the alarm clock, so Connor shut it off and snuck out of the blankets. He dressed for class and readied all his materials before dropping down onto the bed again.

"Hey," he said tentatively, then allowed his voice to grow a little louder. "Hey."

"What?" Jared yawned, but didn't turn around.

"It's…it's Monday morning. Are you going to class?"

Jared yanked up the covers. "I don't know. Probably not."

Connor's hand edged closer to Jared and he squeezed the sheet to keep himself from touching. "Jared, I'm s—"

"Stop apologizing. Go to class."

"O-okay." He took a few deep breaths. "Will you call when you leave?"

"Yeah, sure." Jared burrowed deeper into the blankets. "You should go now or you'll be late."

In other words, *stop bothering me and get out*. Swallowing his guilt, Connor did as he was asked.

By the last class of the day, he had his cell phone glued to his hand. It refused to ring, though, and every moment he stared at the blank screen just served to confirm his fears.

He'd probably never hear from Jared again.

Depression overtook the numbness, and he didn't realize class was over until people began tripping over his legs to exit the row. He followed the crowd, then stood out on the grassy Lawn and tried to come up with something to keep from sliding into complete desolation.

The answer came quickly, and he returned to his cell phone to text Rebecca.

You busy?

Doing a project w/ my film class till late. What's up?

Connor squeezed the phone until his palm hurt, cursing under his breath.

Nothing- it can wait.

Defeated, he trudged back to his room. It was nearing six in the evening when he opened the door, and found Jared exactly where he had left him at nine o' clock that morning.

Jared rolled on the bed to face him. "Hey."

"Hey," Connor responded automatically, blinking through his shock. "Have...have you been in here all day?"

"Nah." Jared stretched. "I left to take a piss a couple of times. Found your stash of Pop-Tarts, though, so I didn't have to go anywhere for food."

Connor almost cracked a smile, but the impulse quickly vanished. Panic took the place of surprise. What was he supposed to say next, now that Jared was actually speaking to him?

Useless ideas like *are you okay?* floated through his mind, but when he sat beside Jared, the first thing out of his mouth was, "Do you hate me?"

"Hate you?" Jared looked at him sharply. "This isn't your fault. I know that."

The words washed over Connor, and his lungs heaved out a breath he didn't know he'd been holding. *He doesn't hate me.*

Jared sat up. "I just…don't know what to do now." He blinked several times, his brown eyes darkened by fear. "What do I do, Connor? Fuck. I'm so fucked."

Connor snatched Jared's hand, forgetting his earlier concerns. He couldn't stare into Jared's face and not try to lessen his pain. "Everyone's always saying Ronnie's crazy. Why don't you just say she made it up? That she was pissed about you breaking things off?"

Jared's gaze drifted to the floor. "I thought of that."

A ray of hope shone through Connor's despair. Maybe things weren't as dire as they seemed. Maybe this could be fixed.

"But if I do that," Jared continued, "if I do that, it would be the end of…*us*…wouldn't it."

Connor's mouth dropped open. *Shit.*

"I mean, the friends thing…it wouldn't really work then. She might have told people about me being involved with you. And going back to the way things were before—"

"I'm sorry, Jared." Connor surprised himself by breaking in. "But I can't ever go back to that."

Jared sighed. "Yeah. I know." He rubbed his face with clenched hands. "What do you want me to do?"

"What do *I* want?" Connor repeated, brows drawing up. "This…this shouldn't be about what I want. It's your life."

"I know that. But…that guy, from the other night…he seemed nice. And he obviously has his shit more together than I do. If that's what you want, I wouldn't blame you. I'm sorry I came back into your life to screw it up. If that's what you want, Connor, if you want me out of the way…"

Moisture gathered in Jared's eyes, and Connor stretched his arm out, intending to take the sheet and soak up the tears before they had a chance to fall. But at the last second, he grabbed Jared's t-shirt instead and yanked him close. He had no idea if what he was doing was right—in fact, there was a good chance it wasn't—but suddenly it was the only thing he *could* do.

He connected with Jared's lips in an abrupt kiss, so forceful it was more like an attack. After a few seconds it melted into something softer, though, and when he finally pulled away, he could feel Jared trembling just as much as he was.

"No, Jared," he whispered. "That's not what I want."

Jared swallowed, his eyes held wide, probably to keep from blinking out the tears. "You know, I don't really think telling people she lied would work. And anyways, Ben already knows—"

It took every ounce of restraint Connor had not to shout from the joy that filled him. Without thinking, he pulled Jared into another hungry kiss.

His face was wet, but he wasn't sure if the tears belonged to him, or to Jared. Or maybe to both of them.

"Does that mean you're going to—"

"Stop," Jared commanded.

Connor snapped his mouth shut and backed away.

"No, listen." Jared grabbed him close again, pulling him down onto the bed. "I don't want to talk about it right now, okay? Not right now." He inched closer to Connor's lips, eyes desperate with an entirely different need. A need that spread to Connor like wildfire.

Even after all the time apart, he fell back into the negative space of Jared's form with complete ease. Urgency radiated from Jared's tense body, but for a while, there was nothing but lips and tongue, frantically reconnecting. They plunged into kiss after kiss, Connor's mouth starved for the contact it had been denied so long.

Except...he wanted more. Didn't Jared?

Connor tried to convey his readiness through his fingertips, clutching fiercely at Jared's shoulders. He received a few deep kisses for his effort.

That wasn't enough. His patience ran out, and he slipped his hand beneath the covers to find the button to

Jared's pants. Within a second, Jared was following his lead, warm fingers sneaking under the band of his khakis.

So Jared had just been waiting for *him* to make the first move.

They tumbled into a rhythmic grinding, and Connor took them both in hand. He coaxed Jared to the edge, panting with pleasure at the little grunt Jared let out when he came. His own cry was smothered in a heavy kiss.

Jared held him tightly, mingling the come between their bodies. He ran his fingers through Connor's hair, and for the first time in over twenty-four hours, the ghost of a smile crossed his face.

Connor returned it, tucking his head in against Jared's neck. He breathed in the sweat-moistened air caught there as the frenzied heat of passion ebbed away. Once it had left, though, doubts and fears rapidly took its place.

What was he doing? Everything about their relationship was completely up in the air, and he'd just succumbed to physical desires before taking the time to figure anything out. Where did they stand? Where would they stand tomorrow, in the light of day?

"Jared..." He invaded the post-orgasm silence. "We still need to talk about things—"

"I know." Jared breathed heavily against his hair. "I know this doesn't fix everything, but right now, I just want to hold you, Connor. Please. I just want to hold you."

Lips pressed against Jared's trembling throat, Connor nodded. "I guess we can talk about it later."

***

Connor awoke early the next morning, still wrapped in Jared's arms. He untangled himself and slipped off to the shower.

The water trickling from the cheap showerhead hit the floor in a steady *pitter-patter* rhythm, and he stood outside the cascade to create a simple accompanying melody.

Eventually he had to step into the stream, though, and the music vanished, allowing his thoughts back in.

Beyond the sexual intimacy, holding Jared had felt *right*. Different than before, but in a good way, as though some of the fronts they'd put up to protect themselves had been stripped, leaving them bare, yet safe. Everything else in both their worlds might have been upside-down, but he couldn't deny that connection.

Still, if Jared were really going to accept what Ronnie had forced on him, he had a difficult road ahead...and there was always the chance he'd decide he couldn't take it.

Connor scrubbed his scalp, fingers jerking erratically through his hair. He hated the feeling of powerlessness—as familiar as it was. He didn't want that in his life anymore.

As Rebecca might say, he needed a plan of action.

When he reentered the room, Jared was still asleep, his dark curls spread across the white pillowcase. Connor sat on the edge of the bed and ran his hand over the greasy locks.

"Morning." Jared rolled over, yawning. "You smell nice."

"That's 'cause I showered. You could take one, if you want."

Jared turned away again. "Subtle. Real subtle."

"Well aren't you going to get ready?"

"No." Jared muffled his reply in the pillow.

Connor kept stroking his hair. "Jared, listen. As much as I like having you in my bed...you can't live here forever. You need to get up and go to class."

"I don't know," Jared mumbled into the sheets. "I don't know if I can."

"Of course you can." The encouragement sounded false to Connor's ears. Did *he* even believe it?

"I'm serious." Jared flipped back around. "I don't know how to do this. My friends aren't like yours. You saw

272

how Ben reacted…they're not going to accept me. And I don't know how to be a friendless loser."

"I can give you lessons, if it comes to that," Connor suggested, which earned him a dour roll of the eyes. "But I don't really think it will."

"Sure, and you know that how?"

"I know that because I know you."

Jared puffed out an angry breath, then shifted to latch on to Connor's shorts, a mischievous quirk of his lips suggesting he might be changing tactics. "Let's stay in today. We could watch a bunch of movies, order delivery—"

"Jared…"

"What? We have a lot of missed time to make up for." He cringed. "That is, I mean, if you and I…I didn't mean to assume…but…are we?"

Connor rubbed his forehead and gave a one-shouldered shrug. "I don't know. We probably need to talk about it some more."

Jared's eyes drifted closed, his Adam's apple bobbing up and down a few times.

Oh, God. Connor stared at the quivering skin of Jared's neck, and his very poorly constructed walls of resistance crumbled. Who was he trying to fool? He didn't want to lose Jared now.

He leaned forward to peck Jared's lips. "Maybe…maybe we could call it a trial period or something? See how things go from here?"

"Yeah?" Jared's eyes flew back open. "Then why don't we curl up here—"

"I meant what I said before." Connor put up a hand to stop him. "You're not staying locked up in my room today. Trust me, it won't help anything. Get up and shower, and then we're going to class. You have astronomy first, right? I can walk with you—it's on my way."

"But…" Jared glanced around the room as if he hoped to find an excuse somewhere on the barren walls. "But I don't have any clothes to wear."

"You can borrow some of mine."

Now Jared shot him a look of utter disdain.

"What's wrong with that?"

"Borrow some of yours? I mean, I know people have heard I'm gay, but that doesn't mean I'm ready to parade around in teeny tiny clothes."

Connor scowled and grabbed his bathroom caddy. "I'll have something that'll fit you," he grumbled, thrusting the caddy in Jared's face. "Now go shower."

Jared ended up wearing his own jeans and one of Connor's t-shirts, which was a much tighter fit on his broader and taller frame. He tugged at the hem as they walked down McCormick Road, muttering about how he wasn't gay enough to want to show his midriff to people.

Their pace slowed as they reached the astronomy building.

"Do you have friends in this class?" Connor prodded gently, trying to distract Jared from his paranoid glances at the crowds around them.

"I have friends in all my classes," Jared retorted. "Or, had."

Connor ignored the revision. "Well just sit with them and act like everything is fine. Weren't you the one who told me you should be assertive even if you're not really sure of yourself?"

"That was different, Connor. That was…before."

Connor held his hands at his side to keep from actually giving Jared a push. "Just go sit with your friends. Maybe they haven't heard, or maybe they have and they don't care. You won't know until you try."

Jared took a few steps forward and then stalled out. "When are your classes over again?"

"I'll be done at two-thirty in New Cabell."

"Okay." He sighed. "I'll meet you there."

Connor watched him take off for the lecture hall, guilt moving in now that the immediate issue had been resolved. Was he doing the right thing, asking this of Jared? After all, if the roles had been reversed—if he'd been the one outed against his will—he wouldn't have been able to face the world so readily. But Jared...Jared should be able to handle it. He could handle anything. He was *Jared.*

Right?

Connor followed him inside, trailing a few feet behind where he wouldn't be spotted. Jared walked all the way down from the back of the hall and took a seat in the first row, dead center.

Somehow it didn't seem likely that was where Jared— and his friends—usually sat. But there was nothing else Connor could do for him now, and he was forced to make his retreat.

CHAPTER TWENTY-THREE

A chorus of *maybes* overwhelmed Connor's mind, leaving no space for the lilting voice of his politics professor. Maybe he'd pushed Jared too much. Maybe Jared had a legitimate reason for avoiding his friends. They probably weren't like Rebecca and the rest of her accepting crowd. Maybe everyone else would react like Ben. Maybe they'd scowl and sneer and point and laugh.

How much disdain could Jared take before his nervousness turned into resentment?

To make things more confusing, little grace notes of glee kept worming their way in between the darker thoughts. They carried with them fantasies of being a real couple—holdings hands, going on dates, perhaps one day kissing in public, without fear. But all that was probably a long way off—if it was even possible—and it wasn't right to be making plans when Jared was clearly so...*lost.*

None of Connor's fears were alleviated when he left class and found Jared sitting against the wall, his head in his hands.

"Jared?"

"Hey." He jumped up. "Ready?"

"How…how did it go?"

"Don't want to talk about it."

"But…did you see any of your friends? Did they say anything?"

"Yeah, I saw them. I saw them fucking whispering and giggling. Now can we please go?"

Jared took off, and Connor hurried to catch up. He squinted as a thought struck him. "You don't think maybe you're giving them more to whisper about by not talking to them?"

"You really gonna lecture me right now?" Jared shot back.

"No, I didn't mean…I just…never mind." This obviously wasn't the right time—though there was a chance he'd just given *himself* a marvelous piece of advice.

"Good. Then let's go back to your dorm."

Back to the dorm? Connor stopped walking. "Wait…this is when I eat lunch."

"Fine. Let's grab some food and go."

"In the dining hall," Connor specified. "With my friends."

"What?" Jared frowned. "Can't we just grab something quick at the Pavilion?"

Connor hesitated as Jared blinked on hopefully. Eating alone would mean they could talk more openly—that is, if he could get Jared to talk—and it would be the only way they could be *close*. Hands holding, skin touching, lips grazing…

But there was much bigger picture at stake than a few moments of cuddling.

"I never see Ben or Veronica or any of your friends at this hour, so I don't think you have to worry about a confrontation. But I'm going to eat lunch with my friends…and I'd really like it if you'd come with me."

Jared tried to stare him down, but he stubbornly held his ground. He could use a little normalcy back in his life.

"Fine. Let's get this over with."

Jared was all slumped shoulders and downcast eyes as they grabbed burgers and headed to the table. It wasn't like him. Jared didn't mouse around from one place to the next—he *strode*. Even knowing the cause, the change unnerved Connor.

"So who exactly is coming?" Jared asked, sticking several fries in his mouth as he spoke. That wasn't like him, either. Right now he seemed to be in a race to finish his food.

"Same people I ate with last semester. They're really cool, I promise. They're all fine with me."

Jared grunted in response and took a large bite of hamburger.

Tate, A.J., and Rebecca joined them a little while later—the boys with their usual pile of junk food, and Rebecca with her greens and soy products.

"Hey, Connor brought a newcomer," A.J. announced.

Rebecca blinked rapidly, as if to clear her vision, then began trying to make eye contact with Connor.

He avoided it. It wasn't like he'd be able to answer her mounting questions with a look.

Jared gave a brief nod but barely glanced up from the burger he was steadily consuming.

"Oh," Tate said, eyes alighting with recognition. "You're the football player Connor was tutoring, right?"

"Jared," Connor supplied.

Jared swung around abruptly to face him. "They don't know?"

"Um," Connor mumbled, and as he spoke all the other faces at the table also turned to stare at him in confusion. "No."

Jared set down his burger. "People I've never seen before in my life probably know about me by now, and your friends don't?"

Connor's cheeks heated as the conversation continued in full view of his bewildered friends. "It's okay, Jared."

"Is it?" Jared locked him in a steady gaze. "Really?" Then he looked over at Tate, a more characteristic glint of confidence peeking out from under the layers of nervousness. "I'm...I'm with Connor."

As vague as the statement was, Connor was pretty sure everyone understood. Only his shock kept him from letting out a joyful cry.

"Cool, man," Tate replied without batting an eyelash, and Connor had to rein in another spurt of emotion. He'd never been so fond of Tate as he was just then.

Rebecca was less smooth. Her eyes flew open and her jaw dropped, but luckily Jared had returned to sullenly eating his food by then.

"I'm going to get some more water." She downed the remainder of her cup and shot Connor a piercing look that obviously said, *come with me right this instant.* "Anyone else need a refill?"

Glancing at his emptied coke, Connor relented. "Yeah, sure. I'll come with."

Jared raised an eyebrow at him. He didn't have to speak to make it clear he didn't want to be left there alone for long.

Connor gave him a quick smile. "Be right back."

Rebecca pulled him away from the path to the soda machine before they even got near it. "All right, what on earth is going on? Yesterday you said 'nothing,' but *this* is definitely not nothing."

He took a deep breath so he could get it all out at once. "Jared broke things off for good with his ex, and I was there afterwards...and she must have seen us. She outed him to everyone."

"Oh my God." Rebecca whistled softly. "What a bitch. How is he taking it?"

"I'm not sure. I always thought he would hate me if this happened, but he doesn't seem to. At least, not yet."

"You think he'll change his mind?"

"I don't know. He's not really acting like himself. He's usually so confident about everything he does…he makes it look effortless. But right now it seems like…like he's…*afraid*."

Rebecca twisted her hair around her wrist as she nodded. "Give him some time. That little announcement was probably a good sign, though…and I take it that means you guys are back together."

"Yeah. I guess."

"Well, is that what you want?"

"I…I want to be with him, but I'm just scared about how he's gonna handle all this. Do you think I'm doing the right thing?"

She sighed and unraveled her hair, leaving it in a loose swirl. "I wish I knew what to tell you. You should always look out for yourself first…but he probably does need you right now. I bet he's freaked out that his control has been taken away—and he has a right to be. No one should have made that decision for him."

"It's my fault she saw us together."

"It is *not* your fault she's a bitch. And blaming yourself won't help anything, anyways. You're the one with experience being out—maybe you should just help walk him through it as much as you can." She gave his shoulder an encouraging squeeze.

Connor rolled his eyes. "Yeah. Like I'm so experienced."

"I bet you have more to offer him than you realize. He needs your support."

"So you're on his side now?" Connor let out a low chuckle. "Don't hate him anymore?"

"I never hated him, Connor. I was just trying to look out for you. If you love the guy, then I will too."

"No one said anything about love," he responded quickly. But his chest tightened and a stomach flip turned into full-on somersaults the second he saw Jared approaching.

"Hey, if you're done, you wanna get going?" Jared murmured, close to his ear.

"Oh, uh…" Connor turned back to Rebecca. She tipped her head and smiled. "Yeah, sure."

Jared gave Rebecca a polite nod and started to walk out.

Connor scrambled after him. "You okay?"

"Sure," Jared grunted. "Why wouldn't I be."

"I just wanted to make sure you were okay with…with what you said. With telling all of them. And I wanted to–" He cut himself off as a group of laughing girls passed by. "I wanted to thank you."

Jared shrugged. "They woulda found out anyway. What's the point of keeping it secret anymore?"

Connor's stomach completed another acrobatic feat, but this time it wasn't with that warm *possibly love* feeling from before. Maybe Jared was only with him now because of *what-was-the-point*. Because he'd been outed and he couldn't have the life he'd really wanted.

"Oh. Right. Well…uh, where're you headed now?"

"I dunno." Jared stopped walking to kick at a black scuff on his shoes. "I don't think…I don't think I can go back to my dorm right now. Ben's…Ben's…he's…"

"All right," Connor interrupted, for his sake as well as Jared's. *Insecure Jared* was like a chord with an out of tune note—grating on his already-frayed nerves. "You can stay with me tonight. But maybe we could stop by and get some of your things."

Jared released a sigh. "We should go now. Ben'll still be in class."

***

The redhead was sitting out in the suite when they entered. He looked over at them, one nostril creeping up as if he'd smelled something bad. Then he gathered his belongings and stalked back to his room.

"Stupid fucking ginger," Jared muttered under his breath. He stomped down the hallway and jammed his keys into his door. Two steps inside, another stream of curses left his lips when he tripped over a pair of shoes that had been left lying in the middle of the room.

"God damn slob." He grabbed a duffle bag from the closet and began angrily stuffing clothes into it, the veins on his neck bulging.

Connor inhaled deeply, working to suppress the queasiness caused by the open contempt. It didn't really take too long to conquer, mostly because it seemed like Jared needed comfort more than he did. "Don't let that guy get to you. He's like half your size."

Jared huffed and ripped a shirt off its hanger. The poor piece of metal bent nearly in half and clattered to the floor.

"You know you could take him in a second if you wanted to," Connor added, then tried for a smile.

Jared paused with a pair of boxers in his hand. "So then what do *you* do when people look at you like that?"

Though that was probably a dig at his size, Connor let it slide. "I...I guess I was already sorta used to people looking at me like I'm strange."

"So you're telling me it doesn't bother you at all?"

"I didn't say that. Of course it makes me uncomfortable...but I'm pretty used to that feeling, too."

Jared returned to his careless packing. "Well I'm not."

There didn't seem to be much hope of calming him down, so Connor sat in the desk chair to watch. He crossed his fingers and hid them under his thigh. *Please, let's just get this done.* Simple pack-and-go—no more confrontations. Maybe he wasn't as attached to the safety of his dorm as he'd once been, but right now they could probably both use a little peace and quiet.

The door swung open anyway, and Connor's teeth snapped shut on his tongue. Blood seeped into his saliva as he remained frozen at Jared's desk, one hand clutching his kneecap and the other smashed under his leg.

Jared turned on Veronica with a steely glare. "What the fuck are you doing here?"

"I'm here to visit my boyfriend," she responded, squinting around like she wasn't quite sure where she was. Dark circles nearly swallowed her haggard eyes, and greasy unwashed hair hung limply to her shoulders. She lifted one stick-thin arm to push a few strands off her forehead.

"Jesus Christ, Ronnie, are you insane?" Jared threw his duffel bag on the floor, where the clothes spilled out in a tangled mess. "We're not together! Even if you weren't a fucking lunatic, I'd never want to be with you. I can't believe you'd even show your face in here after what you did!"

"What I did?" Veronica stepped closer to him. "What do you mean? I just want us to be happy."

"Us? *Us?* There is no us, Ronnie. I'm *gay*, and you fucking know that!" Jared whirled around and gestured toward Connor with a harsh, jerking motion. "I want to be with *him!*"

With him. Finally, Jared had told her. Screamed it at her, actually. The burst of happiness was so intense Connor had to dig a nail into his hand to keep from jumping into Jared's arms.

Veronica tilted her head. "Oh. They told me, but I didn't think it was true. I thought they were lying. They lie all the time."

"Who told you what, Ronnie? What the fuck are you talking about? Why are you always saying shit that doesn't make sense?"

What *was* she talking about? A dull ache started in the back of Connor's neck, probably because he was so tense he'd barely moved a millimeter since Veronica had appeared.

She sat heavily on the bed. "I'm not sure. Did you want to see a movie?"

Jared thrust both hands into his hair, yanking at the curls. "Why did you tell everyone about me? To get some sort of revenge? Do you hate me that much?"

Veronica's eyes brimmed with tears. "I don't hate you. Why would you say that?"

"That's it!" Jared flung an arm toward the door and pointed fiercely. "Get out!"

Veronica hunched in on herself, quivering as giant tears slid down her face. "Don't hate me, don't hate me," she murmured through her sobs.

"Get out of my room right now! I don't ever want to see you again!"

The ache spread to Connor's skull. Something was wrong here. No conversation he'd ever observed from a safe distance had gone this way.

"Jared," he said quietly.

"I said get out!" Jared continued, lost in his tirade. "I want you out of my fucking—"

"Jared!" His voice erupted much louder this time.

Jared whirled to face him. "What? What is it?" he spat, eyes still blazing.

Connor looked back at Veronica. She'd been his enemy since first sight, but right now the only thing he could see was a pitiful, broken human being. Maybe she wasn't the evil seductress he'd always thought her to be.

"Stop shouting for a minute."

"What? Are you actually defending her?"

"No." Connor drew in a startled breath. He'd never expected to be defending Veronica in his lifetime…but something more than romantic rivalries *had* to be going on here. "Um, has she been eating enough lately?"

"What?"

"Eating. Has she been eating? Doesn't it look like she's lost a lot of weight since the beginning of the year?"

Jared turned a skeptical eye toward Veronica, who was still crying in a fetal position. "Oh. I guess she has lost weight," he mumbled.

Connor stood and approached her slowly. "Hi, um, Ronnie?" She blinked at him a few times and stopped crying. "I'm Connor. Do you remember me?"

She shook her head. "Why are you here?"

Jared threw up his hands with a disgusted snort.

Connor tuned him out, hunkering over so he could meet Veronica's eyes. "Ronnie, have you been eating enough lately? You're not trying to lose weight on purpose, are you?"

"Eating?" Her brows furrowed. "We could go out to dinner, if you like. I think I know a place where they can't find us."

From behind his shoulder, Connor heard Jared inhale sharply, as if it had just dawned on him he and Veronica had been having completely different conversations since she'd arrived.

"Fuck," Jared whispered. "Maybe she's high right now."

Connor straightened up. "I think maybe we should take her to Student Health."

"Do you think she's anorexic or something? Is that what's making her act like this?"

"I don't know...but I think there's definitely something wrong."

"Fuck," Jared said again. "Maybe if I hadn't been so wrapped up in my own problems—"

"You can't blame yourself for this," Connor interrupted. Forgetting Veronica was in the room, he stepped forward to rub Jared's arm.

Jared pulled away. "Come on, Ronnie. Let's go for a ride."

CHAPTER TWENTY-FOUR

The brown chair where Connor sat had a tear in its cushion, and he absentmindedly twirled his fingers in the cottony substance that spilled out. By some nonverbal agreement, neither he nor Jared spoke, not even when the nurse whisked Veronica away to check her blood pressure and weight.

He wasn't sure why Jared had brought him along. His dorm was out of the way, he supposed, but there hadn't even been a half-hearted offer to drop him off. What purpose could he possibly serve here?

Shifting in his seat, he began working up the courage to ask, but Jared's drawn brows and pressed-together lips stopped him.

Connor shook his head to clear away the insecurity. He was probably the last thing on Jared's mind right then.

The nurse might have drawn blood, because when Veronica returned she threw herself into Jared's arms. "You won't let them hurt me again, will you?"

Jared's deeply-etched frown grew deeper. "Please just sit and wait for the doctor. You need to calm down."

"Veronica Straton?" a male voice called.

Jared jumped up, pulling Veronica with him. "Yeah, here she is."

The man walked over and offered her a hand. "Hello, Veronica. I'm Dr. Ramirez. Would you like to come into my office for a little chat?"

"Go on." Jared gave her a push, but Veronica dug her nails into his arm.

"Don't let them take me!"

Jared winced, then glanced at the doctor guiltily. "She's been like this for a little while now."

"I won't go anywhere!" Veronica went on. "What if they're in there?"

The doctor nodded like he understood exactly what she was talking about—which hardly seemed possible. "Maybe you'd feel better if your friends could accompany you?"

Connor scooted his chair back until the wall stopped him from going any further. "You go, Jared. I'll just wait out h—"

Before he could finish, Jared grabbed his t-shirt to yank both him and Veronica down the hallway and straight into the doctor's office.

It wasn't the sterile white examination room Connor had expected. Bookshelves lined the walls, and in the middle of the room were several chairs, an old-fashioned desk, and one dark green couch. He sat nervously on the edge of a moss-colored cushion, making himself as small as possible when Jared and Veronica squeezed in beside him.

Why had Jared forced him in here? It wasn't like he really knew anything about Veronica...and if she ever remembered who he was, he rather doubted she'd want him around.

"All right, Veronica, why don't you tell me about how you're feeling today?" The doctor sat in a chair beside them with clipboard and pen in hand.

Veronica pursed her lips. "I don't know."

"You seem a little upset. Can you tell me what's been bothering you?"

"My suitemates are trying to get me." She shrugged. "They say they aren't, but I can tell."

The doctor's eyes crinkled slightly. "What makes you think they're trying to hurt you?"

"They watch me. They whisper things, all the time now."

Jared dropped his head into his hands, and the knot in Connor's stomach threatened to engulf his heart. The couch he was on was too small for all their bodies. Too confining. His left hand sought out an open space, and he began rhythmically tapping out some Vivaldi to calm himself.

The doctor was much better at maintaining composure. "What sort of things do they say to you?"

"Stuff to get back at me. They want me dead."

"What?" Jared exploded, interrupting the Vivaldi and further shattering Connor's nerves. "What are you talking about? No one said that! I thought you guys were just having some stupid girl-rivalries fight."

Dr. Ramirez scribbled something on his clipboard. "Let's let Veronica finish."

Jared did not seem convinced this was the best course of action. He folded his arms across his chest with a scowl.

Connor eyed the doctor, trying to determine what he thought of Veronica's babbling, but he couldn't get a read. He eventually gave up and focused on the door instead. He really had no right to be there, listening to Veronica's business. If only he could slip out...

"It's like a black tunnel," Veronica said when she had the floor again, "and people in there keep *saying* things. Like now they said Jared is gay. They're lying. They want him for themselves."

Jared's cheeks went red, and Connor felt his following suit.

"But we're meant to be together, Jared. You know that."

Jared dropped his head again. "We broke up last semester," he muttered. Then he looked up at the doctor with imploring eyes. "You gotta understand, I tried to stay friends with her. I mean, I knew she was needy, but she wasn't acting this crazy then."

Dr. Ramirez gave Jared the same *professional-understanding* nod he'd given Veronica earlier. "Let's refrain from placing labels right now. Have you noticed any other changes in Veronica's behavior?"

"Uh, she's lost weight, I guess. She started missing class, getting into fights with her suitemates...and sometimes she does say weird stuff, but I just figured it was 'cause she was high or something."

"Why are you always asking about drugs?" Veronica cried. "Who's telling you that? I don't do hard drugs. They told you, didn't they? They're lying!"

Jared turned toward Connor. "This is nuts," he mumbled under his breath. He didn't look away after speaking—he just kept staring at Connor like he was *waiting* for something. Something important.

What could he want? What did Connor even have to offer? Nervously, he leaned into Jared, just barely brushing against his arm. A flicker of gratitude crossed Jared's face before he was back to frowning.

Oh. So *that* was why he'd been dragged in there. It wasn't about convenience, or Veronica...*Jared* needed him.

"They keep lying." Veronica started to cry. "Maybe they'll win. Maybe I'm already dead."

"Ronnie..." Jared groaned.

"Veronica," Doctor Ramirez cut in gently. "Do you believe someone is trying to physically hurt you?"

"We could all be dead," Veronica responded, gazing past him and out a window.

The doctor rose and set down his notes. "Jared, I think you should walk Veronica down to the hospital. I'm going to call ahead and let them know to expect her. I'm concerned about the weight loss, and I'd really like her to stay there a few days for an evaluation."

"The hospital?" Jared lurched forward in his seat. "Is it really serious? What's wrong with her?"

"I can't diagnose anything from this short a session," Dr. Ramirez said, but there was a suspiciously tense note in his voice. "I think it would be best for her to be under observation for a little while."

"Oh, uh, okay." Jared stood, and Veronica hopped up with him, reaching for his hand. He frowned at her but let her continue holding it. "We'll get going then."

They stumbled into the twilight and took off down the short stretch of sidewalk. Veronica still clung to Jared, and Connor looked at anything—a streetlamp, a slew of passing midsize sedans, weeds sprouting in cracks in the concrete—just so he could avoid seeing her hand in his. He had a selfish urge to rip her bony fingers away and place his own in their spot…but for now he forced himself to be content she was pretending he wasn't even there. The last thing he needed was to end up as part of her crazy ramblings.

Jared's mood visibly worsened the second they stepped under the fluorescent lights of the hospital, his jaw clenching so tightly his temples bulged outwards. A petite blond nurse in dancing mouse scrubs had Veronica sign some papers, then escorted them onto an elevator. She smiled at them as the doors slid open on the fifth floor, but underneath the expression was a kind of *I'm-so-sorry-this-is-happening* look that made Connor's stomach turn.

"Well, dears"—she gestured down the hallway toward two sets of imposing double doors—"this is where you say goodbye, I'm afraid. Visiting hours are over for the evening, but if Veronica would like to see you, you can come back between noon and two tomorrow." She draped an arm over Veronica. "Come along, hon."

"Jared?" Veronica asked, her voice wobbling near tears.

"I'll see you later, Ronnie, okay?" Jared pulled free of her hand. "Go and get some rest."

The nurse led Veronica toward the first set of doors. She slid a card through a lock to gain entry, then checked Veronica's pockets before they took the next entrance and disappeared from sight.

Jared sagged against the wall, right next to the sign announcing their location in both Braille and raised white letters: the Psychiatric Unit. "Jesus, Connor." He heaved out what seemed like all the breath his lungs could carry. "This is...out of control."

Connor nodded solemnly.

"Fuck." Jared's hand trembled as he passed it over his face. "Just...fuck."

"Jared," Connor murmured, reaching out to embrace him. Jared moved away.

"Not here," he said gruffly.

"Oh. O-okay." No one was in the hallway, and only an uninterested nurse was anywhere within earshot.

Jared probably had too much on his mind to realize nobody would care about him receiving a hug. But if he wasn't going to accept comfort out in the open, then Connor was just going to have to take action for both their sakes. He grabbed Jared's hand and dragged him into a nearby bathroom.

"Connor...what the hell are you doing?" Jared glared, jerking free. "Someone could see us, and I'm not ready to—"

"Shh. No one is here. Visiting hours are over."

Jared glanced around the empty restroom and crossed his arms. "Fine. Then what are we doing here?"

"You're upset. I...I just wanted you to calm down."

"Of course I'm upset. What the fuck is wrong with her? Is this...my fault?"

"I'm sure she'll be fine." Connor ran his hand along Jared's back. "Maybe she just needs some sleep and some vitamins. Or maybe you're right, maybe she is doing drugs. They'll find out." That sounded reasonable enough. Besides, words of comfort were easier than thinking of the alternative.

Jared's rigid stance slowly dissolved. He unfolded his arms and stepped forward so he could rest his chin on Connor's head. "I hope you're right. This has been one hell of a day. Let's just go home, okay?"

Connor pressed in even closer. He still felt small against Jared's muscular body, but not as small as he once had. "Yeah, let's go."

***

The last light of evening had faded into night by the time they trudged into Jared's suite. Exhausted and single-minded in his desire for *bed-in-Jared's-arms*, Connor didn't slow or even glance up from the tile as he followed Jared to his room.

But then Jared came to a sudden stop, and Connor bounced off his tense back and stumbled into the doorframe.

Ben stood in the center of the room, with Jared's duffle bag in his hands. "So, what, you're moving out? Is that what this means?" He tossed the bag at Jared's feet.

Jared took a step back, and Connor skirted away to avoid another collision.

"Fuck, man," Ben continued. "I realize you guys are probably...sleeping together"—he paused to cringe—"but isn't it a little early to be playing house?"

"Why the fuck do you care?" Jared growled.

Connor bit his tongue in the same abused spot from earlier, reopening the wound. He shrank back against the door as the tension made the air feel too thick to breathe.

Ben opened and closed his mouth a few times. Then he hung his head, staring down at his pile of laundry on the floor. "Okay, look, this is…kinda weird…and I'm not…I'm not sure how I feel about it yet…"

"Well that's good." Jared kicked a dirty towel that lay on his half of the room. "Because I don't give a damn how you feel."

Ben huffed and folded his arms. "I can see that you're pissed, and maybe I didn't react the best way…but how the hell is someone supposed to react when they find that shit out? I mean, you basically lied to me—"

Jared's hands curled into fists. "My life is none of your fucking business."

"What I'm trying to say," Ben cut back in, glaring, "what I'm trying to say is that I don't want you to get lost or whatever. I mean, I've never really had any friends that were…uh, gay…but college is supposed to be about new experiences, right?"

Connor watched the subtle shift in Jared's expression—from anger to surprise in a half-an-inch lift of his furrowed brow.

"And besides," Ben went on, "I'm at least as good looking as your…friend there, and as far as I know you've never tried to rape me, so I figure my ass is safe."

Connor's throat closed up on a swallow of blood and saliva, throwing him into a coughing fit, and Jared's mouth dropped open.

"Uh, that was a joke," Ben added with a lopsided smile. "Sorry, probably inappropriate."

Jared accepted his explanation with a dazed nod, and the room fell silent.

Silent for too long. Connor's eyes bounced back and forth between the two tall men as he waited for someone to speak. But no one said anything…until it suddenly occurred to him he had his own mouth.

He had his own mouth, but he'd never used it for *this* before—for purposefully stepping into an awkward silence. He drew in a halting breath and peered out from behind Jared's back. "S-so, we j-just dropped Ronnie off at the hospital."

Maybe not the best topic to bring up, but it was the only thing that came to mind.

Ben blinked down at him in surprise, as if he'd forgotten Connor was even in the room. "Are you serious? Why?"

Thank God Jared took the conversational bait. "The doctor at Student Health wouldn't tell us what was wrong, but he asked us to take her there."

"Was it like mono or something? Or crap, an…an STD?"

Jared grimaced. "I really don't know. She was just saying all kinds of weird shit, and she's been looking pretty rough lately."

Ben puffed out a breath of agreement, pushing a stack of books over so he could fall back on his bed. "Shit. I always thought something was off with her."

"I guess I should've seen it too."

"I bet it's harder to notice when you deal with her craziness all the time," Ben offered. "I mean, who can tell when a chick is just being their regular kind of crazy, and when there's really something wrong?"

Jared moved to sit on his own bed, and Connor hung back in the doorway until Jared patted the spot beside him. Scrunching his nervous hands into his pockets, he took the offered seat, careful to keep a space between their bodies.

"Nice of you to even give a crap after the shit storm she caused." Ben shook his head. "Don't know that I would do the same if someone had—" He stopped and inhaled sharply. "Wait, that whole gay thing…that wasn't just more of her craziness, was it? You really are a…uh, gay, right?"

Connor's heart skipped its downbeat. This was Jared's out if he ever wanted to take it.

Jared gave Ben a long, pointed look, and eventually Ben nodded. "Right. I get it."

Relief swept Connor into a goofy smile, but Ben caught it and raised an eyebrow at him, effectively wiping the expression from his face. What would Jared's friends find more shocking—that he was gay, or that he was dating someone like Connor?

"Jesus," Jared said suddenly. "I'm gone for like two days and your fucking mess is taking over the entire room." He waved a hand toward a popcorn bag that had spilled its unpopped kernels under his desk, his nose curling up in disgust.

Ben turned to Connor. "Are the gays really into neatness? Is that a gay thing?"

"Uh, um…" Connor stuttered, caught off guard by the direct address. Did it mean he was being accepted, or was he supposed to be the butt of some kind of joke?

Jared saved him from having to respond by launching a shoe at Ben's face.

"All right, all right." Ben ducked and threw his hands up in surrender. "I was just wondering."

"Well you can keep your dickhead wonderings to yourself," Jared retorted, but he didn't really sound angry. In fact, Connor had the distinct impression this was how the two normally spoke to each other.

"Connor—that's your name, right? Maybe you could help Jared with his aggression issues," Ben suggested as he stood.

"Really, Ben? Do you want to take this outside?" Jared's eyes narrowed. "Gay or not I can take your scrawny ass down."

"No, I'd like my ass untouched by you, thank you very much."

A blush rose in Jared's cheeks, and this time he didn't come up with a witty response.

Ben squinted and gave them an embarrassed smile, like he'd sensed his misstep. "Anyways, it's getting late. I'm gonna go grab some food and head off to Clemons to finish my chemistry. Guess I'll see you later, Jer?"

"Yeah." Jared nodded stiffly, still tense. "Later."

He reached out to grab Connor's hand as soon as the door closed. "I'm sorry about him...don't take it seriously, though. That's just the way he is."

"Yeah, uh, I understand. It's okay." Connor squeezed Jared's fingers. The contact was as comforting as always— but who was Jared really trying to reassure? Connor, or himself?

A yawn cut off the train of thought.

"You're tired," Jared said. "And you didn't finish that paper yet, did you."

"No." Connor sighed. "Not yet."

"You should go. I've taken up too much of your time already."

"Oh." Jared was probably right...but it would've been so much nicer if the world could just wait for them to have a moment to themselves. "Are you gonna be okay if I go?"

Jared lifted his hand and ran it through Connor's hair. "Now who's taking care of who?" He chuckled sadly. "I'll be fine."

But as soon as Connor gripped the doorknob to leave, Jared's voice stopped him. "Wait, Connor..."

"Yeah?"

Jared chewed on his bottom lip. It was already a little swollen, making it even fuller than normal. "I know I probably shouldn't ask you this, given, well, everything, but...um...do you think you could come with me to visit Ronnie in the hospital?"

Connor blinked. "Oh, uh..."

"Someone should visit, I think. I just don't know who else would. And I'd go by myself, but I...I *really* hate hospitals."

"Yeah, of course. No problem, just give me a call."

"Thanks, Connor. Thanks for...you know, everything."

Connor brushed past the scowling redhead in the hallway as he left. By the time he remembered he had reason to be nervous around him, he was already out of the suite.

Jared *needed* him. Some things just seemed so trivial now in comparison.

CHAPTER TWENTY-FIVE

A dozen yellow roses lay spread out on the passenger seat of the station wagon. Connor waited patiently as Jared propped open the door for him and tossed the flowers petals-down into the back of the car.

"Hey," Jared mumbled. He stepped on the gas and darted back into traffic, lips tugged downward and knuckles going white from his death-grip on the steering wheel.

Connor buckled his seatbelt and watched Jared's angry movements through the reflection in the window. Maybe this visit was a mistake. At the very least, he should have asked Jared to come up first, so they could have taken some time to talk, hold each other...reestablish their connection. In just a few minutes, they'd be under the scrutinizing eyes of the public, and there'd be no opportunity to be close.

And it suddenly felt like it had been far, far too long since they'd kissed.

"You don't mind that I'm bringing her flowers, do you?" Jared suddenly asked.

"What?" Connor mumbled, then processed the question a second later. He smacked his thigh and forced himself to turn back to Jared before he wasted any more of the precious little private time they had left. "I mean, of course not. She's sick and in the hospital. That's what you're supposed to do."

"Right." Jared squeezed the steering wheel impossibly tighter. "Sorry. Didn't get much sleep last night."

That was already clear from the shadows beneath his sunken-in eyes. "We could always visit tomorrow, if you want to go back to my place and take a nap or something."

Jared shook his head. "I'll be all right."

Connor hunched down in his seat with a sigh. If only Jared would drop one of his hands from the wheel so he could take hold of it—he was positive it would make him feel better. Make *both* of them feel better.

"So…how are things going with Ben?" he ventured quietly.

"Okay." Jared's shoulders jerked in a stiff shrug. "Most of the time stuff seems pretty normal…but every once in a while it gets a little awkward. And when he's around the other guys…I dunno. I guess I'd rather just stay clear for now—let things blow over."

Blow over to what? Although, there were probably worse things Jared could be doing than lying low. Connor returned to staring at Jared's hands, trying to will the right one from its three o'clock grip.

But he never had any luck. For all that Jared claimed to hate hospitals, he certainly seemed to be in a hurry to get there. Hopefully that just meant he was in a hurry to get it *over* with. The creases on his forehead and near the sides of his eyes were starting to leave marks even when his expression changed—perhaps a glimpse of the wrinkles that would one day line his face. They wouldn't make him any less handsome, but it would be better if they were from laughter instead of worry.

A male nurse greeted them this time, with less of a sugary-sweet demeanor than the previous one. He was all business as he opened the first door for them. "Do you have anything sharp on you? Scissors, razors, pocket knife…"

"No, nothing," Jared said, and Connor nodded. "We're here to see Veronica Straton."

"Third door on the right. Visiting hours are over in forty-five minutes." He walked them down the hallway, then took off.

Connor followed Jared past a skeletal blonde, drowning in the starchy white sheets of her hospital bed. Veronica was propped up in her own bed at the back of the room.

"Jared! I knew you'd come!"

Her bright voice didn't match her face. Without a stitch of makeup on, the sheen of the fluorescent lights made her skin appear sallow.

Jared stood there awkwardly for a moment, flowers in hand, until he turned and shoved the bouquet into Connor's arms. "Hi, Ronnie. We wanted to stop by for a little visit."

"That bitch tried to say you wouldn't come, but I knew you would. I know my boyfriend loves me."

He sank into a chair by her bedside. "Ronnie, you know I'm not…we're not…"

"Remember when we went to prom?" She went on, hugging herself and staring up at him dreamily.

Connor's stomach lurched, and he made himself busy by scanning the room until he found an empty plastic container by the windowsill. He took the vase into the tiny hospital bathroom and filled it with water, wishing the faucet would make just a little more noise so as to completely drown out Veronica's voice.

"We were perfect in our pictures, weren't we? I had that green dress."

The roses would wilt quickly without scissors or a knife to cut the stems. But Connor had no intention of asking for either of those, so he just stuck the flowers in the vase and set it back by the window.

"There's green Jello sometimes."

Jared scooted his chair back a few inches. "Maybe we should come sometime when you're feeling better," he mumbled.

Ronnie stretched out to grasp his hand. "How long will I be here? It gets cold at night. And *she* won't stop talking shit." She jerked a thumb at her sleeping roommate, who really didn't look like she had the strength to be that much of a problem.

"I...I don't know. The doctors are going to make you better, first."

Veronica nodded. "I know. I might need a brain transplant."

Jared freed his hand. "No one said that."

"Yes, because of all the voices trying to get to me."

"Ronnie, you're not making any sense." Jared's shoulders twitched. Without thinking, Connor placed his hand on Jared's back. He would've withdrawn it immediately, but Jared surprised him by reaching up to take hold of it. "There's no such thing as a brain transplant. You just need to rest..."

The nurse popped into the room, but Jared didn't seem to notice.

"...eat some healthy meals, talk to the doctor. You'll feel better soon."

Connor nervously tried to pull his hand away, but Jared refused to let go.

"Excuse me." The nurse cleared his throat. "Her parents are waiting outside to see her, and we can only allow two visitors at a time."

Jared released his grip, standing quickly. "Of course. We'll come back tomorrow."

"You're leaving?" Veronica's lip quivered. "Don't you want to stay with me?"

"I said we'd be back." He gave her a weak smile that vanished as soon as they had left.

They passed a couple in the waiting area between the two sets of double doors—a woman in her fifties with graying hair tucked into a harried bun, and an heavy-set man in a rumpled suit. The woman turned red-rimmed eyes on Jared as he approached.

"Mrs. Straton," Jared began, but she put up a hand to stop him.

"You should have consulted us first before you put her in here."

"But the doctor—"

"We're her parents. We should have made the decision. I'm not even sure why you're still around her, since you broke up with her." She pressed her lips into a thin, trembling line and strode off after the nurse.

The color drained from Jared's face and his walking speed nearly doubled. He bypassed the elevators and opted on crashing down the stairs instead, forcing Connor to run to keep up.

"I'll take you home," Jared said gruffly.

Connor barely had time to buckle his seatbelt before the car squealed out of the parking space. *Take him home?* And then he'd have to watch Jared drive off at this breakneck speed—which was entirely too fast for the garage structure they were currently in. Even if Jared really did want to be alone with his distress, Connor wasn't willing to sit in his room and chew his tongue to a bloody nub worrying about him.

"Um, th-that's okay...I have to go to the library later. Your place is closer."

Jared didn't respond. He just sped on past Connor's dorm.

When they reached his place, he stormed inside and nearly slammed the door on Connor. He stood in the middle of the room and stared straight ahead without moving or recognizing Connor's presence.

Then he turned and smashed his fist into a wall. "Fuck!"

Connor jumped back, wincing at the impact.

"Fuck," Jared repeated, cradling his hand. The skin of his knuckles went from ashen white to red as he held it.

Shaking himself from his stupor, Connor ran to the mini-fridge. He tossed aside a few popsicles and found an icepack stored in the back. "Here, use this." He laid it on top of Jared's hand, trying to meet his downcast eyes. "Jared…"

"It's my fault, Connor," Jared mumbled.

"No it's—"

"Her mother blames me."

"No, she—"

"You heard what she said!" Jared pulled back from his touch, letting the icepack fall to the floor.

"She's just upset about her daughter—she probably doesn't even know what's going on yet."

"No. She blames *me*. And why shouldn't she? I shoulda seen something was really wrong. I just assumed it was drugs or drinking…and I thought that was my fault, too."

Connor squeezed his eyes shut. What could he do to break Jared free of this downward spiral of guilt? "How would her doing drugs be your fault?"

"Because I used her." Jared folded onto the bed, propping his feet on the frame so he could wrap his arms around his knees. "I let people believe I was interested in her to keep them from getting suspicious. I let things get physical when she pushed for it…and when she started telling people we were a couple, I just went along with it. I figured, what the hell, she's the kind of girl I'm supposed to be with, right? Attractive, popular…why shouldn't I give it a try?"

"That doesn't mean you're responsible for her getting sick."

"Yes it does. I never should have let her get close to me when I knew…I *knew* I couldn't be what she needed.

Maybe this wouldn't have happened if I'd just wanted her, the way I'm supposed to...the way a normal person would..."

"A normal person?" Connor broke in, the words souring in his mouth. *Normal.* Something he'd never been.

Regret flashed across Jared's dark eyes. "I didn't mean it like that. Shit." He dropped his head into his hands. "I'm gonna screw this up again, aren't I? Maybe it'd be better for you if we just...took some time..."

Alarms rang out in Connor's mind, screeching like a thousand violinists sliding up their fingerboards. He couldn't, *wouldn't* let this happen again—not because of Veronica, not because of fear, not because of undeserved guilt.

"Don't you dare!" He scrambled across the room and gripped Jared's face with both his hands. "Don't you dare pull away from me again!"

Jared gaped at him, his lips parting as a long, shaky breath escaped.

"I don't want to lose you," he eventually said, brushing Connor's cheek with the backs of his fingers. "I just don't think I'm gonna be any good to you right now."

"Then...then maybe I'm good for you."

Tears fought to escape, but Connor held them back, maintaining his focus on Jared's startled eyes. *Believe me.*

Jared watched him for a few more seconds before sinking into his arms. "Yeah," he murmured, clutching him tightly. "You are."

***

"Well if it isn't the prodigal friend," Rebecca remarked as Connor slid into a seat beside her. She stirred honey into her tea with one fair eyebrow arched. "I was beginning to think you weren't going to show."

"Sorry. I didn't realize it was nine already. I was trying to catch up on all my class work...it's been a long week."

"Mhm. We've missed you at lunch. Seems to me you could spare a few minutes to stop by then."

Connor inhaled the rich coffee and cinnamon aroma of the small café, struggling to dampen his annoyance. He wanted the comfort of friendship, but he could do without the guilt trips.

"I told you, Veronica's visiting hours are during my lunch break, and he needs me there."

"I know." She sighed, reaching out to squeeze his hand. "I'm not trying to give you a hard time. I just want to make sure you're still taking care of yourself in all of this. He's looking out for her, you're looking out for him...someone's gotta look out for you."

Connor flushed. How could he be irritated with Rebecca when she was his biggest supporter, as usual?

"I'm doing all right, really. It's Jared I'm worried about."

She brought her cup to her mouth and blew a swirl of steam toward him. "Maybe you two should take a break from the whole nursemaid thing."

"He can't. He thinks it's his fault. The whole thing is just...crazy."

Rebecca offered him a piece of her biscotti. "Still no word on what's wrong with her?"

Connor shook his head and popped the cookie into his mouth. "They won't tell him anything since he's not family."

"Damn." She sipped her tea. "Sounds to me like she's just nuts."

"I don't really think that's a diagnosis."

She giggled. "Sorry. Guess my media studies major isn't helping you out here."

He wanted to laugh, too, but couldn't quite reach that carefree mood.

"Seriously, though, if you want the relationship to work, you need to step out of the nuthouse and get back to real life. Wallowing around in misery is not healthy for him…or you."

"I know, but—"

"Why don't you meet us at Newcomb for dinner? You won't have to pry him away from her bedside then, will you?"

"Well, no…"

"There you go. And what's more low key than meeting up with friends at Newcomb? He's still got a lot of work to do in that whole 'out' department. I mean, he spends all his time with either you or his wacko ex…not exactly being social. You should really—"

"Okay, okay." Connor put his hands over his ears to stop the onslaught. "I get it. I'll ask him."

Rebecca was good enough not to gloat over her triumph.

"Good. I look forward to seeing him again."

Connor rolled his eyes and snatched the last piece of biscotti. "Well I hate to say this, but I really should be getting back to work. I have a bunch of reading to do."

She gathered her belongings and tossed away the empty cup. "Sure. I'll walk you halfway."

He held the café door for her, then stepped out onto the busy sidewalk of The Corner, where he immediately collided with a massive body.

"Oh, shit," the body said. "I didn't see you down there."

Connor opened his mouth to give the obligatory *it's okay*, but the words disintegrated as he found himself staring up at Michael's commanding bulk.

"Oh, shit," Michael said again, the scent of beer carrying on his breath. "It's the little anthro queer."

A dousing of shock left Connor speechless.

Rebecca backtracked to them in two swift steps. With a hand on her hip, she drew herself up to her full six-one, even though Michael still had several inches on her. "Excuse me?"

Michael let out a low whistle, filled with more beer-stench. "Whoa. Call off the queer cavalry. It's not like I'm gonna beat him up or anything."

Queer cavalry? Anger boiled through Connor's system, temporarily muting the fear.

He stepped back around Rebecca and attempted to mimic her move of squaring shoulders and amassing height. If he hadn't been so nervous, he probably would have laughed at the futile effort. "Don't talk to her like that."

Michael did laugh. "Seriously, dude. Chill. I just never thought a little thing like you would have it in you to seduce a big football player right off the team."

"Seduce?" Rebecca fumed. "Listen, asshole—"

"You need to chill." He pushed his hands down in front of her face. "Jared was a lousy player anyway. I really couldn't care less who he fucks. You people should just be honest about it...and keep it out of the locker room. A guy's gotta feel secure there."

Rebecca took another step toward Michael, eyes livid. She was either getting ready to unleash a tirade or a fist, but her fury inspired Connor to make use of his own.

This time he didn't try to appear any taller. He had a hard enough time being himself—no sense pretending to be something he wasn't. "Y-you know, I don't think you ever had any reason to worry about Jared," he said, only a hint of a tremor marring his voice.

Michael crossed his arms. "And why is that?"

"Well...it doesn't exactly look like you're his type, now does it."

Rebecca's hand came down on Connor's shoulder to pull him away from the flabbergasted Michael, and together they dissolved into the mass of student foot traffic.

"Oh, Connor," she choked out, nearly doubled over with laughter. "I could kiss you! But I guess I'll just have to leave that to Jared."

CHAPTER TWENTY-SIX

"Are you fucking kidding me?"

Jared sprung off the bed, his hands clenched.

Definitely not a kiss. Connor stretched out his arms, trying to recapture the hug they'd been sharing moments ago, but missed by several inches. "It's not that big a deal—"

"He's a bigoted asshole to you and it's not that big a deal? I knew he was kind of a jerk, but this…this is fucking bullshit." Jared paced, crossing the length of the room several times. "Why is everything in my life such shit right now?"

Idiot, Connor berated himself. Like Jared didn't have enough to worry about, he had to open his big mouth to bring him more bad news.

"I think he might've been a little drunk. It's not like he threatened me or anything. Really, it's okay." Connor stood and tried to pull Jared back to the bed, but Jared spun around to cast him off.

"Damn it! Quit saying it's okay. It's not! It's not okay for someone to talk to you like that!" Jared thrust his hands into his hair and tugged mercilessly at the curls.

"Jesus, Connor, when I first met you, you were so shy it seemed almost…*painful.*"

Connor's arms warmed in his embarrassment, but he let Jared continue.

"And I wanted so badly to help you get over that…but…but I just made it worse, didn't I?" Jared stopped and blinked a few times, eyes darting left to right and then back again, like he'd just discovered a sheet of answers to read. "I made you feel like you had to keep hiding yourself…like you didn't deserve to be recognized, like people could keep treating you like you were no one…"

The heat rose to Connor's face, and he'd heard enough. He launched himself at Jared, throwing his arms around Jared's waist, and fell onto the bed with his full weight— the only way he could make any impact. He managed to knock Jared's legs against the bed frame and together they toppled over onto the mattress.

"I told you already." Connor took advantage of Jared's shock to interrupt. "You did help me. Even the breaking up part helped me in some ways—I don't know that I was ready for a relationship before…but I am now."

Jared shook his head. "If I helped you so much, how come you let that jackass get away with speaking to you like that?"

"You didn't let me finish the story. I didn't let him get away with anything. I was only afraid for like, two seconds…"

Jared's lips pressed into a firm line, his nostrils flaring.

"…but then I stood up to him. You can even ask Rebecca. And it's okay—"

"Stop fucking saying it's—"

Connor clamped a hand over Jared's mouth. "Let me finish," he said sternly. Jared's eyes shot wide, but he didn't resist. "It's okay because what he said…doesn't affect me. I have good friends, I have you…and I'm happy, just being me."

A smile spread across Connor's lips, growing so wide it stretched his cheeks and exposed nearly all his teeth. Happy just being *him*. It was the first time in his life he'd ever uttered those words.

He released his grip on Jared's face. "Really, baby?" Jared pulled him into a more comfortable embrace.

"Yes. Really."

Jared reached out to tuck some hair behind his ear. "I'd still like to kill him for you, though."

Connor smothered his laughter in Jared's chest, listening to the beat of his heart settle into a calmer rhythm. "Well, it's the thought that counts." He wriggled up to meet Jared's lips, and for that sweet moment, all was right with the world.

But then Jared pulled away. "It's getting late, and I have some assignments to do. You wanna just grab a snack at the Treehouse for dinner?"

"Oh..." Connor rose from the bed slowly, stalling for time. "Actually, Rebecca wanted us to meet up with her and the rest of my friends at Newcomb. Do you think we could?"

Jared flipped over and began smoothing his comforter until it complied with his standards of neatness. "I dunno...I have a lot of work to do if I'm gonna bring up my grades..."

Disappointment threw Connor off for a moment, but he quickly regrouped. He grasped Jared's hand with saddened eyes and a slight frown. "O-oh. Okay."

"Don't do that." Jared sighed, running a thumb over Connor's lips. "I guess I can swing it if you really want. C'mon, we can go."

Victory. Connor smiled in triumph the moment Jared turned to get the door. Maybe manipulation wasn't the best skill to make use of in a relationship, but it was definitely a new achievement for him.

He couldn't help being just a little proud.

***

Only a low rumble of voices came from Newcomb Dining Hall in the evening—the place was much more sedate without the chatter of all the lower classman who frequented the spot during the day. Jared grabbed a tray and loaded up as he normally would, the uncomfortable sideways glances at a minimum.

Relieved, Connor did the same. He headed to the salad station and smothered some greens in cheese and croutons before he caught sight of a petite strawberry-blonde across the dining hall. A few too many spoonfuls of dressing wound up on his lettuce before he accepted he had no choice but to face her.

"Hey!" Beth threw her arms around him as he set down his tray. "Long time no see!"

He tensed, but the flare of nervousness in her embrace was surprisingly mild. And really, after all that had happened, the fact she'd once terrified him now seemed pretty foolish.

Beth murmured near his ear, "Rebecca told me about things. I hope that's okay."

"I told her she could. Beth, I really have to apol—"

She put a finger on his lips to stop him. "Nope. No way. It's completely cool." Then she smothered him in another hug.

Jared approached, but he stood back a ways until Beth had unclasped her hands from around Connor's waist.

She turned to him. "You must be Jared."

"And you must be Beth," he responded, one eyebrow lifted as if to say, *and I know all about you.*

Beth's cheeks went crimson, but a cheer roared inside Connor. This was a sign of the old Jared—the confident man he'd first fallen for.

"Oh." Beth recuperated, her eyes traveling up and down Jared's body. She had to tilt her head a little to capture his full height. "Well, I have to say, I think Connor made the right decision…"

Now it was Jared's turn to blush.

"…but you can't blame me for trying."

Jared lifted his gaze over her head for a second, locking onto Connor's. "No. I can't."

A shiver of pleasure caused goose bumps to spring up on Connor's arms. He ended up blushing as well, completing the trifecta.

"Oh good, we're all here." Rebecca arrived at the table, with Tate close behind. "Jared, I think you met everyone before, except Chrissy." She pointed to Chrissy, who sat munching on some sugar snap peas beside A.J. "Oh, and Beth."

Jared smirked. "We've met now."

"Food's getting cold," Tate mumbled over Rebecca's shoulder, and she turned around to give his arm a light slap.

"All right, let's get to the eating."

They tucked into their meals before making any small talk, and the silence threw Connor into a momentary panic. Would conversation be an issue with Jared at the table? Would everyone know to avoid sensitive subjects? He *really* needed this to be a stress free evening.

But the worry gradually faded. A.J. asked Jared where he was from, and once they discovered they'd gone to rival high schools, they turned the talk to football—which A.J. was surprisingly well informed on, as he'd been in the marching band. Chrissy interrupted to object to the rigidity of musical expression when one was forced to march to the music, and Connor couldn't help but giggle at Jared's amused expression. Chrissy did an excellent job fitting the Brown-residents stereotype he'd always had in mind.

A slight nudge from Tate captured Connor's attention. "Don't look now," Tate whispered, "but I think we're about to get more popular."

Following his gaze, Connor spotted Ben's wiry frame several feet away. He was speaking to someone vaguely familiar-looking—possibly one of Jared's suitemates—and shifting his eyes back and forth between their table and one on the other side of the cafeteria.

Finally Ben seemed to make up his mind, and he turned—toward them.

"Shit," Tate said, speaking louder this time so all could hear. "Everyone act cool. Don't let on how nerdy we are."

Jared's head swiveled around until he spotted Ben and the boy trailing behind him. The rest of the table erupted in giggles.

"Uh"—Ben pushed a hand through his hair as he arrived—"so, I'm kinda used to being the funny one at the table—not so sure how I feel about being laughed at. Maybe we should find somewhere else..."

"Oh, shut up and sit down." Jared scooted over to make room. "Guys, these are my suitemates, Ben and Will." They took their seats, and the rest of the table gave out their names in quick succession.

"I'll forget all those in a second," Ben said, "but I think Will has a better memory—maybe I can just cheat off him."

Will, a shorter guy with a spattering of friendly freckles, rolled his eyes. "Can't remember names of a few people? How'n the hell do you expect to be a history major?"

Jared snorted and Ben gave him a mock glare.

"A history major?" Chrissy repeated, tapping her chin with a snap pea. "And just which version of history will you be studying?"

Ben was silent for a moment, poised with a grilled cheese halfway to his mouth, until his lips moved into a knowing smile. "Oh, that's right." He set down the sandwich. "You guys all live in the Brown dorm. Maybe a better topic of conversation would be...um...let's see...indie flicks?" He stole a french fry off Jared's plate and chewed it innocently.

"Don't be a dickhead," Jared admonished.

"Actually," A.J. piped in, "that sounds good to me."

Everyone laughed, and Ben snuck another few fries from Jared with a self-important grin.

"Hey!" Jared elbowed him in the ribs. "Get your own. The place is a damn buffet. Why do you have to take mine?"

"I'm *sorry*," Ben said slowly. "I thought all you guys were supposed to be really health conscious—I was just trying to lend a hand."

Jared dropped his chicken wrap to grab a hunk of Ben's chest—possibly including some nipple—and give it a hearty twist.

"Ow! Kidding! Kidding!" Ben cried, rubbing the spot after it had been released. "Only kidding."

Jared went back to eating his fries. "Keep it up. There's more where that came from."

A twinge of jealousy welled up in Connor as he observed the playful camaraderie, though he quickly pushed it back down. It had been nice to be Jared's whole world for a while, but it wasn't sustainable. Just like it hadn't been when Jared was his whole world.

The time had come to find a balance.

Beth leaned over the table, her tiny hand on his arm interrupting his thoughts. She got close to his ear so she could whisper only to him.

"Hey, do you happen to know if Ben's seeing anyone?"

CHAPTER TWENTY-SEVEN

The usual male nurse greeted Connor and Jared the next afternoon. "Just so you know," he remarked casually, "I believe her parents are coming by later."

"Yeah." Jared wore his hospital frown—lips thin and turned down, brow crinkled, and eyes half-hooded. "They're gonna see if they can take her home, I think."

They continued down the hallway, relief making Connor's feet light. With any luck, Veronica's parents *would* be able to have her released, so this dark, depressing chapter could end and they could finally return to their regular lives.

Or maybe, get a start on his dream life—the one where he got to see good friends every day, walk around campus accompanied by his incredibly handsome boyfriend...be comfortable in his own skin. It was enough to cause him to skip a few steps, until a glance at Jared's still-troubled expression put him in his place.

This wasn't close to Jared's dream life.

"Everything okay?" He touched Jared's arm to bring him to a stop outside Veronica's door.

"Hmm? Oh, yeah. It's just...this might be the last time we'll be here."

"Yeah," Connor replied, careful to keep his tone neutral.

"And I may never know what really happened with her. I just wish I had some sorta closure, ya know?"

Connor gave him a quick squeeze of understanding before they walked inside. It was all he could offer, but it didn't seem enough.

Veronica peered at him as they approached, her head cocked to the side. "Jared, who's he?"

Jared heaved a short, weary breath. "I've told you before. That's Connor. He's...I'm...he and I are together, remember?"

"Oh." She squinted and shook her head. If she'd grasped what Jared was saying, she'd probably forget in the next second anyway.

Not that it bothered Connor. Acknowledging his presence was at least a step in the right direction.

Jared sat, and she whipped out a notepad to show him poorly done sketches she'd completed during group therapy. Connor pulled up another chair and rested his hand on the back of Jared's neck. Every once in a while he gave the tight muscles a little rub, waiting for them to relax under his touch.

"Will we still be together when I get out of here?" Veronica asked. Connor hadn't followed the trail of conversation—there wasn't much of one when she was speaking—but it was obvious she'd become emotional by the way her bottom lip trembled. "Will you still be my boyfriend?"

Jared's muscles tensed again, and Connor sighed. All his hard work wasted.

"I'll...I'll always be your friend, Ronnie."

"We'll get to go to the formal next spring?"

Connor scooted back his chair, his insides crawling. "Be right back," he mumbled, and darted out of the room. He'd heard the ensuing conversation enough times to know there wasn't anything Jared could say to get through to her. Nothing he could do about it, either.

He leaned back against the wall in the hallway, cracking the knuckles on his hand as the nurse passed by.

"Nice to see she's doing better today," the man said. He got a few steps away before a bizarre thought struck Connor.

It was so far from anything *him* that he almost didn't believe the words were coming from his body. "Um, uh, e-excuse me…"

The nurse turned around. "Yes?"

Connor swallowed hard, his mouth dry and his lips twitching like they were suffering from an electric shock. But now the man's eyes were on him, and if he'd come this far…

"Um, I…I was just w-wondering, about…about what c-could make her sick like this…"

"I'm sorry." The nurse shook his head. "I can't release information about a patient's condition to non-relatives."

"I…I know. I d-don't need to know exactly what's wrong with her. It's just…m-my…my friend…he thinks it's his fault. He thinks he might've done something to cause it, and I was just wondering if it's…if it's something that could have been prevented."

The nurse drummed short nails against the clipboard in his hand. Then he sighed. "Tell your boyfriend it isn't his fault. With a lot of mental illnesses—like schizophreniform disorder, for instance—you can't point a finger and assign blame. We think they might be caused by a combination of genetics and environmental factors…but not by one break up."

He turned and walked off before Connor could summon a response.

Jared popped out of the room a few seconds later. "Hey, there you are. I said goodbye already. She was getting kinda tired and falling asleep. I'm ready to go."

"Yeah, uh, okay." The knowledge—or the *potential* knowledge—Connor had just gained filled him with giddy energy. He bounced after Jared, hands trailing the hospital walls and tapping out a folksy jig.

But the joy was short-lived. When the elevator doors to freedom opened, Veronica's parents stood on the other side. They stepped out but didn't walk away, shuffling their feet and casting uncomfortable glances at the floor.

Jared was the first to break the awkward silence. He certainly deserved points for initiative. "Mr. and Mrs. Straton, how are you?"

"Fine," Mrs. Straton replied briskly. "We're fine."

"I'm so sorry this happened."

Her face contorted, creating deep creases on her forehead and on the sides of her mouth. They remained there even after she schooled her expression. "We've arranged to bring her to a hospital closer to home, so you won't need to come by here anymore." She turned away and her husband gently rubbed her back.

"Patricia, I'm going to grab some coffee. I'll be back up in a minute."

"Fine. Just be quick about it." She took off for the double doors while Mr. Straton stayed behind, waiting for the elevator.

It was the perfect time to take the stairs. More than perfect. Connor rocked forward on his feet so he'd be ready to go. *Please let's take the stairs.*

But Jared remained where he was, lost in thought, until a hand came down on his shoulder. "Son, you in a rush? Or can I buy you and your friend a cup of coffee?"

Rush, rush, rush...

"Yeah, we have a few minutes, Mr. Straton."

Damn.

They stood in line for the mediocre coffee in the hospital cafeteria without saying a word. Once Connor's hands were occupied with a cup, the only thing he could do to calm himself was keep a stream of etudes running through his mind and blink along to the beat. All instincts told him to avoid perturbed parents, whatever the cost, but he couldn't just leave Jared.

"You'll have to excuse Patricia." Mr. Straton finally spoke as they stopped off to add sugar. "This has been…hard on her."

"Of course." Jared nodded. "I understand."

"Hard for me, too," the man added. "She's my little girl, you know?" He rubbed a meaty fist into his eyes, but not before a few tears slipped out.

Jared's eyes shone, too. Seemed like he wasn't the only one trying to shoulder blame. Connor sipped his coffee and accelerated the etude-driven blinks to keep from tearing up in empathy.

Mr. Straton harrumphed, clearing his throat and giving his whole body a little shake. "I'm sorry. Didn't mean to get all emotional on you. I have to get back up there—I just wanted to let you know how much I appreciate you looking out for my daughter, Jared. I know you didn't have to, and I thank you."

Jared shook his hand. "Of course. She's my friend. And I hope she gets better soon."

Veronica's father turned away, and Connor had barely released a sigh when a weight dropped onto his shoulder. "I'm sorry, I didn't get your name…"

That was obviously the moment to supply it, but Connor's lips and tongue inexplicably froze. He wanted to shirk away from the touch, but even that was too much movement.

When he didn't speak, Mr. Straton went on. "Well, I know you've been to visit her, too, so thank you. She's lucky to have such good friends."

He gave them one last smile and walked off.

"Let's go." Jared pulled Connor from his stupor with a firm yank on his arm. "I hate hospital cafeterias."

Connor worked out the remnants of his anxiety with a little mental Mendelssohn during the drive home. Jared was tapping the steering wheel, though, and the erratic rhythm kept messing him up.

"So, that was sorta mixed signals—between her mom and her dad," Jared said.

"Better than all bad signals." Connor abandoned the music.

"Yeah, I guess you're right." Jared shut off the engine by the first-year dorms. He released his seatbelt and shifted toward Connor. "Adults still make you uncomfortable, don't they."

"What?" Mendelssohn started up again, fingers working along the leg of his jeans this time, now that Jared's offbeat tapping wasn't in the way.

Jared grabbed his hand to stop him. "You know, the way you used to be around everyone. Or is it just parents that do that to you?"

Connor scowled through his blush. All his progress and he still wasn't close to perfect. But who was, really? "I dunno. Maybe. Sometimes."

"You know, not all parents are like yours. Mine happen to be pretty cool, in fact."

"Then you're lucky."

Jared chuckled, capturing Connor's face with a hand under his chin. "Hey, you are gonna stand up to them one day, aren't you?"

"A-about what?"

"I dunno. Anything." Jared's fingers danced from Connor's chin to his mouth, where they traced his lips.

"I'll…I'll try."

"Good. Now, we have like a half an hour of private time left." He flung open his door. "Let's not waste it."

Jared peeled off his shirt as soon as they got inside and turned on the fan to air out the muggy room. "Damn. We shoulda gone to your dorm—bet that air conditioning is

320

starting to look pretty nice right about now. Makes the walk out there seem worth it, huh?"

"Mhm," Connor mumbled, for once not melting into a pool of lust at the sight of Jared's shirtless body. He had access to a computer now, and his conversation with the nurse plus the internet just *had* to have the answers he was looking for.

He went straight for Jared's laptop. With the aid of Google, he had millions of results to his query in just a few seconds, and he scanned the first page silently. *Delusions, hallucinations, disorganized speech, onset during late adolescence and early adulthood...*

That was it. There were too many similarities for it not to be...which meant it wasn't something Jared could have caused. He sagged in the desk chair, letting out a long, grateful breath.

"What's wrong?" Jared pulled off his shoes and lay back on his bed. "Why're you over there? C'mere."

"Schizophrenia," Connor said quietly. "I think she has schizophrenia."

"What?" Jared sat up. "How do you know?"

"I...I talked to that nurse."

"And he told you? I've asked before. They said they couldn't tell me anything."

"I didn't ask him for the diagnosis. I just, um...made conversation, and he sorta gave it to me in a roundabout way."

"Schizophrenia. Fuck, that's serious, isn't it?"

"I guess." Connor scanned a few paragraphs under a treatment headline on the webpage. "But with medicine and other therapy, it says patients can get better."

Jared shook his head. "Shit. That's still rough."

"Yeah." Connor fought to keep an appropriately commiserating expression on his face. "But you know, this means it definitely wasn't your fault."

He might not have pulled off the sympathetic look, because Jared stared at him, his eyes narrowing. "So you just happened to 'make conversation' with the nurse to find this out?"

Connor closed the laptop and fiddled with the clasp. "I just couldn't stand seeing you feel so guilty…but you should know…I really *don't* care for talking to strangers—especially adults—so I hope you appreciate—"

Jared leapt up from the bed and dashed across the room. His arms wound around Connor to pull him into a deep kiss. "I appreciate, Connor Owens," he said when he was through. "I may not deserve, but I appreciate."

Emotion choked Connor's laugh, making it come out all watery. He pressed his lips into Jared's and locked them together again, just as Ben barreled through the door.

"Ew, gross!" Ben threw a hand over his face.

Jared pulled away, blushing, but added a glare once Ben looked back at him.

"I mean…uh, sorry for interrupting. I'll just be…reading out in the common room, if anyone needs me."

He ducked away as Jared burst into laughter.

Laughter. Jared had just been caught kissing a boy and he was *laughing it off.* Connor channeled the wild elation into his own giggles, and he smothered them in Jared's chest.

"I bet he'll be gone for a while." Jared's skin radiated even more warmth now that Connor had trapped his breath against it. "Although I guess we should work out some sort of sock on the door system." He pulled Connor toward the bed and they settled in, lying on the same pillow so they were eye to eye. "Or we could just stick to your place."

"I…I don't mind coming over here sometimes. It's closer to campus, and you won't have your car as much now that we don't have to…I mean, now that Veronica's going home."

322

"Yeah." Jared wrapped a leg around Connor's thighs to pull their hips close. "Guess you'll be glad when things get back to normal."

Normal. Connor's heart lurched. There was that sticky word again.

The last time Jared had used it, he'd meant *straight.* Just what did he consider normal? Would his new life, would their relationship, ever be normal to him? Would it ever be what he really wanted?

The question came unbidden to Connor's lips. "Jared...if...if you could have the perfect life, right now, what would it be?"

Jared didn't hesitate. "It'd be one where my father was still alive."

The response hit Connor in the gut, forcing out a rapid exhale. *Idiot, thinking the world revolves around you...*

But Jared stroked his cheek with his index finger, a gentle smile still in place. "It's okay, baby. I know what you meant. Look...for a long time, I didn't know what I wanted. I took a stab at a few things that didn't turn out that great, and tried some other things that ended up better than I ever could have hoped. I'll let you figure out which category you fall under."

A timid grin found its way to Connor's lips.

"And there's something else I've been meaning to tell you." Jared's eyes grew darker, his pupils widening into the ring of deep brown. "I thought I knew it before, but after everything you've done for me in the past few weeks...well, there's just no denying it now."

Connor drew in a breath and held it, his body humming under Jared's touch.

This was it—the moment he'd been waiting for. He could sense it in the air, in Jared's chest as it moved against his, in the serenades that spontaneously burst into his head. Jared was warm and happy and everything was perfect, just as it should be for something as important as hearing those three all-powerful words.

Eyes fluttering closed, Jared sank into his mouth. Connor deepened the kiss, torn between holding onto his lips indefinitely and releasing them so he could hear what Jared had to say.

But they ended up pulling away from each other simultaneously—although not fast enough—as the door swung open. The tail end of Ben's "Mrs. B, wait!" drifted into the room and Connor looked up to see a middle-aged woman with dark, curly hair holding a Tupperware container full of brownies.

"Oh!" she exclaimed, red-faced, then backed up and slammed the door shut again.

CHAPTER TWENTY-EIGHT

Jared sat up. A shudder rippled through his body.

"Jared?" Connor choked out through a rising wave of tears. Why did everything have to keep falling apart? And why *now*? Just when Jared was about to...

He furiously squashed the selfish thought.

"F-fuck," Jared stuttered. His chest rose and fell unevenly as he gulped in each breath—the kind of breathing that led to crying. And not just a little watery eye, but full-on sobs.

"Jared," Connor said again. His voice broke and his vision blurred. "Jared, please don't cry."

The door flew open.

"Jared!" the woman exclaimed as she dashed in. "It's all right!"

Connor flew back against the footboard, getting out of the way just in time for her to throw her Tupperware onto the bed and pull Jared into her arms.

"Don't cry, sweetheart, don't cry."

Jared blinked a few times from where she was forcing his head to rest against her shoulder.

"Jared." She stroked his back. "Jared, I already knew. That's why I came. Veronica's mother couldn't keep her big mouth shut. I'm so sorry you felt you had to hide this from me, baby."

Jared crumpled further into her embrace, and despite his mother's demands to the contrary, several tears slipped out. He tried to speak, getting out a garbled, "I'm sorry, Mom, I'm sorry," before she shushed him again.

Connor watched mother and son for a few seconds, but the *intruder* feeling was just too much to handle. Besides, Jared probably wouldn't want to be seen in such a vulnerable state. He quietly slid off the bed and out the still-open door.

Ben was sitting on the couch in the common room with his head in his hands. "I'm so fucking sorry, dude." He glanced up as Connor entered. "I really tried to stop her. I said he was at the library, but she had those stupid brownies and she just had to put them away in our room..." He tugged at a string from the frayed knee of his jeans, ripping a hole. "Jesus, I'm sorry."

Connor exhaled slowly, sinking onto the couch because his legs probably weren't going to support his weight much longer. "Actually, it's...it's all right, I think."

"Really?" Ben asked, a touch of relief easing the ridge between his brows. "I'm pretty sure my dad would throw a shit fit if I were a...if I were gay."

Connor nodded, eyeing the door to freedom that was just past Ben. He didn't have the energy for conversing, but he couldn't leave without making sure Jared was okay first. He wouldn't allow himself to be that much of a coward.

"So..." Ben said. He slapped his hands on his thighs and looked around at every corner of the room.

If he was trying to keep the conversation from dying, he was failing...and Connor wasn't going to be of much help. He drew his usual blank on anything useful to say and resorted to nodding.

"So, uh..." Ben tried again. "You gonna stick around?"

"Um, I thought maybe I should."

"Yeah." Ben leaned forward on his elbows. "Jared might need moral support, or whatever." He grimaced. "Is he...is he actually crying?"

"Like you've never cried in your life," Connor muttered under his breath.

But the words weren't as quiet as he'd intended. Ben's hands shot up defensively. "Nah, man, no judgment, no judgment. I just mean, you should stick around if he's...you know...that messed up. You'd probably have a better handle on how to help him with that...*emotional* stuff."

"Why?" Connor frowned. "Because I'm gay?"

"No, because you're his...his, uh..."

"Boyfriend," Connor supplied, and Ben cringed.

"Um, yeah, whatever. You know. Hey, do you wanna play some video games?" He grabbed the controllers on the shelf next to the large TV and waved them around.

A convenient change in topic—but Connor was thankful for the shift as well. "I dunno...I kinda suck at them."

Ben tossed him the controller anyway. "I know. Jared told me."

Connor let it fall in his lap, a flash of embarrassment warming his skin. But as quickly as the feeling came, it was gone, replaced by a much more pleasurable thought: Jared was *talking* about him to his friends...and even if it was about his shortcomings, it had to be a good sign. They were a part of each other's lives now.

He grinned and set his eyes on the TV screen. "I guess I can only go up from here."

Hopeful words, but he managed to last only a minute longer than he had in his previous attempt. He scowled and bit down on the tip of his tongue in frustration.

"Man, Jared was not exaggerating about how much you suck at this," Ben remarked.

"I'm trying to shoot." Connor flopped back on the couch. "But when I hit the button it doesn't happen fast enough."

"You sorta need to anticipate, you know. Develop faster reflexes and all. And aiming wouldn't hurt."

"I might be too old to learn new tricks."

Ben chuckled and stood up to place the controllers back on the shelf. Then he sat down across from Connor, tilting his head to observe him. "I think maybe I'm starting to get it now."

"Huh? Get...what?"

"I dunno. The whole thing. At first I just couldn't wrap my head around it. Jared...being gay. I mean, he's like...such a guy, you know?"

Connor's brows rose. *Yes, I'm aware of that.*

"And then you and him...that just seemed even weirder. I mean he's...and you're...but like I said, I think I'm starting to get it."

"Uh, that's good, I guess." Connor licked his lips nervously. Maybe he'd be better off waiting outside.

"Yeah, it's like how guys like different types of girls, right? Like, some like the sexy types, with the pouty lips and the big breasts, some like the peppy, bubbly, cheerleader types...and hell, you wouldn't know it by looking at him, but Will prefers his women extra-curvy, if ya know what I mean."

"Um...okay."

"I think maybe Jared and I have similar tastes after all. I like the cute types—they usually tend to be the nice ones."

Connor blinked as Ben's words gradually sank in. "Are...are you saying you think I'm cute?"

Ben's eyes went wide, and he smacked his palm into his face to cover them up. "Oh my God. This is the gayest conversation I've ever had in my life."

A fit of giggles seized Connor, but the laughter died seconds later, as Jared's mother was suddenly in the room and headed straight for him. Jared followed a few feet behind.

Connor dug his hands deep into the couch cushion and closed them into fists. *Breathe. In and out.* If he could keep that going, and ignore the way his skin prickled with the telltale hot and cold of his anxiety…then maybe he stood a chance of not dissolving into a heap of quivering nerves.

"Connor," she said gently, and he forced himself to look up. She tried unsuccessfully to wipe the smears of mascara from around her red eyes. "I hope we can meet again soon. I have to get back to my other boys tonight, but I'd really like to come down another day when I have some more time. Maybe we could all go out to lunch together." She held his gaze as she waited for a response.

Now he just needed to speak. With words. "Um, y-yeah. Th-that sounds…good," he replied softly.

She smiled. It was sort of like Jared's wide smile, except a few of her teeth were crooked. Maybe Jared had had braces when he was younger?

The spurt of random thoughts faded as she turned to direct her attention to Ben. *Thank God.*

"And you too, of course, Ben."

"Yeah, thanks Mrs. B." He ran a hand through his hair with a sheepish grin.

She walked back a few steps to hug Jared and whisper something in his ear that made him smile, then waved goodbye and left the suite.

Jared slipped into his room.

"That's your cue, man," Ben prompted.

Jared sat on the bed, his back against the wall and his head bent toward the ceiling. His eyes were closed but he opened them briefly as Connor climbed in next to him.

"You must think I'm pretty stupid," he mumbled.

"For what?" Connor pulled on his arm, trying to get him to look over.

Jared scoffed and kept his face averted. "For being afraid to tell her. I mean, I never thought she was going to disown me or anything. She's not like that. But I still didn't want her to know."

"It's okay. I understand."

"I just didn't want her to worry, you know?" Jared went on as if he hadn't heard—like he was arguing with someone. Maybe with himself. "She's had enough to worry about. Losing my dad…raising three boys as a single mother…I think maybe I just got so caught up in the idea of being the man of the house—"

"Just because you're gay doesn't mean you're any less of a man."

Jared clamped his mouth shut, rolling his head toward Connor and opening his eyes. "Yeah. I'm starting to get that. Guess I'm a slow learner."

"I've never thought you were stupid, Jared."

A glossy sheen deepened the brown of Jared's irises. "You know, Connor…you're the best friend I've ever had."

Connor slipped his hand around Jared's waist, a lump of emotion gathering in his throat. "Just a friend?"

"You know what I mean." Jared rolled his eyes.

"I do, but I like to hear you say it."

"Fine." Jared dragged him over and wrapped him in his arms. "Boyfriend. You're my boyfriend. The best boyfriend I've ever had."

Connor smiled into Jared's chest, and the last of the tension drained away. Drowsy from the emotional upheaval, his eyes closed and the weight of his head dropped against Jared's shoulder.

But Jared wouldn't let him rest. He cupped Connor's face in rough hands, sucking on his bottom lip and gently swiping his mouth with a warm tongue. They arranged themselves on the bed and Jared's fingers began creeping their way down to Connor's pants.

For the third time that evening, the door interrupted them.

"I'm not looking," Ben announced, one hand firmly over his eyes. "Just need my laptop." He floundered around with his other hand until he grasped it on his desk, then backed out of the room with exaggerated tiptoe steps.

Jared blew out a long, strained breath. "Hey, uh...do you think I could spend the night at your place? And not 'cause I'm still freaked out about my mom, or anything. I'd just...like to be with you."

Connor jumped up and tugged at Jared with both hands. He might not have had the strength to move him, but it got his point across. "Let's go now."

***

The sound of Connor's door locking signaled a tempo change—from a slow and sleepy passion to a fumbling, frantic pace. Connor tore at Jared's shirt, fighting to pull it up and getting blocked every two seconds by Jared's persistent kisses.

"Why haven't we done this lately?" Jared murmured into his lips.

"Dunno," Connor responded, more focused on the pesky shirt. He wasn't quite tall enough to get it all the way off.

Jared took over while Connor tackled the buttons of his jeans. "Well let's just do this more often from now on."

Jared's pants and boxers became a puddle on the floor, and Connor lifted his arms so Jared could remove his t-shirt. "Mhm. More often," he mumbled through the fabric.

When they were both naked, Jared hoisted him up, wrapping Connor's thighs around his waist to carry him to the bed. He held him there for a while, burrowing his face into Connor's neck and nipping at his skin. But the beat of Connor's heart was up to *vivace* by now, and he was ready for more. He fidgeted in Jared's arms and was promptly deposited on the bed.

Jared stood back for a second and watched him squirm. That wasn't at all helpful, so Connor reached up and clawed at him, forcing him to climb on top. He waited impatiently until they were close enough for him to plunge his tongue into Jared's mouth. His hands closed around Jared's shoulders, and after several long kisses, he used the grip to help him thrust toward Jared's hips...and only just barely grazed his groin.

Frustrated, Connor tried again. Why was there no connection there? Why was Jared holding himself like a plank instead of sinking into the willing body below him? There were only a few inches of space between Connor and the contact he craved, but it might as well have been a thousand feet.

He opened his eyes and found Jared studying him.

"What's wrong?"

Jared didn't respond. He stood and walked across the room to grab something from the desk drawer—all the answer needed.

Connor wriggled into the center of the bed, hips lifting off the mattress in anticipation.

But Jared didn't climb back on top of him. He stood beside the headboard, rolling the lube and condom over in his hand. Then he stretched out his arm to offer them to Connor.

"What?" Connor sat up. "What...what's this?"

Jared huffed. "You know what it is."

"Well, yeah, but...but...you said...you said you'd never...you never wanted..."

Jared sank onto the edge of the bed. "I know what I said. But I've had a lot of time to think about things."

"You...changed your mind?"

"I don't know if you remember, but you told me once that if I loved something, I should give it all I've got. That makes a lot of sense, you know? I guess...I guess that's what I'm trying to do. I don't want to hold back from you anymore."

Confusion rapidly became giddiness, tinged with fear. "You, um…you love sex that much?"

"Shut up." Jared scooped him into his arms. "This…this is for some*one* I love." He bit his lip and looked away shyly. "You know, my whole life I've tried to be in control…but maybe it might be nice to let someone else hold the reins for a little while. Someone I trust." He gently placed the contents of his hand in Connor's. "So how 'bout it? You wanna be in control tonight?"

Control. Connor closed his eyes and ran his fingers over the small, cold bottle of lube. His turn to be in control…and not just with the sex. His life, his happiness—it was all in his hands now. Jared believed in him…and maybe he even believed in himself.

Without warning, a tear slid down his cheek.

Jared wiped it away. "Hey, what's wrong?"

"I don't know." Connor blinked out another tear as he laughed. "I don't know. I'm happy."

"This is you happy?"

"Yeah." He bent down to kiss Jared. "I'm happy. Very happy."

"Now who loves sex that much?"

"That's not why I…." Connor began, but then changed his mind. He could talk when he needed to. Now was a better time for kissing.

Their lips met again and the last traces of the emotional outburst vanished, soaked up by Jared's skin. "It just means a lot to me that you trust me like this."

"Baby," Jared said, cupping his face, "there's no one I trust more."

Connor scraped his fingertips along Jared's jaw. His hand trembled a little, setting it off in a zigzag pattern through the stubble and the softer skin of Jared's cheeks. But he ignored the nerves and focused on the texture—on the little pricks of rough amid the smooth. "Yeah. Okay."

He scooted back so he could kneel between Jared's legs and opened the lube. "Then I'm ready, too."

He used only one finger at first, stopping when Jared's face twitched. "Does it hurt?"

"Quit worrying. It's okay."

"I'm not worried." He slid in deeper to prove his point.

"Jesus!" Jared exhaled sharply. "God you have long fingers."

Connor pressed again at the firm bit of flesh at his fingertip, and Jared shivered. A responsive tremor ran through his body and he added a second finger. He gripped Jared with his free hand and the gasp that left Jared's lips sent an extra-strong pulse through his own throbbing erection.

Jared bucked against him, trying to force his touch. "Connor, I want you."

It was the first time Connor had ever had reason to wear a condom, and he tore into it with a sudden rush of pride—even though he knew it wasn't *really* that thin piece of plastic that was making him feel like more of a man. He slipped it on and used the lube to coat it, then spread Jared's legs wider and angled himself for entry.

A flash of discomfort crossed Jared's face and Connor forced himself to stop with only his tip buried inside. "You don't like it. I mean, it's okay—you can tell me if you don't like it."

Jared whimpered a little, but then licked his lips and smirked. "I wish you'd stop talking so much." He barked a short laugh. "Who knew I'd ever be saying that to you?"

Connor pushed in again to shut him up. "Fine. I won't talk."

Nervousness settled into its rightful place—the background of his thoughts. It was okay to be a little nervous, wasn't it? And maybe things wouldn't be fairy-tale perfect the first time, but that was only natural. Of course, being in control meant he shouldered more responsibility for handling the situation...but he was okay with that.

He pressed in slowly. As Jared had once done for him, he gripped him and stroked, so that by the time he found himself fully surrounded, Jared was hot and hard and slick in his hands.

Inside Jared was *tight*...so tight Connor felt he barely had room to expand with the swells of pleasure. He sank in a little deeper and Jared cried out. But the cry was one of pleasure, and when Connor drew back and thrust once again, a low moan joined the chorus of Jared's gasping breaths.

Beautiful sounds, all of them. And this time Connor got to be the conductor, driving in and out, rocking their bodies to this newly discovered music. He moved his hands up to Jared's chest and clapped them against his tan skin, adding to the percussion as they were swept into a furious crescendo. Cymbals crashing, bodies shivering in *tremolo*, they surrendered to a moment of mutual climax.

After all the spasms had passed, Connor pulled out, using his last bit of energy to tie off the condom before his body went limp. He draped himself across Jared and met his lips, sighing into their kiss.

"I think I could get used to that," Jared whispered against him, the soft accompanying chuckle tickling Connor's mouth.

"Yeah...me too."

Exhausted, Connor closed his eyes. He dozed off until a snore and a little jerk from Jared awoke him.

Jared yawned and blinked at him sheepishly. "I'm sticky. We should take a shower together."

Connor peeled himself off Jared's skin and grabbed a handful of tissues. "I'm not sure how the resident advisor would take to us jumping into the dorm showers together."

"Hm." Jared propped his head up in his hand, watching as Connor cleaned him off. "I know. But Ben and I are talking about moving off campus next year. Hopefully we'll get a two bedroom, two bath. Then we can shower together all we want."

Planning for the future. Another happy rush of emotion nearly burst free. Connor tossed the tissues aside and lay on Jared's chest to squeeze him into a hug. "Sounds good."

Jared took a deep breath, making Connor's head rise and fall a few inches. "You know"—he ran his hand through Connor's hair—"earlier…it was sorta the second time I've said something…and you haven't said anything back. Not that I'm counting or anything."

Connor turned to stare up at him. *Second time he'd said…*Oh. That.

"Nope." He kissed Jared's chest. "Didn't count. Doesn't count when you're drunk, and it doesn't count before, during or after sex."

Jared thrust out his lower lip in a mock pout. "I see. Well, fine. But I am gonna get you, you know. Sometime when you least expect it…and you'll have to say something then."

Connor lay back down against Jared's heart and placed a hand on his own chest to feel the beat. Their hearts played together nicely—maybe not with the same exact rhythm, but still to the same song.

"Yeah." He snuggled in close. "I'm okay with that."

SOCIAL SKILLS

EPILOGUE

END OF THE YEAR CONCERT

The crowd of chatting patrons pressed in around Connor, making it hard to maneuver with his violin slung across his back and the bundle of roses in his hand.

Jared reached him first and pulled him into a hug. "You were great!"

Connor held on longer than he normally did in public, reluctant for the strength of Jared's arms to leave him.

"Hey." Jared's grin dissolved as he drew back, his voice dropping to a whisper. "Are you sure you don't want me to come with you?"

Of course I want you with me. I always want you with me.

But he brushed aside the momentary weakness and shook his head. "I'm sure. I don't want to spring too much on them at once."

"All right, but you gotta promise to call me as soon as they leave. Or if you need me at all, for any reason."

"I will."

Jared reached out and placed a hand on his chest, giving it a quick rub. "Okay. I'll see you later tonight, then."

The contact immediately soothed Connor's fears, as it always did. And now there was even the added pleasure at how much more confident Jared had grown with these small public displays of affection—and how much more comfortable *he* was when receiving them.

"Yeah, see you later."

Their fingers brushed as Connor walked away, and he kept his eyes on Jared's smile for as long as he could.

Once he'd lost sight of it, he squirmed in his tux jacket and loosened his bowtie, scanning the crowd for Rebecca's tall figure. She was easy enough to spot as she climbed the stairs from the stage entrance with her violin in hand. Her normally straight hair was done in loose, flowing curls—a rare styling for her—but as usual she wore no makeup. Connor lifted his case to get her attention, and she waved back with big, dramatic sweeps of her arm, as though she were eager to reconnect with a lost friend instead of the stand partner she'd been next to on stage for nearly an hour.

He held up the flowers as she approached.

"For me?" She laughed. "What for?"

"No reason. I just thought you deserved them."

"Oh, you're such a sweetheart. And where are your roses? None from Jared today?" She gave his shoulder a little shake when he blushed.

Tate appeared by her side, squinting at the bouquet. "Way to upstage me, dude." He swung a meager bunch of carnations in front of Connor's face. "You're lucky you're gay."

Rebecca took the carnations and added them to the roses with a gentle cluck. "Now, boys," she said, kissing each of them—Connor on the cheek and Tate on the lips, "there's enough of me to go around."

The crowd nearest to them abruptly parted to a boisterous, "Excuse me!" and Connor's mother made her way through, followed by his father and sister.

"Hey, Mom!" He gave her a brief hug. Her jaw slackened and Melissa did a near double-take—it wasn't every day Connor greeted her like that. "These are my friends, Rebecca and Tate."

His mother recovered from her surprise and beamed. "Very nice to meet you. I'm Mrs. Owens, and this is my husband and my daughter, Melissa."

"Pleasure meeting you, Mrs. Owens." Rebecca shook her hand. "Connor's a really good friend, and a great musician."

"Isn't he?" She settled her hand on Connor's shoulder. "I'm practically tone deaf, but I wanted to make sure my children didn't suffer the same fate. I made sure to enroll them in music classes as soon as they were walking."

"Well, it paid off," Rebecca responded cheerily as Connor rolled his eyes, careful to make sure his mother wouldn't see.

"Mom, I know you guys have a long drive, so if you wanted to stop by my dorm before you leave we should probably get going."

"Yes, I need to drop off the casserole I baked you. Maybe you could invite your friends over to have some when you eat it?"

"Sure, Mom," he answered quickly, anticipation and dread making him itch to get out of the crowded hall. "Well, I'll see ya tomorrow, guys."

"It was nice meeting you," his mother added. "I'm so glad my Connor has finally found some fr—"

"Mom!" Melissa interrupted, blissfully in the nick of time. "Let's go. I have piano class early tomorrow and I have to get some sleep."

"Oh, all right." She gave Melissa a reproachful glare. Those bad manners had surely earned her a future reprimand.

Connor waved goodbye and got one last half-encouraging, half-worried glance from Rebecca as he escorted his family outside.

***

"It's a little dusty in here." His mother ran her finger along his bookshelf and shook off the gathered dirt in dismay. "You really should keep it more tidy."

"Sorry, Mom," Connor said reflexively. His stomach was tying itself in knots and he was sweating, but at least he hadn't lost his ability to speak as of yet.

His mother bent over to place her casserole dish in the mini-fridge, *tsking* at the expired carton of milk inside. Melissa seated herself on his bed and began picking at the split ends in her hair.

"Hm, Connor." The familiar rumble of his father's throat-clearing filled the room. "I've been talking to a colleague of mine, and I've arranged for you to have an internship at his brother's law firm for the month of July."

"Oh." Connor let out a shaky breath. He hadn't wanted to overwhelm his parents, but there'd be no avoiding it now. "Actually...I've decided to stay here for the summer...and I already have a job."

"What?" his mother interrupted. "You never told us that!"

"I know. I'm sorry, I should have."

"The school year is practically over! Just when were you planning on sharing this?"

"I...I was...um..."

She cut in. "Well, what kind of job is it?"

"It's...It's a boarding school in Keswick for students with dyslexia. They needed a teacher's assistant and someone to help with general music for the summer session, so I applied and got the job."

Jowls formed on the sides of his mother's face when she frowned. "Connor, I admire your initiative, but I really think the work your father has gotten you would be a much more beneficial experience for law school."

"I kind of like teaching, Mom. I think I might be good at it. I think I might want to consider it for a...for a career."

His father cleared his throat again after receiving a scowl from his mother. "Connor, you're too young to be deciding these things just yet. It's not a good idea to cut off any avenues before you've matured enough to make the decision."

"I'm not cutting off any avenues, Dad. I'm pursuing the ones I'm interested in." He paused just long enough to swallow so he wouldn't lose momentum. "I'm sorry...but I'm just not going to go to law school."

Both his parents gaped while Melissa gave a muted snort.

Connor fell silent, using the respite to gather his confidence. Amazingly, it wasn't that difficult a task—probably because this part of what he had to say was not so tremendous in comparison to the rest. "I'm grateful for all the guidance you've given me, I really am...but I've never wanted to be a lawyer. I'm sorry. I know I should have talked to you about this before."

Disappointment shone in his parents' eyes, but they remained speechless.

"And...well, there's something else."

His mother put a hand to her heart, and he cringed. If she got too dramatic, he might not have the courage to continue.

"Now what, Connor?"

Melissa perked up from her reclined position on the bed, suddenly all eyes and ears for whatever he had to say.

"Um, I...I n-need to t-tell you—" His voice cracked and then failed him.

Why on earth had he declined Jared's offer? If Jared were there, holding his hand, or just smiling at him, he would have felt that much stronger...

But he had to learn to stand on his own two feet.

"I need to tell you...th-that I'm...I'm gay."

"What?" his mother thundered, and his father's mouth dropped open.

"He said he's gay," Melissa repeated helpfully.

"Melissa, go to the car."

"But Mom—"

"Richard!" She clutched her husband's arm. "Make her go."

"Your mother said to go to the car." Connor's father spoke on command. He held out his hand to give her the keys.

Melissa took them reluctantly, pouting on her way out.

As soon as she'd closed the door, all eyes were back on Connor, his mother's pupils lit with annoyance—laced with fear. "And just when did you decide this?"

Connor sank down onto his desk chair, weak with a combination of relief at the accomplishment and fear of the repercussions. "I didn't decide it. I just am."

He peeked at his father to see if he'd get any better of a reception from him, but he just sat there with a glazed-over look—probably too stunned to add anything more to their conversation.

"Connor, you're too young to know that for sure. It's natural to be…curious, I suppose, but how can you really know that…that you're…"

"I know, Mom. I've always known."

That shut her up for a moment, and by the look of dismay on her face she was beginning to understand. "And you're just telling us this *now*?" she whimpered.

Connor shrugged and fought the rising lump in his throat. Why did he feel like crying? It wasn't like he was losing some sense of trust he'd shared with his parents—they'd never had that kind of relationship. But he was still terribly lonely all of a sudden…maybe because he couldn't help remembering how Jared's mother had held him after *her* discovery.

But he wasn't going to wallow in jealousy. He just had to accept it—no member of his family would ever hold him like that.

"I…I'm sorry I didn't tell you. I'm trying to be more open now. I just…I just felt it was important for you to know because…well, because I'm okay with it, and I hope you will be, too."

"Connor." His mother shook her head sadly.

Now that all his secrets were tumbling out, he couldn't stop, even if it was clear his mother was reaching her breaking point. "And, well, I also thought you should know because…I'm in love with someone."

Funny how easily the words came to him in the moment, and how true they felt. Despite the current situation, Jared's self-assured grin popped into his mind, and he smiled.

His mother let out a strangled noise, but he still didn't stop.

"You actually met him once, when he was over for breakfast. Jared, remember?"

"Connor, that's enough!"

She stood abruptly and Connor shrank back against his chair. "M-mom." His voice quavered. The sound was as embarrassing as always, but he wasn't going to let her scare him into silence. "You say you're tolerant and accepting–"

"That's not fair," she snapped. "You've…you've just sprung this on me and it isn't fair. You're going to have to give me some time…and I think we've discussed this quite enough for tonight."

"Oh. O-okay," Connor mumbled. Was the *time* his mother needed just another way to say she didn't want to be around him? He'd have appreciated that once…but not now. "I guess I'll…walk you down to your car."

He followed his parents in an icy silence, out of the building and into the humid night air. A mosquito dove near him and he swatted it away just as his mother turned to face him.

"Will you still be coming up for Melissa's piano competition in August? She's been doing an excellent job practicing—all on her own, without me even having to remind her. I think she's going to do really well this year."

Her mundane chatter had never sounded so beautiful. "Of course. Hey, maybe I can even see if Jared would like to c—"

"I said we've discussed that enough for tonight."

Connor dropped his head. "Yeah, Mom. Okay, I'll be there."

But we are going to talk about this, someday.

She nodded and gave him an awkward pat on the shoulder. He received a stiff nod from his father, and together they took off into the darkness.

Other footsteps were rapidly approaching, though. A few seconds later, Connor found himself with an armful of little sister.

Melissa wrapped herself around him and pressed her face into his chest. "Five years," she said.

"Uh, what?" Connor blinked down at her, but he instinctively stretched out his arms to hug her back.

"Five years. That's how long I'm giving them to pull their heads out of their butts about you being gay."

He chuckled. "That seems like a long time."

"Well, that's how long it'll take me to be eighteen, and after that I won't need them anymore. I mean, not as long as I have a big brother to help me out."

The heat that rose in Connor's face was from some internal warmth rather than embarrassment. "But haven't you always thought I was a screw up?"

"Nah." She hit him on the shoulder. "I guess you have some skills, after all. Besides, Amanda says it's really cool to have a gay brother."

"I thought you promised you weren't going to tell anyone."

"Duh, Connor." She rolled her eyes. "I didn't tell her. I used a hyperthetical situation."

"*Hypo*thetical," he corrected automatically.

"See. That's a skill. You can proofread my English papers for me instead of Mom and Dad."

"Oh…um, sure, I can do that."

"And anyways, I'm *so* relieved you told, 'cause now hopefully Mom'll get off my back. I was trying to bring up the topic to see how she'd react, and I think she got really worried *I* was trying to tell her I was gay. She started buying me tons of frilly dresses...taking me out for manicures and pedicures..." Melissa shuddered. "*Way* too much bonding time."

Connor shuddered, too. He could only imagine the horror. "Sorry. Guess you shoulda stuck with that 'don't say anything' suggestion of mine."

Melissa glared, but made it a playful look with a few bats of her eyelashes.

"Anyways, you'd better get going," he reminded her. "You're gonna get in trouble."

She grimaced and finally released him. "You'll talk to me later, right?"

"Yeah, I will."

"See ya, Connor."

He watched her small figure sprint down the path and disappear from sight.

Much stronger arms soon replaced Melissa's thin ones as Connor was embraced from behind. He smiled out into the darkness. "I thought I told you I'd call."

"I know." Jared's chin came to rest on his head. "But I was worried. So sue me. I heard part of what your sister was saying...it sounded like it didn't go so well."

"It wasn't ideal." Connor placed his arms on top of Jared's and laced their fingers together. "But it wasn't too bad. I guess the important thing is, I'm okay...and I think things will get a little better with them, eventually."

"I hope so." Jared's lips brushed his ear. "And...I love you, you know."

Connor leaned into Jared's chest, enjoying the way their breathing settled into an even, matching pace. "I know. I love you too."

The words came naturally again, without fanfare or circumstance. But that didn't make them any less true.

They were a good match, after all. Despite their differences, they'd brought out the best in each other...and really, wasn't that the greatest thing he could have hoped for when socializing with his fellow man?

Well, that, and a little bit more.

Connor turned and stood on tiptoe to kiss the man he loved under the stars.

ABOUT THE AUTHOR

Sara Alva is a small-town girl currently living in big-city L.A. with a husband, two cats, and an avocado tree. She has a day job but loves writing enough to have turned it into a night job. For information, free short stories and news on upcoming releases, visit Sara's website at http://saraalva.com/.